SERPENT IN THE HEATHER

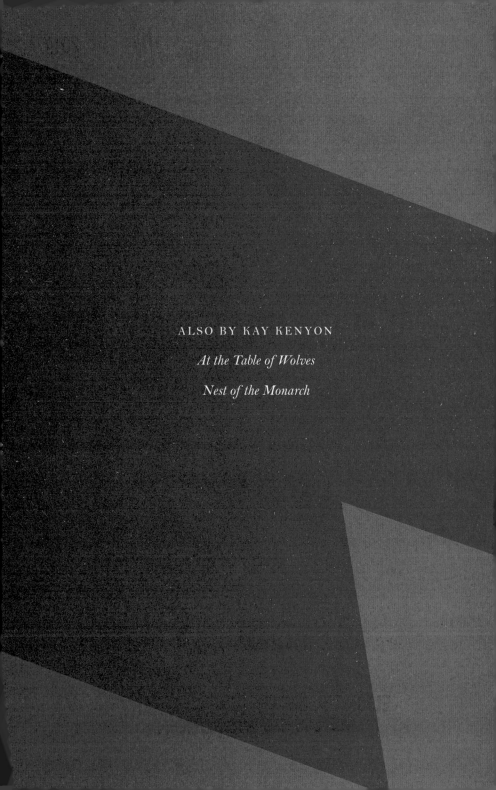

ALSO BY KAY KENYON

At the Table of Wolves

Nest of the Monarch

KAY KENYON

A DARK TALENTS NOVEL

SERPENT
IN THE HEATHER

SAGA PRESS

LONDON SYDNEY NEW YORK TORONTO NEW DELHI

SAGA PRESS

AN IMPRINT OF SIMON & SCHUSTER, INC.

1230 AVENUE OF THE AMERICAS, NEW YORK, NEW YORK 10020

SAGA PRESS and colophon are trademarks of Simon & Schuster, Inc.
For information about special discounts for bulk purchases, please contact Simon & Schuster Special Sales at 1-866-506-1949 or business@simonandschuster.com.
The Simon & Schuster Speakers Bureau can bring authors to your live event. For more information or to book an event, contact the Simon & Schuster Speakers Bureau at 1-866-248-3049 or visit our website at www.simonspeakers.com.
Also available in a Saga Press hardcover edition
Cover design by Greg Stadnyk
Interior design by Brad Mead
The text for this book was set in Bell MT Std.
Manufactured in the United States of America
First Saga Press paperback edition January 2019
10 9 8 7 6 5 4 3 2 1
The Library of Congress has cataloged the hardcover edition as follows:
Names: Kenyon, Kay, 1956– author. Title: Serpent in the heather / Kay Kenyon.
Description: First edition. | New York : Saga Press, [2018] |
Series: A dark talents novel ; 2
Identifiers: LCCN 2017016199 | ISBN 9781481487849 (hardcover)
ISBN 9781481487856 (pbk) | ISBN 9781481487863 (eBook)
Subjects: LCSH: Women intelligence officers—Fiction. | Secret societies—Fiction. |
GSAFD: Occult fiction. | Spy stories.
Classification: LCC PS3561.E5544 S47 2018 | DDC 813/.54—dc23
LC record available at https://lccn.loc.gov/2017016199

PART I

NACHTEULE

1

FRIDAY, JULY 24, 1936. Sometimes, if you run, you attract predators. She knew this but, like a zebra on the savannah sensing danger, she fled. It had only been a man with a doll. Still, she ran. In her second-class carriage seat, Tilda Mazur scanned the railway platform. The train, reeking of oil and scorched iron, collected passengers, but no one she recognized. In the July sun, heat waves wobbled off the pavement, blurring her view of the holiday-goers, families, businessmen. Killers, maybe.

If she had been able to last a few more days, she would have made her rendezvous with "Allan," who was to take her to safety. Allan, she had been told, was six-foot-one, with medium brown hair and blue eyes and would be carrying a leather satchel with a red kerchief tied on the handles. The British embassy had arranged everything: her forged passport, her escape to England. *Escape*, a terrible thing to say. But Poland had betrayed her.

Sitting by the window, clutching her handbag, she crossed her legs. As she did so, a middle-aged man across the aisle noted this, his gaze lingering on her legs. He didn't mean anything by it, but she tugged her skirt down. He was small, dapper, thin. How did you know who was an agent of the Nazi SS? At twenty-three, Tilda Mazur knew little of politics, had never even been out of Poland. She thought Hitler's Black Order would look brutish, with small, hostile eyes.

But they could be anyone.

An old woman sat across from her, a woven basket at her feet. Next to her, a young girl, hair brushed back, with the bright and bored face of a thirteen-year-old leaving for the weekend with Grandmamma.

Tilda moved over to allow another passenger to sit next to her. The woman, with iron-gray hair and smelling of cabbage, heaved her suitcase onto the luggage rack and settled in. Tilda had no luggage, only her handbag, stuffed with two fresh pairs of underwear and her face cream.

The train, which might as well have been cemented in place for all its promise of movement, finally began inching away from the station, venting steam in an explosive hiss. As the train picked up speed, the Dworzec station fell behind, but without bringing even a breath of air into the stifling car.

Nevertheless: in three hours, the embassy in Warsaw, and safety.

Tilda allowed her body to sag into the seat back. The worst was over, but still, her worries spun round and round: the rumors of people like her dying, jumping in front of trains, having heart attacks at thirty. Andrzej, who was her first friend at Sosnowa House, with his sweet demeanor and skill of *hypercognition*, had died in a fall from a bridge. An accident, the papers claimed.

But to her fellow subjects at Sosnowa House, it was an assassination, part of a string of them that the higher-ups wouldn't admit. Dismissing the concerns, their handlers only said no, you are overreacting. She had demanded answers of her case worker. He had claimed she was perfectly safe since the Bureau would never divulge her name. But even if he believed this, perhaps he didn't know if there was a traitor amongst them. Someone who identified Tilda's colleagues to Hitler's paramilitary SS, fanatics who would do anything to further their Führer's aims.

Like the Dutchman.

She had met him in the market last week at the kiosk of antique dolls. She had stopped to admire the beautiful dolls, some with faces so exquisite they seemed to be alive. Many had carefully painted heads with specific character and bright glass eyes. There were even some with feathered brows and real eyelashes.

From behind her had come a voice in an odd, foreign accent: "The one that you are holding. It is a Simon & Halbig. An 1897 bisque doll." She turned to see a stocky man in his mid-thirties, with a squarish face tending to jowls. He wore very thick glasses. A glare of sun slanted off them.

"You have exquisite taste." His Polish was excellent.

Surprised to be addressed, she quickly replaced the doll she had been looking at. "Yes, she is very nice."

As the merchant shuffled forward from the back of the stall, the man in glasses frowned him away. He picked up the Simon & Halbig doll. His full lips glistened as though he had just licked them. "This was among the first dolls to use children's faces. Strange, is it not, that people preferred their dolls to look like women?"

"Oh, I didn't know." She finally placed his accent. Dutch. Actually, she had known about dolls' faces, as antique dolls had always fascinated her. But she did not want a conversation with this man who regarded her with an intensity she found unwelcome. There was something peculiar about his eyes. Behind the thick glasses, his eyes appeared to be crackled with fine lines like old porcelain.

"You like dolls, that is clear," he said. "I, too."

"No, no, too expensive," she said, and made a shrug of indifference before she turned away.

"Sometimes, the price, it is worth it," she heard him say.

She was eager to leave the market square. During their brief encounter, the Dutchman had been staring at her, and standing so close to her, in an over-familiar, disturbing way.

That had been six days before, on Saturday. Then, on Wednesday, she had seen the same man following her, and she had been seized by fear. Did the Dutchman know what she was? Had he come to kill her? Knowing she would have no help at Sosnowa House, she had contacted the British embassy. She must have protection. Surely they would help her, for she could offer them her services. A train ride to Warsaw, and it had all been arranged: her meeting with the man called Allan, her escape.

Her escape on Monday, three days from now. But she could not wait for him.

How had it come to this? Last year, when she had been offered training by the Polish army, she had felt proud of her special ability, but during the last weeks, how she wished she were ordinary! She had never considered how much danger she would be in should Poland's enemies discover what she could do, how her ability was so powerful that she could be of direct use on the field of battle.

At first, it had been exciting. In the vale surrounding the top-secret Sosnowa House, her trainers had led her through precise exercises in the use of her skill: *darkening*. She had learned how far she could reach and how to calmly employ her power under duress. These sessions and her fierce patriotism prepared her for sacrifice in case of war. But she had never thought the Nazi fanatics would come for her in Cracow, that Hitler would begin hostilities early, not bothering to declare war. Andrzej had said that Germany wished to weaken Poland's ability to use Talents in their arsenal of defenses. Poland's army was strong, and the Nazi war machine needed every advantage if they marched across the border.

And now, she believed, a traitor had handed over names of Poland's Talents. Perhaps *her* name.

This morning, when she had seen the Dutchman again, she had telephoned her uncle, begging him to meet her at her apartment and to bring a gun. But then she had changed her mind, suddenly desperate for the safety of the embassy. Afraid to even leave a note for her uncle or mother, she had rushed to the railway station. Within the hour, she was on her way to Warsaw.

The train clattered through the countryside with its endless fields, some harvested to stubble, others with knee-high acres of wheat. Tilda had thought she would feel safer outside of the city, but this emptiness was worse. It felt more exposed, and the close confines of the carriage seemed to strip away her anonymity. How painful it was to be on alert for violence, as though a hand were gathering the nerves in her chest and slowly, softly, twisting them.

On the opposite bench seat, the young girl brought out a sandwich from her pocket. Her grandmamma spread a napkin between them, chatting with the youngster. While Tilda listened idly to their exchange, someone came through from the next car, moving down the aisle.

When Tilda looked up, she saw him. The man in glasses.

Shock coursed through her. He passed by, wearing a rumpled suit, his face glistening with sweat. He did not make eye contact. Oh, he had come for her. She tried to get ahold of her skittering thoughts. Perhaps he was merely a man following her because he wanted her and could not help himself. Still, why was he on this train, knowing she would see him and be forewarned? Perhaps he was one who enjoyed fear, who wanted to savor it.

Panic surged anew as her choice became plain to her: she would run again. The train was coming into a station.

Cradling her handbag, she lurched from her seat, not looking behind to locate the man in glasses. Against the swaying of the train, she staggered down the aisle, then shoved through the door to the inter-carriage compartment, balancing on the shifting floor sections.

The train stopped. Out the window she saw the sign for Częstochowa. She yanked open the door and jumped out.

And brought the night.

She cast a *darkness* around her, over the train, the station platform. She pushed her *darkening* as wide and far as she could, a full acre at least, and rushed along the platform, barely able to see people as they called out in alarm and milled in confusion under the black cloud. Her *darkness* would protect her. The disc of the sun cut through the dark like a baleful, silver eye, casting little light. Pain stabbed at her feet as she ran in her heeled shoes, desperate to be out of sight of the railway carriage windows. She ran past a large outbuilding, and then lumps of what up close she saw were motorcars. The car park.

She stopped to look behind her. But in the gray murk she threw around her, she could see little.

Where could she go? Running madly forward, she found herself in a grassy field. She stumbled on.

† † †

Dries Verhoeven had worried she might bring her Talent to bear. He had known it was powerful, possibly an 8, but he had not known which precise Talent it would be. *Ach*, so it was *darkening*! This was a Talent he was well matched for, especially now as she revealed her panic, bolting from the train as it made its stop.

He followed her, slowly and quietly. He had plenty of time now that she had crossed the car park and entered a field. He could just make out a slightly built young woman—with, he remembered, a very sweet face—stumbling about in the long grass.

2

WEDNESDAY, JULY 22. From the outside, Monkton Hall looked harmless, even homey. Tucked into the edge of the moors, it appeared to be a gone-to-seed brick mansion remodeled too many times and now converted to some public use. But Kim Tavistock knew it to be the clandestine seat of research into meta-abilities, Britain's top-secret project to unlock the mysteries of those unlikely, rare, and oh-so-useful gifts: Talents.

Inside, Miss Drummond, who commanded the great hall at her massive desk, noted Kim's arrival in the logbook and waved her on to the director's office, making friendly eye contact as she passed. No smile, of course. The woman was all business, and this hadn't changed, despite her crucial help this spring with the traitor at Monkton Hall. Waiting at the top of the marble staircase was Owen Cherwell. Kim hardly recognized him without his white lab coat, but the brown suit—ill-fitting but newly pressed—was more in keeping with his new station.

Kim smiled to see the cherrywood desk in his office every bit as disorderly as his small lab table had been when he'd been chief of Hyperpersonal Talents.

"Congratulations, sir," she said as they took their seats in the enormous office of the Directorate.

"Oh, this?" He looked around as though surprised to be there. "Yes. The fate of the highly capable: promoted out of the fun to the rarified realm of administration." Despite the pronouncement, she detected a suppressed glee.

"You look well, Kim. New hairdo, I see." His own hair, having grown in every fifth strand, was a puff of beige around his face.

She hadn't changed her chin-length bob for a decade, but she was not going to be put off with chitchat. "Thanks. But I've got a complaint."

"Don't care for the new fellow?" Owen's replacement in the Hyperpersonal section. "Lewis Whitstone is a bit stiff, perhaps—"

"Lewis is fine. But I'm just his guinea pig while he learns his job."

"You must forgive Lewis's fascination with your excellent rating. Compared to you, a lesser being, say a 2 for *mesmerizing*, is a bit of a letdown." Owen was a snob when it came to Talents. Those without a smattering of it, he called *plain*, though he himself was one.

"Owen." She fixed him with a gaze that by now should signal that she must be taken seriously. "I want a real job. I'm happy to help the new man settle in, but I want an assignment. One that matters."

"How did your training go down at the Estate?"

The intelligence service training site in Hampshire. "Well, I loved it. I know how to unload a dead drop, do a brush-pass exchange of documents, and shoot a Browning automatic. I can create codes, hide them, and break them. All I'm missing is my spy badge."

Owen raised an eyebrow. The work was not a joking matter to him. Nor to her, really, but she did love it so.

"How is Alice Ward adjusting to her new status?" he asked. "Her *trauma view* still under wraps as far as the good folk in Uxley are concerned?"

"She's doing fine so far, as long as her neighbors don't know what she sometimes catches a glimpse of."

"Ah, yes," Owen said. "Views of the dark side of life. Best saved for Office work." Agents called the intelligence service the Office, a charming custom that was merely the first layer of secrecy for an organization so clandestine, the government did not even admit it existed.

Of course, it was not easy for Alice to keep her Talent a secret, especially from the man she hoped to marry, Vicar James Hathaway, who did not hold with such abilities, perhaps did not even think them real. Not that Alice and James were a regular couple; he seemed content to squire her about while keeping an emotional distance.

"I understand Alice took to the code-work aspect," Owen said. In the chain of command, he was her handler and Alice's. "Cottoned on to encryption and numerical analysis, so we'll have to watch she doesn't get recruited to the Government Code and Cypher School."

Kim did not like to think how she would get on without Alice, and hoped she'd never be whisked away to encryption work in London.

"A bit of solidarity now, for the two of you, I should imagine," Owen said. "Fewer secrets between you."

"Yes, of course. But keeping things hush-hush is part of our job. Hard at first. It does get easier." It was true. Secrecy as a way of life had begun to feel so very normal. Even, she had to admit, attractive. For the challenge, for the excitement. Ordinary life paled.

"You had been worried about friends learning of your Talent, so I'm glad to see it's worked out for the two of you. I've always thought that hiding one's Talent cuts two ways. Useful in clandestine work, but a problem if one is vexed on the home front."

An unwieldy subject. It hovered at the edges of her and Alice's life, unresolved, cranky, and unnerving. But she was not here for counseling. "Owen." She fixed him with a pointed look. "I loved my time at the Estate, and now I'm thoroughly prepared. I'm ready. For *something.*"

He got up, moving to gaze out the window overlooking one of Monkton Hall's abandoned gardens. "I know you're eager for action."

"Of course I'm not *eager for action.* Do listen, Owen. I want to be *useful.* I'm your highest score in the *spill.* Give me something to sharpen my teeth on." Sometimes, she feared that the intelligence service would not favor her for assignments because she was half-American. Though born in England, she was really a stranger here, no matter that her family had owned Wrenfell House in the East Riding of Yorkshire for two hundred years.

At the credenza, Owen picked up a black leather-bound book and, crossing over to her, put it in her hands. "You'll be the first to hear when we've got a new operation. Meanwhile, you can memorize this."

The book was small, some five by seven inches. She looked up at him. "What is it?"

His eyes betrayed a boyish enthusiasm. "A new resource. I call it the *Bloom Book*. It's a handbook of Talents, a quick guide to the known abilities, their categories and features."

She wouldn't be deflected in her purpose, but this was worth a pause. She opened the little book to the first page. THE CLASSIFICATION OF TALENTS. Underneath were headings: HYPERPERSONAL, MENTATION, PSYCHOKINESIS. A few pages in, she found the catalogue of Hyperpersonal abilities, among them:

Conceptor. Manifests an unusual level of emotional persuasion, especially in leadership. Not subject to the limitations of geography. Not augmented by proximity. Underlying ability. Examples: Winston Churchill, Adolf Hitler.

Spill. Eliciting from others a spoken admission of a closely held secret, opinion, fear, memory, or longing. The person who spills may evince regret or shame at having shared a hidden thought, but will have no sensation of having been acted upon. An often-unwelcome meta-ability that can be disruptive of social relationships.

"Disruptive of social relationships." Spot on.

Kim noted the slim heft of the book. "How many Talents do we know about?"

"Nineteen so far. The Germans have discovered a few more. As we add to our list of known abilities, I'll have Drummond update it."

She perked up. "But might we be on to a potential new Talent?"

"Actually, no." He held up a hand. "We always have our feelers out for German breakthroughs, of course. As we did for *cold cell.*" The German exploitation of temperature extrusion that had nearly spelled disaster for England in May. "But until we have something exciting for you to do, you can memorize this book. Whatever your next assignment, the more you know about Talents, the better. You'll come here to read it. It doesn't leave my office."

Bringing a secret document home to Wrenfell was fraught with difficulties, not the least of which was her father's troubling ideology and his unreliable, arch-conservative friends. It was a dismal trend, that the upper classes in Britain leaned toward fascism. The political split between her and Julian was hard to ignore, even though they avoided the topic.

"Why didn't we have a catalogue before?"

"We did." He tapped at his temple. "Over a year ago, our former director assigned me to head up a team to create a catalogue, but I made sure the group never got anywhere. It would have gone straight to the Germans. They already know more about Talents than we do, but still, I couldn't bear to write it all down for them. I made sure the committee never made it past goals and objectives."

Kim smiled to think of all the ways Owen—and she—had hoodwinked Fitzroy Blum. "He got shipped out somewhere. Where was it?"

"Fitz is now an undersecretary at the Colonial Office," Owen said with barely concealed joy. "A posting in Southern Rhodesia, so I heard. Not enough evidence to charge him, but at least we never have to lay eyes on him again." He withdrew his watch from his waistcoat pocket and opened it. A waistcoat. She would have to get used to the new Owen.

"Well. I'll leave you with the book. Take your time." He ducked a bow. "I like the hair, by the way."

Kim clutched the book as he shut the door behind him. Their relationship was now one of controller and agent, more businesslike than it had been before, when the case worker and the research subject had been nearly equals, operating by the seat of their pants and outside of government. Now Owen, like her, was recruited into the Secret Intelligence Service, a reward for having performed in exemplary fashion during the recent invasion crisis.

Strange, that intelligence work had so quickly seduced her. She imagined her future assignments with relish; found an odd satisfaction in living a parallel life that few knew about; and craved to know the secrets of SIS. What operations were under way right now? How widely was she known for her part in the Nazi Storm Way operation? Even: who was Owen's controller, and where did they meet? After the first taste of state secrets, you inevitably wished to know more. It could easily become a bit of an obsession, at least for one with a habit of fixation on things. Not that she did.

But while it was delicious to be a part of the intelligence service, with its high purpose and profound aura of mystery, they really must give her something to *do*. She was a 6 for the *spill*. It practically cried out for espionage, if they would just trust her to do her part.

Opening the *Bloom Book* to page one, she savored a list of the types of Talents. It was very satisfying. She did so love lists.

THE BLOOM BOOK

INTRODUCTION

The exact date of the introduction of meta-abilities into the Western world cannot be determined with certainty. Case studies point to 1915 or 1916. The onset of meta-abilities (Talents, as they are popularly called) is at or shortly after puberty. Some individuals destined to manifest Talents who were past puberty in those first years experienced late onset of their abilities. Although data on Talents is incomplete, the proportion of meta-abilities in the population is estimated at a ratio of 1:1115.

Even after twenty years, this profound change in human capability is still considered theoretical by some in the general public, although not among the scientific community. Detractors align the phenomenon of meta-abilities with old associations, considered valid for their time, of hysteria or charlatanism.

When the phenomenon was first empirically described in 1917, it was believed that a cultural-physiological shift had occurred, one that either brought the abilities to the conscious knowledge of those so imbued, or actually seated the meta-abilities within certain individuals. Whether the capabilities had been formerly suppressed, or are uniquely new, the freshly enabled meta-abilities seem to have bloomed in the population like a sudden flourishing of biological organisms. The analogy might be weed or flower, but the name has taken hold. The dawn of meta-abilities, as well as its current reign, is known as the bloom.

Causation has never been scientifically established. It does not appear to run in families, nor to be the result of personal trauma, religious experience, personality, gender, or geography, except that it is a strong phenomenon in Europe, the Middle East, the United States and the Soviet Union. Other areas of the world, less impacted by the Great War, have not been carefully studied; incidences of Talents are less obvious in cultures which have a history of tolerance of psycho-active abilities, and have considered them natural variations in human behavior. Bloom occurrences in non-Western cultures is an area of study ripe for further investigation.

Without proof, it is merely speculation to say that the bloom was triggered by the Great War. Psychologists have a theory that the losses and shared societal suffering created a critical mass of circumstances that, at an unspecified tipping point, erased barriers to abilities that had lain dormant in mankind.

The fact that Talents appear robustly in a proportion of the population, yet not universally, introduces fascinating questions of causation and susceptibility that are just beginning to receive attention.

Highly classified work continues in Britain, focusing especially on case studies, classification, and recruitment of individual practitioners in capacities useful to law enforcement and national security.

—Owen Charles Cherwell, Ph.D., Historical Archives and Records Centre (HARC), Monkton Hall, June 1936

3

SATURDAY, JULY 25. Dawn seeped into Julian Tavistock's bedroom through the half-drawn drapes. He sat up carefully, so as not to disturb Olivia. Swinging his feet to the floor, he savored its coolness after the hot press of the night, when it had been seventy-five degrees even at midnight.

He quickly dressed in shabby trousers and shirt with an overcoat that would allow him to blend in where he was going. Opening the false bottom of his valise, he placed the forged passport the Office had made up for the Polish asset. He glanced at the photo: dark wavy dark hair was pulled back from her youthful face, a few strands escaping. A tentative smile amid strong features conveyed a moment's vulnerability caught by the camera. A heart-shaped face made her appear almost doll-like; but she was not a child. Twenty-three years old, and a highly-ranked *darkening* Talent. Tilda Mazur.

"Will it be dangerous?" Olivia was awake after all and rose up on one elbow to watch him pack.

"There and back," he said, speaking softly as though there was still a chance she might sleep in. "Three or four days at the most. No danger."

"Liar." She smiled at him, letting the sheet fall from her breasts. "If you're undercover in those clothes, it's dangerous."

He would have liked to crawl back in bed with her. "What will you do today?"

"I told my father I'd see the new exhibit at Greenwich. Some naval thing." Her father, the retired admiral. Whom Julian had not met, as he had not met Olivia's mother or sister, and as Olivia had not met his own daughter. Their relationship, all very discreet. It was no trouble; they were used to secrets. It might even be that the clandestine nature of their meetings accounted for the sharply sweet nights—and afternoons—they'd spent together in the last two months.

He snapped the valise shut and tied a red kerchief around the handles. "You could take me with you to Greenwich," he said, as though he would toss over his assignment and have an outing with her.

"But you'll be in Berlin." She made up a city. They couldn't discuss the work of the Secret Intelligence Service, though they both worked for it.

Cracow, he thought. *I'll be in Cracow.* I'll be Allan Howard, and Tilda Mazur will be Macia Antonik. "Yes, Berlin," he said, so now she knew it wouldn't be.

He leaned over to kiss her goodbye, a quick peck that seemed both too little and too much. This affair couldn't last. It was beastly difficult to keep it secret, though *discreet* is what their boss had demanded. And Olivia would walk the plank for the chief, the man everyone called E. He knew that she loved the service; they both did, but it would be a damn sight easier if at least one of them could live without it.

Slipping from the flat, Julian took the stairs to the street in search of a taxi. He'd been on his own since Kim's mother left, so long ago it seemed like someone else's life. Since then, there had been a few women, but nothing stuck. The service didn't mix well with a private life, so it was for the best that he not get too close to anyone. That included his daughter. In her eyes he was a hanger-on in upper-class drawing rooms, attracted to the fascist outlook on the world; a damning view for a woman to have of her father. Most days he was able to believe that the cost to him was small compared to what surely must be coming. That dark wave, gathering at the edges, soon to roll across Europe.

Hitler's rearmament was an open secret. Although a flagrant challenge to the Versailles Treaty, the rearmament was approved by the German populace, providing as it did virtually full employment. Soon the Nazis would be ready for total war. England's own rearmament was underfunded and under-manned, with some at Westminster turning a blind eye in the hopes that Germany would form a bulwark against the USSR. His Majesty's Government could not conceive of another war, could not fund it, and could not survive an election if it did.

Julian slid into a taxi, thoughts already on the extraction of Tilda Mazur. She had requested asylum, and England was anxious to provide it, even if it meant going behind the backs of their Polish allies. It was delicate. The Poles would find out eventually, alerted by their own spies in London, but by then it would be too late. She was a formidable military Talent, testing out as an 8 for *darkening*, near the top of the factor-10 scale. While HMG would not have interfered had she strengthened

Polish defenses, Tilda believed herself in danger, and they could not allow her capture by a potentially belligerent power.

As the cab pulled away from the curb, he looked to the upper-floor window where Olivia had parted the curtains. He thought of her hair tumbling down from her updo, pins scattered on the floor.

"Victoria Station," he told the driver.

COOMSBY, EAST YORKSHIRE

MONDAY, JULY 27. Martin Lister stood in the hallway outside the parlor where his mother was getting an earful from the headmaster. Martin hadn't planned on being in a jam over the Adders; hadn't planned on getting caught, actually. It was *secret.* Who had blabbed? He bet it was Teddy Richardson, that wanker. Now there'd be hell to pay. His da would be steamed about this. He was always steamed up at him for one thing or another. He could hear the lecture coming: *We pay good money for you to be at that school. You think it's easy these days? Where's your gratitude?*

The door to the parlor opened. Headmaster Cairncross heaved his bulk through, slapping his derby hat on his head. "Your mother will speak to you now, Martin. I can't think what you were about, but you'll have to put this right, you know." He fixed Martin with a fleshy stare. "Until you do, I cannot promise you a place in the next term."

Just as Cairncross made his way to his car, Martin's father

drove up, home early from the shop. Another notch against Martin, that his da had to leave the store early. The two men talked outside, as his mother nervously joined him in the hall.

Once inside, his da paused and glared at him. "Kicked out of school, then. I can't say as I'm surprised."

"Headmaster said I could put it right—"

"And for a secret organization?"

"It's not—"

"Don't talk back to me, boy."

It's not an organization. It's a club.

"You've been meeting with two other boys and you're muckin' around with made-up powers. Is that it?" Not really wanting an answer, he looked at Martin's mother in frustration. "Magically seeing the past. I thought he was over that."

She crumpled into the chair next to the parson's table, as though the air had gone out of her. "I told you he was still onto that. I *told* you."

His da snorted and rounded on Martin. "So, who are these Antlers, and what did you think you were doing with 'em?"

"Adders," Martin said. "The clubs are the Adders."

"Clubs? Do you mean to say there's more than one?" He slammed his copy of the *Daily Telegraph* down on the parson's table. "The whole school is infested with this nonsense?"

"There's Adders in lots of schools, all around." Martin had heard there were, not that they were organized or anything. His schoolmates heard rumors; they'd all heard about how the Adders idea was catching on. "The kids want to test out what they can do, but we never did anything that was trouble."

"But it's *trouble*, isn't it, if you're meetin' behind the backs of your own parents and the school authorities. Don't you call that *trouble?*"

Martin knew that anything he said could earn him a cuffing, so he stayed silent, though he'd like to have it out with his da, give him what-for. Problem was his da was a big man and Martin was small, even if he was fifteen.

"Well?" his da demanded.

"It wasn't behind your back. We just didn't tell anybody."

His mum chimed in. "Who can you talk to if it isn't your own parents?"

The last people I would talk to.

His da threw his tweed jacket on the coat rack. "I don't want cheek from you, boy. Here you are, tossed out of school and you don't bother to be sorry. And all on account of this special sight you think you've got. You think I was born in a barn? That I don't know poppycock when I hear it? Talents!" He shook his head.

His mum said, tiny as a bird chirp, "Some people talk as though they're real. Even Maud says so."

His da looked like she'd just told him to bugger himself. He swung his gaze back to Martin, his voice a harsh whisper. "It's your imagination. It's *all* imagination. If you want to puff yourself up, try studyin'. It's what I did, and I have the chemist's, where I'd put you to work tomorrow if I trusted you with the till." He glared from Martin to his wife and back again before storming away.

Martin regarded his mother. "You never think I can do anything."

Rising from the chair, she shook her head, but whether she meant, *No that's not what I think,* or, *No, you can't do anything,* he didn't know. She followed her husband down the hall.

Try thinking for yourself, Mum. Just try it once.

But at least she'd tried to speak up, saying how Maud knew the truth, that Talents weren't just dreamed up. Even the newspapers, and on the wireless, folks knew that some people could do special things. Important things.

Martin sat down in a chair and rested his head against the wall, shutting his eyes. He could feel things in the hallway here. If he let himself concentrate in a place, he could sometimes feel things that had happened there. He'd looked up all the things about his *site view* Talent. Someday, maybe he'd be important because of it.

When he sat up at last, his glance fell on the newspaper. A teenage boy, murdered. It happened outside Portsmouth. He read the article, hoping they'd say how he was murdered. Maybe stabbed; wasn't that how people usually got murdered? But the paper didn't say.

When he put the newspaper back on the table, he noted the snake inked onto his wrist. He pulled down his shirt cuff. No end of trouble if his da saw *that*.

CRACOW, POLAND

TUESDAY, JULY 28. Julian was back in the square, looking for a woman in a green felt hat. He had waited for her yesterday, too, sipping strong black coffee at a cafe in the cobblestoned square, pretending to read a travel brochure.

Tilda Mazur was to pass in front of the Remuh Synagogue and stoop to adjust her shoe. But again today, there was no woman in green, and the women who were there, if they covered their hair, wore babushkas. Nor did any of them need to adjust a shoe while passing the wrought-iron gate of the synagogue. After thirty minutes of observation at the cafe, he had tucked away his brochure and left.

So again today he waited, this time at the planned second meeting time near dusk. The center of the Jewish quarter was beginning to pack up for the day. Stalls dismantled, carts loaded with beets, potatoes, and corn. An old man in a yarmulke, the knotted fringe swaying from his white prayer shawl, pushed his flower cart toward home; a peppering of ravenous doves fell on the little park; a woman in a red blouse met her handsome lover; a beggar approached them, but the couple could not care, with eyes only for each other.

Watching the doves battle for crumbs in the grass, Julian had an unsettling hunch that Tilda was not going to show. It might be cold feet—the momentous step of abandoning one's home. Or it might be something worse.

Despite the long evening shadows that darkened the square, it was too hot to go to his hotel room. Tilda's third and last chance, tomorrow.

He walked from the square but instead of turning toward his hotel, he wandered down the Miodowa to the old Hotel Kazimierz. There he took the lift to the third floor, counting on any tail to wait for him in the lobby. He took the back stairs down. Good tradecraft suggested that he not attempt contact with Tilda, but he found that he didn't want to go home without her. In the Podbrzezie he found a taxi and, in tourist Polish, told the driver to go slowly around the sights. That way, it would be clear if anyone was following by car.

"What sights?" the driver asked in a guttural English.

An explanation confounded Julian's Polish, so he said in English, "There is always something to see."

After a tour of Old Town, he left the taxi at the baroque Izaak Synagogue and walked to Tilda Mazur's apartment on Warszauera.

He knew a great deal about twenty-three-year-old Tilda: her family (widowed mother, no siblings), education (twelve years), occupation (clerk typist), how much English she spoke (none except yes and thank you), reason for asylum request (Germany wanted her, one way or the other).

Well, if she was afraid to come to him, he would have to go to her. He kept watch for German agents, the SS or their intelligence service, the SD. Nor would he want to draw the attention of Polish intelligence. Exposed as an undercover operative, Julian would face unpleasant interrogations. No one liked being spied upon, but at least one's enemies expected it. The Poles would feel justified in a show of outrage.

So, on his own in Cracow, he decided he would not abandon her. Tilda had told a story to British embassy staff. Possibly needlessly alarmist, but disturbing if true: someone was killing Poles with Talents.

At Tilda's door, a man answered Julian's knock. Burly, dark, in the uniform of the Cracow police.

"Yes?" His gaze took Julian in, eyes narrow.

"I'm looking for Tilda Mazur."

"She is not here." He spoke English through a thick Polish accent.

Julian's gaze swept over the man's uniform. "Not in trouble, is she?"

"What is your business, please?"

"Just a friend. We were going to meet in the square."

The man gazed at him a few beats, and opened the door for Julian to enter. Inside the simple flat, a few mismatched chairs, a table with a doily, a coal fireplace.

"So, you are the English. The one who is to help her."

"Just the cinema. I'm in town for business, we met at a cafe." He shrugged. *You know how it is.*

"I am her uncle," the policeman said. He held up a hand. "Do not tell me your name. It is a lie, in any case." He looked out the window into the street. "She was afraid, you understand.

Followed. She asked me to come here, but now"—he spread his hands to encompass the empty flat.

"Where did she go?"

"Yes, where? Where does a girl go who is thinking her own government, or one bad person in government, betrays her to the Germans?"

"An embassy," Julian said.

The policeman nodded. "Perhaps your embassy."

The British embassy in Warsaw. Where she had gone six days before to ask for extraction. Why hadn't she waited for her contact?

Julian looked at the few items of decoration. A framed picture of a saint taken from a calendar, the month of November. A sprig of dried flowers on the small kitchen table. On the mantel, an antique doll in a lace dressing gown.

Tilda's uncle saw his glance. "Her grandmother gave to her." He turned back to the window, parting the curtains an inch or two. "She loves this. A keepsake. But now we have trouble."

Julian waited.

"She went to Saturday market. There was a man who talked to her of dolls. An expert of dolls. He began following her, and she was afraid. Now she goes somewhere, maybe to Warsaw, to escape him." The uncle cocked his head. "But why not go to Polish authorities?"

It was time to be plainspoken, at least to lift the curtain a few inches. "A matter of trust."

"Yes. A matter of trust. No one should know her name. But names, they have a way of being known. My Tilda . . ." He sat at the kitchen table, his face suddenly weary.

"When was this, that she left?"

"I do not know. I watch for her, but she does not come. Maybe, in the end, she did not trust even *me*."

"This man at the market. Did she describe him?"

"A foreigner. Having spectacles. Thirty-two, thirty-three years old, not handsome."

"German?"

The policeman gave an elaborate shrug. "Dutch, so she thought." He snorted in dismissal tinged with incredulity, as though at least a *German*, he could understand. "Dutch!"

6

TUESDAY, JULY 28. Kim cocked the hammer of the snub-nosed Colt and took aim. She pulled the trigger. The shot went wide of the tin can on the fence and sent bark flying off a tree behind it. Shadow lay at her side, muzzle cradled in paws, having given up on her assignment to retrieve the can.

Kim lowered the gun. "Damn it to hell."

Walter Babbage leaned against the fence by the paddock, watching. "Tha's a squirrel that'll live another day."

She glanced at her father's estate caretaker. Walter didn't ask why she had taken up target practice, but his attitude was clear. He sauntered back to the barn, shaking his head.

He would be astonished to learn that she had been recruited into Britain's Secret Intelligence Service. She was, after all, Julian's American daughter, come to live in the country of her birth, but hardly meriting serious attention from the estate care-taker, much less Whitehall. She and Walter got along better now that Kim and his daughter had developed a friendship. Even at nineteen, Rose needed looking after, and Kim had proven herself a worthy protector. The Babbages were her family now, with her father more like a distant uncle, even when he was home.

Julian didn't understand the Nazi threat in Europe. They would never agree about that, especially as he knew nothing of how the shadow of Hitler's ambitions had fallen over England just two months earlier. The island nation had barely escaped. Kim had managed to hide from her father her involvement in that operation. He'd never know what had really happened in the Prestwich Affair—as it had come to be called—on the moors.

Meanwhile the world slumbered, happy to believe Hitler's lies about rearmament, content, even, to send athletes to the summer Olympics in Berlin.

Kim reloaded, bringing her left hand up to support the gun handle. The Olympics. A convivial meeting of international brotherhood, minus Jews and negroes, at least on the German team. To Kim's disgust, German race laws assured that Lilli Henoch, four-time world record holder in discus throwing, would not compete, nor other Jewish athletes. She peeled off two shots, wide again.

This disturbing racial purity idea wasn't confined to Germany. At the last minute, the Americans had pulled two Jews off the long jump team, afraid to offend their Nazi hosts. And this spring, the authorities right here in Uxley had tried to insti-tutionalize Rose, claiming she was feeble-minded and a threat to the community.

Kim narrowed her eyes, held her breath and shot two rounds in quick succession. On the second, the can went flying. Instantly, Shadow bolted from sleep into a border-collie dash.

"Good shot!" someone said. Turning, Kim saw it was Alice.

Taking the can from Shadow, Kim walked forward to replace it on the fence. Returning, she asked, "Have a go at the can?"

"I think I'll stick to knitting needles." Alice's flyaway red hair was pulled into a thick updo that looked like it could hide several needles. After her Estate training, Alice was a pretty good shot, a skill she'd keep hidden.

She leaned against the fence, gazing out. "James took me to dinner at the Three Swans this weekend. I think my being gone for two weeks had him worried. He was solicitous, actually, as though he thought he'd lost me."

"So, when you put out that you were going on holiday at Brighton . . ."

Alice smirked. "He wondered who I'd gone with."

"All to the good?" A little competition might be just what the vicar needed to spark his ardor.

"The thing is, I'm not sure it matters as much as it used to."

Kim put the gun away in its case and looked closely at her friend: Alice leaning comfortably against the split log fence, relaxed, confident and—perhaps her imagination, but—distinctly happy.

Alice met her gaze. "It's not just about the yarn shop and helping out at church bazaars anymore. It's bigger. The world is."

Her attention wandered to the barn on the edge of the paddock, where someone was standing with Walter Babbage.

"There's a young man I'd like you to meet." Alice brushed off her trousers and gestured toward the barn. "Martin Lister. He's been at school in Coomsby, and was helping out with summer repairs to the cricket field, but got in a bit of trouble. He's looking for a summer job."

"What kind of trouble?"

"James tells me Martin was the ringleader at a club for boys with Talents."

"A club?" How intriguing, Kim thought. How wonderful. She knew at once how fine it would be to have a group to share with, if you were a young person with a Talent. And why some schools wouldn't like it.

"They call themselves the Adders," Alice went on. "James says that he's looked into it a bit, and there appear to be clubs like that in a bunch of schools."

"Some parents don't approve, of course?"

"Of course. So, Martin's school got wind of it and treated the whole thing like a conspiracy and told him he wasn't welcome back for the new term unless he apologized. His parents can't get him to, and since the lad's father is friends with James, he asked him to counsel the boy. To see the error of his ways."

Kim sighed. The prejudice against Talents, and sometimes outright denial, was still strong, especially in small towns. "So, they're trying to get him to recant. What's he got?"

"Claims it's *site view*. Seeing past events in a place."

Kim watched as Walter and Martin went into the barn. The kid looked to be about thirteen or fourteen. "So, they think he's faking it."

"And egging the other kids on to believe in special abilities. It might as well be witchcraft, for all they think. He's fifteen, and more than a bit confused, I don't doubt. Want to meet him?"

Of course she did. She was already on his side. Surely, there was something Walter could set the boy to do on the place.

"He'd need somewhere to stay. His dad kicked him out."

Kim hesitated. That might be more responsibility than she could take on, particularly if she got an assignment. But then she saw Alice's wry expression and realized that her friend wanted

Martin at Wrenfell, under Kim's care. James might have some good counsel for the boy, but not on the subject of Talents.

"Just meet him, then?"

Kim put an arm around Alice's shoulders and they headed for the barn.

Inside, Martin was feeding Briar fistfuls of hay.

Alice introduced him to Kim, and he thrust out a dirty hand, thought better of it, and wiped it on his trousers.

"It's okay," Kim said. "Hay in a handshake is good luck around here."

Martin's smile was only a small stab in his cheeks, and then he was back to Briar. The boy was gawky and slender, with pale skin. Her first impression was, *This boy is underfed.* As she looked into his eyes, he shied away, looking at his feet. *Well, then. We'll have to win him over. Briar already has, so it can't be too difficult.* Perhaps he got along better with animals than people.

She noticed a mark on his inside left wrist. A scar, she thought, but with an odd, graceful curve.

He cut a glance at the tack hanging on the barn wall. "Mr. Babbage said I might comb Briar."

"It's called currying, and yes, you may. When you're done, come into the kitchen and we'll see if there's any apple pie."

Walter walked out of the barn with Kim and Alice. "Lad don't know the front end of a 'orse from the rear."

Alice nodded. "He's always worked at his father's chemist shop down to Coomsby."

Walter shrugged and walked back into the barn, muttering, "Old Briar'll teach 'im 'ow."

Alice and Kim went through Wrenfell's back door, finding Mrs. Babbage in the kitchen. The cook greeted Alice, always a favorite, and set out tea.

"Martin seems like a good lad," Alice said. "But his father has taken a hard stance with him. Says he's lazy, can't get out of bed in the morning and hates working in the shop."

"Sounds like every other fifteen-year-old we know," Kim said. Mrs. Babbage nodded at this, carrying a tray of apple pie out from the buttery.

"A few scrapes at school," Alice said. "The kind of fisticuffs boys get into, nothing more. But now he's in trouble for starting a club for Talents, which might as well be witchcraft, for all some people think."

"Witchcraft, is it?" Mrs. Babbage shook her head. "They're just scared of what they don' know, God 'elp 'em." Mrs. Babbage had developed an open mind about these things, now that the family had discovered that their own daughter, Rose, had a major Talent of lowering the surrounding temperature. A previously unknown Talent: *cold cell.*

Kim accepted a wedge of pie. "What would you think of having a hired hand living in for a few weeks, Mrs. Babbage?"

"Stayin' here?" Mrs. Babbage raised her eyebrows. "Well, i' would depend."

"On what?"

"Well, if 'e's a good sort, tha knows."

Martin came in and ducked a bow at Mrs. Babbage. She directed him to the loo to wash up, after which he sat at the lead tabletop with the women and wolfed down two large slabs of pie. He was soon cleaning up the plates in the sink.

Kim had already decided, but she cast a glance at Mrs. Babbage, fixing her with an inquiring look.

Mrs. Babbage nodded with a satisfied smile.

As Kim and Alice were leaving, Mrs. Babbage said, "Did you say you'd be wantin' to bring that gentleman to dinner sometime soon? I could make a nice roast. One o' the nights when Mr. Tavistock is 'ome, too?"

Alice gave Kim a commiserating look and continued on to the back door.

"Stephen, you mean," Kim said, forcing a brightness into her voice. "No, we won't be having him for dinner, I'm afraid."

A little frown of disappointment from Mrs. Babbage. "Oh, I see. Well, tha's all right, then."

Smart, flashy Stephen. An art dealer from York. She could almost laugh, how it had been the standard three-dates-and-you're-out: a chance meeting in the square followed by tea; then a lunch; soon a fancy dinner. Plans for an outing. Then his telephone call. Smooth apologies.

She had quite liked him, perhaps too easily liked him. It had been very like a situation where you were meeting a person who had been highly recommended and you felt duty-bound to find the best in them. Enjoying little quirks, forcing meaningful eye contact. Imagining unbuttoning his shirt. Him unbuttoning hers. After all—tea, lunch, dinner, outing: the next step was his apartment in York.

But then his phone call: So busy, my travels, hard to find time.

She wished he had just said, *I felt I shared too much.* It struck her that they either said too much (a *spill*) or too little (the social lie). That damnable English reserve.

How delicious it had been to be courted—if that was the word—by Erich von Ritter; a man who plied charm with considerable mastery. She supposed it was all right to be a bit enchanted by her former enemy, since he was dead.

And because she had, after all, said no.

7

TUESDAY, JULY 28. At the Dworzec station, Julian hung
back as the train came in. At the last moment, he sprang from
the waiting bench and raced for the door of the nearest carriage.
He hoped that this maneuver, as well as three taxi exchanges,
had shaken the tail. Still, he watched for him, a slim man with a
ferret look.

How could they have found him so quickly? Perhaps they
had been keeping watch on Tilda's flat. He didn't think her uncle
would have reported him.

After he had taken his seat in second class, a man with a
ruddy complexion and muttonchop sideburns sat opposite him,
opening a Polish newspaper.

Just as the train was getting underway, from behind him
Julian heard someone say in heavily accented English, "Excuse
me, sir, but will you come with me?"

Julian turned to see ferret man standing in the aisle. The man tilted his head to the back of the car. He palmed open a warrant card. Polish intelligence. "It is advisable to come."

Christ. He was in for it now. "There is some mistake. I am a tourist."

"Perhaps a mistake, you are right. You will come?"

There was no help for it. Julian stood up and followed the man down the aisle toward the rear carriage door. He had made a stupid mistake in going to Tilda's flat. There was no reason Polish intelligence would be keeping her in view; if they thought she was going to leave the country, they would have just picked her up. A good chance this fellow was associated with the mole who was leaking names of Polish Talents. At her flat they could have been waiting for her to come home. To eliminate her.

Bad luck for him now, here on the train. A traitor in their organization would not be bound by rules of civility.

In the inter-carriage way, the clatter was deafening as hot air rushed up through the metal slats of the floor.

"What's this about?" Julian said.

"We will go into the next car, my compartment. A short journey, and then my superior will be speaking to you. But first, your passport?"

Julian handed it over. Ferret man gave it a cursory glance. "Thank you, Mr. Howard. A weapon on your person?"

"For security. A foreign country . . ." He shrugged.

"Of course. Poland is known for its dangers." Ironic. "I will keep it safe for you."

Julian opened his jacket to show his shoulder holster and after a nod from the agent, handed over his revolver.

"I would like to speak with the British embassy." Not

answering, ferret man nodded to the next car. Julian said, "The WC? Then I have no problem answering questions, of course."

They stopped outside the toilet, and the agent nodded at him.

Inside, Julian tried the window, but it wouldn't budge. As a second choice for ditching the Macia Antonik passport, he jammed it behind the water tank. He flushed the toilet, ran his hands under the tap, dried them, and joined the Polish agent in the corridor.

In forty-five minutes of travel, ferret man had nothing to say. Then, as night came on, the train slowed and the station name loomed into view: Częstochowa. Julian's escort nodded for him to rise.

Apparently they were not going to Warsaw.

At the Częstochowa station office, he sat in a small back room smelling of sweat and burned coffee. Outside, a sudden rain thundered on the pavement. He began to hope, since he was in a quasi-public place, that an interrogation was all they had in mind.

A large man in a good suit entered the room. Bald, self-assured, courteous for now. "Mr. Howard. I am Gustaw Bajek, Polish intelligence."

"Pleased to meet you."

Gustaw Bajek gave an appreciative smile. "Most people are not so pleased. But this is good to hear." His English was excellent. He took out Julian's passport and placed it on the table.

A knock at the door, and in came the man with muttonchop sideburns. He handed his boss another passport, this one a little scraped up from the water tank.

When they were alone again, Bajek took a seat opposite him, sitting heavily in the rickety chair, but looking as though he were ready for a long night of conversation. "Now, Mr. Howard, may I have your real name, please?"

They stared at each other for a moment, a friendly enough game up to now. "Julian Tavistock." They'd find out anyway.

"And your purpose in traveling to Cracow?"

"Tourism."

The bald man regarded him for a few moments. Then he reached over and opened the Macia Antonik passport to the photo page. "This woman, whose real name—as you know—is Tilda Mazur, is the subject of a murder investigation. So, I trust you will tell me what you know."

Julian hoped he meant that she was a suspect. But now, to his dismay, he learned otherwise.

"The woman is dead."

Ah, too late. He glanced at the false passport they had prepared for Tilda, her picture upside down now. Too late.

Gustaw Bajek watched his reaction, then resumed. "You are in a great deal of trouble. Carrying a forged passport—two of them, in fact—and seen at the murder victim's home. You are, of course, a British undercover agent. Jail is next."

If they tried to make something out of this, Julian was on his own, since there would be no diplomatic immunity for him under a false passport. All very unpleasant for him personally and embarrassing for His Majesty's Government.

The agent took out a pack of Gitanes, lighting one, and offering the pack to Julian.

Julian would have much preferred his pipe, but decided not to quibble.

"I believe you were going to extract her," the agent said,

keeping an even tone as though, between the two of them, this sort of thing, however regrettable, was rather common.

"That would be contrary to our countries' mutual respect and obligations."

Gustaw Bajek nodded out the window where Julian could see, under the lights of the railway platform, two policemen conferring. "The local police are quite eager to talk to you. I think you would rather talk to me. I am afraid my police colleagues do not have a refined grasp of mutual respect and obligations."

Julian now had a choice. He could admit his agency's complicity—embarrassing HMG. Or, understanding that in police custody this might happen anyway, he could give them what they wanted, and in doing so, perhaps be extended a professional courtesy from a sister agency.

Julian blew a long stream of smoke to clear his lungs. Wretched Gitanes. "Tilda Mazur was an 8 for *darkening*. She asked for asylum."

A policeman, dripping wet, came in without knocking. He threw a quick, hostile glance at Julian.

"Not now, Feliks," Bajek said. "Please."

After a proprietary stare at Julian, Feliks reluctantly left.

"Asylum?" Gustaw Bajek cocked his head as though confused, which Julian knew he wasn't. "Why didn't she just leave?"

"She thought you had a mole in the intelligence services or at Sosnowa House in particular." Sosnowa House was the Polish counterpart of Monkton Hall. "She believed that this individual was giving names of Polish Talents to the Germans. Talents who ended up run over by buses."

"A mole. Well." He blew a long stream of smoke, a gesture of disgust. "She was right about that, obviously."

"How did she die?" Julian asked.

"Strangled in the nearby field. Four or five days ago, we think, but her body was only discovered this afternoon."

Julian thought of her uncle waiting for her return, the little flat with the doll on the mantel. The rain beat upon the roof of the ticket office, heavy as lead shot. He looked at the passport, still open on the table. The girl's expression seemed to accuse him. *Why didn't you come?*

The agent went on. "So, she could not trust her handlers, could not go to the police. And therefore turned to you. Your embassy, then?"

Julian made a noncommittal gesture.

"Of course, the Germans had no use for her except to make sure we did not make use of her. One cannot force a Talent to work."

Talents were not dependable when the asset's heart wasn't in it; even the Germans couldn't devise an assault on the heart. No, Gestapo plans for Tilda were doubtless to kill her. *Darkening* was too critical a Talent for the Germans to permit the Poles to possess, that is, if Hitler had designs on Polish territory. Where steel was not enough, strong Talents could give the edge. Every military power knew that by now, even if most lagged far behind Germany's research and asset stockpile.

"So, you have travelled all this way for nothing." Gustaw Bajek put his hands on his knees and hoisted himself to his feet with a grunt. "Come with me."

They walked out into the battering rain. On the railway platform, ferret man and muttonchops nodded genially at Julian and handed their boss an umbrella. These Poles were a friendly lot. Well, they were winning the match, so they could afford to be cheerful.

SERPENT IN THE HEATHER

Bajek flicked his cigarette away and led Julian from the platform and across the car park, pavement glistening in the station lights. He gave Julian the umbrella and walked on bareheaded as though, being bald, rain was less of a concern. They walked toward a small group of men in a field lit with makeshift lamps.

They had taken Tilda's body away, and the police were searching for evidence in the long grass.

"You see that old man there?" Bajek gestured at a white-haired, stooped man who stood in the sodden grass with his eyes closed. A policeman held an umbrella over him. "He is our best *site view.*"

Obviously, the Polish police were using Talents in crime investigation, the same as the British. "Has he seen anything?"

Gustaw Bajek shrugged. "His Talent goes to a 4 on the scale. At that level they can pick up only strong emotions which, with murder, is usually the fear and pain of the victim. This time, though, we have something more. It must have been a strong presence in the woman's mind, or the murderer's."

"What did he see?"

"Fire."

"Just that?"

"A large building. Perhaps a government building, or a factory. No details. Still, it is odd." He stared at the men combing the site for clues. "Something else that is odd."

Bajek was bringing Julian into the matter. Perhaps no jail after all.

"This is the first one who was obviously murdered. Until now, the executions were made to look like accidents or suicides. They grow bolder."

So, Tilda was right: there had been a string of killings.

Bajek stared through the downpour at the crime scene. "There is loose amongst us a . . . you would say, *predator*. The Russian bear, the German wolf, yes? But we Poles are so busy arguing among ourselves that we cannot see the shadows looming. It is my belief that this work, it is German." He looked at Julian, appraising him. "The *Sicherheitsdienst*, the SD, have eliminated nine Talents in our country. In France, three. Czechoslovakia, also three."

Fifteen murders. That was an ugly number. "Are you sure it's German work?"

Bajek took the cigarette pack from his pocket. Julian held the umbrella over him as he scratched his thumbnail against a wooden match, igniting it. He took his time, inhaling deeply, perhaps deciding whether to answer. He offered the pack to Julian, who shook his head.

"Because we have been tracking a particular and very interesting code name. *Nachteule*. You would say *Night Owl*. The Germans and their poetry." Gustaw spit out a stray thread of tobacco. "You are not the only ones with spies in good places."

"It's a plan of extermination, then," Julian said.

"Yes. Your French allies, they have not told you this?" Gustaw shook his head. "There should be more trust, *n'est-ce pas?*"

"*Oui.*" Julian went on. "Tilda's uncle doesn't trust you. But he told me that she was followed by a man with thick glasses, looked to be in his early thirties. And that he was Dutch."

Bajek narrowed his eyes. Julian related the conversation he'd had with the policeman.

"Dutch? That is most interesting. One of the recent Talent murders here was linked with a Dutchman. The wife of the victim said a man with such an accent had telephoned the house, and soon her husband left for some kind of meeting. He took a

bad fall off a bridge." He turned around and motioned to someone across the car park.

"The Dutch are allies," Julian observed.

"Perhaps he goes on his own, to the Germans. Also, we have
another very interesting clue that I will tell you. *Nachteule* has a
wealthy friend . . . a benefactor. And British, you see."

British. "Who?"

"We do not know." The bald man smiled without humor.
"Naturally, we would like to."

A car pulled up, and Bajek gestured toward it. Julian slid
into the back seat, followed by Bajek. In the driver's seat, ferret
man handed a towel back to his boss, who wiped off with it.

They sat for a minute while Julian stashed the umbrella
under the forward seat.

The agent brought out Julian's passport, handing it to him.
"I must ask you to leave Poland, Mr. Howard. Today. After that,
the police may create difficulties for you."

Julian accepted the passport with a grateful smile. "I understand." Bajek nodded at ferret man, who handed back the gun he
had confiscated earlier.

Reaching into his breast pocket, Bajek took out Tilda's passport and thumbed it open to the photo page. The little booklet
was just visible from the lights set up in the field. He nodded
in appreciation. "This is very nice work. Not clumsy, like some
we see."

"We try."

"Well. You will not need it now." Gazing for a few moments
at Tilda's picture, he replaced it in his pocket. "From here you
can take the train back to Cracow, and from there you will leave
Poland on the first train. My man will see that you safely make
your connection."

The car pulled around to the station waiting room. Gustaw
Bajek nodded at him to get out. "Good luck, Julian Tavistock."

"Will I need it?"

"We will all need it." He shrugged. "Perhaps Poland more
than you."

8

FRIDAY, JULY 31. "We're making some progress with young Martin, but he won't admit he's making up this . . . special power."

Martin had slept late and had been sneaking down the stairs to get to the barn and his new job when he heard his name from the parlor. He crept closer to the open door.

Miss Kim was saying over the clatter serving tea, "Perhaps he believes it. Suppose, for instance, that I thought I could sing, and told the choir director at All Saints that I should have a solo. But I had the voice of a frog."

"Ah, yes, I see what you're driving at. But it's not the same at all, really. People can be mistaken about the degree of their natural abilities. But powers that are entirely made up?"

Made up, Martin thought with disdain. So the vicar didn't believe him at all, despite acting so friendly and saying he ought to *unburden* himself. He glanced down the hall that went all the way to the back door. Old Babbage hadn't come looking for him yet.

"Do you think it's really quite *settled*," Miss Kim said, "that Talents are just a figment of the imagination? Evidence is building in their favor."

"Evidence? You'd have to show me. Seeing the past whilst holding a hanky belonging to someone . . ." Here the words faded. ". . . just rubbish. Transport a teapot across a room without touching it, seeing things far away when one is not present. Surely you don't believe it." A pause where Martin could imagine the old wanker shaking his head in pity.

"To be honest, Vicar, I have seen a few such things."

"Oh? I must say, Miss Tavistock, I am surprised."

Martin was surprised too. He crept closer to the door to hear better.

Miss Kim was saying, "We should at least keep an open mind, don't you think?"

"Well. One can't argue with an open mind, can one? But in the case before us, the lad's just trying to appear big, what with his poor marks at school and not getting on at his father's shop. I fear this is what comes when young people stray from Christian teachings."

"Well," Kim said, "I'm very glad that the Listers don't mind Martin staying here for a few weeks. We certainly . . ."

A shuffling sound, and Martin spun around to find Walter Babbage staring at him from down the hall. Going down to meet him, Martin said, "I was just coming," though he figured Babbage knew different. *Oh, sod it, anyway.*

He followed Babbage out the door, past the kitchen where the smell of the morning fry-up beckoned him. He guessed he'd missed breakfast, even though it was only eight thirty. He was starving, but Briar needed feeding too, and he hoped that would be his job. He liked looking into that horse's big round eyes. You couldn't tell what a horse was thinking, but he was pretty sure it wasn't *This one's a liar.*

He'd only been at Wrenfell two days, and he had to admit it was grand. All those rooms and *two* toilets, so you didn't have to wait, and the meals with ham and heaps of mash and even butter. And then yesterday for a late-night snack, Mrs. Babbage had put a leftover Yorkshire pudding on a dish in his room.

And now that he knew Miss Kim was on his side, he didn't ever want to go home. But to earn his keep, he'd have to learn fast about horses. It wasn't as though he'd *never* been around a horse, there was that brown and white one up to Aunt Pim's, and Briar seemed to like him. And Rose, Babbage's daughter, she was friendly right off. She'd stood in the hall outside his door yesterday when he was getting settled in Kim's brother's old room and said, "I got me *cold cell.* An' you got *seein' things as happened.*" And then she sort of ducked a curtsy and was gone.

Whatever *cold cell* was. It was one he hadn't heard of. But Miss Kim had said he and Rose might have some things in common, and maybe that's what she meant, that they both had Talents, him and Rose. So, Wrenfell was a bit of all right.

Out in the barn he was rubbing ointment into what Babbage called tack, and Briar in her stall was flicking her tail at flies. He'd never been in a place that smelled like this, a big stew of hay, oiled leather, and earthy turds. His mum would think it dirty, but it wasn't at all.

The vicar had driven off after swilling his tea. Hathaway was against him, against Talents, for sure. Yesterday during his visit the vicar claimed that Teddy admitted he didn't really have a Talent, that he'd lied to the club members. It was just something he'd said to fit in. That plonker! Teddy was new to Adders and hadn't yet done his initiation where he had to show his Talent.

So, it might be true he didn't have one. If he did, he'd be loyal to the club, the one place where you got admired for what you could do, the one place where you knew you were special. He hoped Christopher stayed loyal.

There was only him and Teddy and Christopher in the club, at least up to end of last term. You had to be careful who you asked. Sometimes, you could pull up your sleeve a little to show the ink mark, but if people looked funny at it, you could say you were just playing around. He'd first seen the mark, a wavy line with an eye at front and three crosshatches over the tail, on a batman's hand last fall when they had their match with Lambert's down at Hull. The fellow, Gil, he said he had *attraction*, and did Martin know what that was? And he'd said, sure, that was when lots of people just right away liked you, and it was a Talent, wasn't it? Which Martin very well knew, because he'd studied about Talents at the library. And it was true about Gil; Martin had really liked him even though Gil's team skunked Coomsby St. Mary's school.

It had been exciting to meet someone who was like him, someone else with a Talent. Did Gil ever hear of *site view*? Sure, he says. And then he tells Martin about Adder clubs, and how you could ink on the wavy line, the one that looked like a snake.

That was the first thing he did when he got home. And then he'd started a club at school.

Buffing the reins to a nice, hard finish, he vowed he'd never give up Christopher's name to them. Even if Teddy already had, it was a point of honor when you gave your word to keep a secret. Maybe he did always mess up. But at least he was no traitor.

"All done, then?" Walter Babbage had come back in with a wheelbarrow. When Martin showed him the gleaming bridle, and was looking forward to a break for scones and butter, the old man only grunted and gave him another bunch of crusty reins.

Even with all the work, he'd rather be at Wrenfell than anywhere. Maybe Miss Kim would let him stay for the school year. Somehow, he'd have to prove himself.

"'Youth murder shocks Cambridgeshire.'" Kim slowly lowered the *Daily Telegraph* onto the lead-topped kitchen table, staring ahead, not focusing.

Mrs. Babbage saw her reaction and nodded at the headline. "Another young lad, it's 'orrible, miss."

It was. The idea that a lunatic was running free and had cut short a boy's life sickened her. *Two* boys' lives. So, the first one might not have been an isolated act of rage or madness.

"They will find him, Mrs. Babbage," Kim said. "You can be sure of that."

Mrs. Babbage furrowed her brow, turning back to her biscuit dough on the pastry table.

Sitting next to Kim, Martin patted his mouth with a napkin over an empty plate. He picked up the newspaper.

The authorities weren't giving out details but had confirmed that the murder shared "certain characteristics" in common with the murder of an adolescent four days earlier in Portsmouth. Styled the "second grisly youth murder," the article said the boy had been found near the River Ouse in Ely, Cambridgeshire, after having gone missing overnight. The thought of what these murders might become stirred darkly in Kim. Would the killer be content with two?

Mrs. Babbage put a second bacon sandwich in front of Martin. It disappeared quickly, with the boy hardly stopping to breathe. Kim exchanged glances with Mrs. Babbage, who had earlier opined that with hands and feet as big as Martin's, he was a lad in need of proper meals, fare obviously lacking in the Lister household.

Martin looked up from reading the article. "So, it's the same killer, the one that murdered that student in Portsmouth."

"Yes, it might be."

"It is. You don't just get two grisly murders all the same month."

Grisly. She wondered if Martin even knew what that word meant. And in what way were the murders grisly? It was almost worse not knowing. How awful, just to hope that the youngsters died swiftly. She pushed away her plate with its half-eaten sandwich.

"Two boys gone." Kim shook her head. "It's very sad."

"I don't feel sad," Martin said. "Just angry." He picked up a butter knife and turned it in his hand, as the flatware gleamed in the afternoon light from the window.

Kim looked at him a moment. "Actually, I am too." They made eye contact for a split second, and then Martin shied away and stood to take his plate to the sink.

"So, you'll not be wantin' puddin', then," Mrs. Babbage said, straight-faced.

Martin sat back down.

How the families would cope, Kim didn't know. Or maybe she did. She could still hear her mother's wails from long ago, when the news had come from the battlefront. The way war deaths went, the authorities would drive up to the homes and bring a letter. Sometimes, the parents couldn't open it for their hands shaking. But Julian had slid the letter opener through the top. They noticed Kim in the doorway and asked Mrs. Babbage to take her to the kitchen, and she had held Kim to her bosom as her mother sobbed so loudly that the house itself seemed wracked with pain.

Perhaps it was common that, facing the worst, women wailed and men did not. She wondered, not for the first time, if her father might have turned out differently if he had cried for Robert. Maybe he had stayed silent for Kim and her mother's sake, because someone had to batten things down and keep people from losing their grip. *Steady on*, she'd heard him tell her mother. That had been in the hallway upstairs after the letter had been opened and read. *Steady on*. How strange to urge this on someone in the throes of grief. Perhaps it was the English way, even if your beloved older brother or son died horribly on the Ypres Salient. Above all, one must remain steady.

That night, Martin came downstairs to the pile of newspapers and cut out the article on the River Ouse murder. He was just slipping it under the blotter in his room to join the other one when Rose came by. She stood in the door until he invited her in.

"Wha's tha' on your wrist, then?" she asked.

"Just a wavy line." He'd inked it so many times, it was a part of his skin.

Rose nodded doubtfully. Martin didn't think girls could be in Adders, even if they did have a Talent. The subject had never come up, and besides she wasn't in school, or not in Coomsby St. Mary's, anyway. But that had never come up, either.

"Looks like a snake, though, don' it?" she said.

"Don't you ever draw on yourself?"

She grinned, covering her mouth, as though she couldn't imagine such a thing. Rose was four years older than him, but she seemed much younger. That was nothing to make fun of, Miss Kim had said.

"My da says you got a way wi' 'orses."

"He said that?"

"Aye."

He tried to act like it was nothing big, but he liked hearing that.

"So, what's *cold cell*, then?"

"It's 'ow a big pocket o' cold comes up an' sometimes a lil' storm, too. It dinna last long."

He looked at her, impressed. "You can make a storm?" With that one, she could have got into Adders for sure.

"I guess. 'Cept not when I try." She pursed her lips, thinking. "It's like there's birds flyin' high, an' they look down an' think, *There she is, let's go visit.*"

He knew storms weren't like birds, but he got what she meant. "That's like me. When I see things that went on, it's never when I want to. Like they're hovering there, and one picture steps forward all of a sudden."

She nodded. "Aye, just like tha'. Like a visitor."

When Rose heard her mother calling her, she got up to leave. Stopping at the door, she turned to look at him. "I'm awfu' glad you've coom, Martin." Then she made a curtsy, pulling her white apron to the side like it was a party dress.

9

FRIDAY, JULY 31. "Night Owl?" E repeated. He leaned back in his leather button chair, commanding an imposing desk in front of bay windows with a view of St. James's Park in the distance.

Julian nodded. "*Nachteule*. Polish intelligence has been tracking the operation for months."

"Anything from Woodbird?" Their man in the *Abwehr*.

"He's digging." They'd sent a wireless query out the night before to their asset, who sat smack in the middle of the German army's intelligence section.

E turned a page over in the file before him. "In your opinion this Polish operative—Gustaw Bajek—is reliable? Caught you red-handed, and just drops state secrets in your lap?" Although on the one hand pleased, E was always watchful for misdirection, betrayal, and lies, every secret service's best weapons.

"I think he's playing straight with us. He shared with me that they have a small lead on the assassin, or one of them. A man with a Dutch accent. I think that showed good faith. As for the English benefactor, they'd like us to shut down the funding source, naturally."

E splayed the loose papers of the report on his desk, frowning. "How much money?"

"They don't know, but over a billion Reichsmark have been funneled into the Nazi front company, MEFO, the Society for Metallurgical Research. Some of that's been converted from pounds sterling."

"I don't care if it's the German orphans' fund or the Berlin Philharmonic," E said. "We'll put a stop to it as soon as you find the British donor."

"Giving money to the Nazis is not against the law," Julian pointed out.

"We'll leave it to Whitehall once we have our man." E closed the file. "And what about our own Talents? We may be at risk from this *Nachteule*."

"We could be," Julian said. Hitler's *Nachteule* targets had been Continental so far, but Bajek's claim of a program to exterminate Talents there was troubling. And believable, in keeping with German exploitation of their several years' head start with research on meta-abilities. From the beginning of the Talent outbreak during the war, the Germans had fielded a top research team to find military uses of Talents. Much to E's and Julian's dismay, England had let their war apparatus dribble away, nor were they playing catch-up yet. Except for Monkton Hall. That was something, at least.

"Extra security up on the moors, then," E said. "For HARC." Monkton Hall's code name, the Historical Archives and Records Centre.

Julian nodded. "At the very least a new security fence, and sentries posted, I should think."

"And Churchill?" E flashed a prism of light on the wall from his paperweight, a souvenir from the battle of the Marne. It looked like a piece of shrapnel floated in the glass. Julian imagined it had been dug out of his boss, but he had not asked. They were friends from their Eton days, but as with most people, they seldom discussed the Great War.

"We ought to put him in the picture," Julian said. "With his *conceptor* Talent he could be a target, even if he is out of government." Churchill, a great fan of new styles of weapons, had been tested at Monkton and astonishingly, had been rated a 10.

E nodded. "I'll suggest Whitehall contact him. Put him on alert, though I doubt he'll want security, not on the evidence we have so far."

"And the rest of our strong Talent assets are scattered all over the country," Julian said. "We can't watch everybody."

"Not concerned about Sparrow, then?" Sparrow, the code name for Julian's daughter.

Her Talent of the *spill* was quite strong at 6, with no British asset any higher in her category. Julian shook his head. "No. She's trained. And I have my foreman on watch at Wrenfell, as always." He'd tell Owen Cherwell to alert her to possible danger. Of course, Julian himself couldn't have that talk with her. She might be SIS, but the only case officer she knew was Owen. It was standard compartmentalization, but it played hell with his relationship with his daughter.

Owen had suggested that Kim was restless for an assignment. Nothing to give her right now, but at least she had her new charge, a boy she'd taken in at the farm. He'd rung her up when he'd returned from Poland. She had brought him up to speed on the lad, Martin, and had also wanted to talk about the murdered boys. He hoped the crimes wouldn't haunt her, with her soft spot for youngsters.

E reached again for his glass paperweight and turned it over in his hand, regarding it. "You've been saying that Sparrow is ready for a bigger assignment. What about the Continent? That dust-up in Geneva? Or attach her to the Paris station. Just to listen. Could have some benefit, don't you think?"

He very much *did* think. But E continued to think of her as a passive *spill* asset, a damned limited perspective. Kim was on her way to demonstrating excellent operational judgment. In fact, if Kim hadn't been relentless in the Prestwich Affair, Germany could have secured a foothold in country. Or rather more than a foothold. It remained unclear if Erich von Ritter, heading up the German operation, had had time before his death to tell Berlin about Kim's ability and her role as a spy. Since von Ritter had spared Kim from his suicidal end at Rievaulx Abbey, perhaps he had kept her identity secret. It would make a European mission more likely for Kim.

"I'm keeping my eye out for the right posting," Julian said.

E nodded. "Carry on, then. Inform me immediately if you get a lead on the *Nachteule* funds."

"Chief."

E planned on staying in the city. Most of Whitehall would abandon London for the month of August, but E preferred his London flat to the estate at Litchfield. His wife preferred Litchfield, and that was reason enough.

ALBEMARLE STREET

THAT EVENING. "We could meet tonight," Julian said, cradling the phone receiver to his ear while undoing his tie. It was last-minute to ring up Olivia, but he thought perhaps she'd come. He was free until around eleven, when he was meeting with his team, but he hoped he could take her out somewhere discreet for supper.

"Oh, Julian, I can't. I promised Mum I'd have dinner at their place. She's having some people over."

"Then a drink." He hadn't seen her since his return. "The King's Head?"

A long pause. "Yes, all right. The Savoy, though?"

Closer to her flat, maybe too public. But: "Yes."

He made sure he got there before her so she could slip in and they would not be left standing looking for a table.

She wore a flowered dress with a little jacket. Red lipstick, for his benefit, he thought. He picked her out immediately, with her hair rolled forward in that elegant updo for which she was justly famous in the head office.

"I hope you don't think this is"—she looked around—"too public."

"No. Just this once." In fact, he hadn't liked her choice of the Savoy. Their affair had not stayed under wraps as E had wanted. It had come up more than once with the chief. He ordered a sloe gin for her, whisky for himself. When the waiter left, he added, "We have five hundred other watering holes left in London." This remark put a damper on their mood, that they had to scurry from one clandestine place to the next.

"How was Berlin?"

"It went hard."

A little furrow between her eyes. "Berlin can be that way." She didn't say, *Did you kill someone?* Or, *Did someone try to kill you?* "I'm glad you're back. Sorry this is all rushed. I don't have long."

He was more disappointed than he had realized that she'd be busy tonight. "I was three days too late," he said.

She raised her chin in that way she had of saying, *I understand.* Under the table she took his hand.

He thought Olivia Hennessey was perhaps the only woman he could speak to about his life. Not that he had said much, even now, but still, he felt that she understood, if not the facts, then the upshot of it all. What remained when you came home and tried to sort it out.

When she removed her hand to check her watch, he said, so directly it surprised him, "Would you ever leave the service, Olivia?"

She looked around the room as though searching for an escape route. "Oh, I don't know. . . ."

It was the wrong thing for him to have said, he knew it. Where had it come from? They had known each other for twelve years, been lovers for two and a half months. He wished he hadn't said it, and then he didn't care. He was sixty-two years old, not some youngster afraid of a woman saying no.

"Darling, I have to go."

"I know you do." He called for the tab. "Who will be at your parents'?"

Her gaze slid sideways. "A friend of the family's."

So, just one other. "A friend of *yours*?"

"You're not free to ask me that." They faced off now. "We work for E," she said, simply stating the bare fact of the impediment to their relationship. She collected her purse, but before getting up, she turned back to him. "Would *you* ever leave?"

It was more than fair to ask. Eventually, their affair would become common knowledge in the Office, and then, likely one of them would have to go. It couldn't automatically be her, was unlikely to be her. She had been with E longer, had built her life around that suite of offices on Broadway.

"*Would* you?"

He couldn't answer her, or didn't. She smiled forgivingly, resignedly, then gathered her purse and gloves and went for her taxi.

A SAFE FLAT

LATER THAN NIGHT. Behind shuttered and curtained windows in a flat near Piccadilly, Julian met with his best team, Elsa Rampling and Fin Hewitt. The room was appointed with four mismatched chairs, a desk, a single bed, and a cigarette-burned coffee table that doubled as a dining surface and a table for maps and case files.

On designated evenings, their eleven-fifteen meetings usually lasted until midnight, punctuated by the eleven-thirty wireless transmission from their man in Berlin, Woodbird.

In readiness for the transmission, the wireless set was turned on, spitting static and the faint whine of electromagnetic interference. Elsa sat in the best chair, wearing a dowdy hat and a shapeless chintz dress. At fifty-six, her prematurely white hair added the perfect finish to her little-old-lady role—as well as the excellent befuddled expression that belied her cool nerves and deadly aim with a pistol.

Fin, their best man on Morse code, sat with his feet on the table next to carry-out sacks of scones, smoking another Woodbine. Small and muscular, he was also a superb street fighter, a skill more than one foreign agent had discovered to their chagrin.

He blew a stream of smoke out the side of his mouth. "Birdie's had nothin' for two weeks. Maybe tonight we get lucky." *All quiet nothing to report* was the sign-of-life notice that came in unless there was intel to report.

It hadn't been much over twenty-four hours since SIS sent the query to their mole in the *Abwehr*. Not much time for Woodbird to search out patrons of *Nachteule*, but he fiercely hoped for a little luck. With more than professional interest, he wanted to flush out the British collaborator. It would give Julian special pleasure to staunch the flow of British pounds to Nazi Germany, even if it didn't go far enough to avenge Tilda Mazur.

A few minutes to go before Woodbird's transmission. Fin pulled his feet off the desk, sitting up straight and donning the headset, turning the dials to home in on the frequency.

"I wonder," Elsa said, "why an Englishman would support killing Talents in Poland? It's not as though the Poles could put up much of a fight anyway, if Hitler comes calling." She shifted in her chair, wincing. Since last spring she'd been on light duty after being thrown from a moving train in pursuit of German agents. This exploit had burnished her reputation in the Office; she had lost, but she had also survived.

Julian shrugged. "There were French murders too. They can put up a fight."

Fin snorted at the idea of the French army. The radio band whistled in the background like a profoundly submerged scream. He lit another cigarette from the last of the old one.

"And we think their nasty little plan might migrate here?" Elsa asked.

"We'll take precautions," Julian said.

Precisely at eleven thirty, the tones and clicks of the transmission began. Fin pulled his writing tablet close. After the sign-on code, when he put his pencil to the tablet, Julian and Elsa knew the report had substance. In Fin's right hand his pencil scratched away, while in his left the cigarette ash grew long. After six minutes the transmission ended with the sign-off code.

Fin flicked his ash on the floor and opened the code book. "Our boy was talkative." He bent over the encrypted message and began transcribing as Julian and Elsa waited in silence. "If you stare at me like that," Fin said, grinning, "it'll throw me off." And kept working.

Ten minutes later he handed the message to Julian. "By God, he's got her," Fin said. He looked up at his associates, eyes alight. "Coslett, Dorothea Coslett, is our benefactor. Seventy-eight years old. A dowager baroness in Wales."

Julian read the report twice before passing the tablet to Elsa.

Fin asked, "Ever heard of her, boss?"

Julian paused. "Maybe. The woman's involved in some kind of big spiritualist group."

"Spiritualist?" Elsa asked. "You mean like Ouija boards? Contacting the departed?"

Fin looked at his dead cigarette. "I had a dog once. Wouldn't mind hearing how he's doin'."

Julian looked at the tablet and felt the familiar hungry attention that dead-bang intelligence always produced. Dorothea Coslett, was it? They couldn't admit they knew her connection to *Nachteule* without compromising the Woodbird source, but Julian could imagine the Foreign Office cooking up a story that her charitable donations were being used for underworld crime.

"Work up a dossier on Coslett and her spiritualism set, then," he said to Fin. "Elsa, you're working with Monkton Hall to locate our highest Talents and get them coverage."

"I'm working with Owen on the list," she replied, getting to her feet. As the group made ready to disperse, she said, "Dorothea Coslett. Sounds like a harmless old lady."

As Julian and Fin both gave her a look, she smiled sweetly and patted her straw purse with its .38 revolver.

10

MONDAY, AUGUST 3. Julian tucked his sopping wet umbrella under the pew and flicked water off his hat, which he placed on the pew next to a funeral program that someone had left behind: *In remembrance of Winifred Holt.*

St. James's was a small church by London standards, but it was Julian's favorite. Its galleries on three sides provided a sheltering aspect; a man in tattered clothing must have felt the same, for on the other side of the sanctuary, he slept on a pew. Other than him, Julian was alone in the church.

The carved screen in back of the altar, a spectacular Grinling Gibbons, offered a focal point for contemplation. Today, however, his thoughts were mundane. He hadn't been able to get through to Olivia for four days. One would think that a Secret Intelligence Service officer could find his own mistress.

Right on time, Elsa slid in next to him. Her chalk marks

on an Albemarle Street lamppost had signaled a need to meet.

Julian contemplated the Gibbons screen. "Are you religious, Elsa?"

"Can't say that I am."

Julian couldn't find it within himself to be a religious man, but when he contemplated the art that God had apparently inspired in others, he took comfort that *someone* believed.

They kept their voices low. "But you're not immune to the peace of it all? The beauty?"

Elsa looked up at the vaulted ceiling. "The business we're in, boss. Hard to believe we're all being looked after. Especially today."

He cut a glance at her.

"You might have read there was a child killed yesterday in Cambridgeshire. Fourteen years old." Julian nodded that he had. "Throat cut with a sharp blade. And it followed the same crime scene features as that of another murdered boy, one down in Portsmouth. The victim was found sitting propped up against a tree, as though asleep."

The rain came harder against the stained-glass windows, and the day's darkness seemed to deepen. "The bodies were displayed, then." He shook his head. "Looks like it's the same perpetrator."

"The police are convinced of it. Rather as though the killer wanted to shock with the almost-lifelike position of the bodies."

He heard the muffled sound of the front door of the church closing. Julian turned around just far enough to glance toward the vestibule.

"Rupert Bristow was the second boy's name," she went on. "And here's the worst part—"

"There's worse?"

"Yes. The police have shared with us that the first young person murdered, Ewan Knox, had a Talent. And this afternoon they've found out that the second young murder victim did as well."

"Christ," Julian breathed.

"It could be coincidence. The killer targeted two young people. Maybe they just happened to have, or were claiming to have, Talents."

"Right, could mean nothing." No reason it would be the start of a trend. No reason it would be related to the *Nachteule* murders, either. His mind searched for patterns too much, perhaps.

She went on. "No sexual contact. Both youths were missing only a few hours before being found. No sign of torture, but one of the boys put up quite a fight."

A heavily built man came into the sanctuary, carrying his leather cap. He sat on the other side of the aisle, three rows forward of Julian and Elsa.

"How did they find out the boys had Talents?"

"Their friends knew. Ewan Knox's Talent was *object reading*. And Rupert Bristow, *disguise*."

"*Disguise*, by God?" That was a Talent Monkton Hall hadn't encountered very often.

"Yes, the Bristow boy. His friends said he had the knack of adopting expressions that made him look rather unlike himself. Maybe it was just an ordinary ability to mimic, or else it was the real thing, mentally influencing what others see. But Rupert thought he had one, because he joined a club, supposed to be a secret club. Called the Adders, a bit of a fad in schools these days, apparently."

"I've heard of them." Julian had assumed Martin's club was the only one. But he hadn't asked either Kim or Martin about the group. "We've had a bit of a dust-up about an Adder club in Yorkshire. Are the clubs common, then?"

"They've spread, not sure how far. The clubs are frowned on, and some schools have banned them, but that just drove them to secrecy. It was one of the club members who told the police about Rupert."

"These club members could be lying. Bragging."

"Yes, they could. I expect the clubs are attracting all sorts of misfits."

Julian chewed on all this for a time. Kim was the wrong age for the apparent targets. But Martin Lister fit right in. It was very odd to have two concerns about British Talents at the same time: *Nachteule* migrating to England, and a murderer of adolescents on the loose. Christ God, it was a miserable world.

"All right, Elsa. I'm going to attach you to the police investigation. If we have another murder that fits the MO, you'll track down any correlations amongst the victims. Not that this is going to go further, but if it does, we need to know if the targets have Talents."

"Do you think these two murders are tied to *Nachteule*? In both sets of crimes, Talents die."

"We'll watch for possible connections," Julian said. "The moment any more victims are clearly Talents, that's when we take a closer interest. Meanwhile, let's look into these clubs. If young Talents are the target, then this is one way victims could be chosen. Find out if there's any communication among them, any ring leaders or adult contacts."

The Office's sister organization, the Security Service, wouldn't like them elbowing in on what might appear a domestic matter, but he'd leave that problem to E.

Elsa passed him a dossier. "Fin's report on our British

Nachteule benefactor. Dorothea Coslett is the Dowager Baroness Ellesmere. Lives in North Wales. Her son is Powell Coslett, Baron Ellesmere. The baroness has been an unabashed supporter of the Nazi cause since Hitler came to power, and twice travelled to Germany where she met with some of the inner circle. Her group is called Ancient Light, boasting of two thousand followers scattered throughout Great Britain, but only about eight hundred of them tithe regularly. They are loosely connected, meeting at local sites of standing stones, barrows, and so forth, especially at the equinoxes and solstices. Occasionally, they have fairs, bringing larger numbers together at the Coslett estate. The old woman's grooming her son to take charge of the sect and is also spending down her fortune on various right-wing causes."

"Nothing left for the son, if the money's gone? Or does the estate have an income?"

"Some of the donations go to upkeep for Sulcliffe Castle, considered by the group to be on a sacred site, at least by their standards. Without them, the baron would barely make the tax payments."

"Like a lot of country estates these days."

Elsa gave him a look, as though, since he was landed gentry himself, she didn't care to hear him complain. "Are we going to share the *Nachteule* benefactor information with the Poles?"

"I doubt the Foreign Office will want that. "

"How about sharing with the police?"

"We don't want the authorities following up with the Cosletts. We're involved with a peerage, so we have some sensitivities. And other than the death of Talents, we don't have any similarities between the two sets of murders."

Julian watched as the heavyset man left his pew and walked

past, his face tear-stained. "Stay with the police investigation, Elsa. Dig into the Adder clubs. Meanwhile, on the *Nachteule* front, the Foreign Office has informed Coslett that her contributions to German causes are likely being misused and must stop. She pretended dismay and has complied. So, we've shut down the money flow. That's it for now."

After she left, Julian waited a decent interval, using the time to let his thoughts settle. Two murders, with specific presentation of the bodies. Pray God the killer was done now. But no guarantee. He thought of young Martin Lister. The boy would have to wash off that damn snake drawing on his wrist. He was always pulling his shirtsleeve down to cover it.

Julian picked up his hat, noting the program on the seat beside him. The service included the hymns "Jesu, Joy of Man's Desiring" and "Immortal, Invisible, God Only Wise." He thought of Rupert and Ewan and a wise God.

He had tried many times to reconcile faith with the brutality of the world. He envied Elsa. At least she had given up.

MONKTON HALL, NORTH YORK MOORS

LATER THAT DAY. "How is Pip doing?" Kim asked. She glanced at Miss Drummond's toy spaniel, who slept in a basket by her desk.

"As well as can be expected." Miss Drummond looked over the top of her glasses at Kim, warning her that they were not friends and would not be chatting.

Kim put a finger to her lips. "Mustn't wake him, then."

No one presumed to chat with Miss Drummond, even if

the woman had uncovered Kim's and Owen's artless sleuthing over the Prestwich Affair and had gamely lent a hand. Kim wasn't sure if Drummond had done it for king and country or for Pip. Fitzroy Blum had had it in for the dog. But the woman might well have taken a liking to her after Kim had managed to cover up a doggie mistake on the premises just before Fitz discovered it.

It was precisely eleven o'clock, by her Elgin. She ascended the great staircase to Owen's office on the mezzanine.

Monkton Hall had long been stripped of its Victorian furnishings, but government use of the old manor could not entirely cloak its personality. Decorative gargoyles and carved woodland creatures embroidered the walls and coved ceilings as though trying to free themselves from the plaster. Even better, an ancient chapel lay closed off behind the back wall, a remnant of the sixteenth century, when it had been dangerous to be a Catholic. It was fitting that in this hall of spies, even the stones and walls held secrets.

She knocked twice at Owen's door, and entered to find him wearing a cap bristling with knobs and wires. A dynograph occupied a corner of his desk. He adjusted a knob and stared at the readout that fed out in a stream of paper.

He motioned for her to join him.

"It's the new Sherrington Four," he said. "I wouldn't try it on our people until I tested it myself." He made a note on a pad and then lifted the cap off. His hair sprang back as though electrified.

Kim pulled up a chair. "How do you like it?"

"Remains to be seen, remains to be seen. We'll get you rigged up and see what we can learn." Kim's brain waves changed when she elicited a *spill*. The dynograph showed what areas of the brain were active when a Talent manifested. "Manifested" was the word Monkton liked; while some Talents appeared to be "on" at all times, others came and went, sometimes under control, and sometimes spontaneously, as with the *spill*.

"Lewis is eager to get you hooked up to the thing."

"Is that why I'm here? The Sherrington?"

Owen pursed his lips. "The dynograph? No, no. It's head office, as a matter of fact. Wanted me to have a talk with you about security." He rustled through the long readout piled up on the floor, gathering it up and stacking it in a hopeless tangle on top of the dynograph before taking his seat behind the desk.

"We have some intelligence that our agents could be in danger. You'll want to be watchful and take extra security measures."

A buzz like an electric current spun through her. "Something's afoot."

"Enough to put you on your guard, yes. Nothing direct yet, but keep your eyes open and avoid isolated locations. The usual precautions. I said the same to Alice Ward at her last testing appointment."

Interest surged, but she kept her peace. Clearly, he wasn't going to say more. She thought the "agents in danger" comment rather odd. Which agents, she wondered? And most of all, why?

"Got it," she said. "I'll stay alert. But how serious is it?"

"Could be risky, but nothing definitive." Owen was tapping his pen against the desk, almost a nervous tic, as the conversation ground to a halt.

"They're killing off Talents," he said. "All on the Continent so far, but we really don't know who's in their sights."

Then he closed his eyes a moment, shaking his head. "Did you just do what I think you did?" He flicked a glance at her. "Please do stop."

"I didn't *do* anything, as you very well know, Owen."

"Yes, I know you can't help it, but it's rather annoying when it happens." A slow, rueful shake of his head as he considered the *spill* that had just happened.

"Sorry," she said, hoping it sounded sincere.

This was a part of the controller/agent relationship that they had discussed before. How Owen, as her handler, could maintain the distance he needed, and Kim could be sure she didn't foster a *spill* environment, and potentially damage an operation relying on secrecy. Whatever a *spill* environment was. She could not control her ability, but she had become adept at playing out silences and fostering trustful conversations.

And now: an operation to kill Talents. She would take care, of course, but she didn't worry for herself; she only longed to get in the thick of it. Where on the Continent? France? Belgium? And now England?

"Sorry," she said again. Owen nodded, and it was smoothed over.

While she was rather pleased about what had just happened, at the same time she didn't want her Talent to scare off the paranoid old men at the head office. She was an agent, not a case officer, and therefore she was not in the gentlemen's club of the intelligence services. Nor was Owen. He was the handler for a few Yorkshire assets, and probably preferred it that way.

"Well," Owen said, recovering from having slipped a secret. "I know you're curious. But we must let this play out. If there's a way for you to be involved, you'll be called up. Good enough?"

"Yes, boss." *Wouldn't dream of prying.*

"Sit tight, my girl. We shall no doubt have need of you for something ere long. If it were me, I'd send you off to charm Herr Hitler in a trice."

"I've been studying German."

"*Gut.*" He rose and wandered back to the dynograph.

Poor Owen really had been happier in his lab. And here he was, trying to manage his spy assets and a government operation that was England's best hope for parity with the German war machine. She didn't want to make his job any harder. Still: "Perhaps you could make a suggestion to the higher-ups? About my being eager to work?"

"I shall take it up with my superior, you can rest assured." And he was back poking at the Sherrington Four.

And who *was* Owen's handler? A man who no doubt withheld certain pieces of the truth from him, and so on up the line until, she supposed, only one person had the whole picture. The spymaster, whoever that was. How lovely it must be to know it all.

THE BLOOM BOOK

TALENT GROUPS
INTRODUCTION

Talents may be usefully grouped into three areas: Hyperpersonal, Mentation, and Psychokinesis. Any system that attempts to classify human behavior cannot escape making at least a few arbitrary distinctions. Thus, the composition of the Talent groups may be thought of as a catalogue of convenient reference more than an empirical classification system. The groups described below are widely used among the Allies of the Great War. What follows is a summary. For details, see Meta-Abilities Diagnostic Manual. MADM 4001-5749.37.

GROUP 1: HYPERPERSONAL

These abilities are characterized by close interpersonal transactions, where one individual exerts an influence over another's thoughts, attitudes, or perceptions, or is privy to others' traumatic memories or feelings beyond those that are readily apparent.

Attraction. To manifest around others an aura of appeal ranging from agreeable charm to strong charisma. Research has not identified a strong sexual effect. Underlying ability (always present to some degree), but can be heightened by some practitioners.

Chorister. Can augment the effect of a meta-ability by combining the abilities of several Talents. To operate as a chorister, the individual must possess the same Talent as those he is aggregating.

Conceptor. Manifests an unusual level of emotional persuasion, especially in leadership. Not subject to the limitations of geography. Not augmented by proximity. Underlying ability. Examples: Winston Churchill, Adolf Hitler.

Compelling. Exerts an insistent, sometimes inescapable, persuasion to action. The object of compulsion must be in proximity to the practitioner. Talent is under control. A few case studies exist of abilities under the rating of 4.

Disguise. To effect, in the minds of viewers, apparent changes to the body, especially the face. The perceptions achieved are most commonly youthfulness or advanced age, with other distortions less common. Few case studies. Controlled by the intention of the practitioner.

Mesmerizing. The object of a mesmerizing event experiences a decrease in awareness or judgment. The range of the effect (for high ratings) has been seen to extend to a small crowd. The experience may not be remembered as unusual and indeed is often denied, as though those so acted upon cannot accept the dissonance experienced. Controlled by the intention of the practitioner.

Natural defense. The meta-ability of an individual, known as a natural defender, who cannot be influenced by others' hyperpersonal abilities. The Talent appears to have no effect on other classes of ability, such as psychokinesis, which influences physical systems. Few case studies. Underlying ability.

Suggestion. When in close interaction with an individual, practitioner can sow an impression or conviction in an object's mind. The manifestation may linger after the initial suggestion, and may be refreshed upon subsequent encounters. Few case studies. Controlled by the intention of the practitioner.

Spill. Eliciting from others a spoken admission of a closely held secret, opinion, fear, memory, or longing. The person who spills may evince regret or shame at having shared a hidden thought, but will have no sensation of having been acted upon. An often unwelcome meta-ability that can be disruptive of social relationships. Manifestations spontaneous.

Trauma view. A quasi-real viewpoint of another's negative emotional experience. The ability is dependent upon proximity. Can manifest as a highly accurate view or as a symbolic, dream-like sequence or tableau, or a combination. Manifestations spontaneous.

11

THURSDAY, AUGUST 6. "How are you getting on?"

Martin jumped as though startled. Kim hadn't meant to sneak up on him, but his door had been open.

"I hope you like this room," she said. "It looks north, to the moors. Not that you can see them from here." She looked at his bed, covered with a brown-and-yellow counterpane. Not Robert's. Mrs. Babbage had replaced the items the family most associated with Robert. It was good to give the room a new use, and it seemed to Kim especially fine that it be used by a young man.

"I do like it," Martin said. "Sometimes, Shadow comes in, when you're not around." His suitcase still remained open on the window seat. A plate with biscuit crumbs lay on the nightstand.

"May I sit?"

"Oh. Sorry. Yes." He looked around, and found that the two chairs were both inhabited by dirty clothes. "I have to get to the barn, though. Mr. Babbage won't like it if I'm late."

She sat on the bed. "Well, I just want to see how things are going. Are you getting the hang of the place?"

"The hang?" He brightened. "Oh, you mean the barn and the chickens and mucking out things. I don't mind any of that. It's a lot more interesting than my da's shop. And especially the horse."

"And how do you feel about being here, with all of us? I hope you feel welcome."

A sliding-away glance. "Nothing wrong, is there?"

"No, of course not. We're just happy to have you here. The house is so empty most of the time." She looked around the room with its faded striped wallpaper, the iron bedstead that Robert had once painted black, now flecked like granite.

Martin sat on the bed, half facing her, but at the other end near the pillows. "I've decided not to go home when the term starts. If I could stay, that is." He glanced up to gauge how this went over. "Mr. Babbage needs help. I could lend a hand. And I don't always eat this much. It must be a growth spurt."

"Well." Kim felt relieved to know he liked it at Wrenfell, but the idea of staying on was another matter. "We'll have to see, won't we? Your parents might have something to say about that. But let's not plan too far ahead. You might find that you don't like things quite so much when the newness wears off."

Martin gulped, his Adam's apple bouncing in his slender neck. "Oh, that's not going to happen."

Kim smiled. "You haven't met my father yet."

"Rose says he's the best. Never got mad when she broke things, and besides, he's never home."

"A slim recommendation, don't you think?"

Martin's face cracked into a smile. It slowly faded. He stared at the floor with its faded rag rug. "I see things sometimes."

Well. She had wondered if he would assert his *site view* claims again. "You see things? Like what?"

"Oh, things. Things in this room."

She felt her chest cinch up. "Here?"

He nodded, not making eye contact.

Site view. But of course, if it was real, if it was going to happen, it would be in this room. What had she been thinking of, to bunk him here? They sat in uncomfortable silence for a time. She found herself whispering, "What do you see?"

For a few moments Kim hoped that he would lose his nerve, and the whole thing could just be swept under the rag rug. They would pretend he hadn't brought the subject up.

"Your brother," he said, low and steady.

She could not respond. It had been a mistake to give Martin Robert's room. But when Mrs. Babbage had looked askance at the idea, Kim had insisted. At the time, she had thought it was nearer the lavatory, and boys his age didn't like the morning sun, so a north prospect would suit.

"He was afraid."

Kim heard herself whimper. A horrid little cry deep in her throat.

"Not afraid of . . . of the fighting. But afraid he wouldn't measure up. Wouldn't be what he was supposed to be in front of the other soldiers."

Kim felt that a hot brick was stuck in her chest, preventing her from breathing. She started rubbing the watch on her wrist, polishing the crystal with the sleeve of her sweater. It was eight twenty-six.

"When the bullets came, he wanted to be brave, to not care too much about getting hit and help the others to not be afraid."

"That's natural," Kim managed to say. "One wishes to do one's duty."

Another long pause. "And he worried about you."

"Me?" She risked a glance at Martin, who looked at her from under his long eyelashes, defensively, ready to bolt. "What about me?"

"He worried that . . . if something happened to him, it would go hard with you. That no one would understand, especially not in the village. Your friends, even your parents, that no one would . . . be on your side. That they wouldn't know how you and Robert had always taken care of each other. Like when he beat up that Massey kid who stole your lunch pail."

A few tears slid in hot pathways down her cheeks.

"I'm sorry, I didn't mean . . ."

"Just hush, Martin. You must let me cry." After a moment she wiped her face on her sleeve. She whispered, "What else, what else was there?"

"That he wasn't sorry to go. He wanted to go."

Of course he did. At first they all did, when the war began and it was going to be all glory and honor. They were so trusting, so innocent of the slaughter to come. She repeated numbly, "Wanted to . . ."

"I think so. It sounded like it. That he was proud to be the one to go."

"Sounded? You mean you *heard* him?"

Martin frowned. "No, it's not like that. But somehow, I know what he thought."

Kim took a deep, tattered breath. Her mind clattered on, being logical, even while she was awash in longing. "I didn't know it worked like that. *Site view.*"

"Sometimes." He stood, looking at her in what must be her

obvious distress. "I don't have to stay in this room. I could stay in the barn."

She pulled out her hanky and dried her face. "Oh, Martin, the barn! Of course you must stay in Robert's room." She got up from the edge of the bed. "You were quite right to tell me." She was at a loss for what to say to this youngster who had just slipped her from her moorings and sent her adrift into dark memory. "You did the right thing."

As she turned to go, Martin said, "I don't want to meet with Vicar Hathaway anymore. He's on my da's side, not mine."

She turned back. "I see."

"I mean, I've had two meetings already. He thinks I'm a liar."

She couldn't think about this right now. "Let me see what I can do." She turned to go.

As she closed the door, she heard him say in a resentful murmur, "At least Alice is on my side."

Out in the hallway, she made for the bathroom, feeling dazed. In front of the sink, she splashed her face with cold water. Looking into the mirror, she saw a stranger with black hair stuck to her temples and chin, eyes bright with pain.

It was no accident Martin was in that room. She had put him there. She had wanted his Talent view of the room. It was exceedingly strange how one could make cunning plans and not even realize it. But now that she had had her glimpse of Robert, she felt rather sick, almost as though he had died again.

Sitting on the edge of the claw-footed bathtub, she dried her face. There was a thread of shame woven through the tenderness and old grief. When one heard of desperate family members participating in séances to contact their lost sons, brothers, and husbands, one could only feel pity for them. But was it any different, now, with Martin? Some things we aren't meant to know.

She had learned that over the years with the *spill*. Forcing some things into the light could lose you a friend. Or uncover old losses, making them dreadful again.

She couldn't make sense of it right now. Adjourning to her room, she took out her well-worn copy of the London and North Eastern Railway timetable and traced the columns of arrivals and departures. The stops and connections to other lines. There was no secret to the British railway system. In fact, it embodied an elegant, systematic plan. She had always found the little LNER booklet a comfort, framing the world in an orderly way, which was very important, given the sorts of things that could happen.

A FIELD IN WILTSHIRE

THAT NIGHT. Dries Verhoeven arranged her so that she sat upon the grass, leaning up against the great stone, her head tipped back just so, for good effect. To show how she had died. They wouldn't find her until morning, and no one would disturb her repose until then. He folded her hands in her lap so that anyone seeing her from a distance would think she was looking out toward the view, thus approaching her for a most disturbing discovery.

"For God's sake, leave it be." Bats swooped overhead, feasting on nets of insects. His companion was only a blur in the thick, hot night.

"*Ach*, for *whose* sake?" Dries wiped the blood off his glasses with a rag, deliberately taking his time.

"Just hurry, can't you?"

Dries replaced his glasses. It was no time for a religious

discussion, but he did find it ludicrous to speak of God in a world where a young girl could be slaughtered within a stone's throw of the thatched and rose-riddled village where she had lived. A hapless God, or one who did not care. Either one was not worth one's devotion.

He stood up and regarded his handiwork. Fourteen years old, or perhaps less, lanky hair, a flowered blouse and full skirt. With the moon just rising, colors were shades of gray, her blood black in the lee of the stone. He expelled a noisy breath. It really gave him no particular pleasure to kill, nor was he indulging an irrational hatred of young people. It was something people didn't often realize, that there might be logical and compelling reasons to put out a life.

The girl's mongrel dog, however, that was a different matter. Quieting the yapping thing did bring some satisfaction.

He couldn't help needling his nervous companion. "Do you like to say a prayer for her, perhaps?"

"For God's sake!" came the outraged whisper, conveying the panicked desire to leave before anyone could stumble upon them.

For that reason Dries paused longer. There were times when one's tasks were worth methodical care. As a restorer of antique dolls, he knew that excellence could not be rushed. "We have put out her light. You see how dark she is?"

"*You* have done. You."

"Oh, there we must have a difference, my friend. I used the knife, but you brought her to the car, *ja*? A reasonable person will say we have both done this thing."

His companion walked away, not wishing to hear more.

Dries sighed. Some people could not bear the truth, that the world was cruel and without pity. People in these times had grown soft. Even the ignorant tribe that had dug these barrows and set these stones knew that the gods were brutal and life, terrifying.

He shook his head. Humanity was devolving. It was what he liked about dolls. They, at least, never changed.

12

SUNDAY, AUGUST 9. In the darkened park, Julian approached the agreed-upon bench and sat next to a diminutive man with sparse, flyaway hair wearing a suit a decade out of date. He set his package down between them.

The statue of Achilles was just visible through the row of trees that separated them from the busy intersection at Hyde's corner. "The statue used to be naked," Julian said.

Owen Cherwell looked about until he realized that Julian was talking about the great statue of Achilles. "It *is* naked."

"No, shortly after it first went up, they put a fig leaf in place. I expect it was required when it got about that the statue's face was based upon the Duke of Wellington."

"Well, quite right, then," Owen said.

Julian couldn't tell if he was being ironic or not. He didn't know Owen very well yet, even if the man was one of his. "Have you been reading about the youth killings?"

Owen cut a glance at Julian. "A third death on Thursday. Avebury, I read. At the location of the massive henge and standing stones."

"Yes, the stone circle site. The dead girl, Frances Brooke, came from the village next to it. The police believe these are signature killings, since the crime methods are identical."

"The papers have been saying so. Horrible. But our lot is involved?"

"We may have a foreign connection."

"Night Owl, you mean?" Owen frowned. "I thought those were military assets being eliminated."

"Yes, but we've got a new angle to consider. The young murder victims may all have had Talents."

Owen shook his head and swiped at his brow as though he had walked into a cobweb. "*Talents?*"

"I'm afraid so. We knew the first two adolescents claimed to have Talents. Yesterday we learned that the third victim did as well. That's the foreign connection. It's tenuous, but in the Continental murders and the British ones, the victims are Talents."

"Talents," Owen murmured. "Terrible news." He shook his head. "But the victims here are children! It can't be the same at all."

"Clearly, there are differences. But we'd like to follow up on the possible involvement of Dorothea Coslett."

"Coslett? You think an English baroness could be involved in murdering young people?"

"Worth a look, we think. There are some resemblances: You know that the *Nachteule* Talent assassinations are partially funded by Coslett. So, she already has her hand in murder. Then, as I said, in both crime strings so far, the victims are Talents.

Finally, the location of the latest murder at Avebury. As a Neolithic site, it might be significant for the spiritualist crowd."

"Good Lord," Owen said, "the woman's a peer. Funneling money to Nazi Germany is one thing, but this . . ."

"It's a stretch, but we've decided to take a closer look. Nothing official. We'll work up an excuse to get next to the family—undercover—and see what might turn up."

Owen shook his head, still trying to absorb it. "But how do you know these youths had genuine Talents? We certainly haven't been testing young people in my shop."

"If they bragged, or told the wrong people, the killer might *think* their claims were true."

Owen frowned. "Ah. They may have been *accidental* victims." The thought seemed to cheer him, that his potential future test subjects might not be at risk after all. "But you mention the *wrong people*. Who would that be?"

"Worst case, sleeper cells throughout England. Spies living here who are only activated when needed. That would mean that many young people are at risk of exposure. In any case, we're still trying to grasp what's going on. The two sets of Talent murders aren't identical. On the Continent, as you know, the victims are adults and the killings have been arranged to look like accidents. Here, the crimes target youth and are obviously murders. So, things don't line up enough to properly question the Cosletts."

Owen asked, "Does this spiritual group believe Talents have religious significance? Is that a connection?"

"I don't think so. In their literature there isn't much mention of them, except to imply that some people may have gifts—perhaps their term for Talents—that make them suitable for leadership. Dorothea Coslett started Ancient Light, and her convictions appear to be standard crackpot mysticism. Part of the cult's appeal could be that people are dazzled by her claim that Sulcliffe Castle is some kind of spiritual center, and when she opens up the grounds to followers, there's free food and hob-nobbing with the great lady herself."

"Well. But it sounds like we don't have much so far," Owen said.

Julian agreed. They were all slim leads. But once the third youth victim turned out to be a Talent, Julian had wanted to contact SIS counterparts in friendly European countries. Especially Gustaw Bajek in Poland. But E wouldn't have it, fearing that soon foreign agents would be sniffing after the Cosletts and stumbling over local operations.

Owen was shaking his head as though he were still trying to deny it all. Finally, he came up with, "But this is *England*."

Poor chap. Despite all he'd been through with the Prestwich Affair, he still believed that their island nation would be spared what was coming. "Herr Hitler has been known to suffer from boundary confusion." Julian went on. "We'll be checking into this baroness but treading carefully. We need someone who can investigate without appearing to do so."

"One of our Talents, then," Owen surmised.

"Yes." Julian looked at the statue, and that famous, vulnerable heel. "Someone with a credible journalism background to provide cover."

"I see. Despite the fact that the individual I believe you have in mind has a Talent and could be in danger herself."

"I'm afraid so."

They sat for a few minutes as the evening deepened. In the distance, they heard the shouts from a cricket match as the day faded.

"It's none of my business," Owen said, "but it seems a pity Sparrow doesn't know you're on the same team."

"Can't be helped, I suppose," Julian said. The Office had a way of isolating one. It was always king and country first. Lately, it seemed as though the dictum had become king and country *only*. He'd already lost his daughter in many ways, and now Olivia. Perhaps Olivia. The thought had occurred to him that he had chosen her for that very reason. Because at a deeper level, he wished to be alone.

"We have a cover story for her," Julian said. He patted the manila envelope. "It's all in here. Top priority. No time to lose."

"Of course."

Julian walked back the way he'd come, leaving Owen with the briefing packet that would soon be in the hands of his daughter. Worry for Kim was not very far from his thoughts. But he couldn't spare her from the hard things. She would hate him if he did and she found out. This was her job. It was his to see that she did her job.

Work your magic, my dear, he thought. He very much wished he could say it to her out loud.

A COUNTRY ROAD, YORKSHIRE

TUESDAY, AUGUST 11. Kim and Owen leaned on the split-log fence, watching sheep lazily swinging their undocked tails as they grazed. Owen's car, parked on the verge next to her own, creaked as it cooled. Kim found the lovely checkered fields of the Wolds a jarring contrast with Owen's unnerving details on two sets of murders.

The German code phrase for the Continental plot was *Nachteule,* which she knew from her German studies meant "night owl." And the connotation of the word did not elude her, either. Predator. One that struck without warning, gliding silently on heavy wings. Fifteen murders in France, Poland, and Czechoslovakia.

And now a new outbreak of Talent murders, targeting young people. She glanced at the packet Owen held, containing, he'd said, pictures of the crime scenes. She did not look forward to opening it. With the third adolescent murder, public fears were rising that the killer would strike again. It was front-page business now, with even the *Coomsby Herald* calling the crimes a "grim rampage."

"We're not sure our local murders are related to the Continental exterminations," Owen said. "If they are, this is going to be a major operation. In any case, you'll be one of several people working on it."

He'd already mentioned that she would go to Wales to attempt a *spill* from an elderly baroness reportedly quite ill from cancer. Dorothea Coslett, Lady Ellesmere, had been sending funds to support the *Nachteule* operation, and Kim would be angling for any clues that might tie the woman to the youth Talent killings. Owen had revealed the murder method used with the young people: their throats cut, the disturbing lifelike tableaux. Her imagination conjured the scenes. There were worse things than violent death, she knew. *How* a person died added terror to sorrow. She knew this. And found herself darkly zealous to track down this killer.

Owen looked down the one-lane road, watching for any vehicles. He had chosen this tucked-away pasture of the Landry farm for emergency meetings by virtue of the isolated locale.

"At Whitehall's direction, the police are withholding the information about the youths having Talents. No point in causing
the families of Talents alarm right now. And it could ruin our
registration numbers," he added heartlessly.

"How likely do we think it is that the Continental murders
are tied to our own?"

"Only a hypothesis. The timing is suspicious, certainly. And,
three Talent murders . . . Young Frances Brooke, the latest
victim, was known in her village for *precognition.*" He held up a
finger. "Which is?"

She quoted from the *Bloom Book.* "The ability to view potential future events." Owen was taking refuge in analysis, but she
kept thinking of the innocence of the victims, and the utter waste
of it all. Frances had only been fourteen. The fat manila folder
drew Kim's eyes, where it balanced on the fence under Owen's
hands.

"As I said earlier, your main target is Dorothea Coslett,
Lady Ellesmere, who until Whitehall put a stop to it, was funneling cash to the German operation. She heads up a spiritualist
group called Ancient Light, and apparently they attach a mystical significance to cairns and stone circles and the like. Ever
heard of it?"

"Not really. There are quite a lot of mystic groups around
these days." It was a phenomenon of the Great War. After those
horrors, people sought comfort in contact with the departed, or
if not that, then at least intimations of a nearby realm of lost
ones. So much more comforting than some far-off heaven. She
knew the impulse, for it had come in the guise of a *site view*
Talent in Robert's old room.

Owen went on. "This Avebury murder has piqued our interest in Coslett. Young Frances was killed at a standing-stones

site, the type of Neolithic and Bronze age ruin the Ancient Light group sets store by. We intend to follow every lead, no matter how fragile." He noted her skeptical look. "The Office does *not* assume the baroness or her cult is involved. You'll proceed with utmost discretion, staying strictly in touch. Everything through me.

"So, you'll get next to the Cosletts," Owen went on, "and hope for a bit of luck with your *spill*. Ingratiate yourself, write a flattering newspaper piece, and establish any bonds that you can. Get invited back."

"I'm to write up this group, that's the cover story?"

"Yes, you'll write an article for the *London Register* on the earth mysteries movement in Great Britain with the angle that Ancient Light is a good example of the trend. We've asked the editor at the *Register* to arrange for your interview with the dowager baroness. And the paper will run the piece, so your credentials will hold up." He lifted the fat package. "Here are the details of the murders, and background on Dorothea Coslett and this fellowship, as they call it, of Ancient Light." He handed her the folder. "Read it and burn it. If you gather any evidence, we'll take it from there. Dorothea Coslett comes from a frightfully good family. We can't afford a misstep."

It was so typical of the British that the upper classes got astonishing leeway by virtue of their position in society. It still galled her, having spent most of her life in the States, that such gilded treatment was simply the way it was, even if the person *from a frightfully good family* might be murdering young people.

"One other thing. Not that the two sets of murders are necessarily connected, but we have a description of someone who may be involved with the Polish murders, perhaps the assassin himself. His description is in the file. There may be other *Nachteule* killers. But for now we're thinking there's one. Code-named Talon. And our operation against him, of which your infiltration of the Coslett group is a part, will be Crossbow."

"How are the targets identified? We don't wear signs saying, *I have a Talent.*"

Owen flattened his mouth. "That's a troubling aspect. On the Continent, it could mean they've breached government secrets."

"But in the case of our murders, the young people weren't registered with Monkton Hall."

"You'll see we have one lead, clubs called Adders in secondary schools. They're not approved of, and the students involved keep them secret."

With a small shock, Kim realized it should have been the first thing she thought of when she'd heard the young people all had Talents. "I know a little about them."

"Yes, well, it's all in the report. We've got people on that one. However, neighbors, family, friends could all be unwittingly helping. There are a lot of ways for the truth to leak out, aren't there? But the fact is, we don't know how the victims are identified. Scotland Yard is setting up a National Task Force. We're working closely with them, but without sharing the *Nachteule* side of things. One of ours has been attached to the task force to cover our interests."

"You're sure the Monkton Hall log is secure?"

"It's in my safe when not in use. But of course, the horses might be out of the barn. My predecessor may have disclosed all of our assets' names to the Germans."

They locked gazes. *Including mine*, she thought.

"On that score, be aware that the baroness herself could have a Talent. The Ancient Light literature suggests that they feel great leaders are gifted in some way. Nothing definitive, but try to find out early on what ability she might have." Owen handed her the envelope. "Tread carefully with this Coslett woman, Kim. We're only allowed a limited operation. You must deploy your witless-American mode to perfection."

She snapped a look at him. "I didn't know I *had* one."

"What? Oh, yes, quite a good one. Charging around all innocent and eager. Top-notch." He patted his coat pockets for his keys. "If you make headway, it comes straight to me and I pass it up the line. Understood?" Owen waited. "You do understand."

"I do, you needn't repeat yourself."

"Yes, I do need to repeat myself. We won't have you blithely ringing me up to inform me that you're haring off on your own."

She had taken the initiative in the Prestwich Affair. When no one else would. Now with SIS, she knew she'd have to toe the line. She'd already run one line of work into the ground, her reporting career that ended abruptly at the *Philadelphia Inquirer*. They had not approved her eagerness to report on animal laboratory testing. *Initiative. Eagerness.* Women must be careful about earning those labels. Unless one just couldn't help oneself.

To placate, she threw out, "That was before I was official."

Having found his keys at last, Owen fixed her with a piercing look. "Well, good luck, then, Kim. It's a risk to use you in an operation where Talents are at hazard, but I know that won't stop you."

No, it wouldn't. Dorothea Coslett was going to *spill* her guts—if Kim could control her keen wish to *have* a spill, an intention that tended to keep confidences at bay. And this was the first she'd heard that the woman might have a Talent. How annoying that a spy agency couldn't find out which one or how strong.

"One last thing," Owen said. "The police are using *site view* artists at the crime scenes. They're picking up on some intense emotions, as would be expected, but one anomaly has popped up. Images of a conflagration. A fire."

"In the victims' minds or the murderer's?"

"They couldn't distinguish." He shrugged. "Doesn't seem to tie in, does it? Well, it's our job to connect the dots."

Connect the dots. It was so satisfying to view the world as a puzzle. If one stood back and yet kept it all in view, the solution would emerge, inevitable and complete. She held on to this enduring belief even in extreme doubt. Perhaps then more than ever.

Owen pulled away in his old Vauxhall, trailing a cloud of exhaust. Molten sunshine pressed down on the country lane and Kim's shoulders. It would be best to read the file in the comfort of her parlor, but she wanted to get the pictures over with.

She slid out the handful of glossy prints. The top picture was of a girl leaning against a stone. One side of her dress, black with blood. The gash at her neck . . . Kim put out a hand on the fence to steady herself, breathing deeply to dispel the fist of pain in her stomach.

She quickly looked at the photos of the two boys. Ewan Knox and Rupert Bristow.

Her mind reeled. It was one thing to hear about the killings, but seeing them . . . Three young teens with their throats cut, and in those casual, seated postures. She went back to the Avebury victim, Frances. The girl had been treated a bit differently from the boys, with that awful clump of flowering thistles lying across her lap. The killer was beginning to elaborate on his methods.

With shaking hands she shoved the photos back into the file.

As she drove home, the world with its green and gold fields and bleating sheep seemed wrongly tranquil. There should be a lowering sky and weeping.

The sun shone on.

PART II

A CROOKED LIGHT

13

FRIDAY, AUGUST 14. "I'm taking you off the earth mysteries story." Maxwell Slater rolled up his shirtsleeves in the stifling office of the *London Register* and stared balefully across his desk at one of his reporters, Lloyd Nichols.

Lloyd couldn't have been more surprised if Slater had told him to drop his trousers. "What're you talking about? We're just about ready to put it to bed."

"Well, it's not going in the direction I want."

"And what direction might that be? You haven't read it yet!" Lloyd felt his face grow hot, and he barely managed to remain seated.

Slater had his big fist around his pencil and was making doodles on a notepad, like always. "Last time I checked, I was still the editor of this rag, and I'll make the calls on the assignments. Fact is, we've got an opportunity, someone who's onto the topic and is going to make a splash with it." He wrote "splash" with two underlines.

"You've giving it to someone *else*? Who the hell is he? Not Gardiner. Tell me you're not giving it to Gardiner, that bugger!"

"No, it's someone new. Name's Kim Tavistock, she had a stint with—"

"A woman? From the outside?" Lloyd had passed from chagrin to outrage. "What the devil are you up to?"

Slater went on as though he hadn't been interrupted. "—a stint with the *Philadelphia Inquirer*. Happens to be living in Yorkshire now, and we've taken her on for a few pieces."

A Yank paper. A woman from Yorkshire. He couldn't believe this was happening.

"I need you on a different story, Lloyd."

"Well? I can write two stories at once. This ain't grammar school."

"No, I mean a major feature. On unemployment." He made a note of that, writing it out big on the notepad.

Lloyd stared at the notepad in disbelief. Once it ended up on Slater's doodles, it was set in stone. "Unemployment? Unemployment? Might as well talk about the price of hogs. Nobody wants to read about that. People live it every day. It ain't news, or have you lost your touch?"

Slater picked up a well-chewed cigar and rolled it around his mouth. He'd given up smoking but still liked the taste of the rolled tobacco. "Pack it in a moment and listen. The unionist movement is gaining steam, lots of controversy there. And you can tie it into that Soviet five-year plan and get folks heated up on the socialist issue. It'll sell papers."

Lloyd lowered his voice as though talking to a madman. "It'll *kill* papers. It'll kill *me*. Give *that* one to Gardiner." He felt suddenly vulnerable. They were trying to give him a dog of story in order to have a reason to sack him. Three jobs in the last two years. The *London Register* was the end of the line. "Please, Maxwell. At least read what I've got so far. It's damn good."

"For Christ's sake, you're not some rookie who can't bear to have a piece cut. Get out of here before I lose my battle with cigars and light this fucker up."

Lloyd slouched to the door, then turned around. "Say, put *her* on the unemployment scoop!"

"Out," Slater said, pointing to the door with his cigar.

SULCLIFFE CASTLE, WALES

LATER THAT DAY. The impression that Sulcliffe Castle was at the edge of the known world was greatly magnified by the long, deserted roadway following the contours of a rocky headland, with the Irish Sea pounding below. As well, there was the four-hour train ride from York and, once in Wales, those end-of-the-world-sounding names: Penmaenmawr, Llanfairfechan, Dwygyfylchi.

Kim's ancient driver, who had introduced himself at the railway station as Awbrey, drove furiously along a road hugging a cliff. The car was an older model from the twenties, with patched mohair upholstery. She hoped its engine was in better repair.

"No speed limit, then," Kim said, gripping the seat with whitened hands.

"Not seein' so well as I once did," Awbrey rasped. "But I kin find my way home blindfolded."

The last stretch lay across a rugged plateau. In the distance, silhouetted against the sea, she spied the castle, squat and stony, its corners anchored by four jutting towers. Anyone approaching Sulcliffe would be visible for several miles. Kim wondered if they watched now, peering from the slit windows. She wondered what they knew about the slain young people. But at this distance, Sulcliffe did seem the sort of place that would guard its secrets.

With a last-minute careening turn, Awbrey pulled into the castle's car park in front of an imposing wall of stone. Once out of the car, Kim noted an iron-banded door that must do for a front entrance. Fat raindrops began pelting the bonnet of the car.

As thunder rolled in off the sea, Awbrey shouted, "You hurry in. I'll be comin' behind with the bags." He waved her toward the door.

Once inside the castle, the Crossbow hunt for the youth killer would begin in earnest. At least Kim's end of the operation. She must not presume anyone here was guilty, but neither would she relax for a moment in her pursuit of possible connections. It was for those murdered young people, Ewan, Rupert, Frances. She could not help but imagine how their parents, their brothers and sisters, must grieve. She knew, she did acutely know, how they must grieve. Her own mother, her anguish. That day they learned that Robert had died, and especially how he died.

Kim tried the latch of the iron-encrusted door. It gave way, and stepping through, she found herself in a small vestibule with a stone stairway leading up. She ascended the stairs, coming out on an expansive stone porch where she spied a formal entry of arched double doors. As rain pelted down, she tapped the door knocker against the wood, and when no one answered, she entered. She found herself in a long gallery with lancet windows along one side. The castle was as quiet as a museum at night.

In another couple of minutes Awbrey was puffing past her with her valise and camera box. "There's the sittin' room," he said, nodding his head at a gaping doorway before disappearing down the hall.

She wished that she had carried the camera equipment herself, for Awbrey, despite looking every bit of seventy-five years old, seemed to do everything in the greatest haste, and none too carefully.

There was nothing for it except to go in and wait for her hostess or whoever was going to greet her. In the large salon, a fire smoldered in a fireplace big enough to park her Austin 10. She took a seat in an enormous wingback, removing her gloves and patting the rain from her hair. The room was lavishly appointed in brocade, silk damask and Indian carpets.

Here she was again, in another grand British country home, another article to write. But this time, she need not lie that she was on assignment. She would write up her topic; she would have a byline in the *London Register*. The days when that alone would have been exciting seemed long ago. In her newspaper reporting days, the world had been morally straightforward. People must not experiment on dogs. The newspaper ought not put her on obituaries. One might be excused from telling the truth, but it must be a white lie. And now, deception was the essence of her undertakings. And she'd found it was not difficult, not difficult at all. It was what spies did, she thought with circular logic. Good enough logic.

Rain pattered at the mullioned windows and thunder rumbled like the old castle clearing its throat. The lamplight quivered beneath the heavy Edwardian lampshades. She savored the moment. *How excellent. I am alone in a castle in a thunderstorm.*

At that moment a shadow passed by her chair, and a figure in brown robes drifted through the room. Kim gave a start. But it was merely a slight, gray-haired woman in a calf-length brown knit suit. Moving past Kim, the figure knelt at the fireplace and began poking at the embers until a flame erupted. Rather than putting in more wood to take advantage, the old woman stood up and held the poker as she stared at the meager fire. When she turned around, Kim saw that she was even older than Awbrey, with a long, mournful face. By her dress—shapeless knit, but of good quality—this was not a servant.

For an opening, Kim said, "You still have fires in August!"

The old woman stared at her with a bland expression, as though Kim were merely one of many people in the room and in no need of special recognition. Then, placing the poker in its holder, she departed as quietly as she had come in.

Kim certainly hoped this was not Dorothea Coslett. If it was, and she could not even be bothered to say hello, conversation, upon which Kim depended to ply her craft, could be hopeless.

"Oh, there you are!" A man's voice hailed her from the entry-way. She stood up to meet the newcomer.

"Awbrey said he'd left you here, but I thought at least Rian would come to bring you tea." It was a tall, strapping man, per-haps in his mid-thirties, dressed in country tweeds. Striding into the room, he pushed back a forelock of thick brown hair.

"You're Kim Tavistock, I take it. Well, of course you are. We only have five guests a year and we know each one!" His smile was large and lit up his face, making it rather handsome. A whiff of eau de cologne. "I'm Powell Coslett." They shook hands.

This burst of energy was very welcome, and instantly dis-persed the gloom of the place. Kim stepped forward. "So glad to meet you. I hope I've come on the right day!"

He grinned sheepishly. "Yes, you might wonder. We are a tad disorganized. Mother isn't feeling well, and we are all tiptoeing about, I'm afraid. And I see you've met Idelle." He looked behind him where the women in brown had floated off. "I hope you didn't think her rude. She doesn't speak."

He charged over to the fireplace and pulled on a cord. "Well, tea, shall we? You've had a long trip. Unless you'd like to freshen up?"

"Did you say her ladyship is unwell? I didn't realize . . ." She knew very well the baroness was ill, but as the family kept this private, she must pretend to be surprised.

"She has good days and bad. But I shouldn't worry, Mother said I'm to fill in for now. Poor you! But I tell you what, if you don't get what you want from me, we'll get you an audience with Mother so that at least you can have a smart quote. She's rather good at the cogent phrase!"

He led her out into the gallery. Thunder shook the long row of windows.

"Sounds like the Scots using their cannon, doesn't it?" They walked down the hall and up a flight of stairs curving around what must be one of the four towers. "Mind you, Sulcliffe has never seen a battle. I think it's because, with these walls, and with our back to the sea, we would rather overwhelm any invaders. One might as well ravage the countryside and leave the castle high and dry!"

"I hope my visit won't be disruptive, Lord Ellesmere. With your mother unwell."

"Please do call me Powell. And you mustn't think of leaving. Besides, you can't escape now. The drawbridge is up."

She pretended not to find this a bit ominous. "And the hounds are loose?"

He nodded. "That too." He steered her up the stairs with the merest pressure of a long arm. His enthusiasm helped to counter her first impressions of the rather forbidding castle, more isolated than she had imagined, and with the bizarre treatment she had received from the woman in the sitting room. They stopped on the first landing, where Powell opened a door.

Her room was enormous and filled with overstuffed furniture, heavy red drapes and carpets, the whole scene an alarming shade of raspberry.

Powell put her valise on the four-poster bed piled with dusty pillows. A tray with cakes and tea occupied a footstool. Powell frowned. "I'm afraid the tea is cold. Rian does her best, but she's getting on a bit. I'll send her up with fresh."

"No, don't put her to trouble, really." Out the windows in the curved wall of her tower room she saw black, craggy rocks and a silver strip of the sea beyond.

She turned back to him. "I've never spent the night in a castle." She noticed his jacket had an emblem on the breast pocket. Perhaps a coat of arms.

He squared his shoulders. "Tell you what, we'll have our talk while taking a tour of it. You do write-ups of British grand houses, don't you?"

"How did you know that?"

"Oh, Mother looked you up. We know all about you."

His face lit up with a wide, spontaneous smile. She would have to remember that technique. One could say anything one pleased and make it go down well if followed with a dazzling smile.

So, Dorothea Coslett wasn't too ill to check up on her. She trusted the investigation produced the right story, the witless American one.

Powell looked around the room. "I hope you'll be comfortable. Mind you, the electricity can be dicey. There's a flashlight
on the mantel if the lights go out."

"Is there a telephone I might use?"

"Yes, in the sitting room. Connections fail at the worst times,
but you're welcome to try it."

Of course. She would expect no less of Sulcliffe. If it wished
to keep you, it would fill the moat, douse the lights, and kill the
telephone.

The pipes clanged as though being attacked with a pickax but
eventually produced a hot bath. Washrooms were obviously an
afterthought in old castles, and this one was barely large enough
for a claw-footed tub and toilet. As Kim bathed, it struck her
that, in her short career as a spy, this was her second time in close
company with an eligible lord of a manor. Like Lord Daventry at
Summerhill, Powell was charming, but not in Hugh Aberdare's
insouciant way; more artless and unaffected.

She wondered if agents very often fell for people who, in
the eyes of the service, they oughtn't. Not that she found Powell
Coslett such a candidate; she had just met him.

As she dressed, she indulged the fantasy of being a titled married woman. She imagined three happy children, several dogs, a
French governess. And oh dear, perhaps a domineering mother-
in-law who would rule the roost. Well. She had no ambition to
live in a castle, though a country house—say in York—came to
mind. She wondered what a husband would make of the line of
work she was in. He would certainly have to make do. Lately, she
had tried to imagine the sort of man who *would*.

In a wool skirt and sweater set she made her way down to
the parlor, where she put in her call to Knightsbridge and Nash

Photo Finishing. Someone from the Office answered appropriately and said her photo prints would be ready on Wednesday. Her sign-of-life call complete, she turned to find Powell had entered the drawing room.

"I was just checking on the prints from my last job."

"Oh yes, you're quite the photographer, aren't you?" He glanced at the camera case slung over her shoulder as he led her into the gallery. "I should tell you that Mother isn't keen on snaps of the place, though."

"Well, I do hope for one of her. My editor will expect that, and I'd hate to come away without it. Perhaps one of her on the battlements, hair blowing a bit in the wind?"

When his ready smile faltered, he looked rather lost. "You might not want to go in that direction. It's easy to see us as a fringe group—not that you do—but we're quite used to being dismissed."

"Oh, I didn't mean . . ."

"Never you fear. It's where most outsiders start with us. We're used to it."

He led her into the window-flanked hallway and around a corner, where a stone balustrade separated them from a large hall below. They looked down on it, a cavernous room with trestle tables lined up in rows.

"It can seat two hundred for dinner," Powell explained. "Not that it ever did. I think the king and queen dined here in the sixteenth century. The food must have been frightful, because royals haven't been back since."

He pointed to a shield over the fireplace. "The Sulcliffe emblem."

Kim took note of the green and yellow. Around a castle representation in the center field were two symbols, one of waves, one of a flower. Stylized swords jutted from the castle, dividing the spaces like pieces of pie.

"Lovely," Kim observed. "Your own coat of arms, then."

"No, it's not an official coat of arms in the heraldic sense. My father designed it as a symbol of the estate."

She pulled her notebook out of her pocket, jotting a note. "Bowen Coslett, wasn't it? I believe I read he died in the Great War."

"Yes. That was his sister you saw in the sitting room. My aunt Idelle. She took a vow of silence not long after he was killed. We're all quite used to it. And she and I have always had a knack for understanding each other. She has trouble these days with her memory and concentration. Hard to watch, I must say. Though she remembers the old days as though they were yesterday! Her silence doesn't make a lot of sense to outsiders, I suppose, but it's how she was able to keep going."

"Some losses are too much to bear without . . . effects."

He looked grateful. "You don't seem old enough to know that."

She flashed him a solid smile. "Where's the chapel?"

Powell led her onward through wood-paneled corridors with dressed stone floors, a mixture of country manor and fortified keep. Deep in the castle, a heavy chill descended.

They stood outside an archway leading to the chapel. "Our Ancient Light fellowship doesn't hold with Christian dogma," Powell said. "Some of your readers will be shocked by that. But when you pull away the embellishments of two thousand years of idolatry, one is left with the grounding of it all, of our lives: the landscape, the earth itself. If we go back to pre-Roman times, people were connected with those things. That's where we take our inspiration." He made it all sound four-square, the essence of reason.

The chapel was a plain affair, oddly dour despite an attempt at tracery and vaulting. Hewn ribs marched down the peaked ceiling like the rib cage of a stone beast.

"We don't use the chapel, obviously. Mother had all the statuary taken out, and did try to reclaim the place, but really, it still keeps its papist form." He watched as she took down a note. "I expect that you're not a believer, are you?"

"A Christian?"

"A believer in earth mysteries."

"I'm not, I'm afraid."

"I didn't think so." He regarded her intently. "But you do have a practical aura about you. I hope you'll keep an open mind."

"Oh, leave the girl alone, Powell." A woman's voice from the chapel doorway.

A generously built elderly woman appeared there, framed by the gothic arch. As she stood motionless, with her broad outline and heavy shoulders, she looked rather like a dwarfish spirit emerging from a cave.

"Mother," Powell said, in obvious surprise. He went to the dowager, taking her arm.

Dorothea Coslett leaned on a cane on one side and Powell on the other, slowly moving forward to greet Kim. So, here was the target. The woman with the close Nazi ties. And a person who might have a strong Talent, even the *spill*. A ripple of anxiety traveled through Kim.

The baroness wore a fur-trimmed vest over a dark green dress with her hair pulled high on her head and arranged in a circular braid rather like a crown.

"Mother," Powell said, "may I present Kim Tavistock. Kim, Lady Ellesmere."

The dowager extended her hand, and Kim grasped it lightly. "It's a pleasure to meet you, Lady Ellesmere."

"Is it? Most people are unnerved by me."

Kim smiled. "It's the burden of being a strong woman. One gets blamed for it."

Lady Ellesmere brightened. "She has opinions, Powell. Mark that. This might be more agreeable than we first thought." Her lively blue eyes assessed Kim's appearance. "You're younger than I expected," she said in a loud and slightly wavering voice. "They said they were sending an experienced journalist, and here they've sent us a wisp of a girl, Powell."

"I think she knows her stuff, Mother. From the *London Register*."

She looked at the notebook Kim held. "Writing it all down, are you?"

"Yes. I had just got to the part where you had . . . redecorated the chapel."

"Oh, he told you that, did he?" The dowager beamed at her son. "He might not have said how I ripped out the horrid crucifixes and statues of saints."

Kim had an image of Dorothea Coslett in her younger years taking a sledgehammer to the walls. "What did you do with them, if I may ask?"

Lady Ellesmere turned to Powell. "Bring my wheelchair, would you, my dear?" As Powell left them, his mother turned to Kim. "I regret not being able to greet you on your arrival. I hope you will excuse the lapse."

"Of course. Powell has been showing me about."

As her son approached, pushing a wheelchair, Lady Ellesmere frowned. "You started without me, dear." He helped her settle into the chair. As they left the chapel, she stabbed her lap blanket around her legs. "You shan't get rid of me as easily as that. I'm not dead yet!"

Powell raised an eyebrow at Kim, sharing a moment of *it happens all the time.*

"I have my devotees," Lady Ellesmere snapped. She clutched her cane across her knees as they passed down the gallery. "I've done everything for them, and they're grateful, of course. Someday, Powell will lead them. But not yet. Not . . . *yet.*" At this, she reached back and patted her son's hand.

As they bumped along the uneven floor, she held forth. "Only the gifted can rule. Think of Germany's chancellor, how far he has taken that poor, shattered country. He has called people to a cleansing nationalism, giving the common man an alternative to Communism. It would not have been possible without his gift of persuasion." She glanced up at Kim. "From your reading of history, wouldn't you agree it is essential?"

"Well, in the States, we've had a few simply dreadful presidents. Voters can make mistakes."

Lady Ellesmere made a disgusted face. "Oh dear, now we are talking about *democracy.* In any case, if Powell can't make the grade, dear Helena is waiting in the wings to guide the faithful. She is a most efficacious young woman with a strong spiritual gift, you may be sure."

Interesting. So, there was competition for the cult's leadership. Likely a sensitive topic for Powell.

They were just passing the sitting room. Shaking the subject off, the dowager pointed her cane toward the main door. "Have you seen the view from the high terrace?"

"No, it was raining when I arrived, and I came straight in."

Powell said, "It's cold, Mother. Oughtn't it wait for morning?"

She turned a tender look at him. "Oh, darling, you mustn't coddle me. But if you would fetch my wrap?"

When he left, Lady Ellesmere struggled to get out of the

chair. "It's rather trying, being seventy-eight years old. Everyone thinks one is likely to topple over at any moment." She stood, planting her feet firmly, then gestured with her cane at the door.

Kim obligingly opened it and stood aside as the baroness shouldered herself out onto the enormous stone porch. Wind barreled in off the sea, snapping their clothes around them.

Lady Ellesmere led the way to the crenellated parapet overlooking a grass-swathed headland.

"Sulcliffe has occupied this place, some three hundred acres, since 1588," she explained. "There's a tidal beach about a mile from here, but Sulcliffe land is girded by rock cliffs. This headland is a sacred location, where land, cliff, and sea join. That's why Sulcliffe is the spiritual center of the Ancient Light fellowship and why our devotees will make sure the land remains intact and the castle maintained for the future."

Kim jotted in her notebook as Lady Ellesmere looked on approvingly.

"Sulcliffe is blessed with a very special site of power. I've given Powell permission to show it to you, if you're up to a hike." She waved Kim's inquiring look away. "We'll keep it a secret until tomorrow. Powell wants to surprise you." Turning from the inland view, she led Kim to the other side of the battlements, where they looked out on the vast expanse of the Irish Sea, stained golden in the afternoon sun.

"It's breathtaking," Kim said.

The old woman leaned on the parapet. "Bowen loved it so. He was the one who taught me that land and sea have powers. Then I lost him to the war, the war that ought never have been fought." She remained silent for some moments. "Eighteen years. When does it cease to matter?"

Kim stared out to sea. "I don't think that ever happens."

Lady Ellesmere turned to her, murmuring, "Ah, then. You know, don't you? You have your own loss."

Kim was startled by the comment. "So many do."

"Oh, but it is always *particular*, isn't it? There were so many, but for each of us, only one is a stone in the heart." She put her hand on Kim's, a surprisingly personal, and not entirely pleasant, gesture. "I have the gift, you know. It's no use to keep things from me, particularly not here."

Kim affected nonchalance. "By 'gift,' do you mean a Talent?"

Lady Ellesmere waved a hand in dismissal. "Not a term we care for. We take the spiritual viewpoint."

It's no use to keep things from me. . . . She so hoped that it wasn't the *spill*.

Lady Ellesmere spoke again, nodding shrewdly, as Kim's stomach twisted. "I've always known people's strong feelings. It's a burden, but also quite useful, if one is in the public eye."

Kim considered the phrase about people's strong feelings. It came to her then, from the *Bloom Book*: *hyperempathy*, tracking emotions in another person. It wasn't a fatal advantage if the dowager had it. But it would be bad enough.

Powell returned, carrying a fur coat. He placed it over his mother's shoulders.

"Such a good son," the dowager said to Kim. "All this is his, of course. But it is Ancient Light that he wants." She turned to Powell. "Isn't it, darling?"

"I hope to deserve it, Mother."

It seemed like a ritual exchange, a safe formula to bring out a nasty problem and let it breathe before burying it again.

"Just one picture, Lady Ellesmere?" Kim patted her camera.

The baroness threw up a hand, palm out. "You may take

Powell's picture. The heir, as it were." She turned a look on her son that was half-doting, half-despairing.

"No, Mother, it should be you."

She pointed to the parapet. "Stand there and strike a manly pose."

Kim was beginning to pity him for having such a mother, with her hostility and sarcasm. So far, annoyingly, he was letting her get by with it. She fumbled with the camera case and drew out her Leica before they changed their minds. Or their single mind, since clearly Dorothea Coslett's was the only one whose preferences seemed to matter.

Self-consciously, Powell moved to one of the gaps that cut into the battlements.

"A little to one side," Kim directed. "We'll get the sea behind you." She adjusted the rangefinder and framed Powell next to the parapet with a gold-and-silver sunset infusing the clouds. Setting the shutter speed, she took a few shots. "And one smiling," she said, because when he smiled, one felt one could follow the man anywhere.

"Oh, excellent, Powie," Lady Ellesmere said dryly. "Now you look like a cinema star."

"I'll take that as compliment," he said, apparently enjoying himself and surprising Kim by daring to talk back.

As Kim snapped the camera back into its case, Lady Ellesmere beckoned to her. "You asked about the chapel statuary. What happened to it."

She pulled Kim into the stone embrasure. "See?" Her hand pressed on Kim's back, requiring her to look down. The side of the castle formed a curtain wall, and below that the rock cliff fell another five hundred feet.

"I sent them down the cliff."

Kim bent forward to look over the edge of the battlements, not that she would have been able, at this remove in time, to see the shards of the banished relics. The rocks below were slick in the last of the sun.

The dowager watched Kim in some amusement, as though throwing the icons over the wall had been a rather clever solution. "I shouldn't wonder they're well out to sea by now. The earth cleanses all."

Powell helped his mother back inside, her form covered with the full-length fur coat, making her look rather like an old bear returning to its den.

14

THAT EVENING. "Thank you for having me in your home," Kim said to Idelle, who stopped sawing at her mutton for a moment before ignoring the statement. At one end of the twenty-foot-long table, Kim sat across from Idelle and Powell, the only others present. A place had been set at the head of the table, but the dowager would not be joining them tonight.

Powell responded for his aunt. "Glad you've come! Sometimes, it seems Sulcliffe is in a forgotten land." He wore a sweater under his fine wool jacket, and Kim wished she had brought one as well. Neither the dining hall nor any of the castle was heated, making sweaters and furs obligatory, as at a Russian palace. The hall, although not the one with the trestle tables, was as large as the whole ground floor of Wrenfell.

Despite being served on fine china emblazoned with the Sulcliffe emblem, the meal was hopeless: bland roast potatoes and a rather tough mutton. A savory pea soup saved the meal, though it was served tepid from a kitchen that might, for all she knew, be a furlong away.

"What did you think of Mother?" Powell asked. Idelle glanced up, waiting for her to answer.

"Her ladyship is a most remarkable woman. So *suited* to this place." In fact, she could not imagine Dorothea Coslett anywhere else.

Powell beamed. "Yes, she's quite the heart of Sulcliffe. I can't think what it will be like when . . . when she's no longer here." He pushed a potato around his plate. "I expect I shall be wanting a wife then."

Kim could think of no rejoinder to this statement, but Idelle, looking at her nephew, produced a sweet smile. Powell returned it.

"Lady Ellesmere mentioned having a *gift*. Do you know what she meant?" Kim took a sip of the very dark red wine which, tasting dusty and overripe, reminded her of her bedroom upstairs.

Powell dabbed at his mouth with a brocaded napkin. "Yes, she has the gift of perceiving a person's true feelings. It's what makes her such a success with people. I know that at first she may not seem empathetic."

"When you say gift, do you mean what most people call a Talent?"

"We find 'Talent' a bit crass. So much of the popular conception is the product of tabloid sensation."

Idelle pushed her unfinished plate aside. Rian, who had been standing by a sideboard watchful for any needs, moved forward to remove the plate.

Powell said, "Please, Iddy, you must try to eat. Just a bit more?" Idelle looked distressed, prompting Powell to nod at

Rian, who helped his aunt from the table. They made their way toward a small door next to a wall tapestry and disappeared.

"She's not used to a formal dinner," Powell explained, "but I thought she might enjoy a little company. My aunt has lived with us my whole life. You ought to have seen her when she was young! An expert horsewoman, keen interests in everything. She taught me to ride." He glanced at the door through which she and Rian had gone.

"But we were talking of Mother." He took a sip of wine and appeared to gather his thoughts. "She is really extraordinarily perceptive. Her personal magnetism is what has kept our fellowship together for so long. I may never be able to fill her shoes. I just hope that I won't make a hash of it." He put down his knife and fork. "I say, you won't write that, will you? I didn't mean to state it that way, and it's probably not true."

How delightful, when people said things they didn't mean to! A *spill*? She tried to read Powell's expression. It had a tinge of alarm, she thought.

"I'll come into my gift at some point, of course, we all believe that."

"Is a gift earned? Say, through good works or spiritual practice?"

"Oh, I wouldn't say so, no. One has to be *receptive*, is how we think of it. But gifts are a mystery of earth. And truly, they are only notable when they're visited upon a potential leader. A person who can inspire the masses. A leader must be able to persuade and inspire, or movements tend to dissipate. Gifts in the hands of the rank and file . . ." He shook his head. "They can't really be meaningful." He glanced at her notebook. "I'd rather you didn't mention this in your piece. It might appear snobbish or a bit authoritarian."

"It does, rather."

"Well, Mother and I do think a strong hand is needed in large affairs, but it can be misinterpreted."

Indeed it could, Kim thought. "Tell me more about places of power."

"The idea may sound like superstition to you, but it is really the essence of our beliefs. Have you ever been to one of the ritual spaces of the country?"

"You mean like Stonehenge?"

"Yes, that's one. But most people don't realize there are hundreds of such places scattered throughout Great Britain. Orkney. Pentre Ifan. Callanish in the Scottish Isles. Silbury Hill in Wiltshire. Hundreds."

Kim nodded. "And aren't they all evidence of ancient cultures? Tribes who used them for ceremonies and burial and primitive worship?" She had done a bit of homework beyond the Crossbow dossier. "Surely, you don't ascribe meaning simply by virtue of it having been an early belief system?"

"No, no. But those primitive tribes were more open to the true forces of the landscape, and they created memorials in those places of power."

He went on as Rian cleared the plates and served coffee. "They were simple people—which can be a very good thing. Their monuments are markers of places they felt had a non-material influence. They were attracted to sites with energy fields, as we still are today. So, it isn't the standing stones, barrows and mounds and suchlike that have power, but the places such things stand upon. That is what we are trying to say."

"And are these places unique to Great Britain? Surely, they must exist elsewhere in the world."

"Our island is a place of great power. But every land mass is its own sphere of power, nested within the larger spheres of continents and hemispheres. Ancient Light is focused on Britain. The most powerful places are always where we live and where our ancestors have lived. It's why Hitler was keen to reoccupy the Rhineland, and quite right, too. These things are not just lines on a map."

"You admire the German chancellor, then?"

He considered this for a moment. "Well. He's one of the few to take a clear stand against the Communists. Our way of life is at risk if these revolutionaries have their way."

"He does seem to have done some good things."

He brightened. "Exactly. The economy. Getting people back to work. And why this man and not another? Because of his gift for oratory and persuasion."

It was rather an alarming stew of ideas: the fascist-sounding politics, the mystical powers of leadership, the devotion to charismatic individuals.

Powell set down his napkin. "I say, I wrote a book about Ancient Light, did you know? The history, the family involvement. Perhaps you'd like to borrow it." Kim said that she would very much like to, and he excused himself to fetch it.

Alone now in the dining hall, Kim sipped her coffee and made some notes. Not all would find their way into her article, especially things like the Coslett approval of the Nazi party; Powell's bleak obstacle of needing a Talent to inherit the leadership of Ancient Light.

A shuffle behind her gave Kim a start. Turning, she found that Idelle had returned. The woman had a knack for moving so quietly, one could almost believe she floated. She gazed at Kim's notebook and lifted her chin as though in inquiry. After a moment, Kim slowly put her pen down on the table, thinking that Idelle might take it up. She did.

The woman drew the notebook closer and wrote something. Kim looked into her very dark eyes, and for a moment they seemed brimming with words never spoken. She imagined the years, the decades creeping by, none commented upon, except inwardly. It might be the most profound peace. Or a wild storm never let go.

Kim looked down at her notebook. In a lovely, copperplate script, Idelle had written, "Flory Soames."

She looked up at Idelle. "Who is Flory Soames, Miss Coslett?" She hoped for another note, but Idelle put her finger to her lips and backed away. She wandered to the fireplace, leaving Kim surprised and intrigued. She wondered how much Idelle communicated in writing, or if this had taken a rare effort on her part. The woman was regarding her with keen interest. Idelle might not always be tethered to the moment, but whether she had been perfectly alert just now or had behaved irrationally, Kim couldn't judge.

When she heard Powell come into the dining hall, she slipped the notebook into her handbag. They pored over his slim volume, titled *Earth Powers*, as she tried to pay the strictest attention to his spiritualist view. He took pains to elucidate it, turning to chapters where he had treated the topics. But she kept thinking of Idelle and how she was not susceptible to a *spill*. Unless the *spill* might be in writing.

If this were the case, then it was possible that Idelle might wish she had not written what she did.

Kim thanked Powell for the book, which he intended her to keep. He collected his aunt, who was gazing into the fireplace as though seeing, or imagining, a nice fire, and the three of them left the hall together, parting ways at the corridor with the long march of windows.

In the red bedroom, Kim sat propped up in bed in her night-gown, reading the LNER timetable to settle her nerves. It had been an unusual day, and the arrivals and departures of the London and North Eastern Railway line, as always, calmed her. What connections from Edinburgh to Hull before 11:00 AM? And from London to York on a Sunday?

Tomorrow, she hoped for another interview with the baroness, and she was to accompany Powell to view a location of spiritual import on the estate.

Ancient sites of earth power. It was one, perhaps minor, thread of the Crossbow investigation. But she must remember that the major one was Dorothea's tie to the Nazi movement and the *Nachteule* assassinations. In so many ways this case was as convoluted as her last, with minor clues, misdirection, false leads and the fickle role of intuition. But at least then she had known her enemy, the *Sicherheitsdienst* officer, von Ritter.

As she settled in to sleep, she thought about Ancient Light's twisted version of Talents, distorting the *bloom* to support their philosophy of a Sacred Earth. It must have an appeal for those who had no use for the Church of England. But it worked against the family's hopes for leadership of the cult, if Powell was never to have a Talent. And he wouldn't, she knew. He was the wrong age to acquire one as an adult. He would have been an adolescent during the outbreak of the *bloom*. So, it seemed the Cosletts were stuck with their own curious requirements for leadership. Upon Dorothea's death, the next leader would be installed. Powell did not have long to prove himself. He must be in the most dreadful hurry.

As for the baroness, perhaps she did not greatly care who led Ancient Light, as long as it was a person with a *gift* as she defined it, and the fellowship made sure the estate was generously supported after her passing. They would likely do so if they believed Sulcliffe was Britain's spiritual center.

Late that night, she woke, confused for a moment about where she was. She had heard something; was it a cry? By the time she had rearranged her pillow, sleep had retreated. She turned on the lamp and went to the bathroom, thinking that she had read too many ghost stories. Wailing, indeed.

As she crawled back into bed, she heard once more, and unmistakably, a faraway cry. Someone was hurt.

Lacking a robe, Kim grabbed a fringed shawl from the back of a chair and ventured out onto the landing of the winding staircase. The way down fell into blackness. Back in the room, she found the flashlight and returned to the little landing. Following the flashlight's yellow cone of light, she made her way downward, her bare feet immediately icy.

She came to the long hallway near the sitting room and hurried along it toward the area she knew the dining room to be. It unnerved her to be about the stony place in such darkness. There were light switches somewhere. . . .

An appalling cry erupted from one of the rooms up ahead. It was half a moan and half a startled scream. She thought she should have a weapon. The only thing she could think of was the poker by the fireplace in the sitting room, but no time for that now. Another scream. It led her around a corner to another stairway. She heard someone shouting, "Now! Now! You damned shrew!" Lady Ellesmere's voice.

Kim slowed her climb up the stairs, uncertain whether she would interrupt a murder or a family dispute. At that moment, Idelle appeared around a turn and stopped in surprise to see Kim.

"Miss Coslett! I heard screams. Is everything all right?"

"Who's there?" came the dowager's wavering cry. "Who?"

Idelle flattened herself against the stairwell wall and gave no signal as to whether Kim should proceed or leave. Kim climbed past her, up to the first landing. A large door lay open, and inside a massive bedroom a figure moved in the dim lamplight.

"Hurry, you great sow," moaned the dowager.

A woman in a nightgown bent over the prostrate figure of Lady Ellesmere on the bed. She administered an injection, and the dowager fell back onto her pillows.

Noticing Kim, the nurse, elderly and rotund, barked from beside the bed, "Who are ye?"

"I'm a guest. I heard screams. I thought someone had been hurt." She started to back away. The nurse ignored her then, bending over her charge. The room, heavy with the smell of vomit, had been converted into a hospital ward, with tables containing bottles and equipment.

Idelle came into the room, carrying folded blankets and began stripping the top coverlet off the bed.

"Ye'd better go," the nurse said. "Her ladyship will be quiet now."

The patient groaned, "Is it the girl?"

Kim came to the near side of the bed. "It's me, Lady Ellesmere, Kim Tavistock."

The baroness looked in her direction, her eyes watery and vacant. "You've come back."

The nurse shook her head. "Her ladyship dinna know you're here."

As though to contradict the nurse, the dowager grabbed Kim's hand. Her grip was weak but insistent. Not knowing what else to do, Kim sat on the edge of the bed. The room was filled with a miasma of decay and chemicals. From the dossier she knew that Dorothea Coslett had an advanced cancer, but that idea was hard to reconcile with the robust woman she had seen earlier that day.

The nurse loaded a tray with cups and various implements and carried it from the room as Idelle went to the curved wall of windows and opened large French doors. To Kim's relief, fresh air fanned into the room. Idelle stood in the doorframe, looking out on the sea, where moonlight silvered the calm surface. When Kim's eyes had adjusted to the gloom, she saw a portrait of Adolf Hitler hanging over the mantelpiece. He was dressed, as was his habit, in a brown uniform with a swastika armband, a stern expression on his face.

From the newly smoothed covers, the baroness whispered, "I can't go yet." She had opened her eyes and reached for Kim's hand, gripping it forcibly. "Not yet!"

"You must rest," Kim said.

"Not until his gift comes, you see?" The old woman's eyes were keen, the last vestige of what the woman must once have been. "No son of mine can be common. How dare he be common!"

Idelle was watching them now, her face troubled.

"Your son has become a fine, strong man," Kim said softly.

"Oh, all grown, then?" she whispered, her eyes open but unfocused. "Time he took my place. Did he ever marry? He's not supposed to. How can he be receptive to his gift if you're always hanging on him, Margret? I thought you were gone for good!" With surprising strength, she pulled Kim toward her, hissing, "You promised. I paid you, didn't I?" From behind small yellow teeth came her fetid breath. "Only the gifted can rule. It's the ancient law." Her fingers dug into Kim's hand, and Kim endured it, wondering if a woman demented by painkillers was more or in fact, less, capable of a *spill*.

She yanked her hand away from Kim's. "The King was here, how do you like that, you wretched girl!"

Lady Ellesmere's face was drawn into a pronounced sneer, her eyes darting across Kim's face, looking for a point of entrance. "Oh, yes! Edward himself. The summer solstice, that time of power. If you don't leave, I'll tell the King." She produced a hideous smile. "He'll make sure you're gone for good."

Idelle crossed the room to the door and held it open, a clear invitation for Kim to leave. Kim would have liked to stay, but she moved away from the sickbed, passing Idelle, who avoided her eyes.

The nurse returned and insisted that her ladyship could not be further disturbed. Reluctantly, Kim left and wound her way down the stairs, finding that the lights had come on in the corridor.

Powell hurried up to her. "Kim! What the devil are you doing about?"

"When I heard cries, I thought someone needed help."

"I was just going up. I can't bear to see her suffer. But the nurse will administer her shot. . . . You must go to bed. There's nothing you can do, nothing any of us can do."

With that, he charged up the steps to his mother's room, disappearing around the bend in the turret stairs.

15

SATURDAY, AUGUST 15. Gustaw Bajek was a man not easily concealed. He had long ago been promoted out of surveillance, but a man standing six foot and two draws attention everywhere. Here in the Jewish quarter, old men in prayer shawls and women in their knotted headscarves stared at him in his tailored jacket and pressed trousers.

Carrying his package, he walked down Na Przejsciu to Bartosza, each turn bringing him deeper into the industrial sector. The Tilda Mazur case had given Polish intelligence their best lead: the man who had been following her was one who appeared to be an expert in antique dolls. Also, Tilda thought that he was Dutch, a characteristic common now to two Talent murders in Poland.

He made his way down a rutted street, past a building materials factory and a redolent slaughterhouse. Workers' houses clustered along an open canal, looking as though they had been sucked into a cyclone and deposited again. But this was the place where the antique doll seller lived.

Gustaw's asset had said that the doll seller's home could be identified by its blue-painted door, but in this neighborhood painted doors and lintels sprouted everywhere, like poppies growing from cracked cement. He knocked on a blue door.

"Moriz Henschel?" Gustaw asked when it opened.

The occupant of the shanty, a gnome-like man with a full, dark beard, stared up at Gustaw. He noted that the visitor had his hat in his hand—proper manners—and nodded. "I have the honor of being Moriz Henschel. Some days, more honor than others."

"My name is Gustaw Bajek. I have come to ask a question."

"A question. Ah." Moriz nodded, wrinkling his lips as though already considering his answer. "It is not about taxes?"

"No. It is about dolls." Gustaw smoothed his bald head in a mannerism left over from the days when he had had hair.

Moriz opened the door and gestured for Gustaw to enter.

Gustaw sat on the hut's only chair, his package wrapped in twine at his feet. Moriz took a place opposite, on a chest draped with a white cloth framed by a crocheted edge. A bronze samovar crouched on a stove within reach.

"So," Moriz said after Gustaw had stated his business. "It is not a doll you are interested in but a man. I remember the one you describe, the man with the spectacles. He had a crooked light in his eyes."

Gustaw brought the teacup to his lips and slurped gratefully. The stench from the abattoir was strong enough to tint the air green. It had taken two weeks for Polish intelligence to find Moriz Henschel. The man had not returned to the square with his kiosk of dolls, having nursed a boil on his foot.

"Did you know the man?" Gustaw asked. "His name, perhaps?"

"No. He was a foreigner, maybe German. But the young woman, ah, that one! She had been to my stall before, patting the dolls with the tips of her fingers, like she would caress a baby."

"How were the man's eyes crooked?"

Moriz made a fist and then released his fingers in an exploding gesture. "Like a glass ball shattered. Blue, cracked eyes. I never forget such eyes." He picked up the samovar and replenished Gustaw's tea, but not his own. Tea was precious, perhaps saved for guests.

"The young lady," Moriz said, his brow furrowing, "did she come to harm?"

"I do not say that she did."

"You are police, then?" Moriz suddenly looked more ingratiating, and slightly regretful for having offered tea.

"No. Border security," Gustaw supplied at random. He flicked a glance in the general direction of Russia.

"What security? You cannot fill a torn sack."

"This is true. Now I come to Cracow, and perhaps I will do a better job of things. So, tell me, Moriz Henschel, was this man a collector? Perhaps a collector of very old dolls such as yours?"

"No, no collector. He did not love my dolls." Moriz stood up and lifted the cloth off the trunk. Opening the aged chest, he exposed an arrangement of neatly stacked dolls. Like a family, the dolls varied, large and small. Some were clad in pressed but shabby smocks with aprons, and some in old silk and lace.

"This man with the crooked eyes," Moriz went on. "He looked for defects. He picks up one, then the other, squinting at them. He settled upon a fine Kestner Heubach. It was this one." Moriz picked up a doll and held it at arms' length. "He said it would be very nice, but the head, it is not original. Not a Kestner Heubach head."

Moriz shrugged. "My response: 'Perfection belongs to God.' And he: 'Or to a gifted restorer of dolls.' 'Such as yourself,' I say, though I am guessing.

"He answers me: 'Yes.' He said he was not working that day, that he was on holiday."

Ah. So, now confirmed. The Dutchman was an expert indeed, a restorer of antique dolls.

The doll seller nodded to himself, remembering. "Then he looks after the young lady, who hurries away." He shook his head gravely. "If she had not come to my stall, she would have been better off, is that not right, Gustaw Bajek?"

Gustaw wondered. Had she been betrayed, or did the Dutchman stumble upon her? "She loved old dolls, there could be no harm in that."

Moriz looked at the package at Gustaw's feet. "Old dolls such as are in your parcel?"

Gustaw unwrapped the doll that Tilda Mazur's uncle had let him borrow and handed it to Moriz.

The old man nodded, smiling. "She is lovely. A *Mein Liebling* doll, this one. You know the German, *Mein Liebling*?" Gustaw shook his head. "'My darling,' it means. Kammer and Reinhardt, thirty years old, very good condition. Except."

Gustaw nodded. "The arm."

"The missing arm, alas." Moriz gazed intently at his guest. "But she can be repaired."

"Yes," Gustaw said, rewrapping the doll.

Moriz nodded meaningfully at his guest. "It would take a gifted restorer, though."

Gustaw rose, smiling at Moriz. "Yes. I will be most particular."

16

SATURDAY, AUGUST 15. "You say it's a sea henge?" Kim asked as she and Powell hiked across the headland. "I haven't heard the term."

"Just wait! You'll understand immediately, once you see it."

The day had dawned with a fresh, blue sky and a few scudding clouds sharing the channel between there and Ireland. Nothing was said at the breakfast table about the previous night's events. Idelle, quiet of course, was perhaps mournful. Kim wondered if Idelle could possibly be close to Dorothea Coslett; it had seemed last night that she was helping to minister to the baroness. Curious as well, the cryptic note of "Flory Soames," delivered with such stealth when Powell was out of the room. All filed away for further thought.

Though Kim had hardly slept and was still mulling over the disturbing nighttime commotion, Powell was in high spirits. "You've come at an especially good time. If the tide table doesn't lie!"

She looked at him inquiringly as they scrambled up a draw to another shoulder of rock overlooking the sea. As he handed her up the last rise, his cologne mixed with the breeze off the sea.

Powell seemed invigorated by the fine day and the view of the estate, massively green and rippling with vales and hills. But it could not dispel the disquiet Kim felt about how the baroness cast such a dark shadow over her family. She alternately put Powell forward and then belittled him. Her control over her son extended to an apparent bribe to a woman to stop seeing him. Perhaps worst of all, her conviction that *only the gifted can rule*, a dictum that allowed her to criticize her son for something he could not remedy and that kept him from the future leadership of Ancient Light, which he obviously was keen to have.

"Powell, who is Helena? When the baroness mentioned her yesterday, she implied the woman had an important role with the group."

"Well. That's Helena Cumberledge, a woman of the fellowship. She's got her hooks into Mother. Supposedly has the qualities I lack." He stopped, mopping his forehead, looking disconcerted.

It was certainly candid. Inwardly, she smiled.

"A perfectly nice woman. People think she has quite the knack for emotional persuasion. Nothing to write up, mind you."

Perhaps a *conceptor*; certainly helpful for a leader. "No, no," Kim said. "I was just wondering." They resumed their walk.

In the little valley that nearly bisected the headland, they crossed a field that Powell said was used for Ancient Light encampments. A stream cut through it, and on the far side of the field large irregular stones formed a ring.

"A sacred stone circle?" Kim asked.

"No." An ironic smile. "Not every circle has power, you know."

"How can you tell which ones do?"

"Mother and I rely on the ancients. That's one we made, actually. It isn't authentic, but our people like to have a circle for our gatherings."

They ascended a rocky hillside and reached the summit, where the panorama of the silver-green sea unfurled before them. From there it was a short walk over deeply folded bare rock to the cliff's edge. He pointed down. "There it is!"

She joined him, looking down on a cove with a generous crescent beach. It was protected on three sides with black shale cliffs. He pointed at the cove. At the tide line, a series of stones was revealed, too regular in their occurrence to be quite natural.

"I see it," Kim said. "A line of stones like shark teeth."

"But it isn't a line, it's a circle, you see." They watched as the tide receded rather swiftly, revealing first a crescent and then a nearly full circle of upright stones. It looked from this vantage point to be some forty feet in diameter.

"And the stones are only visible at low tide?"

"That's right, and it's what has prevented people from desecrating the stones. If you were to rush out there now, you wouldn't make much progress in dislodging a stone before the tide came in again. It's ancient, possibly over two thousand years old."

"But how could it have been built if the tide had it underwater most of the time?"

"That's the wonderful part. When they built it, this headland had a permanent beach. Over the millennia the builders gradually lost their henge. Mind you, it isn't really a henge, which is a ditch and a bank. But these days people like to call any ancient circle a henge."

A bracing wind slapped at their cheeks. "The tide comes

in fast. It's why Mother always has fretted about my coming here. It disappears at high tide. The whole beach." He flashed his high-wattage smile at her. "There is something profound and enduring about all this. And my mother is a part of it, almost as adamantine as the cliffs."

"You admire her very much, don't you?"

He looked out to sea. The sand around the henge was starting to lose its saturation of water and turned a creamy brown in the morning sun. "Yes. I want to measure up, to continue her work."

"Surely, though, you have the work of the estate to carry on."

"Well, there's not much of a resource there. Mother has given most of her fortune away on charitable causes, and although the estate is mine, I'll need a position with an income. I'll need Ancient Light. Its supporters are very generous."

She'd known it wasn't just ambition. He needed the money.

He went on. "It would be so much easier if my gift came to me. I've been told it's struggling to find expression. It's why I come here and make visits to places of power. To be receptive."

He buttoned up his jacket further against the brisk wind. "It really isn't fair that some people have great success, almost automatically. They just burn brighter than others do."

"I think you could burn brightly." *If your Mother let you*, she wanted to say. Instead, she finished, "If you let yourself."

"I don't think that's how it works."

"The fault is in the stars, in fate?"

A smile started and faltered. "Something like that."

From around the headland came the muffled sound of waves crashing against the rocks. "Last night—"

He interrupted. "That was one of Mother's bad ones. I'm sorry you were distressed. We have to ask you not to make that public, of course."

"We don't need to mention it."

He nodded gratefully.

"You are very watchful for her. With her poor health, it can't be easy."

"Well, we have a live-in nurse to care for her. I can't claim to do much, and I have a demanding travel schedule, to appear at fellowship gatherings here and there."

"You have some important people among your devotees. Even the King, Lady Ellesmere said. He came for an observance of the summer solstice, she said."

He looked surprised. "She told you that? His Majesty would like his privacy. It was not a visit the palace announced."

"Of course. I won't mention it."

"Awfully good of you. The King's expected to be Church of England, but his interests range rather wider."

"An impressive friend for Ancient Light, I must say."

A rueful smile. "He does what he can for us. We are very grateful." He gestured toward the cliffs. "Shall we go down to the beach before it's gone? It's a bit of a slog, I warn you!"

"Oh yes, I'm game."

"That's the spirit," he said. "I'll lead the way so that you can follow my footholds."

They began picking their way down a narrow path along the cliff face, where a missed step on the uneven track could mean a nasty fall to the beach.

He looked back to encourage her. "You aren't afraid?"

"So far, so good!" Halfway down the cliff, the path narrowed even further. She picked her way with care. Ahead, Powell moved sure-footedly and quickly down.

With some relief she planted her feet on the hard-packed sand. Sheltered from the morning sun, the cove was in cold gloom, with the headland throwing its shadow past the sea henge.

Powell looked out to sea. "When I was young, I used to sneak down here and search for agates. Mother forbade me to come, but she was always too fearful for me. Only son and all that." He stooped down to examine a small rock. Seagulls rode thermals above them, shrieking, but in the sheltering bay the wind had subsided.

"Can we walk out to the henge?" The tide had withdrawn from the forward curve of the circle, and Kim felt drawn to stand among the monoliths.

Startled, he came over to her. "No. That one *is* sacred ground. I hope you don't mind."

"Of course. But they do rather beckon, don't they?"

"I've always thought so." He smiled. "I'm glad you do too." He put an arm around her. "You aren't cold?"

The move was forward of him, but she felt she couldn't move away without insult. "Oh, not at all, really." The memory surfaced of Erich von Ritter sharing his coat in the cold and rain of the gazebo. An excuse to be close, and though she had felt certain von Ritter was a spy and she should not let down her guard, she had felt it would be prudish to say no.

"Kim, I have a bit of bad news. I'm afraid that Mother's turn for the worse means we won't be able to have your company for the whole weekend."

She had feared that she was going to be sent home a day early, but she could hardly ask to stay under the circumstances. "Oh. I do understand, of course."

"Have you enough information for your article?"

"Perhaps I could call if I have follow-up questions. Or, I would love to come back when Lady Ellesmere is feeling better."

"I would like to say yes. But we have to see how Mother

fares." He turned to her, bringing them face-to-face. "I've enjoyed our conversations. More than you know."

He was going to make a pass at her. But she had now had a few more hours in the man's company, and the initial spark she had felt had not rekindled.

"I would like to kiss you," he said. "If that's all right. If you wouldn't mind."

She thought it the most awkward proposition she had ever encountered. "Perhaps, given that I'm on assignment, it may not do."

"Surely, that doesn't matter."

She thought of Lady Ellesmere and suddenly wished to thwart the woman. The scene in the sickroom left little doubt that the dowager would disapprove a kiss on the beach. As well, the thought flickered: she would be more likely to get a return invitation. "Well," she said, "perhaps it's not a rule."

He put his hand on the back of her head and, turning her face up toward him, he kissed her, inexpertly but sincerely.

This had been a bad idea. She had now passed a rotten milestone: pretending affection to further her aims.

Awkwardly, they moved apart. "I wish you didn't have to go. My lady friends always go," he said artlessly.

I'll bet they do, Kim thought. If not put off by Powell's clumsiness, then driven off by Dorothea.

Their moment of intimacy suddenly over, he bent down to retrieve a beach stone and hurled it at one of sea gulls. He had no chance of hitting it, but she was unpleasantly startled by the gesture.

In the silence that had fallen, she searched for something to say, coming up with, "What gift would you like to have? If you could choose."

"Well, you'll laugh."

"I won't."

"Well, I should like the gift of charisma. Of people liking one at once."

I liked you at once, she thought to say, because it was true. When he had met her in the sitting room on Friday, he was immediately appealing, though less so now. It was difficult to admire a man who allowed himself to be so manipulated by his mother. But she could see why he wanted that "gift." He might wish for the devotion that his mother had enjoyed all these years. He did seem to thrive on admiration; and no wonder, with his mother an expert in dispensing and withdrawing of approval.

She felt sorry for him. But now she was being sent home and found herself much sorrier on that score. How hard it was to ply such a subtle thing as the *spill*; how disappointing when others were counting on you and you had not come through.

They began their climb up the cliff face, and her thoughts went to Ewan, Rupert, and Frances. *I'm not giving up*, she assured them.

PENGEYLAN

At the railway station, Awbrey waited with her, peering down the track to catch sight of the train.

Kim looked at the old retainer and thought it likely that he didn't miss much of what went on at Sulcliffe. She wished she could ask him about the name Idelle Coslett had written down for her, but Idelle had been at pains to keep it secret. To reveal that she knew the name might put the Cosletts on guard.

Before she left the castle, she had seen Rian and told her that she'd like to thank Miss Coslett for her hospitality. Rian allowed as how Idelle liked to help in the kitchen, and showed Kim the way. But then there were the three of them in the scullery, with Idelle looking alarmed—and pointedly continuing to peel potatoes. No chance to ask her a private question.

Now SIS would put their people on the task of uncovering who Flory Soames might be.

Her intelligence product for Crossbow had certainly been disappointing. The Office would sift through her report, following up on anything they found interesting, but it was hard to think what that might be. The Cosletts were Nazi sympathizers, a viewpoint shared by many in England. Oh, to be a higher rating for the *spill*, she thought, and to have uncovered something of real import.

Such a wish surprised her. She knew the downside of her Talent; she had lived with it, and had often longed to be free of it. How quickly she had slipped into the role of spy, wishing to cull yet more secrets, wanting to know. Willing to live with the consequences in her personal life.

For a purpose, though. And this time, to prevent the slaughter of children.

Crossbow could not be a leisurely investigation. It had been nine days since Frances Brooke had died at Avebury. No one assumed the killer was finished.

Awbrey still watched down the tracks. A taciturn and loyal Coslett retainer, but conversation was her art, and she must put it in play. "Lady Ellesmere told me the King came to visit at the summer solstice. Did you get to see him?"

He screwed up his lips, regarding her with skepticism. "D'ye mean to say her ladyship was talkin' of that?"

"Why yes, just briefly. Were you on the premises for the visit, then?"

He paused, obviously unsure, but finally went on, "Aye, but not close, like. We was all kept well back. An' told to keep silent."

"Well, it won't go in my article. The baron asked me not to mention it."

Awbrey nodded, perhaps eager now, to brag. "And that woman, she come too. Not royal, that one, but in his favor, y' know."

"Oh, Mrs. Simpson, you mean." Most people were well aware that the King was besotted with Wallis Simpson, not only married, but married twice, and despised by many for her influence over Edward.

He frowned. "Might be, might be, but no business of mine."

The train came into view. On the trip home she would write down the possible *spills* or indeed any salient details. Flory Soames; Powell's determination to lead Ancient Light despite the gift/Talent obstacle; Helena Cumberledge, a possible rival; even the sea henge, where few visitors were allowed. Any of these divulged matters—as well as seemingly innocuous things people said—might be *spills*, and therefore important. As always, the question remained, *Was there a spill, or more than one?* And if so, *Which utterances were they?* The thing about the *spill* was that it was often the very thing you needed most to know, since the subject had a desire *not* to tell it.

The train chuffed into the tiny station with clanking couplings and hissing brakes. Having assured Awbrey that she could manage her two bags, they said their goodbyes and she boarded the train.

In her private railway compartment she found a copy of the *Times*. The issue was full of the Berlin Olympics. She read with pleasure, JESSE OWENS WINS 4TH GOLD. That *should give the lie to*

Hitler's myth of Aryan supremacy, she thought. In fact, Owens was the most successful athlete at the games.

Eventually, she took out her notebook and began recording her observations from Sulcliffe. One phrase that gave her pause was *Only the gifted can rule*. Dorothea and Powell Coslett placed great importance on the special qualities needed for leadership. It was something Erich von Ritter had believed, too. That the *bloom* meant that people of great Talent would lead the world, improving it. How wrong that was. She didn't know the significance of the *bloom*, but it wasn't a brighter future. It might mean a far more dangerous one. The reign of the unscrupulous, with powers they should not have. She thought of Hugh Aberdare during her first mission and Lady Ellesmere on this one, and how they abused their powers. In people like that, uncanny abilities were dark Talents, indeed. Hard, sometimes impossible, to contain.

Unless there were equal Talents ranged in opposition to them.

The compartment door swung open. She looked up to find a man in an ill-fitting suit. He clicked the door shut behind him.

"This is a private compartment," Kim said.

"Oh, I kin see that. Nice posh seat you got there." He was about fifty years old, a man on whom a slim frame had become rangy. His face was tense, but lit with energy, perhaps fueled by a pint or two.

"What is this about?"

"I might ask you the same, Kimberly Tavistock."

That couldn't be good, that he knew her name.

He swayed at the door, as the train rounded a curve. "You come marchin' into the *Register* claiming you're onto a story that we happen to be already workin' on." He nodded at her. "That's the question might be asked."

"What story?"

He rolled his eyes. "What story. Earth mysteries, that's what. It was my story, my idea to chat up Baron Ellesmere. All arranged, nice like. And then the boss, he says he's got a girl onto it, and she's some big writer from the States, with *credentials*, and we sodding well don't need Lloyd Nichols."

Kim drew herself up. "I think we can leave it to your editor to decide. If you have a better story, you'll have to convince him. Meanwhile, I'll thank you to leave or I'll summon the conductor." She carefully closed her notebook.

He noticed this. "Oh, so that's your interview, is it? With her ladyship and her son? That was to be *my* scoop. Far as I'm concerned, you pinched it."

"I'll thank you to leave. Now, Mr. Nichols."

"I know all about the mess you made of things at your big Yank newspaper." He came closer, looming over her, his breath reeking of gin. "Got yourself sacked, is the truth. And now you come looking for *my* job, so I'm buggered, ain't I? Buggered."

"If you don't leave, I'll call the conductor." She rose to push the bell.

Nichols wiped his chin and its faint stubble. "This ain't the end of the discussion."

"Yes, it is," Kim replied. "And I plan to be in touch with Maxwell Slater."

Nichols bit his lip. "You don't need to get Maxwell into this. I'll lose my job."

"If I don't see you again, we'll leave it at that."

Nichols swayed out of the compartment and slammed the door.

When she changed trains at Chester, she glimpsed Nichols waiting at the platform for the train to London. He'd had the look of a heavy drinker, red-faced and disheveled, and she wondered that he was still employed at all. She considered reporting him to Owen, but she mustn't give the service any reason to think she was particularly vulnerable for being a woman and one traveling alone. She had had to keep Owen firmly reminded of this fact to counter his bouts of overprotectiveness. In any case, even though Nichols *had* investigated her—to the extent of her stint with the *Inquirer*—he was just a harmless, if aggravating, drunk.

THE TOWN WALL, YORK

THAT EVENING. "The problem always is," she told Owen Cherwell, "that it's impossible to know for sure if I've gotten a *spill.*"

Dusk had already claimed the Old Town area of York, its medieval warren of streets a faintly glowing maze. Here on the city walls, the day lingered. At Kim's last call-in from Sulcliffe they had arranged this meeting place, a stopover on her way home.

"I mean, if someone tells me they're having an affair with their cousin, and they blurt it, I might suspect it was one. But even then . . ." It was hard to explain. So much of the *spill* was a dance of intimacy and avoidance.

"You don't have to be *sure*, you just have to be *aware.*" Owen leaned on the wall abutment, looking north to the York Minster with its soaring Gothic towers. "What sounded *off*? When did the conversation suddenly veer away?"

"Yes, I know, but that's how all conversations go, if they're very long." She drew her notebook out of her coat pocket. "Well. Here is my list of things I learned, whether *spill* or not."

Owen squinted at the list. "The estate is in financial trouble; Powell Coslett fighting for succession to Ancient Light's leadership;

the dowager sending away a girlfriend of her son's; the name Flory Soames." He glanced up. "What's that one about?"

Kim described Idelle Coslett and her vow of silence that apparently did not prevent her from writing notes. "She may dislike the baroness. She's a hard woman to like. But if she meant to speak against Lady Ellesmere, she didn't give me much. And if it was a *spill*, it's of a sort I've never had before. Written. Also, Idelle Coslett is elderly and losing some of her competency."

Owen read on. They stood on one of the main gatehouses of the York city walls, the one called Bootham, its pathways and stairs worn smooth by eight hundred years of sentries and tourists. The stones were still warm from the sun, unlike the stones of Sulcliffe, which perhaps never lost their chill.

When Owen came to Edward VIII and Mrs. Simpson's visit to Sulcliffe, he raised an eyebrow. "The King?"

"Yes, Lady Ellesmere told this to me when she was heavily sedated. Later, Powell said that the King is also a donor to Ancient Light."

"The Cosletts are solidly in the highest circle, then." Owen frowned. "And a visit at the summer solstice, no less. Do you suppose His Majesty is partial to spiritualism?"

"Why else would he go there on the solstice, a rather significant date for the spiritualism crowd?"

"Indeed. But it may complicate things. We're already warned away from unnecessary meddling with the baron and the dowager. Now this." Owen tore out the pages from her notebook and stuffed them into his breast pocket.

She had only a few minutes before the 9:40 to Uxley. "You'll see in my notes that the dowager has a Talent. I'm guessing it's *hyperempathy*. She's very shrewd at deducing moods and things left unspoken." Such as when the subject of the war came up.

All losses are specific, she had said, as though she had seen into Kim's heart. "She thought she caught a glimpse of unease in me. It gave me a start, but I don't think she could identify my . . . duplicity."

"Don't think of it like that. It's not a lie, it's a cover."

Well. It was both. But it didn't hurt to use the right words, the ones that helped you live with yourself.

Kim looked at her Helbros wristwatch. 9:04 PM. In their last minutes Owen expertly debriefed her, teasing out details for later consideration in that formidable mind of his, the one for which he had been plucked from the Cambridge psychology department to work at Monkton Hall.

"Good to keep a watch on the baron, as you've done." Owen said. "He may be keen to impress the Germans. He could even be Talon."

"Hard to think why he would be."

Perhaps the Nazis would reward him for killing English young people. But why? If they wanted to assassinate military Talents, they would come after *her*—and others whose names were listed in the logbook at Monkton Hall.

In any case, she must work on Powell Coslett, who liked her and who was less on guard than Lady Ellesmere.

Sulcliffe Castle was a dark well of secrets and longing. It was like the sea henge, its secrets covered by fathoms of water. But even the sea henge came into view sometimes.

She would go back. She must. A little more time, and the truth might be revealed.

But for the killer's next target, time might be the one thing they did not have.

THE BLOOM BOOK

Mentation capabilities are characterized by heightened mental processing. An individual can perceive facts, outcomes, conclusions, events, and associations derived from people, objects, or a setting. The nature of these perceptions appears to be tied to human emotional experience. The class is distinguished from the Hyperpersonal Group by the absence of personal interactions.

Hypercognition. Enhanced speed of deduction. This ability manifests in a manner that can be compared to what is commonly referred to as intuition. The individual grasps, in an unconscious manner, minor events or statements that point to an accurate conclusion. The insight so derived is often instantaneous. Manifestations spontaneous.

Hyperempathy. When in close proximity to a subject, practitioner perceives the presence of suppressed or hidden emotions. At the lower end of the rating scale, the specific emotion may not be identified, but merely its apparent strength. Underlying ability.

Object reading. Upon physical contact with an item, details relating to the object's owner are perceived. The details may be clear or shrouded by a number of historical associations. Some observations of the ability show an object's entanglement in an owner's life such that perceptions can be gleaned whether or not the item was in the presence of the emotional event. Controlled by the intention of the practitioner.

Precognition. This ability manifests as a quasi-real viewpoint of a potential future event. It is highly variable in accuracy. Researchers are divided about how the skill operates. One theory holds that it is a variation of hypercognition, wherein the practitioner makes a powerful logical extrapolation. The very nature of our current understanding of time and the future is brought into question with this most intriguing of meta-abilities. Manifestations spontaneous.

Site view. Practitioners gain a perception, visual glimpse, or deduction derived from a past event in a specific location. (In contrast to trauma view, which is a viewpoint derived from a person.) The sensitivity is to emotion-laden occurrences that have happened in a place where the practitioner is present. In addition to impressions from the event, the practitioner may perceive emotions of actors present in the view. This ability is often used in law enforcement. Manifestations spontaneous.

17

SUNDAY, AUGUST 16. *"May I come in?"*

Julian stood at Kim's bedroom door, watching as she unpacked from her trip. He would have liked to know the results of her efforts in Wales, but he'd have to learn that secondhand, from Owen Cherwell.

Inviting him in, Kim tipped the last of her things out of the valise. She continued her sorting and folding of clothes. He knew from experience that once Kim had a little organizing in hand, she would keep at it until it was completed.

"How was your trip? You haven't been to Wales before, have you?"

"No, I haven't. It was rather dark and windblown. The castle inmates were quite a crew." She glanced at the little book he held in his hand.

"Inmates?" He felt he had license to follow up *that* remark.

"Yes, a doughty old baroness and her peculiar son, plus all

the servants at least seventy years old." She removed a cardigan sweater from the suitcase, refolding it before laying it in a drawer. "But I got a good story on the fad of finding mysticism in prehistorical sites. Sold it to the *London Register*."

He heard Martin on the stairs; the lad always seemed to take two stairs at a time. He walked over to Kim's door and closed it.

As Kim looked at him inquiringly, he sat on the edge of her bed. "Mrs. Babbage was in Martin's room the other day. She decided to unpack for him since he was still grabbing clothes out of his suitcase. In the chest of drawers, she found this." He looked at the book in his hands.

Kim sat next to him. "A journal?"

He didn't know how to say this to her other than straight out. "It belonged to Robert."

"Robert?" Kim whispered.

"His diary. From the battlefront."

"Oh, God. Is it really? Is it really from Robert?" She looked at the journal with a mixture of tenderness and dread.

"Yes. I considered not reading it. His private thoughts. But I couldn't not do so."

"She found it in Robert's dresser drawer?" She looked as confused as he must have when Mrs. Babbage had brought him the notebook, saying that she hadn't presumed to read it, of course, but had looked at it far enough to know that it was Robert's.

The leather of the cover was well worn, as though Robert had carried it for a time in his kit. Many of the water-stained pages were hard to read. Julian had gotten through it to the end, but had not slept that night.

She reached out to touch the leather cover, a tender gesture, as across someone's cheek. Her gaze went to the hall. "I thought those drawers were empty."

"They were." He shook his head. "I spoke to him about it. Martin said that he found the diary on the top closet shelf, pushed so far back we must have missed it. And that he meant to tell us, but he didn't know what it was and didn't think it important."

Kim frowned. "I see."

He handed the diary to her.

He wanted to say that Robert's words had been very hard to read, but that he treasured them for all that. That they were so very fortunate to have this remembrance of him, even if right now it hurt to the core to read the words. But he and Kim were not accustomed to sharing such thoughts.

Kim gripped the diary with both hands.

"I'll let you make your own decision about reading it," he said.

She looked up at him, and nodded.

Kim listened to Julian descending the stairs. Since she had heard Martin run up the stairs a few minutes before, she surmised he was in his room, waiting for her. Putting the diary on her bed, she went to his room.

He sat on the window seat like a prisoner awaiting a sentence. "I was going to tell you," he said miserably.

"No, I don't think you were." She kept her voice low and even, controlling her anger. "You were planning to use the contents of my brother's diary to try and prove a *site view* Talent."

"No, I—"

She interrupted him. "Martin, you lied to your parents and the headmaster about the clubs. You lied to your fellow members of the Adder club about having a Talent. And now to me." She saw his misery, but she could not soften this for him. He had terribly abused her trust. "Even knowing how we still grieve for

Robert, you were going to withhold this diary from us for your own aggrandizement."

"My what?"

"For the sake of making yourself important. That was an awful thing to do."

"I was going to give it to you."

"But that wouldn't work, would it? Once you had leaked to me the facts from this diary, you could never let me read the same things in its pages. Isn't that right?"

His voice went so soft, she could hardly hear it. "I didn't think where it would go. That if I started with the diary, I could never give it to you."

"But *why*, Martin? Why do this?" She waited.

"Because I was afraid you'd send me home. When school starts."

"So, you risked stealing from us?"

"Yes, because I knew my da would make me come home, and I don't know about the barn and horses and I'm not strong, not even as strong as old Babbage, and I thought I'd have to go home. Unless . . ." He hesitated.

"Unless you told me my brother's private's thoughts."

He swallowed but kept silent.

"Oh, Martin." She shook her head at the mess of it all. "What shall we do?"

He looked up at her fiercely. "You should call the police. I did steal the diary, and I'm not worth it, not worth your trust. Obviously."

She looked down at him as he sat on the window seat. She wanted to shake him and also comfort him. "Is home so awful?"

He wiped his nose with the back of his hand and nodded.

"What's awful about it?"

"My da. He hates me because of my Talent and how I always screw up everything. And that I don't like the chemist's shop, and my mum goes along with whatever he says." He cut a wounded glance at her. "But I do see things. Lots of other times, I have."

Looking at him, Kim saw a boy who desperately wanted people's regard and had taken up lying to get it. He felt a failure at home, even with the wretched gambit to claim special powers. Which undoubtedly had just made matters worse. But she couldn't send him away. He had done a terrible thing, but he deserved a second chance.

"All right," she said. "For starters, we won't talk about Robert ever again. I'm going to let you stay until school starts as long as there are no more lies. Not even one. Are there any lies you want to tell me about now?"

He shook his head.

"I don't think you always screw up. I think you're fifteen and are willing to try things and sometimes fail. And from what Mr. Babbage says, you don't fail very often. So. We're going to start over." She gave him a small smile, one that she thought she meant. At least now, since he'd made up his Talent, she would worry a little less about his being a murder target. Except the killer couldn't know who was real and who was fake.

Neither could she, it was clear.

"One more thing," she said. "I want you to wash that ink drawing off your wrist." The Crossbow dossier had described the Adder club mark. It was too dangerous to advertise a Talent, even if it wasn't true.

"Oh, Mr. Tavistock already told me to."

"He did?"

"But it won't come off. I really scrubbed it." He pulled back his plaid shirtsleeve. The little snake emblem on his pale skin looked like a blue vein running the wrong way.

It was odd that Julian had asked him to wash the symbol off. Normally, household matters went utterly by him.

"He said the school wasn't going to like it."

"I think that's right. *Or* your parents."

It seemed so out of character for Julian to have mentioned this to Martin. But he was right about the school objecting, though he couldn't know the larger reason why getting rid of the mark was a good idea.

Martin shook his head. "I don't think I can get rid of it."

"Of course you can. Keep at it, and eventually it will fade." He seemed completely crestfallen now. Well, that made two of them.

She went to her room and locked the door.

Her anger having passed through her like a sudden squall, she felt hollow, as though the emotion had burned away smaller things. It left her a bit weak, unless that was just dread that she would be filled back up again by things she did not want to feel.

Finally, she picked up the journal and sat on her bed. She slowly opened it and began to read.

Friday, 11th September, 1914. They say there'll be an all-out attack on Sunday. Some of the boys are up for it, because anything is better than the mud, the trenches, the waiting.

Kim closed the book. *I cannot do this*, she thought. It was already like ripping a plaster off a wound. But she opened the diary again.

Wednesday, 16th September, 1914. Back of the lines I'm drilling raw recruits in target practice, and wouldn't be surprised to catch a stray bullet from one of them. Now they say the offensive will come on Tuesday a week. They'll start with a bombardment at dawn, but all that will do is wake the Germans up. We wait.

Saturday, 3rd October, 1914. We lost Peter today. A sniper shot as he left the command bunker. Still raining. The world is mud.

That innocent line, *The world is mud.* It prefigured what was to come, and her heart crimped, confronting it yet again. The horror of Robert's last minutes still had power over her.

She opened the diary and continued to read.

WHITECHAPEL HIGH STREET, LONDON

Lloyd Nichols looked up from his desk as his boss came by. "Working on a Sunday, then, are we?" Slater said, who was obviously working himself.

Nichols scratched his chin, wondering how sarcastic to be. Plenty, he decided. "Fascinatin' topic, unemployment. It cries out for a snappy title. Do you fancy SOCIALISTS SCREAM FOR BALDWIN'S HEAD or MEN ON DOLE HAPPY AS PIGS IN MUCK?"

"How about NICHOLS AVOIDS THE AXE?" Slater said, shrugging into his suit jacket and heading for the door. "Just write it up, old thing, and leave the headline to me."

Point taken, you blighter. When he heard the downstairs door slam shut, he reached for the bottom drawer, bringing out a bottle of Gordon's gin. He looked at the work in front of him: one typewritten page. A complete cockup.

That Tavistock girl, now. Stuck up, and plain as a yard of water. *I plan to be in touch with Maxwell Slater.* A regular countess, she was, talking like that to him, who'd been in the business for twenty-five years, and her just a Yank havin' a rich father in Uxley with a hand in the whisky trade. And her getting sacked from the *Inquirer* for stickin' her nose into things blokes'd rather not read, like torturin' dogs for science.

He drank a toothful, and then another, staring at Slater's door. The boss was jerking him around, assigning him a feature one day, spiking it another. What was the man up to? He'd have a little look in the boss's office. Maybe he was slipping Tavistock Lloyd's own copy. If that was it, he'd put a stop to it, right enough.

Slater's door was unlocked. Checking to be sure the newsroom was still empty, Lloyd went for the big stack of files on the table, finding one labeled ANCIENT LIGHT a few inches down. Nothing in it but notes from Lloyd's original assignment and some old tear sheets from the society pages of the *Times* involving the Cosletts.

Leaving that aside, he found a dozen of Slater's lined pads, filled with his notes and doodles. Like the man couldn't be on the phone or in a meeting without jotting down dates, circling words, making designs.

After a few minutes of scanning the notes, he found a page with the name *Tavistock* and two big underlines. The same page, a date: *17 Aug.* And circled, *R. Galbraith.* He heard the outer door shut and dropped the tablet, skirting around Slater's desk, trying to get to the door. Too late.

Slater was coming right for him. And he had the bottle of Gordon's.

The editor's bulk filled the doorway. "What're you doing in my office?"

The blighter must have forgotten something. Lloyd was in

a jam but decided to brave it out. "I'm having a look around, is all. Thought maybe I'd see my feature story in here. The one you asked me to write but that all of a sudden ain't wanted."

Slater's eyebrows raised up. "Did you lose it? The story we killed? I figured maybe you'd get it framed or something."

There'd be a row, no way of avoiding it. Nichols squeezed by into the newsroom. He turned, facing off with his boss, his anger overcoming his fear. "You shaggin' her? Is that it? That why she got my interview with Coslett?"

Slater's face closed down.

"You gettin' your knob shined by that twit from Yorkshire?"

Slater's lip curled so far, it showed his canines. "Pack your stuff, Nichols. I want you the hell out of my newsroom."

"You're sacking me?" Lloyd licked his lips, thinking how to get things shoved back into their place. "So, that's it, then?" he asked, knowing it was. He was so pissed, he couldn't think straight.

"That's it, you arsehole. Get the hell out of here." He slammed the Gordon's into Lloyd's hands. "And take your bottle with you before you're chucking your guts out in my newsroom. Bloody wanker."

Before he knew it, Lloyd was staggering down the stairs, carrying a box with his belongings. The whole thing was a total balls-up. The only fix for it would be going on the piss with his bottle of Gordon's. He knew the morning would bring worse.

He'd be unemployed.

WRENFELL, EAST YORKSHIRE

Past 11:00 PM, Julian had his pipe out on the back stoop. The warm night air surged with the sound of crickets, somehow always invisible in their multitudes. Shadow had come out with him, watching the yard, the property. Julian looked up toward Kim's window. The light was still on.

Shadow came to attention and dashed off through the kitchen garden and out toward the paddock. Whatever he had seen, it wasn't visible to human eyes in this darkness before moonrise.

In the Babbage cottage a stone's throw away, a wan light glowed from the kitchen window. It was a peaceful scene, marred only by Julian's thoughts of the youth murderer. It had been ten days since the last death; the interval between the other murders: seven and five days. They all expected the killer to strike again.

"Shadow!" he called, not shouting it but loud enough. "Shadow!" Perhaps he'd gotten wind of a fox.

He finished his pipe. It was too late to call Olivia. Just as well. Their telephone conversations had been stilted lately. Once or twice he imagined she'd been with someone—that friend of the family of whom he was unreasonably jealous without even knowing the man's name.

E forbade personal involvement among his agents. It was a security risk on several levels, and he believed that romantic entanglements spoiled office peace and protocols. The fact that he was allowing this one to go forward was an indulgence. Olivia was not an agent. But as E's secretary she was more integral to operations than any agent, keeper of all secrets great and small.

He felt she was slipping away from him; and why wouldn't she, when they had no future? Perhaps he should retire. The notion came to him lately, always aslant, testing for the reception it would receive. But the thought of having nothing productive to do, of giving up what had become his calling . . . No, he could not do it. Until he thought of Olivia, and then the needling thought

came, of them sharing his Albemarle flat and then weekends at
Wrenfell. Times he wanted that. Times he didn't. Good God.

"Shadow!" And the dog came racing from wherever he had
been.

Climbing the stairs to bed, he saw light in Kim's room. Her
door was partway open.

As Shadow nudged past him into her room, he saw Kim sitting propped up in bed with the journal, her dinner untouched
on the tray on the footstool. "How many times have you read
it?" he asked.

She managed a smile. "A few." The border collie got thorough rubs from her before assuming his position curled up by
her nightstand.

"Does it help or make it worse?"

She looked up at him with a soft but haunted look. "Both, I
think. He was so young." She set aside the journal on the counterpane. "They were all so young."

"Yes." He thought he knew how she felt but didn't dare say
so. She had always believed that Robert's death hadn't registered
with him as it had with her and her mother. She was wrong, but
he felt he oughtn't have to say that he loved his son. When she'd
come back to England and found him apparently enamored of
the Nazi cause, it confirmed her view that he had no loyalty to
Robert. As though hating Germany was proof that one loved
those they had slaughtered. It was a wearying subject, one they
avoided.

Robert had died on November 11, 1914. Two weeks later
Julian and his wife learned of his death. Then, as the loss took
hold of them in its stark permanence, they learned *how* he had
died. The army had originally said it was during a cavalry charge
on the salient near the village of Ypres. But Robert had not been

mowed down by enemy fire. As the charge went forward, the
saturated ground over which his unit surged collapsed into an
enormous crater, trapping Robert and two of his comrades on
their horses. As the infantry poured over the nearby ground, the
sides gave way in a thunderous slurry of mud. It had taken only
a few seconds to engulf and bury the soldiers and their mounts.
Robert's men—he was in command that day after his captain
had been killed—tried to dig the doomed men out, but under
the German barrage it was hopeless. Robert had drowned under
tons of mud, along with Baron, his favorite black.

When at last they had heard the complete story of the disaster, Robert's mother had utterly broken down. Then, at some
time during those awful weeks, Ellen sought comfort from her
remaining child. She had told Kim, though their daughter had
been only eleven. It had all been grief and madness. Within two
months Ellen had gone back to the United States, taking Kim
with her.

This event spiraled on through their lives, breaking the
family apart. With Kim's return to Wrenfell three years ago,
for a time Julian had hoped they might patch something of it
together again.

Of course, it could never be put right. He knew that.

18

WEDNESDAY, AUGUST 19. Kim knelt in front of the open trunk and surveyed its contents, the last things they'd kept of Robert's.

"There's not much left," she said to Alice. "We gave his clothes away." Well, Julian had. She wasn't sure she could have done it, so perhaps it was best he hadn't told her.

Alice drew up a dusty stool and sat down. Behind her, morning light streamed in through the gable window. Her flaming red hair always gave the impression that something dramatic was going on in her head. At any given moment, it might even be *trauma view*, a vision of people behaving their worst.

Kim carefully placed the diary on top of Robert's papers and mementoes.

Here on the unused third floor of Wrenfell, the smell of dust and old timbers was strong, especially as the sun flooded over the floorboards. Her heart felt raw after a night of reading entries in Robert's journal. In mid-October of 1914 he had come home on leave, and it must have been then that he put his journal in the upper shelf of the closet.

"This business with Martin faking his visions," Alice said. "An awful thing to do."

Closing the trunk lid, Kim sat on the floor next to the chest, cradling her arms around her knees. She wanted to forgive Martin, but it was hard. "Maybe he didn't know. If you've never experienced the death of someone you loved, maybe you don't know how long the pain lasts."

Alice was having none of it. "His parents did say he had a problem with lying. And this was just bloody awful of him."

"Well, I'm giving him another chance. I don't want to kick him out on a first offense."

"A rather large offense," Alice sniffed.

It was a death twenty years past. She was getting over it. Surely, in fact, she *had* gotten over it. "Mrs. Babbage says Rose is excited to have another young person around. They're doing crossword puzzles together. She's already devoted to him."

Alice sighed. "If James gets word of what happened, it'll be more proof that Martin is a rotter."

"We won't tell him. But can you see if James will relent on the counseling sessions? He's only making Martin feel more worthless."

"I shouldn't think I'm the right person to bring it up. Not at the moment."

Kim shot a look at her.

"You see, I'm going to tell him. James. I'm going to tell him I have a Talent." She noted Kim's surprise. "And I don't care what happens. It's just bloody well time to let it all out."

"Oh, Alice." She hadn't realized how relieved she would feel to hear her friend say something just like this. Surely, if anyone was to know something so personal, it would be the person you hoped to marry. "But you do care, of course. You are being frightfully brave."

"Not brave, just steamed up. I picture myself barging into his study and blurting it out all at once, then defying him to make something of it." A self-deprecating smile. "Probably I'll be more tactful."

"When?"

Alice smirked, pushing a strand of hair back into her updo. "When I get my courage up."

All very well to urge honesty on other people. Kim thought of her own web of secrecy, going back twenty years.

"Never mind about James. We have work to do." Alice nodded meaningfully. "The operation." She cut a look at the doorway, then lowered her voice. "Kim. I'm going to be brought in on it. On the Crossbow mission."

Surprised, Kim put her hand on Alice's. "Good. That's *very* good. The two of us plying our Talents, then?" Her mood soared. She got up to close the door. Not that anyone else would be up here on the third floor, but advisable just in case.

In case it might be her father who would eavesdrop.

She checked down the hallway. No one there. The thought came to her: *I don't trust my father.* Her discomfort with him had increased since she had been inducted into the service. Julian could not be spying for the Germans. But then why did she feel he had secrets of his own?

Closing the door, she turned back to Alice. "What have they told you?"

"The murders. The Nazis. The bloody red baroness."

"*That's* what they're calling her?"

"It's what *I* call her. I'm catching up on the dossier. Powell Coslett and his leadership ambitions, the Dutchman, Idelle Coslett's mention of Flory Soames . . . The baroness isn't just funding *Nachteule*, she's funding the youth murders as well. The two operations are related. Killing Talents. That's the link."

"Well, it's proof we need. And we can't investigate the Cosletts properly until we establish motive or more suspicious ties. Ones that will convince Whitehall. Polish up that *trauma view*, my girl."

"I shall. And when you go back to Wales, I'm going with you. I'll be your traveling companion. Women shouldn't travel that far alone. The old woman would appreciate that idea."

"*Am* I going back?"

"That's where the baroness lives, our only suspect. So, to Sulcliffe." Alice grinned. "I've *got* to see this place."

POPLAR, EAST END, LONDON

THURSDAY, AUGUST 20. In the front hall, Lloyd Nichols smelled the greasy odors of Bill Dorne's morning fry-up. Spotting Dorne's copy of the *London Register*, he bent down and picked it up. Riffling through it, he soon found the Tavistock article.

Oh, it was a big, grand feature, just like Slater had planned for his own story. He snorted. "Places of Power: The Earth Mysteries Movement." A headline taken straight from a tourist circular, it was. He stared at what should have been his scoop, spread across the page like a bruise. The usual pictures of Stonehenge, and henge this, henge that, as well as a picture of the baron, grinning his arse off.

And there it was, the cockchafer's byline: *Kim Tavistock*.

He read it through to the end, so intent that he didn't notice when old Dorne opened his door.

"'Ere now! My paper, ain't it?" He was wearing a sweater over his pajamas, shuffling into the hall in his bloody slippers.

Lloyd glared back. "Guess I thought it was mine." He handed it to the old scrote, and made a show of looking around the hall for his copy.

The old man slammed the door, leaving Lloyd to climb the stairs to his flat, his little corner of the empire, a drab nest in council housing. But not for long if he didn't find work.

He stopped just inside the door to his flat, looking at the mess of the last four days since Maxwell had sacked him. Plates crusted with dried gravy and gobbets of jam, a greasy pan on the small gas ring in the corner, a sweater thrown on the coffee table, his trousers crumpled on the ladderback chair.

On the kitchen table, strewn notes from his own article on the subject. He planned to sell it to the *East End Express*, and it was worth ten pounds at least, he figured. Maybe fifteen. But now hadn't the bitch beat him to it, so it would look like he was riding her coattails? *Riding her coattails.* She purloined his story, her with her toff airs and big *Register* byline. It galled, it did.

The smell of Dorne's morning sausages wound up the staircase, reminding him that he was hungry. He turned on the gas ring to heat up the leftover grease in the pan. When it started to smoke, he mopped up a hunk of bread in it, turning up the flame for a nice crust.

As he chewed, he thought about asking Slater for his job back. But the blighter might take it amiss if he sold a story to another paper, a story he might claim was written on the *Register*'s time. The fry bread sat in his gut, churning.

CHEAPSIDE

THAT EVENING. It was a delicate matter to find a child to kill in London. And in the exact right place. Patience and luck were needed. Lately, Dries Verhoeven seemed to have both.

So as not to attract attention, when they emerged from Bank Station, he and his companion had separately strolled down Cheapside. Dries looked in store windows, watching reflections, waiting for the right youngster. Across the narrow street, St. Mary-le-Bow would suit perfectly.

And there she was. A girl of secondary-school age entering the church in company with adults. Dries leaned against the brick wall, reading a map of the Square Mile, as Londoners called their financial district. He could sense that his accomplice across the street was not happy about stopping. They both knew it signaled they had a possible target.

Then the stroke of fortune. From the door that was thrown open to the warm evening, the girl wandered out. How cruel of St. Mary. God and St. Mary were no cowards, he observed, to dare him this way. Inside, he could see a few parishioners gathered in the hall. The girl, wearing a navy-blue dress with a charming white yoke, walked out the door, away from the group, along the long wall of the church.

Dries crossed the street to join his helper.

His companion was always nervous when it came down to the act itself. "We can't!" he hissed. "Her parents . . ."

"Are talking to the vicar."

"Too many people! We'll be seen."

It was infuriating to have to deal with his helper's possible defection at this moment, but he spoke reassuringly. "I must take this girl. She has presented herself to me, you see."

"Don't you understand? This place is too public!"

"Another feature that recommends it. We strike at the heart of the City. And at a *church*. Don't you see?" Oh, the handsome baron didn't see. His face was always bland and guarded except when he smiled in that way that he assumed charmed everyone.

"You're barking mad!"

Dries took a long, appraising look at Powell Coslett, the man he had been saddled with for a helper. He said, slowly and with relish, "I'll tell your mother."

It was the line Dries had been wanting to use on Coslett since the beginning. And, indeed, it had the desired effect. The man's rebellion wilted, he could see it.

"Ga nou!" Dries hissed. *Come on!* He pushed his accomplice toward the side of the church. Coslett would administer the anesthetic, and they would lower her to the ground and drain her. It had to be now. The opportunity was begging for consummation, with her over there, already in shadows.

He must leave England soon. His demanding masters required him elsewhere, for more important work. England was a side issue for them. However, for Dries, it was of the essence. For the record—if there would ever be a record—he did not enjoy killing these youngsters. What he must have in satisfaction came from the terror of the British. He lived and relived the finding of the young bodies. He savored the panic and despair that now slowly crawled over the country. He was quite willing to conduct the work of the French murders, and the Polish . . . yes. Ah, but the British work, that was of a different order.

He grasped the scalpel in his coat pocket. Now, in the moments before the cut, came the flames, surging down the long hall of memory, curling the wood, paper, bones. Coslett was at his side, bringing out the reeking cloth. How slowly the ritual unfolded. Blade, flame, rag.

Coslett stepped toward the girl, as he must, the one without an accent, the one with the handsome appearance and inimitable air of breeding.

Dutiful now, Coslett said, "Excuse me, can you help me?"

The girl turned to look up at him, her face framed by the square, hand-stitched yoke. She glowed with—what would most people say? *Health*, perhaps.

As his helper clumsily slapped the cloth over the girl's face, Dries moved in behind. As always came the memory of scorching, blistering heat, and skin—so frail a barrier. Through it all, he thrust out quickly, pulling the blade under her chin, severing the artery of the neck. She was already unconscious, dying, as they lowered her to the ground. They grabbed her by the armpits to sit her upright, just so.

Dries removed his coat, now stained red, and turned it inside out, throwing it over his arm.

He and his companion slowly walked from the square, picking up their pace once on Cheapside. Well on their way to St. Paul station, they heard distant screams. Dries Verhoeven stopped a moment, closing his eyes to savor it.

A PUB NEAR COVENT GARDEN

It took the distraught baron two pints to stop shaking.

The patrons in the pub had no idea what had just happened in Cheapside. In the morning they would read about it, knowing with certainty that the rampage—as the papers delightfully called it—wasn't going to stop.

Dries watched as Coslett, this fine specimen of British aristocracy, sucked down his beer. It was an odd alliance, the aristocratic Cosletts and Heinrich Himmler. Himmler wished for *Nachteule* to come to England. Dorothea wanted a slight change: could the targets be adolescents? She bragged to Dries how Himmler had been happy to comply, proving how high was her regard in the eyes of the Third Reich. And it was true, she had important inroads with a person Hitler wished to influence: the English King.

Coslett had begun to calm down. "You are better?" Dries asked.

The man nodded, his face grim, eyes beginning to soften with drink. "I should be getting back."

"There is no hurry. Have your drink." A little warmth was in order, for the man had performed rather well, at the end. "You must bear in mind that we have only done what is necessary."

"I know, I know. But you're wasting time. The youngsters needn't be gifted. It's enough that they're young."

"Ach, but what can I do? You have your purposes, Himmler has his own. He wishes me to continue the . . . Talent *theme*, you might say. You know this, it is not new." The baron always found reasons to whine and bleat after one of their outings. Dries continued. "You and the baroness did not mind so much when I hunted down Talents in Poland and Czechoslovakia."

"That was on your own time. And Mother recognizes that military assets like those could affect the outcome of the next conflict. They must be controlled—"

"Please. *Eliminated*. Do not be squeamish."

"But you are here now. And the time it takes to find them! Any young person would suit, and we would be done the sooner. When *will* we be finished, man?"

"Soon," Dries said. "You are maturing. Your power grows within you, this is evident to me. If you do not have faith, however, you will push it away. People will follow you—in fact, they have begun to do so. I do, you see."

Coslett snorted. "That's utter nonsense. I follow *you*, God help me."

Dries made a placating gesture. "Together. We are—what shall I say? A *team*." This was the last thing the man wanted to hear. He wanted to keep a seemly distance from a lowborn antique doll restorer. And a foreigner. One mustn't forget the British disdain of their Continental inferiors. "Yes, a team."

It was a curious thing. The more people wished to be superior in the world, the easier it was to make them suffer. The low had no hope to rise, and therefore were inured to existential anguish.

Dries lifted a finger to the waiter to bring another round. "One more," he soothed. "You can sleep on the train."

"And you?"

"I will sleep in some cheap hotel in Hackney. One place or another. It is where your countrymen expect one like me to sleep."

Coslett lifted hopeful eyes to meet his companion's. "You said I was *maturing*. Is that what you really think?"

"I have said so. It is what I hope for. We will see." Another two pints appeared in front of them. Dries softened his tone again. Coslett was accustomed to it: support and belittlement. One, then the other. Dries used it like the old serpent herself.

"You will have your normal life back soon enough. And you will be stronger, able to carry on the family legacy. And it is time for you to marry. A nice fat wife is something to look forward to."

"I think of that sometimes."

"I am sure that you do."

"Not a woman just to get children on, if that's what you mean. Someone to care for me. And me for her."

To replace your mother, Dries thought.

"I've met someone, actually. I think she fancies me. Not at my station, but I do like her. Her name is Kim."

"Well, you must be able to *support* her, Coslett. Ancient Light will keep you and Sulcliffe going. You can dress your Kim in robes and chant away your days."

"If you're going to mock me . . ."

"Do pardon. I am just envious."

"She's a reporter. Her article came out this morning. It's very good, even Mother will be pleased."

Dries had not heard of this. An unpleasant surprise. "What article?"

"On the earth spiritualism movement. It featured us. She came out for a weekend at Sulcliffe."

"You let a reporter come to Sulcliffe? A bit rash, was it not, given our enterprise?"

"All she wanted was a newspaper feature. Lovely girl." Coslett cocked his head, remembering. "She let me kiss her."

"What newspaper?"

"The *London Register*. It's damned good, too."

"And pictures? Of you, for example?"

"What of it?" Coslett raised his chin, taking that superior tone that came so naturally to him. "It not as though she's writing anything new."

"What does the dowager think of her?" Wicked to ask, but one must.

"Oh, leave off. It hasn't gone that far. And won't until Mother passes, I suppose."

It was a false step, inviting this Kim to Sulcliffe. He stood up. "You have had enough, Baron."

Coslett rose to his feet, throwing down coins to settle the bill. "I have. Enough of everything."

"Your mother and Heinrich Himmler will be disappointed to learn that. But I have work elsewhere, so I do not care."

His companion frowned. Powell would do well to remember that this was a German operation, graciously modified to suit Coslett preferences. Hands across the water, he thought the expression was.

19

FRIDAY, AUGUST 21. Martin sat on the split-log fence, watching Rose surrounded by a clucking fury of hens. From her bag she tossed a kernel of corn at Martin as he ate his sandwich.

Reaching to catch it, he almost fell off his perch.

"Nah then, ol' thing," Rose said, twirling around to avoid ambush by a large black hen.

"Who're you calling 'old thing'!" Martin said.

Rose looked up. "You, if you fall in the muck!"

"More like you, if you let those hens push you around."

She came over to him, handing the bag up. "You give it a go, then." She climbed up beside him, and they threw kernels with impunity. Rose nodded thoughtfully. "You're awfu' smart."

"I'm not, just sitting on a fence." He aimed a kernel and hit a hen solidly on the comb.

"Martin! Tha's not the proper way." She held the bag of corn to her stomach. He tucked into his liverwurst sandwich, wishing it were bigger.

Rose lowered her voice. "There's bad people round aboot." She nodded toward the house. "Like 'im that killed that girl yesterday."

Martin turned a startled look on her.

"Aye. No older than you, and at church wi' her parents just inside the doors, so they said."

He felt his gorge rise. *Not again.* It wasn't going to stop, then. Sometimes, if you didn't think about things, they went away. Not this time. Hopping down from the fence, he stuffed his unfinished sandwich into his shirt. He had to get inside and read the article before it went for kindling.

Rose went on. "A bad person, 'e is, and me mum, she says 'e's a nutter."

He handed Rose down from the fence. "He'd have to be, wouldn't he? Someone so crazy, he couldn't help himself."

"Vicar says we kin 'elp ourselves, or we're no better 'n animals. But I think animals are better anyroad. My Blaze, she don' hurt no one." The big hen ruffled her feathers as though she'd heard the praise.

"I saw her take a peck at that rooster, though." He grinned at her to get a smile, but she was out of the mood now that it came to murder.

Alice rushed up the steps at Wrenfell, clutching her copy of the *Coomsby Herald.* She knocked on the door and then let herself in without waiting. Hearing someone in the dining hall, she went in, to find Kim looking over architectural drawings for another Wrenfell remodel.

Kim looked up as Alice strode into the room. She registered the look on Alice's face. "What? What is it?"

"Have you seen the paper?"

Kim shook her head. "I've been hunkered down all morning, wrestling with drawings. . . ."

"Another murder." Alice handed her the newspaper.

Over Kim's shoulder Alice read the headline again. FOURTH VICTIM OF RITUAL KILLER.

Kim swore under her breath. "Damn it to hell."

There was a photo of a girl, round-faced and smiling, holding up a trophy. Jane Babington of Notting Hill, London. Winner of school honors for music. Murdered in the courtyard outside the church where they'd held a political meeting. She had strayed out. The discovery of a cloth with anesthetic on it.

Kim looked up, her eyes hard. Most people, when reading about these murders, expressed shock and dismay. A few were in the angry camp. That would be Kim, protector of the innocent, especially the young innocent. She would never be done with her crusade of justice, one that she was not even aware of waging. Though she put her brother's death in one compartment and her determination to do the right thing in another, the boxes leaked, Alice felt certain.

Kim pushed herself up from her chair. "This creature . . . must be stopped." She paced to the window, where a riot of hollyhocks could be seen poking up from the soil like flowered lances.

She turned her back on the garden, striding to the table to read the article a second time. The *Herald* described the work of the National Task Force, the summer camps cancelled, the groups of parents clamoring for more police protection, and the police calling for citizen vigilance.

"We'll be going to Sulcliffe, won't we?" Alice said, lowering her voice. Julian was in London, but the Babbages might be about. "We'll find something. I'll *see* something or you'll *hear* something, even if I am only a 5."

"Only? Well, I'm only a 6."

"Anyway, we'll do it together. Two is better than one. You'll see."

Kim wandered over to the mantel, adjusting the spacing of the Royal Dalton figurines, and then the four candlesticks, all in a row. That done, she turned to the architectural drawings and began aligning the sheets.

Alice pressed her hand down on Kim's, stopping her. "Maybe we should pack."

Kim shook her head. "I'm not sure the baroness will be open to a visit. She's sick. And she doesn't like young women to be around her son."

Alice had heard how the dowager was determined to keep her son to herself.

Martin barged into the dining room, stopping when he saw Alice. "Is it true? Another one?"

Alice sighed and passed the paper to him. A fifteen-year-old should not have to read about such things, but he was of an age that the news couldn't be kept from him.

He looked up from reading the article. "What's a ritual murder?"

Kim paused, then jumped in. "It's where the killing looks particular. As though the murderer wanted it to look a certain way, or be a certain way that's unusual."

"Unusual like what?"

"The papers are sensationalizing it, Martin." Kim glanced at Alice, conveying *and we'll say no more.*

He pulled the newspaper very close to his face, peering at the photo of the girl. He whispered, "God, what's happening?"

Alice pulled out a chair and pressed him into it. "What is it, Martin?"

He held the paper in shaking hands. "It's the girl, she—" He looked up at Alice. "Oh, nothing. It's nothing."

Mrs. Babbage ducked in, noting the expression on their faces. "Anythin' needed, miss?" she asked Kim.

"Tea might be welcome, thank you, Mrs. Babbage." Mrs. Babbage nodded, heading to the kitchen.

After a few moments Martin looked up at Alice. "Do they suffer? The victims?"

"No. The murderer uses chloroform so they don't cry out. They felt nothing." Or at least they didn't feel it for long. The discussion was plunging Alice into a profoundly dark mood.

As Kim spoke soothingly to Martin, Alice went to the kitchen to help Mrs. Babbage. They worked in silence, arranging a tray. Wrenfell was a comfortable home, one that Alice could imagine having one day, if not quite so grand. With or without a husband. She had not yet had her chat with James, something she was postponing until she got back from Wales, if she was going to go.

She followed as Mrs. Babbage carried the tray into the dining room. The biscuits would help. Martin was always hungry.

We will stop the creature, Alice thought as they arranged themselves for tea. The country's best *site view* teams had been at each murder scene. Just a few more pieces, and they would have him.

Then Alice saw it. In her mind's eye, the scene came to her vividly. It was happening. Her *trauma view*. And it was from Martin.

His father hauled his fist back, punching Martin in the stomach. The boy crashed to the floor. From the kitchen door Martin's mother wrung her apron into a twist. "You worthless bastard," his father spat. He picked Martin up by his arms and held him in front of him. "You worthless sod!" He struck him again, a slap that sounded like a whip cracking. His mother pulled up the apron to cover her face. As Martin lay sprawled on his back on the floor, he lifted up on his elbow. He stared his father down, daring him to strike again. After a long pause where he appeared to be considering it, he stormed from the room, pushing past his wife.

Alice closed her eyes to steady herself. What a Talent this was, to collect the dark matters of the world. And why not the joyful ones?

But now she knew the real reason that Martin didn't want to go home.

ANTWERP, BELGIUM

FRIDAY, AUGUST 21. The antique dealer turned the doll over in nimble, fat hands, inspecting the number impressed on the back of the head, under the wig. "An average doll," he said in French. "German made."

Gustaw nodded. "*Oui.* Kammer and Reinhardt. *C'est correct?*"

Wincing at Gustaw's French, the shopkeeper tried English. "It could be Kammer and Reinhardt." He shrugged. "You sell this doll?"

"No. It is the arm. Someone to replace it?" The doll was just interesting enough that it always got antique dealers talking. So much more effective than him showing up as a police officer. "You know of an expert, perhaps."

The dealer scratched his double chins. "An original arm, ball and socket . . . it is difficult. The doll's value, half what it was. Best to sell and save yourself difficulty."

Gustaw patted the doll. "Sentimental value."

"A *Mein Liebling* doll. My darling." The antique dealer gave a pitying smirk. The business of dolls should not be clouded by sentiment.

"You cannot recommend someone?" Gustaw had a list, but it was long. A gifted restorer might be the first name that came up in a chat such as this, shortening Gustaw's mission.

"*Non,*" the man said, looking up as another customer entered the shop. Well. A buyer of dolls wishes to purchase at a discount, not help with repairs, Gustaw reflected. Still, the doll and its obvious need for repair was his best ruse to obtain information on doll restorers who might specialize in antique varieties.

He left the shop, his fourth on a list of antique dealers provided by a very helpful woman in Brussels. It would take many days to track down all the names, even though his counterpart in Belgium, with the *Sûreté Militaire,* had half the list. The Dutch and Belgian authorities were all eager to crack open *Nachteule.* Unlike the British, who kept their cards hidden.

Gustaw sat on a bench in the Grote Markt and considered the long list of antique dealers. Unfortunately, the occupations of those who sold, traded, and repaired dolls and other antiques were not distinct professions. Anyone might both sell and repair. It would be a tedious investigation, but what else could they do except pursue an expert of antique dolls, one who wore thick glasses and might be Dutch. Nine murders in Poland. It must stop.

He looked up at the lavish guild houses that fronted the square, standing like self-satisfied burghers. How quickly the world had returned to commerce after the slaughter of the war. Peace had returned to Antwerp, and all was well.

Yet it was difficult to believe it would last. Even if alliances between governments proclaimed that acts of aggression against any country would be met with military aid, how firm would nations be in the face of Germany's might? Already the Third Reich prepared for war. Last year, army conscription, the expansion of the German naval fleet. Amid all this, who guaranteed Polish borders? France claimed to, and Czechoslovakia, yes, but who could believe them? The Czech army was weak, and the French did not wish to share military secrets, even with an ally. No, Poland could not depend on such friends. When five starving men sit down to divide a leg of mutton, honor goes out the window.

He would stay in Belgium for a few more days. They would stop this predator of Talents, this tool of Hitler. Gustaw sighed. He had seen how lofty missions made fools of all men, so he put it to himself this way: Someone would pay for murdering Tilda Mazur. Perhaps not soon. Perhaps not from tracking down doll restorers. But they would not give up the hunt. Even in a craven world, a small justice mattered.

With his thick pencil, he reluctantly struck the French names off the list. He would concentrate upon only the Dutch.

On his lap lay the package wrapped in brown paper and bound in twine. Tilda's *my darling*, loaned from her uncle. Since his investigations of the Dutch assassin had begun, he could have sold the doll several times. Of course, it was not for sale, but for his cover as a man with a family heirloom needing repair . . .

Yes, Gustaw, very clever you are. So far, three days in Belgium, and no one knows of an expert of dolls with thick glasses and a crooked light in his eyes.

THE EMBANKMENT, LONDON

Rain fell in relentless sheets on the Victoria Embankment. The storm had begun yesterday and lingered over the city, as though the cross on St. Paul's had speared the clouds.

Hunching under his umbrella, Julian leaned against the retaining wall, looking at the Thames in the shadow of Blackfriars Bridge. Where the blazes was Elsa? Normally punctual, she was already ten minutes late, and time was a precious commodity now that the youth murders had risen to four. Baldwin's government felt up against the wall, as the murderer struck with impunity.

The latest victim, thirteen years old, had been slain in the City. Elsa was attached to the National Task Force headed up by Scotland Yard, and had said that they did not yet know young Jane Babington's Talent, but she had likely been in an Adder club, by the tiny snake symbol inked onto her wrist, in plain view. They were still questioning the parents.

The job of the police was to catch their man, but so far they were just catching hell from the tabloids. Especially today, when the papers were making much of the church setting. The killer struck at will, spreading shock and fear throughout the country. The method of execution and display of the victim was generally the same. This murder site, however, was not Neolithic as the Frances Brooke murder had been. That association with Ancient Light, always slight, now appeared to be nothing more than coincidence. Nor was the Adder connection consistent. Of the four victims, only Jane and Rupert had been members. They were getting nowhere. He hoped that the investigation of the Babington murder would by God yield *something* they could work with.

A taxi pulled up on the street. Elsa. Since she'd come without an umbrella, he met her on the strip of grass to share his. They made their way to the pavement beside the Thames. She scowled at the river, its gray surface like pockmarked tin. "Filthy weather. Couldn't meet in a pub?"

"Will I need a drink?" Julian hoped she had something for him. Even bad news was better than this holding pattern.

"No breaks yet. We're interviewing the Babington girl's parents again this afternoon. The mother is quite off the rails." Rain spilled from the umbrella in a round sheet, giving them even more privacy than that afforded by the deserted embankment. "The task force is interviewing students and school authorities on the Adder clubs." She shrugged. "There are dozens of them, most members are boys, but the occasional club is mixed."

"Talon could be tapping a network of informants that have no connection to school clubs."

Traffic rumbled over Blackfriars like thunder. "Right," Elsa said. "Sleeper cells, identifying young people, the ones that boast."

"Is the unit pursuing that angle?"

"After a fashion." Elsa handed Julian a card. "Here's the bloke who's supposed to be in charge. Bernard Weaver. But he's not even competent. A bloody blowhard."

"You don't fancy him, then," Julian observed with as much irony as he thought she could stand.

"Right-o. I do not. He's made it clear I'm in the way, and it kills him that I'm along for the ride."

A tug churned by, towing an old dreadnought toward the Tower Bridge, now beginning to rise to let it pass. It seemed to Julian that it was an emblem of England's preparedness for hostilities. A battered hulk with twelve-inch guns left over from the Great War, unable to move under its own power.

"Elsa," Julian murmured. "We haven't turned up anything so far. Not on the Cosletts, not on the Adders, nothing. So, I want you to follow your own leads, around about."

She cut a glance at him.

"Any leads that you can follow discreetly, do it. And bear in mind, the last thing we need is the police going up to Sulcliffe and putting them on their guard."

Elsa's sneer was eloquent. "So, we're to have nothing going on in Sulcliffe."

"I wouldn't say that. Sparrow's going back in." He opened his copy of the *London Register*. "Her article appeared yesterday."

She glanced at the spread. "That was quick."

"We fast-tracked it. It's been well received, which gives us a basis for going after a follow-up article. And this time our asset will have a *trauma view* with her."

Elsa brightened. "So, Whitehall comes through, after all."

The downpour continued, relentless. August in London. Julian pulled his coat collar more tightly closed. "I'm afraid Whitehall hasn't come through. It won't do to openly pursue someone in the King's circle. Not yet. We're on our own."

She raised an eyebrow. "A bit dodgy."

Sending Sparrow in without the Foreign Office's approval was the kind of call that could cost one's job. This wasn't the first time E had gone his own way. But pursuing a friend of the King on flimsy evidence meant the whole team could be on the line.

"And we're going to send in a *trauma view* asset. To get next to the baroness or her son and see what deviltry they've been party to. No guarantee she'll pick up anything, but if she does, we'll feel a damn sight more justified on the resources we're putting into the Coslett end of things."

"One more thing," he went on. "Let's put Rabbit on watch at Wrenfell for a few days while Sparrow is at Sulcliffe. The Babbages will be spending the weekend in the manor, so Martin won't be alone, but Walter has his duties around the place and I want a close watch on Rose and Martin. Particularly the boy who's more the age of the victims."

"He'll be on his way this afternoon," Elsa said. Preparing to leave the shelter of his umbrella, she pulled up the collar on her raincoat. "What's your hunch, then? Can we pin this on the Cosletts?"

"You know how these things go. You've got a whole lot of nothing, and then the dam breaks."

Scowling, she took her leave, muttering, "Could use a little dynamite."

20

SATURDAY, AUGUST 22. "It's nobut a thorn," Walter said, examining Shadow's paw. "We'll 'ave it out, if ye keep 'old of 'im." He went off to find something to pry out the thorn while Shadow looked trustingly up from the bale of hay where he lay.

"There's my boy," Kim soothed, petting the border collie's warm coat.

Walter had found his implement, a pair of large iron pliers that looked like it could extract a hippo's tooth.

"Nah, then," Walter said, taking the paw, and without further preamble, clasped the thorn with his extractor and yanked. Shadow cringed, but honor forbade yelping. Walter wrapped the paw in a length of torn rag, winding medical tape around to secure it. He pronounced that Shadow should stay in the barn until morning, since there'd be no "runnin' aboot on a bum paw."

She patted Shadow again and helped him down from the bale. A quick look at her watch showed she'd be late if she didn't

hurry. Kim was seldom, if ever, late, but when she was, it was
likely to be for an animal.

Owen's phone call, a wrong number, had by prearranged
code terms announced a meeting at Abbey Pond at one o'clock.
Time to set out.

As Walter and she parted ways at the kitchen garden, Flint,
her father's best hunting dog, cocked his head and pricked up
his ears, unsure whether to follow Walter or her. Flint whined,
then trotted after Walter into the barley field, where Martin was
cleaning out an irrigation trap.

Kim headed past the Babbage's cottage and the paddock and
was soon traversing the south field, its grasses just lifting in the
sun after yesterday's drenching rains. Surrounding her were low,
checkered hills pillowed with barley and grasses. Wrenfell nestled
in the soft hills of the Wolds, and in August at this time of day the
heights shimmered in golden light. She was glad that Owen was
meeting her at Abbey Pond—a place that had hundreds of years
ago sported an abbey. She was drawn to the place, though some
of its memories were dark. The dogs from the animal shelter. As
a young girl she'd liberated them one night. The worst winter in
memory. The next day they discovered their bodies on the frozen
pond. Wolves. Who knew that there were wolves in England?

Her meeting with Owen must be important if he was willing
to drive the forty-five minutes from Monkton Hall. It was sure
to be her assignment for Wales. Time to wring the truth from
Sulcliffe Castle, mute as Idelle, dark as the old widow. Once,
Kim had longed to be free of her Talent, the ability that caused
friends to fall away. Once, she had felt like a voyeur, or intruder,
learning things that were best left hidden. With the Office, all
that changed. There was a point to it, a necessity. Until that
sense of mission, she had always felt that there was something

wrong with her. Not only had that belief subsided, but, remarkably, she felt like now there was something *right.*

She came to the overgrown road, little more than a deer path, and crossed it, descending the hillside to the pond, glinting between the trees.

A man was waiting for her by the fallen log. Owen.

"My editor is thrilled with my piece on earth mysteries," Kim said over the telephone. "Did you see it?" The *Register* had given it a nice splash, something that in former days she might have relished. But her intended audience this time had been only Lady Ellesmere.

The baroness's voice rang clearly, rather unsettlingly so, through the earpiece. "We might have changed a phrase here and there. But on the whole, I'm quite pleased."

"Oh, I'm *so* glad, Lady Ellesmere."

"I must say it's not often that an outsider quite grasps what we're about."

"It was essential for me to hear your views on the subject. We've had such lovely reception to the feature, including a flood of phone calls. It's as though the country was just waiting for someone to bring the concepts more forward. For the common man." She paused to give emphasis to her next words. "I'd love to do a follow-up article, Lady Ellesmere."

A long pause. "I see . . ."

"To keep momentum going."

"Momentum?"

Kim imagined the cold, deep castle breathing in the background, warning the old woman.

"To go more in depth on earth spiritualism. While people are paying attention." She added a casual laugh. "While my boss is paying attention."

"Ambitious, aren't you? That surprises me. I took you for more of a dabbler."

Kim soldiered past this. "Well, this has been one of my successes. And another article might explicitly bring home to people what their alternatives are. For those who've given up on the church."

"People like you?"

The woman would have a nose for lies if she had *hyperempathy*. "I don't know what I believe. But I'm interested."

"*Interested*. You seem to have put your profession before your spirit, I must say. However, if you're asking my permission, I don't mind if you write another piece."

"Well, I was asking that, but I'd need a more thorough interview. On the deeper aspects of Ancient Light. Nothing intrusive, just what you feel might take people to the next stage."

Silence at the other end. Kim wondered if there was someone else in the parlor where Lady Ellesmere's telephone lived. Perhaps the dowager was waiting for her sister-in-law to drift out of hearing. Idelle, a woman who had perfected the art of silence, and might be in any castle room, but unobserved. Or perhaps Powell was there, urging his mother to allow a young woman to visit.

The dowager said, "We're having a fair next weekend. You might come then, I suppose."

"Oh, that's—"

"It might suit better," Lady Ellesmere interrupted, "if you came for just a few hours. Must it be overnight? I don't mean to be inhospitable, but I am not well."

She needed more than an afternoon. "My goodness, that *would* be a long day. . . ."

At length, the baroness gave in. "Oh, very well. Come on Friday. We'll manage."

"That's excellent, thank you. It's such a long way from Uxley, though. I wonder if I might bring a companion. She's a close friend and very discreet. A woman traveling alone isn't always the best."

"I'm afraid it won't do." Kim heard a crack like the old woman's cane thumping down on the stone at her feet. "We'll have a hundred people camped on the field. And I am expected to minister to them. The strain. I'm sure you understand."

When Kim hung up, she had succeeded in her primary objective: an invitation to Sulcliffe. Alice, however, would not be going with her. There would be no *trauma view* in this phase of the operation. And no best friend with whom to share the dreadful raspberry room.

But at least she was going to Sulcliffe. The place did not want her to come, she felt sure. It preferred its stony isolation, and its cold embrace of a dying woman, the unhappy son.

As she turned toward the stairs, she found that Martin had come down.

Usually, he clambered down the stairs. Well, he had tried to be quiet for the sake of her call. Lately, Martin had been making a very good effort to mind his p's and q's.

She smiled at him, but since the diary incident he had resumed that lonely, skittering-away glance.

A MANSION FLAT IN MAYFAIR, LONDON

THAT EVENING. Lady Sarah Desborough waylaid Julian in the hall outside the drawing room. "Julian! I had given up on you."

A tall woman, Lady Desborough had an athletic figure

admirably suited for riding, a pastime she shared with her older husband, whom Julian had known for years at his club. She took his hand. "Lovely to see you. Do let's get over this being my birthday, I don't look forty, say it, and we'll have done."

From the drawing room came the drowned roar of guests. "You don't look forty, of course not."

She smirked. "Hardly effusive."

"But sincere, Sarah. You won't get much of that here." He glanced cheerfully toward the salon, as though looking forward to mixing. It was his job to see and be seen, polishing his contacts and exuding what charm he could manage, even if a German plot was intent on killing British young people. The Babington girl. In the Adder club she had joined, her Talent was reportedly *attraction.* Imbuing one with approval, charisma. He'd always wondered whether he had ever met someone with that Talent, and how it differed from plain appeal. It might explain how some scoundrels were rather enjoyable.

Lady Desborough took his arm and steered him into the Georgian drawing room, with its ornamental plaster and somewhat out-of-place Italian vases brought back from the grand tour. Her well-appointed guests stood in clusters, women in stylish silk, men in dinner jackets. Servers wound among them with trays of champagne.

"You know everyone, I think, except for Lady Graham, perhaps? Well, she's having a political discussion on the divan, so you won't want to get in the crossfire." She brightened as she saw someone crossing the room. "Guy," she called, bringing Julian along to meet a fair-haired, slightly built chap with a receding hairline. "Julian, I don't believe you've met Guy Ascher. Guy, this is Julian Tavistock." They shook hands. "Guy is my cousin, and he managed to bring a date this time, didn't you, sweet?"

After Lady Desborough had spun away to shepherd her guests, Julian got through a conversation about the Desborough passion for riding, and whether Julian would go down in October for the grouse at the Desborough estate. Pleasantries concluded, Julian sought a drink, which he hoped would not have to be champagne but was. He headed for the political discussion at the divan but caught a glimpse of a woman standing in front of the open verandah doors.

Olivia. She stood alone, looking out on the garden.

He made his way to her. She wore a light pink dress with something shimmery in it. It was intriguing to see her so transformed: gone, the workday updo, her hair now pulled back from her face and elegantly collected at the nape of her neck.

"Good evening, Olivia."

She turned, and for a second her expression wobbled, and he could not quite discern if she was happy to see him.

"Julian!" she said. "Oh, do you know Lady Desborough, then? How nice to see you."

He glanced at the room full of people. "I've known her and her husband for years." She looked exquisite, so much so that he reminded himself not to stare.

There were a few moments of silence. "May I get you a drink?"

"Oh, please."

She was still there when he returned with her champagne. Accepting it, she leaned in toward him. "You should know, E is here." She glanced at the fireplace where a group of men stood.

He had already noted E's presence. Julian occasionally found himself in company with E—Richard Galbraith to everyone except those in the Office. When they met, they conducted themselves as two men who'd known each other at Eton, and were on distant but friendly terms.

"I'm sorry we haven't been in touch," Olivia said. "It's my fault."

"You've been avoiding me, I think," he said mildly. If he was never going to see her alone, he would press her now.

"Oh, I . . . I think perhaps we've been—"

"Don't say 'avoiding each other.' It isn't true. I've missed you."

"Have you?" Her voice was shaky. She looked around, as though hoping for an excuse to include someone, anyone, on a more agreeable topic. He hated this dance of avoidance, with them unable to say what was really going on. And what was going on? For him, nothing more than that he loved her, and was miserable because of it.

He lowered his voice. "Olivia, please look at me." When she finally did, he said, "I love you. Where have you gone?"

She closed her eyes as though to reset her thoughts. Taking her by the arm, he led her out onto the terrace. It was surrounded by a small garden that faced on Berkeley Square, where couples could be seen strolling the pavement in the lingering warmth of the evening.

Olivia turned to him, her face losing its studied control. "God, Julian, what are we to do?"

"Talk to E."

She shook her head. "I already have."

"Then E be damned." They'd had this conversation before, and Julian was offering nothing new, except this bluff to dare E to sack one of them.

Glancing in Galbraith's direction in the drawing room, she murmured, "You might ask him for a word in the garden." Her voice was wistful. If she had sounded bitter or angry, he would have known what to say, he would have drummed up a response. But her tone of kindness, hopelessness, threw him off guard.

She looked up, turning as someone approached them. It was the fellow Lady Desborough had introduced him to.

Olivia smiled at the man and asked Julian, "Do you know Guy Ascher?"

"We just met." He nodded to Guy, who held two glasses of champagne.

Guy put one glass down on the balustrade. "Thanks for doing the honors," he said to Julian. He sipped his drink, eyeing the two of them. "Splendid out here, isn't it?"

Not by any measure. Guy was Olivia's date, perhaps the friend of the family that he had suspected was his rival. "I thought I'd smoke," Julian said, "but since Olivia likes gardens . . ." He shrugged.

"Do you?" Guy asked her.

"Other people's." She turned to look out on the grounds, dark except in the spill of light from the drawing room.

"Olivia's father served in the navy with mine," Guy said. "How do you know Olivia?"

Olivia's face grew tight as Julian rushed in with the answer. "Since we both know Lady Desborough, we've met several times."

A chime from inside. "The gong for dinner, I'm afraid," Guy said, and held out his arm for Olivia. The three of them followed the other guests to the table. As he passed E, Julian greeted him, and E shook his hand. Further pleasantries were easily avoided by the press of diners and Julian's cooled enthusiasm for the gathering.

It was the longest dinner he could remember enduring. He sat between an earl's sister and the niece of Lady Desborough, one being too old and one too young for him, if he were seeking a wife.

He managed not to look very often at Olivia and Guy. And

with despicable cowardice, sneaked out early, with apologies to his hostess.

ALBEMARLE STREET

It was very late when the knock came at his door. A discreet knock, but loud enough to wake him if he'd retired.

He hadn't been sleeping. It was Olivia.

Wordlessly, he drew her into the flat. "Have you come with bad news?" He took her wrap. "If so, let me have it all at once."

"No. I've come for a drink."

He smiled in relief. If she was going to leave him—and they had only been seeing each other three months—at least it wouldn't be tonight. He poured two whiskies and sat next to her on the sofa.

"You are stunning," he said. "I left early so I wouldn't stare."

"And men always look good in dinner jackets. You bastards." She smiled, and attacked her drink.

"Olivia, I . . ."

She put a hand up to his mouth. "Let's not talk. I just wanted to be with you for a moment's peace." She put her hand in his, and they sat side by side, looking at the drawn blinds of his window onto Albemarle Street, the parlor shadows helping to suppress the words that kept rising to his lips. *How are you really? What have you been doing? How can you be with this Ascher fellow?*

After a time, he brought the decanter and poured. And still they were quiet.

He stroked her hair at her temple. "Are you hungry? I have bread and butter."

"No. If you had offered cake or sandwiches . . ."

He laughed softly. "Not much of a cook, I'm afraid."

"Me either."

She stood up, extending her hand. He took it, rising from the divan. She was right; there was no need to talk. Well, there might be need, but sometimes silence was best.

As she led him to the bedroom, she pulled the pins from her hair.

21

SUNDAY, AUGUST 23. From the corner of the abandoned stone hut, they watched the boy heading in their direction, toward the pigpens. Low clouds spilled off the moors to the north, cloaking the farmhouse and outbuildings with a mossy-green fog.

A harsh whisper. "Is this the one?"

"*Ja,*" Dries hissed.

A pail in each hand, the boy plodded his way from the farmhouse, hidden around the curve of the wooded path. The pigsty, out of sight from the main buildings, was a perfect setting, giving them the privacy for a bit of mayhem. It had taken several days for Dries to find the right spot, the right young person. Then, a phone call to the baron assigning the meeting place on a road outside of Stourbridge. All that was left was to apply the scalpel.

"He's big," Coslett whispered.

This was more evident now that he saw the boy again. "We are two against the one," Dries soothed.

The lad drew nearer, walking along the path, careful not to spill the contents of his pails. He was thickset, with a shambling gait, his face a serene blank, his high forehead harboring no thought except to feed the pigs.

Dries wondered what the boy's Talent was. He had, of course, a curiosity. For one of the slayings, he had been sure: the woman from Cracow. She had given him an elegant demonstration that day at the railway station, with those stygian shadows flowing from her. She must have been a 7 at least. Perhaps an 8.

The boy lifted one pail and tipped it into the trough. The pigs grunted and thrust their noses through the rails. Setting the first pail down, he emptied the second pail, held away from his body so the slop would not splash upon him.

"Now?" Coslett mouthed, grabbing Dries by the arm.

The hogs growled and squealed. The boy lingered a moment to see them jostle at the trough.

Dries nodded. It was time.

They came out into view, with Coslett having an arm around his companion, who limped. "I say, could you help?" Coslett said. "My friend's been hurt."

The boy looked at them in consternation a moment, no doubt trying to figure out why two men would suddenly come from behind the hut. But they were well dressed, and the boy took this in, pausing just long enough to allow them within range.

Dries separated himself from Coslett, bending down and groaning. As he did so, the memory came at the edges of consciousness, little flickers of heat and flame.

Coslett spoke up again. "If you could just help me get him to your house, perhaps your parents could get help? I think his foot is broken."

Dutifully, the boy stepped forward to help, as Coslett fumbled in his pocket for the rag. Wrong pocket, the idiot! Then the other pocket, an odd action the farm boy noted. He stopped in his tracks.

Dries groaned louder, looking up with as pitiable an expression as he could muster.

The boy took another step forward, but toward Dries, not Coslett.

Coslett was now behind the boy. "Thank you, young gentleman," Dries said.

Lurching forward, Coslett tried to push the stinking rag into the victim's face.

Then they both set upon the boy. He struggled, pushing the cloth away and, using the pail as a weapon, smashed it against his assailants. Coslett slipped in the mud, dropping the cloth. Dries threw himself against the boy, toppling him. Cold mud on his knees, the stench of pig shit. Sensory perceptions surrounding him in a wooly miasma. He struggled with the boy, trying to pin down his flailing arms but clumsily missing his connections.

"The rag, you fool, the rag!" he shouted at Coslett, who now crawled forward, trying to get it into the boy's face. The boy jammed his fists into his assailants as the three of them grappled in the mud. Dries flailed as Coslett wallowed like a drunk. *Godverdomme*, he thought. *This one has the* mesmerizing.

In a supreme effort, Dries raised his scalpel and stabbed, thrusting it into the boy's back. A bellow. He rolled away with the scalpel still in his back, trying to rise but failing to get traction in the mud. Coslett finally got the rag over his face, holding it secure. As the boy jerked on the ground, Coslett practically stuffed the muddied rag down his throat.

Their victim fell quiet, and Dries extracted the knife from his flesh, trying to get in position to finish the job.

Coslett looked up the path. "Someone coming!"

Through a haze of flames that snapped at the edges of his eyes, Dries saw a man hurrying down the path from the farmhouse, shouting at them. He stopped and raised a shotgun. Fired.

A searing impact sent Dries staggering. The man on the path bellowed and let fly another blast, this one just clearing their heads. Coslett pulled Dries away, dragging him back from the pig sty toward the dark trees.

"I can walk!" His companion finally let go of him.

Dries craned his neck for a glimpse in back of them. The farmer knelt by the boy, jerking his head up to see where the attackers were. He and Coslett staggered into the cover of the forest. They wove through the trees, trying to recover their wits. Dries's chest was cold and wet with blood.

He leaned on Coslett as they rushed through the bracken-choked ground. After a hundred meters or so, the fog of confusion lifted; *mesmerizing* could not reach so far. At last they reached the car, where Coslett helped him into the back seat.

Dries lay there, bleeding. Amid his pain, his thoughts came clearly. *If I die, let it not be at the hands of the British. Kill me in France or Austria. But, you blasted God, not in England.*

THE STONE GALLERY, ST. PAUL'S, LONDON

MONDAY, AUGUST 24. "Talon is wounded," Julian said straight out.

E took a long, deep breath. He kept his gaze on the view, those intermittent slices of London seen from 175 feet up through the stone balustrades. Against the massive, darkened sky, the gold spires of St. Paul's caught the afternoon sun like a flame in a storm.

"It happened during an attempted execution at a farm near Stourbridge in the West Midlands," Julian said. "The victim was George Merkin, a fifteen-year-old. The boy's father came upon the scene and hit one of the assailants at mid-range with a shotgun. It was a man in glasses. Sounds like our Dutchman."

"*One* of the assailants?"

"Looks like Talon has an accomplice. The father heard the boy yell and rushed down with a shotgun. He saw them struggling, and risked a shot. The men fled."

"Good man with a gun," E said with satisfaction. "Any description of the second man?"

"No. The father was too far away, and once one of them was hit, they ran into the woods. The youngster hasn't regained consciousness."

"Any trail?"

"Not so far. Our assassin was bloodied but strong enough to get through a half mile of woods back to a car. We may not be done with him yet."

"But by God, a strike back." Gazing out at the view, E looked more and more these last few minutes like a commander surveying a battle scene, one that was going in his favor.

They fell silent as tourists poured out of a doorway onto the gallery, having made the long climb from the floor of St. Paul's and the whisper gallery. When the group wandered off, following the curve around the dome, E said, "Something else, then?"

"The National Task Force is still withholding the information that the victims are Talents. Isn't it time to let the papers loose with that piece? It would give the parents of adolescents with Talents—those that are aware of their children having an ability—a chance to be on the alert."

E shook his head. "I've spoken to the JIC about this already, and they're adamant that we forestall any fearmongering around the Talent question. We must encourage people to register as Talents. National security is at stake. We might not match German conventional arms, but we have a fighting chance with Talents. This *Nachteule* thing could knock us out of the game."

Julian knew better than to argue when the Joint Intelligence Committee had weighed in.

"One more thing, then: I think it's time to pass intel more freely to our Continental counterparts. We should coordinate. Talon may be wounded, but he may live to kill again. Or he'll be replaced by another, just as deadly."

E shook his head. "We don't want foreign agents tracking *Nachteule* on our soil. They'll be in the way, the Security Service will howl."

"Then make an exception for the Poles. For Gustaw Bajek. We share intel with him, and he lets us know what the Czechs, French, and Dutch have. He passes on to them only what we approve, and meanwhile, we stay abreast of *Nachteule*."

E looked at Julian directly for the first time. "It puts at risk his ties with his counterparts. Why would he agree to such a lopsided arrangement?"

"Because of Tilda Mazur."

"The woman we almost snatched from the Polish army?" Julian nodded. "I should think that is a reason he *wouldn't* cooperate."

Julian saw that E was starting to close down, to fall into a mood of leave-well-enough-alone. "Bajek wants Mazur's assassin. He hated that it was his own countrymen who leaked names of Polish talents. And Tilda Mazur . . ." He struggled to find words that would convince an old army man that emotions swayed decisions. "Mazur put a face on the exterminations. She ran for her life and was put down in a field like a deer. He wants the killer."

"So, he activates his people here—"

"No. He works with me, period." If Julian was wrong about Gustaw, it could compromise Crossbow. But without a break in the case, more youngsters would likely face a brutal death. They couldn't wait for Talon to expose himself; they had to take some risks to finally track him down.

E pulled his jacket collar up against a smattering of rain carried in on a freshening breeze. "All right. Bring your Pole in on it. Time to shake things up and see what falls out." He shared a glance with Julian. "It ends now. Five murders are enough."

He didn't correct his boss that only four had died. George Merkin wasn't dead yet.

Julian descended the narrow stone stairs to the cathedral's main floor and crossed the south transept, noting that Elsa had just arrived at the south door and was preceding him down to the floor below. The crypt.

After paying his respects to Lord Nelson's sarcophagus, Julian wandered over to the William Blake plaque. Elsa knew her poetry, but all Julian had of William Blake was *Tyger, tyger burning bright, in the forests of the night.* And something about *fearful symmetry.* What was fearful about symmetry, he wondered, and why must poetics be so obscure one always felt like one had rather missed the point?

"Young man," Elsa said, looking worried, "might you know where they've buried Wellington? I'm afraid I've lost him."

"He's over there," Julian said, pointing. "I say, you can have my guide if you like." He passed it to her along with his letter to Gustaw Bajek, prepared ahead of time in the hope of E's approval.

"Oh, thank you very much indeed. If you're sure you don't

need it." She turned to the Blake plaque. "Didn't he write about flowers in the crannied wall? Or was that Kipling?"

Julian squinted at the inscription. As he did so, Elsa murmured, "Courier to our Polish friend?"

"Yes, quick as can be done."

He turned to leave, saying over his shoulder. "A great soldier, Wellington. You won't want to miss him."

"Oh, gracious no. But we need the poets as well." Delightfully, she wandered off in the wrong direction, holding her guide upside down.

22

TUESDAY, AUGUST 25. Ed Gardiner clutched his beer and regarded Lloyd with a fishy stare. "Bum luck, getting sacked."

"Don't worry, I got prospects." Lloyd hoisted his glass in a toast to something, didn't matter what. He took a long pull. "Got a big piece coming out in the *East End Express*." His own earth mysteries article. "Mind you, if you hear anything, I'm willin' to consider other offers." Gardiner was still on with the *Register*, lucky sod.

"Right-o."

Gardiner didn't give a rat's ass about Lloyd, of course. Just the same, he didn't seem to like the way Lloyd got fired. In favor of a Yank, a *woman*, who nosed in on a story, and not even on the *London Register*.

"Ever see this Tavistock girl at the office?" Lloyd asked, picking at the sore.

Gardiner shook his head. "She's going to do another in the series, too."

"Series? What series?"

"On spiritualism."

Lloyd felt sick.

"Same as you were doin'," Gardiner added, as though it needed saying. Lloyd thought maybe Gardiner was enjoying this.

"Purloined it, she did," Lloyd muttered. "Purloined."

It was odd how you could hate someone you hardly knew. Kim Tavistock, lately of Uxley, Yorkshire. But the injustice was almost too much to bear. Where was he going to find another position, with three million able-bodied men out of work? Come to that, how was he going to pay his rent? And he knew that Maxwell had given her his idea for earth mysteries, and his contact with Lord Ellesmere, as well. He'd be happy if the twit had a run-in with a bus.

"I know a shop that needs some help cleaning up. Evenings," Gardiner said, avoiding his gaze. "Until your prospects pan out."

Lloyd struggled with himself whether to answer. Truth was, he needed a job, any job. Gritting his teeth, he said, "I might pass a name on. Lots of people in my predicament."

Gardiner wrote down a name and telephone number on a scrap of paper, pushing it across the table.

Lloyd slid it into his pocket. "You ever heard Maxwell mention someone named Galbraith?" That was the name, underlined twice, written on Maxwell's tablet along with *Tavistock* and *Coslett.*

"Why?"

"Just, did you? I'm runnin' down some leads on a story to sell."

"Well, you know about the medal, right? Max used to know this toff, a Galbraith, in the war. Colonel Galbraith, the one in the picture."

"Picture?"

"Right. Max was his batman, and got a citation out of it. Has that picture on his wall, from when he got his medal pinned on. Don't tell me you never heard about the sodding medal?"

"Can't say as I did. Colonel, was it?"

"A regular toff, and Maxwell dug his latrine holes for him."

"Where's he now?"

Gardiner shrugged. "Don't know. I could ask Max."

"No, this is a private matter." The urge to follow a lead reared its head. Galbraith. R. Galbraith. The one time in his life where Maxwell Slater's path had evidently crossed that of gentry. He might have been on the telephone with Galbraith that day he scrawled his doodles. And it might be that this Colonel Galbraith asked for a favor for the twit.

Well, now. Seeing as how he had nothing else to do, Lloyd might just track down the fellow. Get to the bottom of things, wrap up the story, like.

He twirled a finger at the barman for two more. Gardiner was all right, a waster on the job, but in a pinch, he knew how to come through. One more pint, and he'd take a little jaunt, drop in on some mates with a hand in policing. A bloke in the business always had a few colleagues at the Yard, people who knew people or could find out.

He had plenty of time on his hands. And he was curious as hell.

WRENFELL, EAST YORKSHIRE

In the loo, Martin scrubbed at the snake on his wrist until his skin grew bright red. He had inked the line into his skin so many times, it wouldn't come out, but it was fading. He hated to admit it, but his da had been right. The Adder clubs were a stupid idea. And now an awful one.

The clubs wanted secrecy so that adults wouldn't interfere, and the rest of the kids wouldn't badger you. But now one of the Adders was squealing, he'd bet. One of them was revealing names. How exactly could they do that, though? There was no list of Adders, not that he ever heard of. The clubs were all separate. He always thought they just caught on, as word got around. But maybe other clubs were part of a list, and his club all the way off in Coomsby was just ignored. Or worse: somehow his club was on a list and the killer could come after him next, or Christopher or Teddy, and he would feel responsible.

Leaving the toilet, Martin crossed the hall to his room. He took the newspaper articles out from under the mattress. There, in the newspaper photo of Jane Babington holding up her music trophy: the Adder on her wrist. Add that to Rupert Bristow, the one murdered by the river in Cambridgeshire, with the little wavy line on his neck. Martin had to squint, but he was sure the line had three crosshatches across the tail. The sign of the Adders.

And someone was killing them. He didn't know about the other two kids; maybe they had Adder marks that didn't show up in photographs.

Maybe the murderer had come into one of the clubs, pretending to have a Talent, acting like one of the group, but secretly hating them all for what they were. Maybe, like a lot of people— like Reverend Hathaway—the murderer thought Adder abilities were wrong. Something that must be wiped out.

He looked at his pile of newspaper articles. From the beginning, with Rupert Bristow, he'd been hoping that the mark on his neck wasn't an Adder mark, or if it was, that it was only a fluke that he'd been murdered and had a Talent.

But now two Adders. He had a sinking feeling, a hunch that had been gathering strength since Rose told him about that girl's murder at a church, that these were Talent murders. And that the police knew and were keeping it secret. Because, like Miss Kim said, the police didn't tell all the details, so as to keep the killer off-guard.

He put the newspaper articles back under his mattress. Would he be adding to them?

Since the police weren't stopping the murders, it was time for people to fight back, like that fellow in Stourbridge did. They tried to kill him by the pig trough at his farm, and his da, he came out with a shotgun, and fired at whoever it was. Regular people ought to help out. Maybe people like him.

It was hard to stop thinking about how he might be able to use his *site view* Talent to find clues. That would be fair, to use a Talent to catch a Talent-killer. Maybe people would finally believe him, if he could prove he had *site view*, and if he could do something important with it.

He couldn't use his ability at the pigsty, because he didn't know where it was. But that church in London should be easy to find.

St. Mary-le-Bow.

23

WEDNESDAY AUGUST 26. The tractor lay half-buried in the cornfield. In a hired motorcar, Gustaw Bajek drove past a group of men using a team of horses to extract the machine from a deep hole.

Driving through the storied battlefields of Passchendaele, Gustaw saw that the war remained imprinted on the land. Cemeteries corralled white gravestones like ghostly dominoes, row on row, many noting only, A SOLDIER OF THE GREAT WAR, KNOWN UNTO GOD.

There were many such. For the fallen who were recovered weeks or months or years after death, the bones had become separated, the clothes torn or just gone. When authorities could find nothing else, they buried a skull or a foot. And though the war had been over for nineteen years, the Belgians were still burying the dead when farmers plowed up remains. It was good of them to maintain the graveyards, as they did with meticulous care, clipping the grass and straightening the headstones, which tended to sink into the earth as though the land wished to be done with remembrance.

Today a great sinkhole had opened up in a cornfield, swallowing a tractor, but it was not unusual. The combatants had dug miles of tunnels, which were now slowly collapsing. During the war, both sides had laid massive amounts of explosives in tunnels next to enemy enclosures, exploding them with devastating effect. In these trenches and tunnels the war had been fought, an unimaginable war. A bad war, all the way around. Pointless, some said, including Gustaw. Now the next one was coming. Perhaps it had started already, with Tilda.

Well. These were dark thoughts for a warm summer day. He drove on, into the small hamlet of Beselare.

This was the sixth doll maker on his list. His directions were to a house of a restorer who, like many, worked out of his home. Gustaw left his car on the rutted driveway before a tidy home with a deep-sloping roof pierced by a gabled entryway. He knocked, but finding no one answering, he went round to the back, where a dilapidated stoop looked out on a field with a moss-covered gun emplacement, long abandoned.

He peered in a back window. An orderly kitchen. Next, a small bedroom. Sunshine lapped at a white counterpane where a girl appeared to be resting. No, a doll, but so lifelike it gave Gustaw a start. The house hardly looked lived-in.

Back in the village, he stopped at a pub for a luncheon of smoked sausage and a pint of bitter. He placed his package secured with twine on the bar. He had practiced how to say *a very good doll with an arm missing* in French and Dutch. The owner looked at the package, and mentioned the name on Gustaw's list, Monsieur Verhoeven, who lived nearby, but he did not know where the man was at present.

"He is not in here, then," Gustaw said amiably, looking around the dark pub, well occupied with a crowd for lunch.

"*Non,*" the innkeeper said.

"Spectacles?" Gustaw said, as he always did, for he had little else to describe his Dutchman. "Does he perhaps wear glasses?"

The innkeeper shrugged. "*Aveugle sans eux.*"

Gustaw's French was not up to this remark. "*Pardonnez-moi, je ne comprends pas.*"

The innkeeper turned back to the work of rinsing glasses in the sink behind the bar. In carefully enunciated English, he said, "The man eez blind without them." He twisted around to look at Gustaw, perhaps wondering if the man even spoke English. He made a gesture, rounding his hands and bringing them up to his eyes like binoculars.

Gustaw's attention was now riveted. "Do you know how I can reach him? Please, it is for a very special doll. My daughter's."

"*Non.*" The innkeeper shrugged expressively. "Many people repair the toys. Not only Monsieur Verhoeven."

Gustaw kept his face neutral, but his excitement propelled him from his half-finished sausages. "*Merci, monsieur. Merci.*"

As he made his way to the door, a middle-aged woman followed him out, tucking her hair into a scarf that fluttered in the wind. "You were asking for Dries Verhoeven. You know that he lives just up the road?"

"Yes, I have stopped by, but he is not at home. Do you know where I can find him?"

"I do not, but Auberte may know. She knows most things."

"Thank you so much. Who is Auberte?"

"Auberte Cloutier." She pointed down the street.

† † †

Across from the village post office was the ground-floor apartment of Auberte Cloutier. But today, it seemed, was a day for no
one to be home. Madame Cloutier did not answer his knock.

Gustaw was not discouraged. He was close to the man with
the crooked light in his eyes, he was sure of it.

And if he was, then Julian Tavistock would be most interested
to hear. It had taken five days for the message to reach him, having
gone first to Polish authorities, who finally found him in Antwerp.

The British intelligence service had decided to share what
they knew. With conditions. Ah, well, it was a start. And very
interesting: *Nachteule* had come to England, but in a changed
form. What it could mean, he did not know, except that, now that
the British were in the game—with the best intelligence services in the world—Gustaw had new hope to find the assassin.

He drove back to the steep-roofed house.

At the rear door he withdrew from his pocket a small piece
of hardware and jiggled it in the lock until he heard the tumblers
fall into place. Pushing open the door, he entered Verhoeven's
house. Inside, it was not so clean as it had looked from the window.
Everything was in order, almost rigidly so, but the stove shone
with a film of grease, and broom sweep marks suggested a resi-
dent who was tidy but not thorough.

A narrow hall led away, and Gustaw followed it to the front
of the house. The parlor had been converted into a workroom,
with two long trestle tables with benches, and a line of shelves
around the walls at shoulder height.

On every surface, a doll, or part of one. Arms, feet, torsos,
legs. And clothes: tiny shoes arranged by size. To the left of the
fireplace mantel, a shelf for heads, some with the eyes open, and
some closed, as though some would sleep but others could not. It
was a workshop that must be typical of those who repaired dolls.

Here were spare parts for missing hands, legs, and heads and, as well, the dolls who came to find what was missing, such as the porcelain doll nearest him on the trestle table, a rosy-cheeked girl. The right hand gone at the wrist. Next to it, a small hand just emerging from a block of wood. One of the fingers was beginning to show evidence of a fingernail.

A man who would work at carving and repairing in his parlor was one who had no other life. Possibly no friends to invite in, no interests outside of work.

Well. He had been interested in Tilda Mazur. Perhaps Dries Verhoeven had a sideline. Murder.

He went to the large front window and drew the curtains aside. Past his car parked on the verge, a hundred yards away was the roadway to town. A hay truck rumbled by.

In the small dining room across the hall, a place mat showed where Dries Verhoeven took his meals. Lace curtains, once white, but with holes repaired, filtered the sunlight from the sun just summiting the steep roof.

Upstairs, three more rooms, tiny, sparse, and stale. In one room, the chest of drawers contained folded sweaters for a cooler season. The closet contained a neat rank of coats and jackets. On the floor, shoes and boots, arranged by type: loafers, lace-ups, boots. For the big doll, Gustaw could not help thinking.

He made his way downstairs to the room where a doll lay against the pillows like a pampered lady. The specimen was clearly fine, clothed in a smoky-blue silk gown, with high-heeled black shoes. Most striking were the large and lustrous blue eyes. Open, but with eyelids that might close. The steeply arched eyebrows and perfect rosy mouth gave the doll a grown-up aspect, even with the childish body.

In the closet and chest, Verhoeven's simple wardrobe, folded and hung. On the bureau, a framed photograph of a woman holding an armful of books. She stood on the steps of what might have been a library. The picture was of poor quality, the face barely visible. Wife? Mother?

Back in the dining room, where Gustaw had seen metal filing boxes, he flipped through files containing orders, receipts and invoices. Dutch, French and German addresses. He would like to comb this house more thoroughly, but he would need something convincing that tied Verhoeven to the murders.

He returned to the parlor. Standing in the dim and cold of the fading afternoon, he gazed at the scattered limbs and heads. The macabre thought intruded that the doll heads—the ones with open eyes—were ready to speak. They knew the doll maker who lived and worked here, his darkness and his shattered life.

Come, Gustaw. It is no crime to be in possession of broken dolls, and to fix them.

But he wished the dolls could tell what they knew.

THE BLOOM BOOK

This group of meta-abilities produces changes to objects and environments that are not acted upon by any measurable force. Military applications, as well as use in crime and terrorism, make this group a vital field of study. Particular notice must be paid to the role of those individuals with the ability to link with others for a common, more profound effect (choristers, described under the Hyperpersonal group.) The Psychokinesis category requires further definition based upon case studies.

<u>Cold cell</u>. Practitioners cause a rapid decrease in outside temperatures over a territory. The effect is often accompanied by precipitation and other locally anomalous weather disturbances. Manifestations are variously initiated. Depending on the practitioner, they may be spontaneous (often initiated by emotional experiences) or may be under conscious control.

<u>Damaging</u>. To cause disruption, breakage or wounding at a distance. Few case studies. Controlled by the intention of the practitioner.

<u>Darkening</u>. To cause the blockage of light. A heavy shadow, though not absolute darkness, may be exerted over a wide area, often several acres. Neither the practitioner nor those around the individual are able to defend against it. Controlled by the intention of the practitioner. Few case studies.

Sounding. To produce high-decibel noise that may sound variously as a crack, explosion, distant boom, or shelling. Witnesses report reactions of fear, but it has not been established whether this is a natural reaction or induced as a separate effect. Few case studies.

Transport. To exert upon an object a force that can move the object. The range in size and weight of objects susceptible to be acted upon are proportional to the strength of the Talent rating. Individuals studied have not demonstrated control over direction and speed. Existing studies have been limited to practitioners of ratings 3 or lower. This circumstance has suggested to some that transport Talents at higher levels may not exist, although it is an unconfirmed theory. Controlled by the intention of the practitioner.

PART III

BLOODLINES

24

FRIDAY, AUGUST 28. "I say, you've got the wrong timetable there, you know."

In the first-class compartment, a rotund, amiable man sitting next to Kim and wearing ill-fitting tweeds offered her the timetable to Chester.

Kim smiled at him. "Oh, yes, I know. But I do prefer this one." He blinked in confusion and, murmuring an apology, tucked the timetable into a breast pocket.

The timetable in her hands was her usual, for the London and North Eastern Railway, which did very nicely for most trips, if not this one. It always soothed her nerves to see the connections one could make right out of Uxley, and she had committed a great deal of the LNER timetable to memory. Helpfully, it included a map of England on the back, complete with designations of other railway lines. One could hardly get lost in England if one knew the railway system, and as a kind of newcomer—born in England, yet a stranger—she had long depended on the railway system maps to make sense of things.

The train clacked and swayed, heading southwest to Chester. She had just had time, when changing trains in York, to pick up the *Yorkshire Post*, with its blazoned headline, FOILED IN STOURBRIDGE.

Frank Merkin, the attack victim's father, was suddenly a national hero, and communities throughout Great Britain had begun prayer vigils for young George, who had awakened but was still weak. According to Owen, the boy's memory of the assault had not returned as of Thursday night. She thought how satisfying it would be if Frank Merkin had managed to kill Talon. He had been wounded, or his accomplice had, and so he was possibly dead or dying. Devoutly to be hoped. But they couldn't count on that.

She gripped the LNER timetable, glad that Martin, who was of an age to be a target, was well under guard at Wrenfell. From her window seat, she gazed at the undulating pastureland. Not far out of Leeds it began changing to uplands, with graceful dry stone walls weaving up scars and fells, separating the farms.

She missed Alice's company, with her strength and surety. Alice's opinions were not often shaken by ambiguities. It was the right disposition for an agent, unlike Kim, who was always thinking, and crawling around to the other side of issues to see the truth of things. Her adversaries were masters of deception, causing one to doubt first impressions and, often, to distrust outright proof. One never knew if a realization had been planted as misdirection.

She wondered how Alice's confrontation with James would go, when she finally told him the truth about who she was. In any case, Alice, having been disinvited by Dorothea Coslett, would now try to gain anonymous entrance to the Ancient Light fair. To do so, she had gone ahead to stay at Pengeylan, the village near Sulcliffe. She was settled into lodgings at the Llewellyn House, where she had been able to make contact with people gathering for the fair. Kim's last update from the dead drop in Uxley had provided the hotel name and phone number.

This might well be her last chance to gather the intelligence that would allow the authorities to descend on Sulcliffe. But it would have to be a convincing link to the murders: knowledge they might have of the murdered young people, details of the method of the murders that they could not otherwise know, or a motive for the killings of young people. Once SIS felt they could justify an investigation, they would hunt down the Coslett connection, whether they were friends of the King's or not.

As an American, she found it difficult to accept the British deference toward peers of the realm. It wasn't just a heightened sense of courtesy toward the upper classes. It was more deeply ingrained than that, and more infectious to the workings of justice: the establishment simply could not imagine that one of their own would be involved in treason. They did not wish to think it, and for the most part, they never did.

As mistress of the *spill,* all Kim could do was wait for the Cosletts to incriminate themselves. Had she been a higher-rated *spill,* such as an 8 or 9, she likely would have had her quarry by now. But even as a 6, Kim was the intelligence service's best in that arena. Nor did the police have anyone with a better rating. Alice was a 5 for *trauma view.* If Britain had been testing people as long as Germany, by now they would have had time to find their 9s and 10s, those higher, rarer ratings. And Kim would be relegated to smaller operations. She had to admit she did not wish for it, not at all, now that she was in the most exclusive club in England, the SIS.

That she had been recruited into the intelligence service still thrilled her. It was an outcome, a livelihood, that even six months earlier she could not have imagined. Fascination with the work had soon gripped her imagination, stripping away a faltering interest in journalism and replacing it with a fierce sense of purpose and challenge.

The rhythmic beat of wheels on tracks lulled her, bringing to mind her first opponent in espionage, Erich von Ritter. She vividly remembered that rain-soaked afternoon at the abbey. Blood seeped from his wound as they huddled together, waiting to die. The soldiers, heading into the trap. The suitcase, with its wires and explosives. The gunshot from across the ruins.

She didn't think that von Ritter would have approved the murder of children. Yes, he had been Nazi SD. He had been in the advance guard for a planned invasion of England. But when she thought of her former adversary, she often reflected that there had been honor in him, no matter how misguided. He had freed her, at the end. And he had taken his own life, granting a reprieve to the soldiers who pursued him onto the moors. No, he would not have been party to a twisted version of *Nachteule*.

The train slowed to a stop, waiting for the signal to change at a roadway crossing. Then a whistle blew and they shuddered forward, the wheels squealing and gripping. Her camera box rattled in the luggage rack, sharing space with her revolver, a piece of equipment she would have a hard time explaining at Sulcliffe if it were found. Owen said she was to go armed this time. She hoped pictures would be more the requirement. But she would do what needed to be done.

So much easier if the dowager did not manage to discern that, this time, her guest came armed.

She changed trains at Chester. Powell would meet her at the station at 11:16. Powell, an unhappy man, who visited spiritual sites to be "receptive" to a gift that the heir of Sulcliffe Castle must surely be destined to receive. She knew, however, that a meta-ability would never come to him. He was, according to his dossier, thirty-five years old, which would have made him an adolescent during the mass outbreak of the *bloom*. If he were to have a Talent, it would have come to him then.

And yet, a spiritual gift could still be a motive if Powell believed in some kind of communion with Sacred Earth. Did he think, pagan-wise, that the gods wanted blood? When he had mentioned being open to his gift, perhaps he hadn't meant through meditation. It was hard to imagine gentle Powell going down such a dark path.

But if he wasn't directly a part of the operation, his mother well could be. She with her framed portrait of the Führer and the bleeding of her fortune into the Nazi cause.

An hour and a half later the attendant brought coffee and newspapers, this time the *Manchester Guardian* with its three-inch headline: VICTIM #5 SURVIVES. She sipped from the china cup and thought again about the Adder clubs. It might be a dead end, since only two of the victims, Rupert Bristow, who died near the River Ouse, and Jane Babington in London, were confirmed members. Then there were the possible sleeper cells, spies who might have taken note—and passed on to their handlers—the names of those in various towns and hamlets who claimed to have gifts.

The train clattered on as they sped toward Wales. Out the window she caught views of the Irish Sea. In barely glimpsed fiords along the coast, the August sun shone brilliantly, warming the land, the village roofs, and the sea. It did not seem a day when she would be entering a vale of killers.

The train slowed for Pengeylan, where Powell was waiting, unless he had sent Awbrey after all. She would certainly try to coax more from the old man if he were her driver.

As the train pulled into the tiny station, she saw people crowded on the platform, wearing holiday attire: broad hats and sturdy walking shoes and carrying rucksacks and picnic baskets. Fair-goers, she guessed. Alice might be among them. She peered out the window.

She saw Powell on the platform, standing in front of the ticket office, watching for her. The sun glinted harshly off the waiting-room window behind him. The sudden burst of sun made him seem to *burn brightly*, as he had termed it.

She stood to retrieve her suitcase from the rack. And hesitated.

The train had stopped. Doors slammed along the length of the train as people began to debark. She pulled her suitcase from the rack and rested it for a moment on the bench seat. She chased an odd, sudden thought.

Might *that* have been a *spill?* That some people burned brighter . . . Could Powell have meant that the gifted actually shone with a visible light?

Was it possible that someone in Ancient Light was able to discern such things?

Seeing him on the platform just now with the sun glinting in the window sparked this idea, perhaps an absurd one. And yet, might it be a Talent to see such things, a Talent not recorded in the *Bloom Book?* But perhaps one known to the German military. It could explain how the youngsters with Talents were identified.

She gathered up her camera case, along with her suitcase and handbag and walked in a daze down the corridor.

It was a crazy idea. And yet: *to burn brightly*. Was this something that Powell desperately wished to hide, so that he was susceptible to *spilling* it? Talents were generally related to human emotions. Fear and guilt and strong desire to hide things were the emotions that the *spill* thrived upon. So, when Powell said that some people burned more brightly than others, he might not have been referring to luck and privileges. He might have meant something completely different.

She found herself on the station platform, facing Powell Coslett. The sun was no longer reflecting off the window. Powell was an ordinary, dark human being.

But she wondered: *Do* I *burn brightly?*

ST. MARY-LE-BOW CHURCH, LONDON

LATER THAT DAY. Martin had twice been to London with his father, but never alone. He had even been to St. Paul's, but standing in its shadow now, he hardly cared to look at it. It was the other church he had come to see, the one where Jane Babington had died.

He turned away from the crowds in St. Paul's churchyard, walking down Cheapside with what assurance he could muster. He thought people looked sideways at him, but why should they notice him or figure out that he had come to London and would be in trouble about it? At Wrenfell, though, they were probably already wondering where he was. Miss Kim had gone to Wales to write another article on that earth-worshipper group, so she wouldn't find out until she got back. But when she did, she'd kick him out for sure.

He saw the spires of a building that had to be a church. It wasn't at all regular how this church was crowded in with other buildings, but there it was, with its tower and little courtyard. Turning into the courtyard, he glanced around but didn't have to guess where the murder had happened. Flowers lay heaped near the deeply shaded, moss-covered wall of the church.

He knew that he wasn't the only one with visions who had been at the scene. The police would have had their best *site view* people there, he figured. But he had to see for himself, to know what had happened to Jane Babington. If he had one of his visions, he might be able to see an Adder mark on the murderer, or hear them talk about the Adders. Well, he had come here on the chance of it. And if he was honest, also with the hope of proving that he had *site view*. Had it so strong sometimes it scared him.

The day was hot, and he was thankful for the shade. Over there, on the other side of the open space, was a man having a cup of tea or something from a cart. He didn't watch Martin, but he was the only other person in the courtyard.

Martin bent down to place the flower he had brought from Miss Kim's garden on the paving stones.

The day fell into gloom. Not just the shade of the buildings surrounding the courtyard, but the fog of *site view*. His chest cinched up in preparation. He was going into *the sight*, as he thought of it. Falling, falling into it.

There was a young girl, startlingly pretty. Her skin was pale, her clothes the color of oyster and storm clouds. The visions were always like this, soft grays and murky white, as though the effort of pulling the past into view could not manage the bright, vibrant things.

Her face was at first serene, then curious, then alert. His view of her and the little patch of courtyard was dim, but charged suddenly with loathing, and at the edges, something fiercer: fire.

Two men walked toward her. The courtyard jumped with flame, surging, receding. But what was burning? The two men did not feel the flames; they brought the fire with them, spasmodic thrusts of horror and pain.

One of them said, in a strangled *site view* voice, *Can you help me?*

Just as her expression turned to alarm, a rag came up in one man's hand and swiftly covered her face. Her arms flailed out wildly. The fire spurted and seethed, rushing to consume her long brown hair. She wobbled and sank, resting back into the arms of the man with the cloth, as though grateful for his support. Another man slid in close to use the knife. A scream died in Martin's throat. *No! No!* But already, a black liquid streamed from her neck, down the front of her dress.

Martin tried to rush forward to help her, to staunch the flow, but he could not move.

The two men lifted her up and pushed her into a sitting position against the church wall. Then they walked away, leaving Jane Babington sitting there, the black stream still pumping with the rhythm of her heart. She lay still, her eyes softly closed. One man, with thick glasses. The other . . . was one he recognized. He had seen him before, the man with the handkerchief, the man in whose arms the girl had reclined.

"You're Martin Lister, aren't you?"

Martin turned. Someone had come up to him, a man in a green-and-brown plaid cap. The day was back in its proper order. Martin's voice cracked as he tried to answer. *What business of yours?* was what he should say, but he was confused by coming back from *then* into *now*. The paving stones were strewn with flowers where her bleeding body had been.

"Martin, isn't it?"

"Yeesss," Martin whispered.

"Everything all right? I've come from Wrenfell. Miss Tavistock asked me to come for you."

Martin staggered back. Miss Kim knew he was here? How could she?

"Who are you?" He had begun to shake.

"My name's Louis. I can take you home now, if you're ready."

"No," Martin said, staggering back. The man had been watching him. He turned to run, but the man had him fast by the shoulders.

Martin yelled. "Help, somebody help!"

"Settle down, lad. No need to . . ."

Martin thrashed away from him as someone came running to his side, a young bloke with an angry face, breaking up the man's grip on his shoulder. "Here now, let go of him!"

"I don't know him, he's trying to kill me!" Martin yelled, backing up as several people moved in, faces dark, starting to clamor against the man in the plaid cap.

As more men came forward to restrain his attacker, Martin pushed through the crowd and tore around the corner of the church onto Cheapside. He heard shouting from behind, in the courtyard, as he ran down the street. He ducked into an alley, a narrow canyon with well-dressed people walking, some with briefcases, who stared at him as he pushed forward in a frantic dash. Panic fueled his strides as he skidded around another corner into an even tighter street, with pavements an arm's length wide. He ran until he saw some market stalls. Slowing, he turned in. He walked, pretending to look at merchandise, as his heartbeat slowed. Out of the heat, the perspiration on his face went cold like a mask. He looked at watches and bars of soap and little statues of St. Paul's.

He didn't hear shouting anymore. Deep into the market, he watched the entrance with its blinding wall of sunshine. The man in the plaid cap hadn't followed him, but who had that been? The man had been watching him. And had almost kidnapped him, or killed him.

Thoughts banged around in his head, fueled by the memory of what he'd seen, the murder . . . and a face, a face he recognized. The man with the cloth who covered the girl's face, it was the same person he'd seen in a photo. The man from the castle.

Miss Kim had shown him her newspaper article, and the man with the big smile, standing in front of the stones and the sea. It was the same man. In his vision the smile was gone. He had held Jane Babington while a man with glasses cut her open with a knife.

The startling realization came to him that Miss Kim had just that morning set out for her assignment. And wasn't she going back to that same castle? She didn't know; she thought it was a place that could give her another newspaper article.

But it was more than that. It was the home of the killer.

SULCLIFFE CASTLE, WALES

At the tea table in the raspberry room, Kim sat before the box of cartridges and the snub-nosed Colt revolver. She could hardly remember the drive across the headland to the castle, so hard had she been concentrating on acting naturally. Powell drove, charming as always, but with a reserve she hadn't seen in him before, except when he was recognized on the railway platform and surrounded for a few moments by Ancient Lighters arriving for the fair.

She removed six cartridges from the ammunition box and lined them up in a row.

She had no proof for her theory, but if someone had an ability to see other Talents, perhaps like some kind of aura, it would explain so much. How the young people were identified, and the Continental victims as well.

This might be the man with glasses—the Dutchman, the perpetrator they had been calling Talon. Or perhaps two people with this *seeing* Talent, since there were purportedly two at the scene of the Merkin attack. Or the second one might be an ordinary person, one who believed the gods wanted blood.

Picking up the revolver, she knocked out the Colt's cylinder and pushed the rounds in, rotating the cylinder until it was fully loaded.

The thing about guns was that she had never shot anyone. In her training at the Estate, she had mastered the various types of guns, and had made progress at target practice. But shooting someone would be a different matter. She regarded the heavy gun in her hand. She hoped that she would never need to kill someone; in the back of her mind she always thought that she would wound them instead. Even though at the gun range her trainer had often said, *Never draw your gun unless prepared to kill.*

An agent couldn't afford such doubts, yet she had them; and hadn't shared them with anyone, not even Alice.

She clicked the cylinder into place and tucked the gun in her shoulder bag.

Checking her watch, she noted the time, 11:56. Powell would

come back to the castle from his field duties at 1:30 to walk her to the fair.

She stared at the sandwich waiting for her on a tray, her mind moving too fast to consider food. Might Talon have a terrible ability to identify a Talent's visual signature? Well. It was more likely that she had conjured up a theory that conveniently explained how the murder victims were selected.

And yet, might this be a meta-ability that the Germans had discovered and were using to their advantage?

A Talent that could discern Talents. If it existed, people like her, like Rose, and Martin, might be as obvious to such a Talent as a person wearing a strong color or holding a sign: *I have a Talent.*

Kill me.

25

FRIDAY, AUGUST 28. At 54 Broadway, Julian led Owen through the office of Veteran Benefits and up the back way to a third-floor landing with false office fronts. The security guard unlocked the door to the office of Empire Press, and they entered the suite of the Secret Intelligence Service.

"Now I *do* feel like a spy," Owen muttered.

Julian made a silent laugh. "And you didn't at Monkton Hall? The Historical Archives and Research Centre, indeed. Your lot wouldn't know history if it reared up and bit you."

"Point taken. But in case of need, if I come up those back stairs, the guard lets me in?"

"'Fraid not. Let Miss Hennessey know you're coming. She'll arrange it." As they approached her, Olivia was conferring with a colleague by the window. She nodded at Julian and returned to her conversation.

"The secretary gives me clearance?"

Julian stopped for a moment among the cluster of cubicles. "Hennessey is E's assistant. She wields more power than the deputy director and has orders to shoot anyone on the third floor she doesn't recognize." He led Owen onward. "Or who calls her a secretary."

"Quite." Owen was learning the politics of the Office, nearly as important as tradecraft. Since nothing could be more political than the academic environment at Cambridge, the man would no doubt quickly grasp the workings of a new one.

In the conference room, Elsa and Fin were setting up the displays. As Owen took a seat at the table, Fin crossed over to Julian. He was dressed for the street, looking more like a dock-worker than an agent.

"Martin Lister's run away."

Julian frowned.

"Left Wrenfell this morning an hour or so after Kim. He's in London, but Rory lost him."

"What the devil is he doing in London?"

"That's what we don't know. Rory decided to tail him when he went into the village. He wasn't expected to get on a train, but when he did, Rory followed him."

"And where is he?"

"He *was* at St. Mary-le-Bow." A pause while Julian absorbed this piece. "Rory approached him. Tried to get him to come home, but it turned into a bit of a row, and Rory lost him in Cheapside."

E entered the room, nodding to Julian and Fin, and took a seat at the table. Julian murmured, "He went to the place to try his hand at *site view*."

"Too bloody right."

"So the boy still thinks he can see the past. And the murdered girl was an Adder, the same as Martin."

The group was waiting for them at the table. "We've got the police helping to find him," Fin said. "We're watching Kings Cross station to see if he tries to get up to Cambridgeshire."

"The River Ouse murder," Julian said. "Rupert Bristow, also an Adder. All right, keep me informed." He frowned at Fin. "Good God, couldn't Rory bring home a fifteen-year-old?"

"He couldn't contact us for instruction, so he decided to keep him in view."

Julian moved to take a seat. Martin was a young idiot, still trying to claim a Talent for himself.

As he passed E, seated at the head of the table, E looked up. "Tell me Crossbow's got something, Julian."

"A dozen fragments, but nothing that connects. We've sent in a *trauma view* asset to try and penetrate the Ancient Light fair."

"*Trauma view.*" E's tone told what he thought of the Talent idea: undependable; slightly unsavory.

"Well, she helped crack the *Sturmweg* operation this spring," Julian said. He got a scowl. E did not seem in the best of moods.

Julian introduced them all to Owen, and waved for the briefing to begin.

On the chalkboard was a list of the crime victims and their locations:

Ewan Knox—Portsmouth, Hampshire, *object reading*;
Rupert Bristow—Ely, (River Ouse) Cambridgeshire, *disguise*;
Frances Brooke—Avebury, stone circle, Wiltshire, *precognition*;
Jane Babington—London, St. Mary-le-Bow, *attraction*;
George Merkin—Stourbridge, Worcestershire, *mesmerizing*.

Elsa began to tape up photos of the victims, but E shook his head. "We'll do without portraits." This wasn't Scotland Yard, and his sense of propriety didn't tolerate pictures of children with their throats cut.

Elsa began. "The *Nachteule* killer, or one of them, was identified in Cracow as a man in his early thirties with heavy glasses, having what might be a Dutch accent—although it might have been mistaken for German—and likely an expert in antique dolls. Although the slayer's method and the victim profiles have been different in Britain, the targeting of Talents connects the two operations. At the Merkin farm, when one of the attackers was wounded, the father identified a thirtyish man wearing glasses. The youngster, George Merkin, is still in hospital and struggling to regain his memory of the attack. There was an accomplice. White male, beyond that the father wasn't able to provide a description."

"If the farmer was a better shot, we'd be done by now," Fin muttered.

Elsa ignored this. "The boy might have used his *mesmerizing* Talent to fight off his assailants. It might not be a strong Talent, according to his parents, but it could have given him the edge. He's a big boy."

Moving on, Elsa pointed to the map of Great Britain, with large Xs on the crime sites. "As you can see, we don't have a meaningful geographic grouping of the murders. The victims were variously taken in an alley, by a river, a stone circle, a farm, and a church in London. They ranged in age from thirteen to fifteen, all with Talents, or purportedly so."

E turned to Owen Cherwell. "You're sure none of the victims was registered as a Talent?"

"Not a one. We don't normally test youths, but sometimes their parents register them. The few we know of now have had police protection since the third murder."

"Discreet protection, I presume." E had his marching orders from the intelligence committee; there would be no public announcement of Talents as targets.

Julian weighed in. "Local police are keeping an eye out. The families have been asked not to discuss it with anyone."

"How robust is the National Task Force in the whole pursuit?" E asked.

"Since Jane Babington," Elsa said, "they've seconded officers from six regional crime squads to work on it, and they're coordinating with local forces. The task force doesn't know about *Nachteule*, so they aren't pursuing the ties to Dorothea Coslett." She looked at E. "The Security Service is sniffing about."

"I'll have a chat with them," E said. "They had their chance." With the first two murders, the Security Service had deferred to Scotland Yard since they didn't know the counterespionage connection. It was a crime spree, as far as they knew. By the time SIS came in on it through Gustaw Bajek, it seemed best to run the operation from the intelligence side. The Security Service was weak, still building its organization after cutbacks following the war. It was hard to take them seriously.

E looked around the table. "So, how does the killer identify those with Talents?"

Elsa ventured, "Sleeper cells is one theory. People in towns and villages, activated to see who's known to have meta-abilities, or who's bragging about them. Someone in the Adder clubs may also be blabbing. With all these sources, the Germans could have put together a list."

She wrote *Adder clubs* on the board and circled it. "These are secret Talent clubs in some of the secondary schools. With their cult of secrecy, members of the clubs don't like to expose each other, but so far we believe that only Jane Babington and

Rupert Bristow were Adders. They often self-identify by drawing a snake symbol on themselves, on the wrist or neck, so other Adders can recognize them." She drew a wavy line with a swelling at one end and three crosshatches across the tail.

Julian nodded at Fin. "Better tell them the piece about Martin Lister."

All eyes turned to Fin, as he related the morning's events, including Martin's background and charade of having a Talent. E gave Julian a skeptical look as though Kim were in trouble again. Her reputation should still be golden after the Prestwich Affair, but even Julian had to admit that this wrinkle was pure Kim Tavistock: take in a stray; make a mess of it.

E affected a look of long-suffering patience and waved Elsa to continue.

"We're interviewing about a hundred kids involved with the Adders, but nothing of interest so far." She paused with a cynical smile. "Maybe we should interview Martin."

Got to find him first, Julian thought. "Adders aside, I'd like to know why our Dutchman isn't going after bigger fish. Why would the Germans care about a fifteen-year-old girl with a Talent of *attraction*?"

"Maybe to make people afraid to register by striking at a vulnerable population," Elsa said. "Or terrorize the British people into keeping their noses out of Hitler's territorial ambitions."

Fin snorted a laugh. "When it gets out that the Germans are behind this, we'll have a hundred thousand blokes lining up to join the army."

"You say our Continental partners aren't sharing the *Nachteule* threat with us," E began.

Julian interjected: "Except for my contact in Poland."

"Yes, well then, what do you hear from him?"

"We've got a courier packet out to him," Elsa said. "Nothing there yet." She nodded at Fin to pick up the thread.

"We're looking at Ancient Light finances and the Coslett fortune. The organization has cash assets of three quarters of a million. The Sulcliffe estate is in arrears on taxes and has no income to speak of. Dorothea Coslett has given most of her fortune away."

"To the Germans?" E asked.

"*Nachteule*, for one, but we're still tracking her Aryan charities."

Julian added, "All of which puts Powell Coslett in a world of hurt."

"Right enough," Fin said. "He's popular with the Ancient Light crowd, though, and a shoo-in to lead it when the old woman pops off."

Elsa said, "It's hard to see what he'd get out of murdering students."

E turned to Julian. "You're big on the Coslett connection. When did you say our people are going back in?"

"They're in place now."

Fin went on. "We're also digging for any information on a piece of intel that Sparrow picked up from Idelle Coslett, the dowager's sister-in-law. Flory Soames. The name was delivered in a manner that led her to the conclusion that it was important. We haven't got a handle on the name yet."

"His Majesty's Government has three hundred agents and police officers working this," E grumbled, "and after four weeks, we've got damn little to show for it."

"There's one more thing," Julian said. He handed Owen a roll of plastic and nodded for him to go to the display board. "Ley lines."

He'd gotten the ley line idea from Lloyd Nichols' article on the

Earth Mysteries movement that had been published by the *East End Express* on Wednesday. The piece was a lurid account of supernatural claims for stone rings, long barrow sites and the like in the British Isles, but the ley line idea had caught Julian's attention.

Owen smoothed the plastic over the map of Great Britain and taped it into place. It showed an elaborate crosshatch design of straight lines. "This is a reproduction from a recent newspaper article, showing a possible network of 'archaic tracks' that may have been used by ancient British cultures to travel to places they considered powerful. Powerful in a spiritual sense."

"Good God," E muttered.

Owen hesitated at this remark, and Julian nodded for him to go on.

"The concept of ley lines cropped up in the early twenties as an archaeological term for major Neolithic routes. It seems that a mystical interpretation has attached itself, entirely discredited. Various spiritualist groups have latched on to it. They ascribe spiritual meaning to certain landscape alignments, imaginary lines connecting natural and prehistoric structures. Taking this belief into consideration, the murders may have been planned to occur on these alignments."

He took a marker out of his breast pocket and drew a triangle in southwest England. "If you're looking for important alignments, you can find them. For example, we have a notable geometric shape between Stonehenge, Grovely Castle, and Old Sarum, the site where the first Salisbury cathedral was built. The three lines form an equilateral triangle. Now, that's just an example of one striking geometric shape. It's doubtful that Neolithic cultures put stock in straight lines between widely separated landscape features, but the ley line idea has been co-opted by fringe groups."

"Are we going somewhere with this?" E asked with elaborate politeness.

Owen pointed to the map, drawing the pointer counter-clockwise. "Avebury, Portsmouth, London, Cambridgeshire, and Stourbridge in the West Midlands. We can also make two triangles with London sharing a point of each. That makes it London, Cambridgeshire, Stourbridge, and London, Portsmouth, Avebury. Or we can create a starburst pattern, setting the center point here." He pointed to Oxfordshire.

"There's a bit of a problem, though," Owen said.

"A *bit* of one?" E said.

Owen pushed on. "The statistical probability of finding patterns of lines between geographical sites is no different than connecting the dots between, say, all the phone boxes in England. In other words, everything can be connected to everything, and can even provide rather interesting designs."

"Then why bring it up?" E asked.

"I asked Owen to look into it," Julian said. "If our Dutchman has a design in mind, it might be discovered by connecting our murder sites. If someone in Ancient Light has a plan for alignment, and the alignments connect our murder sites, it means that the movement can be implicated in the killings. And the *motive* is spiritual power."

"So, the pattern of connecting lines might mean something to our dowager or her son," Fin said.

"Or someone else," Elsa chimed in.

"Or someone else," Julian admitted. "But it brings back to the table the idea that the killer may attach mystical significance to the murder sites."

"But why would the victims be Talents?" E asked. "Wouldn't any human sacrifice do?"

Julian shrugged. "Talents might seem more important. Or it could be related to German goals with the *Nachteule* killings."

E shook his head, pushing back his chair. "I'm afraid you've got nothing. This goes nowhere, do you understand? It gets out, we're a laughingstock." He looked with distaste at the shapes drawn on the map. "We are *not* pursuing triangles and human sacrifice. We need answers. The PM wants this wrapped up before the school terms start."

He turned to Julian. "I'll give the Sulcliffe inquiry three more days to produce evidence. Without it, we can't pursue the Cosletts, given that the King likes to drop in now and then on the dowager's pagan events." He shook his head, glancing at Owen's map. "We need something more than wild conjecture and *spiritual geometry*."

He rose from the table. "One more look at Ancient Light. Then we move on."

"Meet me at the bridge?" Olivia had found a moment alone with Julian in the hallway outside the conference room. "I'm taking a late lunch."

Fifteen minutes later, Julian stood on the Blue Bridge looking over the lake in St. James's Park toward one of the most beautiful views in London: Buckingham Palace, the Horse Guards and the stacked spires and roofs of London.

He watched for Olivia on the footpath. A week before, they'd been in each other's arms for a few hours' reprieve from their difficulties. He hoped it had signaled an accommodation to each other's lives, because sometimes there weren't solutions. One had to make do. And wasn't it a good thing that they had found each other at their stage in life?

He looked down the path toward Broadway, watching for

her. Where in London, he wondered, would Martin Lister be right now? He had seemed happy at Wrenfell, after stumbling at first. Walter Babbage liked him, and certainly the women-folk were keen on him, even Rose, with whom Martin had an easy way, as of equals, since he was a greenhorn at most prac-tical matters, and Rose had lived on the estate all her life. He thought of E's looming deadline. Three days to implicate the Cosletts or decamp. If it were a less prominent family, they would have by now hauled Lord Ellesmere in and interrogated him and, for the sake of the murdered students, perhaps applied a bit of pressure.

Olivia approached at last, wearing her gray-and-black plaid suit that hugged her small waist. She had that smart and focused look of a woman who got things done. His equal. It was an enor-mously attractive thought.

Smiling at him, she stepped to the railing and looked out on the view. The obligatory pelicans of St. James's, four of them, hove into view from under the bridge.

"I'm sorry to hear about Martin Lister. I'm sure he'll turn up."

"The young idiot." He turned to look at her. "Let's go to lunch if you like."

"Oh, I'll grab something at the canteen." The basement watering hole at Broadway.

A shadow passed across Julian's mind. They stared at the pelicans swimming in a row as though forming up at the Horse Guards, and the silence turned leaden. He looked down to where Olivia's hands rested on the bridge rail. A diamond ring on her left hand.

He swallowed, beating back his dismay. It was Guy Ascher. He tried to think of a gracious response when what was going to be said was said.

The pelicans sailed on, but the day had lost its color. What was there to say? How did one respond to a woman who had chosen someone else? "It's Guy Ascher, then."

She closed her eyes for a moment, then opened them, looking serenely at the view. "Yes."

Surely he had steps at his disposal, something he could do. At the least, he would not disgrace himself with some bitter remark. But the more sanguine you were about it, the less you would seem to care, and only a craven man would want a woman to think she had never been wanted.

"We're to be married," she said.

The waiting was over; the triangle was over. The war was settled and he hadn't even been in battle.

She gave a little laugh. "Seems silly, at my age, doesn't it."

"No, not silly at all." There were little lines around her eyes, that was true, and her face could not be mistaken for a schoolgirl's. But he thought her beautiful.

"Do you want to be married, Olivia?" It was a miserable remark, suggesting that marriage had never been a subject between them. True, they had never said "marriage," that word.

"Yes, I suppose I do." She went on with dreadful equanimity. "I think it's more that I want to plan for the future and do it *with* someone." She looked at him for the first time. He looked for tears or doubt. Found none.

He hated it. Hated Guy Ascher. Hated his own life, his pigheaded insistence that things were good enough as they were. They were no longer young, less so every day. He almost proposed to her at that moment, to put his hat in the ring, but of course he was not going to do that. It would be unseemly now that she was engaged and all the barriers between them remained. Guy Ascher would be her husband, and it wouldn't matter that she still worked, for of course she would have made that a condition of the marriage.

"Julian," she said. "Don't be cast down. I've decided for both of us, because we couldn't decide together, could we? And it doesn't mean that I didn't love you, because I did." She turned back to look at the skyline of the city. "I do, even now, I will admit it. But it doesn't matter. People live all the time with things like that. In time I'll get over it, and so will you."

Well then, all settled. He would *get over it*, thank God. He felt anger rising. He would so much rather have had a row than this bloody awful, dispassionate execution.

"You must try to be happy, Olivia" was the best he could say. But good Christ, who could stand to live with the likes of Guy Ascher?

She smiled ironically. "I *will* be happy. It's a decision you make."

"Is it?"

Her expression, he noted with satisfaction, faltered a bit. "Yes. I hope so." She made that little laugh again. "My father said he'd like me to be married before he dies."

"Well then, good for your old man." He winced at himself. "That was unforgiveable, Olivia. Please pardon me."

"Oh, Julian." She bit her lip. "I'm just glad one of us has the honesty to be angry." She took his hand and pressed hers into it, the one without the ring. Then she walked away, dragging his gaze with her.

26

FRIDAY, AUGUST 28. A large orange cat pressed up against Gustaw's pants leg, meowing with great strength.

"You must pardon Flaubert," Auberte Cloutier said, "he thinks you have a little something for him." She was offering lemonade, but at her advanced age of what Gustaw guessed was over ninety, it was a process of many minutes to bring glasses and the jug from the icebox.

"I am sorry, Flaubert," Gustaw said. "I am a man without presents."

Auberte Cloutier was thin, a birdlike woman, and short as well. She smiled coquettishly. "Ah. He likes a man who is not afraid of talking to cats."

While the old woman fussed at the sink, Gustaw looked around the tiny flat. Framed pictures of days gone by, crocheted doilies, and leaning against the back door, an axe. Pressing against the kitchen window, a fully laden lemon tree, the fruit like molten sunlight. On the pillows, floor, and overstuffed chairs he counted four cats, three of them warmly curled upon themselves.

"How did you know that I was looking for Monsieur Verhoeven?" He had already offered to help her bring glasses, but she had pretended not to hear him.

"Everyone knows," she said in heavily accented English. She set down two mismatched little glasses, then turned away for the pitcher. It would be another five minutes. "At the market, they said, 'An important man is here for Dries and must speak to you, Auberte.'"

She made her way to the table with a pitcher and poured out his portion, golden-green with fresh lemons, but when he sipped, almost no sugar. He managed to smile. "Thank you. Delicious."

"People say a lemon tree, it is impossible here. Pfft. It survived the Great War."

As she poured for herself, he drew out the brown-wrapped package and untied the string. "My daughter has this favorite . . ."

Auberte began to sit at the table, and he waited while she completed the maneuver. She sipped at her drink, her mouth the locus of a hundred tiny lines running in all directions. "It is sour, but it is good for the digestion, *n'est-ce pas?*"

"*Oui*, madame." He took another sip for the digestion.

She pressed a hand upon the doll, which now lay unwrapped on the table, as though comforting it for its lost arm. Her eyes, watery and sharp, looked suddenly to be a stormy gray. "Dries has been on holiday this past month, so he does no work."

That put the conversation on an awkward path. What reason could he now conjure for pursuing a repairman on holiday?

But he asked anyway. "Do you know where on holiday?"

"*Non*, I am sorry. You are disappointed?"

"No, madame. But the doll . . ."

She waved a hand in which the bones lay in ridges under a thin draping of skin. "The doll, missing the arm, yes. But you wish to know about Dries in any case. This is what I think. Having come all the way from . . . Poland, is it?" Gustaw shrugged, admitting it.

Flaubert was now sitting at attention and staring at him, as was Auberte.

"Does Monsieur Verhoeven have an interesting story? Since we have our lemonade, and I am not in a hurry." He sat back, beginning to think that she saw straight through him. Some people have an instinct for the police. You are born with it, or have suffered beatings enough to spot them.

"Interesting? No, it is not interesting. Why would it be? You have driven through our country, and seen the stories all around you. Thousands of stories: how this one died, and that one, and a thousand more, ten thousand more. Some stories, they are very bad. Do you know how many ways there are to die?"

"Who can count?"

She snorted, but allowed, "A good answer." She nodded her head in a little rocking motion that Gustaw recognized for her thinking mode. Judging him and how much to tell him or whether to pack him off with just the lemonade. But she went on.

"I know Dries Verhoeven. From long ago. A good boy, and a smart one, you see. His mother taught at the school. You drove past it when you came into town, but you would not know that. The stones in the grass are all that is left." She clucked a tongue against the roof of her mouth. The lemons had gotten to her after all.

"We liked him, dear little Dries. But then his mother died and he was never the same."

"He was attached to her."

Her eyes narrowed. She did not like to be interrupted. "No. Not more than most children. It was that she was murdered, that is why.

"It was during the war. The battle of Glencorse Wood. They thought the school housed armaments. How foolish, for it was just a school, and contained only children and their teachers, and that day it included Dries and his mother. But they had their opinions and they had their spies who said the school was just a pretense and so came the bombs.

"We saw the front of the school—two stories tall it was, and made of lovely banded brick—we saw it collapse like toys falling, and such dust there was! But now a fire. Dries's mother and a few of the other teachers, they took hold of a child or two and ran out into the field."

Gustaw considered this revelation: The school on fire. It was the source of the assassin's vision of fire, reported by the police *site view* Talents. It was all he could do to keep from leaping up from his chair. Dries Verhoeven was, he must be, the murderer of *Nachteule*.

Auberte held her glass in a claw-like grip. "But when the soldiers came, they saw there were no secret guns or stores in the building, that they had killed the schoolchildren instead. And so they had, twenty-six children. Two soldiers came around into the field, and here, Dries's mother was kneeling next to a child dying of terrible burns. She screamed at them, how it was a school, and they were murderers and she would have justice. Dries Verhoeven was thirteen years old. He stood there, and later he told me how it was, and I knew he could not bear it, but what could I do? What could anyone do?"

She took a sip of lemon water, and it steadied her. "His mother became, what is the word, for crying too much?"

"Hysterical."

"Yes. And when they heard her German accent, they became angry and shot her. The gun against her forehead. For she was German, you see, and Dries's father, Dutch, from Beselare."

Gustaw frowned. "But why were the German soldiers angry that she was German?"

Auberte leaned down—it was not far to go—and petted Flaubert. "Because they were British soldiers, *mon ami.*"

Ah, *British* soldiers. The fire, so terrible, and then the great calamity, that having almost survived, they shot her in the field. So this was why Dries Verhoeven was slaying children in Britain, as Julian Tavistock had reported in the packet.

Auberte went on. "We tried to help him, of course. But there was more to come. He began to act strangely, and to say things to people that they didn't like. I told him to hush and not to talk about such things, that some things are best left alone. But he was young and angry, and he liked having power to say things."

"Things?"

She cut a glance at him, weighing him again. "He saw the secret powers, the powers to place a hand on a ring, and know to whom it belonged or to sense hungers of the heart. He had only to look at such a one, and he knew."

Flaubert abandoned the conversation and found a good place on the sofa to settle in.

"You call it the *blooming.* That is one opinion, and it is not mine. The powers did not come all at once, like a lemon tree blooms. Some of us have always held powers. And died for it, too."

Like many of her generation, she had specific notions about the *bloom,* whether it was so or not, and how it had come about.

She went on. "So, some people spoke against him, causing problems for Dries. He became unpopular."

Gustaw murmured, "Because he could see these powers."

A slow rocking of the old woman's head, like a doll's head on a hinge. "His eyes, you understand. Wild eyes, a thing you could notice when he took off his spectacles."

Of course the Germans had recruited him. And now they had a weapon of great import. "A crooked light," Gustaw murmured.

Auberte shrugged. "You could say. I would say broken. Ruined by the war, you see, like so much. A broken light."

It was a great relief to know that Polish intelligence did not have a mole. Tilda had not been betrayed by one of their own. She had been discovered, by accident even, at the doll seller's stall in Cracow.

"So," Gustaw said. "Dries Verhoeven has a great power. He knows each Talent by looking at a person."

"*Non, monsieur.* He only knows how strong it is, but not *which* one. He told me that I shine with the great light, but I did not need our Dries to tell me that. You wish to know the name given for what he could do? Seeing the powers? Some call it *aura sight,* because Dries said it was a glow that surrounded one."

Gustaw thought that this birdlike lady did not need people to tell her much of anything. The woman outside the pub said that Auberte knew most things.

She fixed him with a critical look. "You do not have a daughter."

Gustaw began rewrapping the *Mein Liebling* doll. "No, you are right."

"The owner of the toy, she is dead and buried."

"Yes. Her name was Tilda Mazur."

Auberte's nodding became shallow and she closed her eyes. She was falling asleep. Gustaw stood up, dazed by the yellow afternoon sun sliding in the window, the sleeping cats, the axe with wood chips fallen around it, the old woman who knew too much. Who had the Talent of *object reading*, which had not come into her at the *bloom*, but which she might have had for nearly a hundred years. They said that Talents might have visited people through the ages. But for the masses, it was the war that broke through the barriers. The barriers. Whatever they were. Denial, superstition, religion, propriety. So many ways to deny the truth.

Standing, he put his hat under his arm and when Auberte started awake, he softly thanked her for her hospitality. Unspoken between them was what Gustaw Bajek would do with Dries Verhoeven, and what awful thing he had done—for why else would a policeman come so far to find him?

As he stood at the door, Gustaw turned. "Have you forgiven the British, madame?"

Auberte gave a small, alert smile. "Never."

27

SULCLIFFE CASTLE, WALES

FRIDAY, AUGUST 28. With her sun hat, camera case, and shoulder purse containing the loaded Colt, Kim had just come down the turret stairs into the gallery to meet Powell.

Dorothea Coslett stood in the archway to the salon, conferring with a few servants. Kim recognized the cook and a few others. Idelle was present too, gazing out one of the tall windows flanking the hall. She wore a Victorian-styled black dress with buttons from neck to mid-calf.

It was a very new feeling for Kim, to think that her Talent might be obvious to someone else. Even before the intelligence service, she had always kept her ability secret. That it might no longer be—might never again be absolutely hidden—filled her with unease. How would she handle social settings, if confidences could be ascribed to her prying ways? And in clandestine work, it could jeopardize her pretense of artlessness. She might be dead wrong about the "burning bright" idea. She hoped that she was.

The dowager noted Kim's arrival. "Miss Tavistock," came her voice, wavering and sonorous. "They told me you'd arrived." She wore a gray Edwardian skirt with a long matching felt coat.

Kim stopped to greet Idelle, who nodded to her. The view out the windows showed an almost-blinding afternoon sun warming the terrace.

As Rian bustled off, Lady Ellesmere approached Kim and Idelle, accompanied by the *thunk* of her cane on the flagstones. "Don't sulk, Iddy," she said. "You know I would join you if it weren't for the fair."

Idelle smiled wanly and tucked a lacy handkerchief in her sleeve. She turned away and wandered off down the hall.

Lady Ellesmere watched her go. "Tomorrow is the anniversary of Bowen's death. We usually visit his grave together on that day, but we are rather getting on to be traipsing about. Idelle will go alone, but she's sulking since I am not accompanying her."

"Is your husband buried here, on the estate, Lady Ellesmere?"

"No, at St. Alban's, the little church in Pengeylan. We have a lovely memorial headstone, carved at great expense, from France."

Kim was stuck on *in Pengeylan*. Idelle was going to Pengeylan.

"My sister-in-law *can* speak, you know. But has chosen not to. She has been betrayed by life and protects herself from further loss. This is her attitude, though we accord her every comfort."

Kim glanced out the window, in the direction of the village. "I'm sure she's very grateful to you."

"How nice that would be. Well, I expect you're looking for Powell. He's down at the camp right now. Awbrey will accompany you there. He's just outside, assembling supplies."

"I'm looking forward to seeing everything," Kim said. "It was so good of you to invite me."

"Well, you invited yourself, didn't you?"

Kim felt a smile flutter over her face. "I suppose I did. Please pardon my manners, if they're too American."

"Allowances must be made, I expect." Lady Ellesmere rested her hand on her cane and regarded Kim with a penetrating gaze. "There's something brash in you, I must say. Perhaps it's the American manner. But there's something underneath, something you don't let out."

"Oh. Do you think so?" Kim shot back. "I hope it's nothing disagreeable!"

A thin smile. "So do I."

They faced off. "My dear," the dowager said, suddenly shifting her tone. "Is there something troubling you?"

"Of course there isn't." It sounded too defensive. She must give something up to this woman who prided herself on getting to the bottom of people.

"Except . . ." Kim stammered.

The blue eyes narrowed, paying strict attention. Kim could imagine that this was a dowager maneuver of long standing. To claim to sense an emotion and then demand that the other party elaborate. She found her lie slipping out easily. If one was to be a spy, everything was grist for the mill of deception. Lives depended on it. Hers, perhaps.

"Well, my family is not the happiest."

The dowager shook her head in slow regret. "That's an evasion, my dear. You know it is."

"An evasion?"

"It's not your *family*."

What did the damn woman know? She tried to remember what the *Bloom Book* said about *hyperempathy*. *To perceive suppressed or hidden emotions.* But which of her feelings was the woman picking up on? She was a jumble of emotions, including suspicion, wariness, and a nasty sense of being entirely out of her depth.

"It's not the family in general," Lady Ellesmere said. After a hulking pause, she added, "It's your brother, isn't it?"

She had it wrong, thank God. But now she faced the disagreeable prospect of telling her about Robert. She could not, no more than she would shed her clothes on the hallway floor.

Still waiting for her to answer.

"That was long ago," she finally said.

"But for you, it is like yesterday, I shouldn't wonder."

The old woman liked to suck the darkness out from people. And Kim must feed her. "Yes. I always remember." It was like a forced entry. Into her heart. And she was allowing it, for fear the old woman would see even more hidden things.

"How did he die? You can tell me. Most people feel better when they do. Which battle was it?"

It was Ypres. He drowned. "I beg your pardon." Her voice lower, almost a growl. "I never discuss it." An unwelcome flash of insight: she never discussed it; not with a nosy old woman she hardly knew, but not with anyone, really. The woman of the *spill* might not just lose friends from knowing too much, but for sharing too little.

Lady Ellesmere narrowed her eyes, as though detecting her discomfort. She murmured, "Buried things have the most power over us. In time you will learn that."

She hadn't expected wisdom from this woman. It was quite disagreeable.

The dowager shook her head with a pitying smile. "You can't hide things from me, you know. Especially about Powell."

"Powell?"

"He's not for you. You do see that, don't you?"

"Oh! I don't think of him in that way."

Lady Ellesmere gave an indulgent smile. "Well, if you did, you can stop now." Glancing at the camera, she said, "No pictures. Some of our people need their privacy. Leave it in the salon and I'll have someone return it to your room."

Eager to be away, Kim went into the salon to place her camera case on the table beside the telephone. She had hoped to have some pictures of the castle and the estate; snaps could be pored over later for evidence, but it was not to be.

Looking at the telephone, she made a plan to get back to it when she was alone. For Idelle was going to Pengeylan, and that could provide a chance for Alice and her *trauma view* if Alice could contrive to get next to her at the cemetery.

Descending the entryway steps, she opened the door to the terrace. Idelle was waiting for her, close to the castle wall, where they would not be seen from above. The woman's scalp was pink underneath the sparse mat of her hair. Fragile-looking, Kim thought, but tough. And she could speak, she reminded herself.

"Idelle," Kim said. "Who is Flory Soames?" The woman's expression turned pained, but she said nothing.

She thrust something small and hard into Kim's hand before turning away and slipping through the terrace door.

Kim glanced down. It was a key.

PENGEYLAN

Martin sat in the village green, devouring a scone, with one still to go, watching as motorcars tried to back up on the street, away from an upended cart. A horse still hitched to the cart reared and pawed at the air.

The scones had taken the last of his coin, the last from his Wrenfell wages, but he'd made it to Sulcliffe. Or nearly. Three train changes from London, each one gut-wrenching with worry. Which platform, which direction? The station masters could tell you, but they weren't always nearby, and if you asked someone on the train, they all said different things.

He'd hoped that he might see Miss Kim at the railway station, or even in the village, but she'd left six hours earlier. She must be at Sulcliffe Castle by now, probably *in* the castle, so he didn't know how he would get to her. But since it was a fair, and she'd gone to report on it, his best hope was that she'd come strolling through with her camera, and he would sidle up to her and tell her about the murderer. That the man who lived there— gentry, with a title, even—he had helped kill that girl. Martin had *seen* it, so he knew. Maybe other *site view* Talents working for the police had seen it too, but they didn't know who it was. It was the man in the picture, sure enough.

He set aside for now the fact that she was never going to believe him, since he had lied about her brother. Why did he always lie?

But he'd had to, because of seeing things. Because of how his da looked at him with a corkscrew face when he knew something he shouldn't know. If he didn't want the back of his da's hand, he had to come up with reasons for knowing things and acting on things that were none of his business. So when he started having *site view*, he'd lied, and everyone was happier for it.

But then one day he finally told his mum, and she went and told da that he had what everyone was calling a Talent. And from then on, it was no good between them.

The thing was, he supposed he was still a liar, because of what he'd done with the book he'd found in his room at Wrenfell.

In the street, the horse was pulling at the traces and kicking as the man tried to control him, and no wonder, because the cars honked and people were shouting.

Martin tucked half of a scone into his pocket for later and went into the street. He spoke up and offered the man some help with the horse, and the man said, no, the beast would calm down, but he didn't, and then Martin was talking to the horse like he did with Briar. Pretty soon, he was feeding him the scone, and the horse stopped rolling its eyes and settled down. The man said, "I told you to leave 'im alone," and Martin backed off.

Then he realized he'd just given his supper to a horse.

THE SULCLIFFE ESTATE

Under a brilliant sky towering with a few stacked clouds, Kim and Awbrey tramped across the meadow. The flag on an erected tent shuddered in the wind, blowing hard off the Irish Sea.

"We'll have a right good crowd by tomorrow mornin'," Awbrey said. Already there were a half dozen workmen bringing in boxes of supplies. He gestured to the wide dale creased by a rippling stream. "It'll be somethin' to see, all her ladyship's followers come together."

"I expect they'll set up tents, then?" In the stiff breeze, the corners of a collapsed pavilion flapped like a great, wounded bird trying to fly. Idelle Coslett's key was nestled in Kim's trouser pocket. It looked like a door key, but she had thrust it away quickly without a proper look. Even so, she was furiously imagining opening a door to the castle skeletons.

"Aye, an' we put up the big tents in case of it rainin'."

Powell had come into the field from the tree line, and seeing them, waved. Kim waved back. "Will Lady Ellesmere come down, do you think?"

"Oh, 'course she will." Awbrey looked up at the castle visible over the short rise of hill, where it massively jutted from the headland. He gestured at the edge of the field to what Kim could now discern was a stone circle veiled in grass. "Her ladyship will join hands around the circle. Nor distinctions made, is her way."

Powell had come up to them, and nodded to dismiss Awbrey.

"Kim," he said, his smile broad and quick. "Sorry I didn't come for you. Mother has me on last-minute tasks."

"Quite all right. Awbrey said the fair really starts tomorrow. Can anyone come?"

"Open to all, but you do have to stand for a pledge as a seeker, at least."

She had read of the pledge they asked followers to make; perhaps their way of fending off skeptics, but of course, one could easily lie. Kim gestured to the stone meeting circle. "You can't all fit in a circle there, it's too small."

"Circles within circles." He led the way toward the stone ring, now appearing to be larger than it had before, some twenty-five feet in diameter, the grass scythed in patches, sprouting in tufts beside low stone slabs. The central area was built up as a berm, where a speaker might stand. "People join hands and eventually, we are all standing together without broken links."

They stood within the stone ring. "Sometimes this is where we have our chants and singing. A few of those were in my book."

"Which I did read," she said. "It was fascinating." One gift the man certainly did not have was writing, the whole tome dry as a school thesis.

"I'm glad you liked it." A smile started up but failed to

complete. "You know, you'll be the only one here who isn't a believer or a seeker." He cut a glance at her. "Unless you *are*."

"I have an open mind. I can't promise a conversion." She smiled to be playful, but he seemed distracted and didn't notice.

He sighed, taking a seat on the nearest stone bench. His face looked older, without his cheerful aspect to soften it. Kim was determined to pursue the idea of what he had to do to be receptive to a gift. In case it was murder. It was dicey to approach the topic, especially since she did not want to desire a *spill* too much. Neutrality was a stance she had to work on. It was very difficult not to care.

She sat next to him on the stone. "Were you down at the henge just now?"

"The sea henge?" He hesitated. "The vicinity. How did you know?"

"You said you meditated on the cliffs there. I know you work at your spirituality."

"More people should," he said. "Most live their lives so conventionally, as if what's on the surface matters so much."

"Self-examination is so lacking these days."

"You would put it that way."

"Too mundane for you, I know."

He leaned his forearms on his knees, clasping his hands. "It's as though you reject what I'm doing."

"I'm sorry. I don't mean to judge things before I have any experience." She paused. "But you believe it improves you, that's what counts. Do you feel it *does*?"

He shook his head, murmuring, "Don't you think I ask myself that every hour of the day?"

"But, Powell. What if you are already fine? What if you are ready to inspire and guide people *now*? What if your gift has in fact come? You have an attractive way about you. I thought so from the moment I met you."

In a violent movement he rose, turning on her. "No! It hasn't come. It's not about being attractive or likable. It's about the power a man must have to lead. And that power is still waiting for me." The movement startled both of them. His face was filled with an unreadable expression, one that might have reflected a sickening doubt.

Because if he was wrong, and all the gifts he would ever receive had already long been a part of him, then murdering innocents was a disastrous mistake.

She pressed on. "Haven't you been receptive to powers all along? What more must you do?"

He stared at her. She had come too close to the key question. Deflecting his attention, she went on. "And what of the thieves who have a *darkening* power, or leaders who are *conceptors*, trampling on freedom? What if further power made you worse?"

He ran his hands through his hair. "But you're looking at the outside of things. No man can judge another."

Oh yes, they can.

He took a deep breath. "I beg your pardon. Do excuse me, I'm not myself today. Too little sleep, with the preparations and all. Let's go back."

And just like that the conversation was over. She gathered up her handbag and followed him toward the pavilions now taking shape on the field.

After a few strides he half-turned to her. "What you said . . . I know you're trying to bolster me. It's really very good of you."

She had been twisting his hopes in front of his face, hoping to crack his facade, so it was not *very good of her*. The farther she walked down this road, the more deception and manipulation she used, almost effortlessly.

It was reassuring to know that she had it in her.

She glanced toward the castle, looking like a distorted crown encircling the massive rock on which it sat. Someone here might have a way of detecting Talents. Would it be someone at the fair tomorrow? Or would SIS have to follow Lord Ellesmere until he led them to such a man? The family was full of riddles. But the more they wished to hide, the more likely they would be to *spill*.

It was one reason why she thought Powell might have given her a *spill* of his darkest secret. That some people burned brightly. He might have meant it metaphorically, but how extraordinary if it were real.

28

FRIDAY, AUGUST 28. Dries leaned against the worktable, regarding his visitor. A roll of bandages, disinfectant, and a scissors lay scattered behind him. Outside the heavily shuttered windows, the night was disturbed by a gusting wind off the sea, setting the woods to thrashing.

The dowager sat in a torn, overstuffed chair, her body sagging into its depths as she recovered from her trek. The oil lantern on the table threw a murky light around them, as though they were a fathom deep in water. As well, she bore her own light, a pallid one, from her inconsequential Talent of which she made such a fetish.

"You should never have come to Sulcliffe. It exposes us to danger," Dorothea said, blithely ignoring the danger that Dries himself was in, wounded and pursued by the police.

"But where else could I go, Dorothea?" Coslett's decision to bring him here—his father's old woodland retreat—had been shrewd and rather brave, given Dorothea's certain opposition.

"Please do not call me that, Monsieur Verhoeven."

She hated familiarity, especially with someone below her station, and a foreigner. But what could be more intimate than murdering together? Even family or sex could not match the tie.

"I see you are feeling better," she said.

He touched the dressing on his neck. "*Ach.* It takes more than the shotgun to kill me." The pellets might have taken his face off, but instead the blast had gone wide, only raking his shoulder, chest and neck. He was much improved. Ready to go on, in fact.

His time in England was almost at an end. Himmler wished for him to return his efforts to the Continent, and next it would be Paris, where he would watch in the dark for the strongest lights. Germany's might grew stronger every day, soon to be unequaled. But in the realm of Talents, this was not the case. Meta powers had been bestowed broadly, wastefully. Cropping up in French peasants, Czech Communists, even Jews. Hitler understood the danger of undesirables rising in power. And for Dries, it had long been a conviction, as well.

He glanced in the direction where the woman's son waited outside the cabin, having brought a lantern to guide the way. "Powell is coming along very well. Yesterday I saw a light around his head. Almost a halo."

Her face lifted at the mention of Powell. The need for a private discussion of him was the reason her son stood outside. "You still believe the gift will come to him?"

"I do think so. There are . . . little flickers. More all the time."

She nodded, letting out a ragged breath. He could almost smell the miasma of her cancer. "Receiving a gift can be such a difficult birth. With me, it was a natural thing, like awakening after a long night, and finding oneself anointed. And Powell struggles so!" She looked up at him with an expression of longing. Somehow this bloated woman managed to harbor love for one person. Her son. A moment of pity sliced through him before he remembered that she was British.

"But you do see the little flickers?"

"Like St. Elmo's fire along a ship's mast." That was rather good, he thought, though he could no more see the approach of a Talent than he could pick out a train a hundred miles away. Once a Talent broke through, only then was it apparent to him. But, for his very satisfying work on British soil—pursuing young people—he must keep the old woman's hopes alive.

"I do wish you had not spilled blood at the church," Dorothea said, peevish. "It arouses the enthusiasm of the police to find us."

"They are enthusiastic because we are killing *children*, I think."

She sniffed at this correction. "Well, young, innocent blood. That is most powerful, of course."

Her wish was for power. His wish, terror. Everyone in it for their own reasons, a perfect collaboration.

She went on, "No more churches. And the stone circle choice. Another mistake. That place of power could have brought to mind our reverence for ancient sites." He could not help but show his irritation, and she shot back, "Himmler has seconded you to my cause, my leadership. Perhaps you should remember that."

She would invoke the one man he was afraid of. He remembered their meeting. The man with the weasel face, made strong only by his austere manner. The stylish black uniform. The offer of tea and a conversation about a certain Talent Dries that might serve the Reich. How Himmler had heard of Dries, he did not know. But when an SS subordinate came to his home, he had been pleased to leave his village in a sleek Mercedes, to ride down the Wilhelmstrasse in the heart of great Berlin. To be ushered in to meet a man who was the second most important person in Germany. Of course Dries would assist in the operation. His politics? None, but the racial goals of the National Socialist party, yes, so correct. He would gladly take an oath to Hitler. Himmler had smiled. An agreement. But Dries Verhoeven never forgot those swastika-draped halls and this diminutive man's power over life and death. Dries admired him, and feared him.

He allowed Coslett her point. "Himmler, yes. I am directed to help you, it is true. You wish the blood spilled along the lines." Her absurd ideas had no end. Not only earth worship and sacred sites but the infernal *lines*. "And I do my best for you. The stone circle and the church, both were ideally situated. Do you know how difficult it is to find a youngster in the correct place? I must watch and wait. It is not easy, Dorothea."

Turning to the table, he fingered the old baron's compass and maps. She did not like him to handle her husband's things, and so he persisted. "Bowen Coslett," he mused. "The one who began it all, *ja*?" He looked up, but found no response. "These plotting instruments. He was a surveyor in the war, Powell said."

"He began things," Dorothea conceded. "There were others. But they were minor figures."

"Your husband departed from the strictly scientific. The others had not his imagination in regard to the *lines*. Yes?"

"They were men of intellect, but lacking the spiritual dimension. There were disagreements about significance and spiritual connection. My husband continued on a solitary way."

"A man who . . . followed his own drummer, is what you say?"

She raised an eyebrow at this attempt to define her husband. "His competitors were conventional, rigid men who could not see beyond the surface of things. Who refused to acknowledge Lord Ellesmere's insights on ley lines. They derided the very idea."

"I can imagine this. Envy. A common story."

"Envy of us both. It was my idea to share our insights as broadly as I have. Ancient Light has been my contribution."

"That and the murder of children. That part, it is new, *ja?*"

Her gaze flared up at him. "How dare you goad me! You, of all people."

"Yes, your humble servant, Dries Verhoeven. Who undertakes things that would soil your hands."

She murmured, "I soiled my hands, on that score you are wrong. The first to die—it happened here."

That did surprise him. "Here?"

"At the castle. It was a clumsy affair. The girl was a runaway, a child of no account, dirty and ragged. She would not be missed."

The old serpent had some courage, after all, he thought.

"I had long wondered if the vitality of blood, as many ancients believed, held power for those who spilled it in the proper way, at the proper place."

"And of course, your fine castle is situated on holy ground."

She flicked a look at him, alert for sarcasm. He had managed to say it in his best sincere manner. She went on. "Afterward, as the girl lay dying, I felt the power of Sacred Earth flow into me. The gift that I had long possessed surged more strongly, leaving me breathless. How I longed to go on! Think of the following I might have amassed, had I an even stronger gift for knowing each person's true feelings. But to spill more blood, no. Had there been more deaths, I might have been suspect."

"And then too, the patrons of your Ancient Light, they would not have understood, *ja?*"

"Every religion preserves the highest secrets for the initiated few. In any case, the girl's death was my inspiration. But the violence of the act—I had not the taste for it."

He felt a smile come to his lips. "Then you found me. And the taste, it returned, yes?"

Dorothea straightened. "Monsieur Verhoeven, you are a man who makes me uneasy. You have no *raison d'être*, no great longing or cause. I hope that you are not merely a murderer."

"No *cause*? I believe we share an admiration for the Nazi movement."

"Yes, yes. But the Führer does not hate our island. He respects the British people. While you . . ."

He felt his heart contract into a smaller space. "I *what*?"

"You are not a normal man. I perceive that you have a great hate inside you. And I believe it is for the British. It is why you agreed to come."

Her drawing-room psychology, it might aggravate him were it not so pompous and foolish. Her Talent had taken a turn he had seen in others many times. She had become enamored of it. With *hyperempathy*, Dorothea had come not just to see feelings but to require them.

"Can you not give it up?" Her voice needled at him. "Let whatever wrong has been done to you fall away?"

His left hand touched the scissors on the table. "I believe you refer to forgiveness."

"Yes. Hate is a heavy burden."

"Also an inspiration."

She drew back at this, murmuring, "It is better to kill for love than for hate."

He moved away from the table so that he would not be tempted to silence her.

"And so," he said, changing the subject. "Do we go on?"

"We do, monsieur. I feel we are close to a breakthrough." She looked up at him with an almost flirtatious expression. "Perhaps one or two more?"

Until Himmler ordered him home. "One or two only." The police were too near; they might have a description of Coslett from the pigsty fiasco.

She stood, leaning so hard on her cane, he thought it might plunge through the rotting floor. "You must remain hidden. The fair . . ."

He nodded. Room enough for Dries as well as her besotted followers on such an estate.

She turned for the door.

"By the way," he said. "The woman who came into the field today, talking alone with Powell—"

She swung around to stare at him. "You were at the field?"

"I stayed hidden. But this woman, she has a strong gift."

"Do you mean to say the Tavistock woman? She is just an American, a writer of articles."

Ah. So, this was Coslett's lady. "Nevertheless, she sheds the light." He estimated she would be at least a 6. He hoped it was not for *trauma view*, for it would be Powell's downfall, for anyone to see the things he had done.

"What is the nature of her gift?"

"I do not know. To me, she is only a light."

Dorothea wrinkled her brow. "Well, it may do no harm. She has not the guile to use a gift properly."

"It would be best if Powell avoided her." He shrugged. "Our enterprise, you know."

She glanced in the direction of the castle. "That may be difficult to arrange. They have become friends."

Since Coslett had first mentioned this woman, Dries had

been considering her with growing unease. "Any person with a gift can be a danger. To see things, to perceive things."

"Well. I am sending her home tomorrow. Just make sure you do not lurk around the fairgrounds and risk being seen."

He might keep his distance. On the other hand, he was attracted to the light. Like a moth to the flame . . . The memory came, of fire surging down the hall. Papers on bulletin boards erupting in fire and the hair of schoolchildren.

He stood at the door, watching the mother and son walk into the woods, one of them bright, one dark.

29

THAT SAME EVENING. Kim's dinner sat on a tray at the table: squab and mash, Rian had declared. There would be no formal dinner tonight. She tried to remember what squab was and feared it was dove. She gazed at the food, straightening the tableware just so, lining up the fork with the knife, the napkin, and plate.

Out the windows of her suite, the rocky headland caught the last rays of sun glaring off the sea. On the highboy was her camera, which had been returned to her. She adjusted the salt and pepper into a nice line with the butter dish. . . .

She could sit still no longer. Rising from the table, she left the apartment and stood on the landing, listening for activity downstairs. Faint voices—Rian's? And another woman's, possibly the nurse. There were no guests other than herself lodging in the castle.

Here she was, thoroughly infiltrated into the nest of suspects, and yet she'd be making no progress for the rest of the evening, since the entire household was consumed by tasks relating to the gathering.

The stairs curved around to higher floors. She climbed. Through stone slit windows rectangles of light lit her way.

On the next landing was a closed door much like her own. No voices or movement inside. Removing Idelle's key from her pocket, she slipped it into the lock, but it did not fit.

Ascending, she found herself on the last landing. Electricity had not come to this level of the castle, leaving the shallow landing in semi-darkness. The door to the apartment lay ajar. She pushed it open to reveal a room identical in shape to her own, but long unused, the only furniture a black Victorian bedstead too massive to move down the stairwell. She wondered who had ever slept here, and whether Sulcliffe might once have rung with the cries of children playing or couples laughing or making love. It was very hard to imagine.

One of the windows looked out toward folded hills, a reminder of her isolation here. The glass was very old and appeared to be sagging, as though after a very long time it could no longer keep its shape.

She turned to another window in the semicircular wall. It looked out to Sulcliffe's long north wall, massive and capped at the far end by another turret, and beyond it, the Irish Sea. On the top floor of the north turret she could just make out someone moving inside. Perhaps it was Powell. Lady Ellesmere's suite was on the other side of the castle. Who else besides the baron would have an apartment commanding what must be an extraordinary view of the sea?

As she stood at the window, she wondered what she would look like at this distance to someone who could see Talents.

She imagined her body shedding light as though electrified, or her skin suffused with a phosphorescent glow. To a person who could discern such things, the world might appear to be full of ghostlike creatures, stripped of their personalities, distilled to one thing only: light. It might be possible to think such people easier to exterminate.

If there was such a Talent, she hoped it was very rare.

The shadow at the far window had disappeared. If it had been Powell, perhaps he was sitting down to his dinner.

On the landing, she quickly descended all the way to the broad, gallery-like hall.

Sconces lit her way in the deserted corridor. She slipped into the drawing room, looking around in case someone might be reading a paper on the divan or stoking the fire. But the room was empty. She lifted the receiver of the telephone. The operator came on, and she gave the telephone number of Alice's lodging.

After a few moments of clicking, a man's voice came across the line. "Llewellyn House, may I help you?"

"I would like to speak with a lodger, Alice Ward."

"Could you speak up, please?"

Kim looked toward the hall. "Alice Ward, please," she said more urgently.

A very long pause. She thought perhaps she had been disconnected. The moment stretched on interminably. Then: "I'm sorry, she is not in her room. Would you like to leave word?"

"Oh, it's perfectly all right." Although it wasn't. "I'll call back."

"Wait a moment, please." Kim heard a conversation at the other end, just out of earshot. "My wife found her in the dining room. Here she is."

A beat and a rustle on the line. "Hello, this is Alice."

"Alice! Oh, hello, this is Kim. How are you?"

"Very well indeed. And you?"

"I just wanted to let you know that I arrived in good order, and expect to have a lovely weekend. I hope you're enjoying your holiday. You might like to tour the little church tomorrow. Saturdays are such a nice time to do a little sightseeing. I've heard there's quite a significant monument in the churchyard. These old churches are so edifying."

"Good idea, I'll give it a go. I wonder if I'll see anyone I know."

"Your sister-in-law said she'd go sightseeing, so you might run into her."

"I'll watch for her, then. By the way, I just heard some news from Vicar Hathaway. Martin has gone off to London, of all places. He left a note saying he'd be back, but there was something he had to do. They're looking for him. Just thought you should know."

"Oh no, Alice." This was disturbing news. Why on earth would Martin do such a thing? "Will you call with any developments?"

"Of course."

Martin in London. It was no place for a boy his age by himself. What could he be thinking? "Well, must ring off. That little cold I had has gone, so I'm feeling in the pink."

"Oh, good. Have fun, and get some good snaps."

"I should be home on Sunday evening, so see you then." She replaced the receiver, and wiped her sweating hands on her skirt. *In the pink* was her code for all well.

Martin was missing. After the episode of lying, she thought he would be keen on redeeming himself. And now this. She worried about a boy his age traveling alone, and to London! Alice shouldn't have injected family matters into an operational message. A newcomer's mistake, but frankly, she was glad to be informed.

She sat for a while, thinking about Martin. Despite what had happened with Robert's diary, over the past month she had grown terribly fond of him. She had watched Martin grow from guarded and diffident to something approaching lively and actually happy. Everyone in the house enjoyed him, and, she had to admit, especially her. Someday, she would have children of her own; it was not too late. But for now, it was lovely to have Martin.

A noise at the archway. Powell had entered the drawing room.

"There you are!"

She smiled up at him. "How is everything going at the fair?"

"Top-notch. Sorry we all had to have dinner in our rooms; that's how it is these fair weekends." He frowned. "I say, is everything all right? You look a bit cast down."

"Oh. Well, yes, I'm fine. But I just had a telephone chat with my friend Alice, to tell her I'll be home tomorrow. She told me that a boy I'm fostering has run off, or I should say, took an unapproved trip. It's a bit worrying."

"I shouldn't wonder! I didn't know you had a foster child."

"Martin isn't officially in my care, but he is staying on the farm for the summer." It was better to encourage Powell to talk about himself rather than her, so she quickly deflected the questions he seemed on the verge of pursuing. "I should have come with you to the field. Did Lady Ellesmere give a talk at the big tent?"

"No, she'll wait for more to arrive, but she did join in for a bit of the singing at the stone circle. Quite lovely. It does inspire, to have music and the nice fire under the stars. In fact, I was just coming to find you. There's something to see from the terrace."

"What is it?"

He smiled. "Just come. You won't be disappointed."

They crossed the gallery hall and went out onto the terrace. He draped an arm over her shoulder and led her across the paving stones to the parapet. They looked east onto a series of vales shadowed by soft hills.

There, far down, were lights. A string of them, moving past the castle, like Chinese lanterns floating on a river.

"We've had an omnibus pick our people up at the village green, and they'll be bivouacking on the field tonight. It's a fine sight, isn't it?"

"Oh, yes! It looks like a river of gold." Though an almost-full moon lay on the eastern horizon, the headland remained in dramatic darkness. "Do they have lanterns, then?" *Do some glow on their own?*

"Yes, and flashlights. Our people come prepared. See over there?" He turned her shoulders toward the fairgrounds where a dim firelight pulsed. "We've lit a bonfire to shed some light so they can make camp."

"Too bad I couldn't get a snap of this! But I guess there won't be any pictures at all, Lady Ellesmere says." She tossed her head to rid herself of his arm. "Well, we'll make do."

The wall of the castle provided some refuge from the wind, so the high terrace was quite pleasant in the heavy dusk. From the gallery hall, the lancet windows threw ingots of light onto the flagstones. Kim could imagine a soiree out here, had it been any other family who owned the place.

"About the lad you're fostering—Martin, is it?" At her nod, he said, "You don't feel you have to be going home early?"

"No, I don't think so. I'm sure it will be all right." She knew she was under Powell's particular gaze, and wondered why he had really brought her to the terrace.

"I'm glad. When you're done with your articles, we'll be friends. Won't we?"

"Of course we will." With his back to the windows, his face was not so much in shadow, as missing. It reminded her that she had no idea who he truly was.

"It wasn't only for your newspaper that you came this time, was it?"

"Well, I *am* keen on writing you up."

"All right, then, I'll just ask you. Do you like me, Kim?" He let out a little laugh. "Or has Mother completely scared you off?"

The question was so fraught with mines, she didn't know where to step. And how desperate for affection he must be, to presume to say this on so little encouragement. "She did say I wasn't for you."

He snorted. "And what did you say?"

"I . . . I said . . ." She didn't know how to sustain some pretense of affection for the sake of the operation. She was a *spill* artist, not a spy trading in sex and secrets.

"I told her I didn't think of you in that way."

He hadn't moved. "Did you mean it?"

"Powell." She paused, gathering her words carefully. "I don't know you very well. So, of course I am here to write an article. We have time to become better acquainted if we decide we should."

She watched as he moved to the other side of the battlements, the one that faced the sea. His voice came to her faintly. "I thought you said I had *attraction*."

He had heard that clearly enough, but she hadn't meant it to pertain to her, only to his followers. "You do. You have a great attraction." She drew closer to him. "But between a man and a woman, a gift for it—that can't be what goes on. You do see that."

He turned to her with a forced smile. "It was my test."

"I failed it."

"No," he said. "*I* failed it. I failed to attract you."

The wind blew her hair in her face, into her mouth as though trying to stop her from talking, but she couldn't leave this. "Everyone who meets you must feel at ease, must feel your warmth. I felt it, Powell, truly. You'll make a good leader of Ancient Light." She hesitated but added, "If Lady Ellesmere would only *let* you." If Powell was innocent, he needed to hear this. If he wasn't, then nothing could save him.

He looked at her without responding, for really, what could he say? She was not for him. His mother was not for him. It was too bad, but Powell had probably been dodging the truth of his mother's rejection his whole life.

After such a conversation, it was best to call it a night. There could be no small talk, no *spill*, after this. She turned at the doorway. "Personally, I don't think you need to meditate anymore."

Pushing open the door, she made her way down the gallery hall. He didn't follow her. As she passed by the hall windows, she saw him standing on the terrace, gazing out to sea.

30

SATURDAY, AUGUST 29. The pipes shuddered and banged as Kim drew a hot bath. It surprised her greatly that there was hot water, but this morning she could have steeped a chicken in it.

She slipped into the giant claw-footed basin, and watched her skin turn rosy red. The bath needed to refresh her, because she had hardly slept, expecting some dramatic occurrence in the middle of the night. Her gun under her pillow, her door locked. *Why* did clandestine work demand overnights?

By her watch lying on the low table next to the tub, it was 9:17. Terribly late, because she had only dozed off shortly before dawn. Reluctantly, she pulled the plug. With a little sleep and a bright sun charging through the windows, her theory of secret sight seemed a bit foolish. It no doubt came of wishing to bring a villain to trial before he killed again. But the real murderer could be in Sussex or Cornwall, for all she knew.

She was dressed when the knock came at her door. Rian.

"There's kidneys and fry for breakfast down to the dining hall, miss. But it's cold by now. Did ye not hear the gong?"

"Oh, thank you, Rian. I'll be right along. It's a big castle for a gong."

Rian sniffed. "It brung the master from the cabin many a year."

"Good ears, then, I imagine."

Rian looked at her as though having good ears was hardly the point. Kim grabbed her light jacket and her handbag with its extra heft from the Colt and made her way to the gallery hall. Looking out the windows, she wondered if she could see any fair activity from the castle battlements. She hurried down the hall to the massive front door and stepped out onto the terrace.

Hearing voices from below, she leaned over the parapet to see Idelle getting into the family car. She was dressed in dark maroon with matching felt hat. But instead of Awbrey opening the door for her, it was Powell. They drove off in a spray of gravel.

A setback. If Powell was with Idelle, it would not be possible for Alice to get close to her at the cemetery and strike up a conversation, as she had directed her to do during their phone call. *Your sister-in-law said she'd go sightseeing, so you might run into her.* They were interested in *Flory Soames,* in case the name had some importance, as Idelle seemed to believe it did—or why would she have taken such pains to be sure she had told Kim the name in private? All Alice might need was a few minutes alone with her. With luck, her *trauma view* could cast light on the name. Well, perhaps not possible now.

The damnable Coslett luck. They had escaped everything that Crossbow had thrown at them.

She ate alone in the dining hall, feeling very small indeed at the massive table and with chandeliers hanging on twenty-foot chains overhead. The fireplace was spacious enough to roast a boar. While she ate, she brooded on the dance of agents and their quarry. Four young people slaughtered near their homes, farms and churches. One badly hurt. More to come, she didn't doubt. Hundreds of agents and police mobilized.

Surely Talon would make a mistake somewhere along the line. If not here, then wherever he was.

But he had not.

THE SULCLIFFE ESTATE

12:30 PM. "Please do not *hover*."

Kim watched as Lady Ellesmere bent crookedly over her cane, her face distorted. "It will pass," she said making a guttural slur of the final word. The sounds of the fair came from just over the rise.

Her young and eager-faced attendants, Donald and Royce, stepped back, faces creased with concern.

Kim thought the men likely had been chosen by Lady Ellesmere from among her followers. At least, Kim hadn't seen them before. Red-haired Donald was bright-faced and eager. Royce, jug-eared and solid, watched the dowager as though at any moment she might topple.

When the old woman straightened up, she inhaled deeply and struck her cane into the ground, walking on. The spasm and pain seemed to have passed, but it had left its mark in the deeper lines of her face. How strange that Dorothea Coslett could not just give her son the reins of Ancient Light. She had not long to live, and what might have been comfort in having her son carry on had turned into a test that he could never pass.

The fierce morning sun lit up the vistas before them: the distant Snowdonian Mountains, the near hills thick with green grasses and the massed heather a bruised purple. The four of them began making their way up the next rise, behind which Kim could hear the droning of a crowd, pierced by bright shouts.

The dowager wore a heavy knit dress and three-quarter-length coat, more suited to a cross-channel ferry deck than a warm day at the fair. The wind had subsided, making the August day balmy. "Did you see the circle?" Lady Ellesmere asked.

"Oh, yes. Is it an ancient locale or did you bring the stones in?"

Lady Ellesmere paused to rest for a moment. "We brought them in. But they're in the right place."

"How do you know?" Kim took out her notebook and pencil.

The old woman shook her head in exasperation. "You people are *besotted* with stones and barrows. Stonehenge, Barclodiad y Gawres, Silbury Hill. But they're all connected by the sacred ground, Earth itself."

"Of course, but some places have great power. Isn't that a principle?"

As they approached the top of the rise, Kim saw pennants first, bright primary colors against the cerulean sky, then the tent peaks.

"Oh, if you must dwell on it." She glanced at Kim's notebook. "For the popular press," she said, making clear how low that was.

"Would it be wrong to think of the henges and megaliths as, in some way, the churches of Ancient Light?"

"Never use that word," Lady Ellesmere managed to say through gritted teeth. Kim couldn't decide if she was still in pain or just suffering a fool. They looked down on the tents and pavilions of the gathering, with the happy chaos of fair-goers cooking over small fire pits near their tents and shouting amid games in the meadow. This was more like a gathering of friends than any tent revival or religious meeting.

"I see that Powell took Idelle into the village," Kim said. "Will he spend time at the churchyard with her?"

But people had seen them on the hill, and began to run forward, first the small group from the closest tents, and then others, some issuing from the main pavilion, seashell white, anchored with ropes.

A ruddy-faced woman in leather trousers and blousy shirt reached Lady Ellesmere first, her eyes shining with not a little adoration. "Helena," the dowager murmured, "lovely to see you." They chatted for a moment as people jostled around them. So, this was Helena Cumberledge, Powell's replacement if it came to that. She did have a robust presence, a ready smile; perhaps she was the leader Ancient Light would get.

Soon there was a knot of excited people surrounding them as they walked into the encampment, bringing an undisguised pleasure to Lady Ellesmere's face. It was, Kim thought, the appeal that Powell must have seen his mother exert many times, a room-dazzling charisma that only a few could lay claim to. Perhaps for some, it came from a Talent of *attraction*. But with Dorothea Coslett, it appeared to be a combination of personality, presence, and even joy. For the old woman did find joy in these people, and no wonder. Hoping for a glance, a word, a crumb of power, they flocked to her.

As the matriarch toured the encampment, Donald and Royce kept the path open before her. Kim allowed herself to drift behind. She wandered into the main pavilion, where tea urns were set out on tables along with sturdy cups and little collections: flints, broken pottery vessels and tools made out of what might be antlers. She dutifully took notes, but her purpose was to slip away unnoticed.

Ducking out of the tent, she wandered to the outskirts of the field, and then turned into a draw leading in the direction of the castle.

She had rushed up the stone stairway and entered the sitting room, without having seen any of the servants. Debating about whether to make her check-in call now or later, she decided to do so now, in case there was anything that Owen needed to convey to her. Moving quickly to the telephone, she tried to raise the operator. The line was dead. Powell had said that service came and went but, replacing the earpiece in the cradle, she felt a moment's acute discomfort. The castle had been so *good* up until now.

With the heavy metal key clutched inside her pocket, she slipped into the gallery hall and turned into the intersecting south corridor leading past the dining hall. At the foot of the south turret, what she thought of as Dorothea's tower, she hurried up the stairs. Approaching the first landing, she found the dowager's bedroom door open. Heavy curtains shadowed the room.

Pausing to listen, and hearing nothing, she ducked inside. The room smelled of iodine and something sweet. A breakfast tray lay on the unmade bed, with a crockery filled with stewed fruit.

Gaps in the brocade drapes metered a thin light into the room. From the balcony came the sound of pounding swells. In his place of pride over the mantel, Herr Hitler looked resolutely into the space over her shoulder.

Well, if her *spill* could not break the case open, a little old-fashioned snooping might do.

Beginning with the dresser drawers, Kim riffled through folded linens and small clothes. She hoped to find records, photographs, papers—some connection to Ewan Knox, Rupert Bristow, Frances Brooke, Jane Babington, George Merkin. Or to the places of mystery where they had been sacrificed for reasons of power.

A chest anchored by metal corners and clasps contained a man's frock coat, unfamiliar instruments, some in handsome leather cases, and a military kit. Mementos of Lady Ellesmere's husband. A framed wedding picture, with a slim Dorothea standing next to whiskered and doughty gentlemen who looked of an age to be on a second marriage.

A sound on the stairs.

This was the essential problem with searching Lady Ellesmere's suite. There was no escape from being overtaken. She rushed to the bedroom door, thinking to flee up the stairs, but sensed she hadn't the time.

Dashing across the room, she opened the balcony door and shut it softly behind her. With any luck at all, it would be Idelle. But it could not be she, since she had gone to the village. So, it would only be someone who would report her: Rian, Awbrey . . . She peeked through the gap in the drapes.

The nurse, moving about.

The sea lay open on every side, massive and glittering. After the dusky interior, the sight hit Kim's eyes like bird shot. *The view, Lady Ellesmere, how splendid!* No, if discovered, she would be caught dead to rights, spying. Below the stone balustrade, the curtain wall of the castle fell straight to the surf, swelling and dipping. She was afraid, practically holding her breath, and only dimly aware of the crash of the sea below.

She pulled her sleeve back to check her watch, a nervous tic that nevertheless often steadied her. It was a quarter after one.

A jangle of noise from inside. She guessed it was the nurse taking up the breakfast tray. Pray God the nurse would not throw open the French doors to let in fresh air. Victorians didn't believe in fresh air, did they? Everyone in the castle seemed to be carrying the nineteenth century with them like great, dismal bundles on their backs.

One twenty-two. Time to risk a look through the curtains. The breakfast tray was gone.

Kim emerged back into the bedroom and crept to the door to listen as the clattering tray made its way down the tower stairs. Cautiously, she followed.

At the bottom of the stairs, she walked calmly down the hall. Home free. She moved away from the precincts of Dorothea's tower, passing the long row of windows just off the drawing room. No one had seen her, but she'd found nothing for her trouble.

She passed the stairs to her own turret bedroom, and went farther down the corridor. Here was the unused great hall visible over the balcony rail. She imagined a king and queen having their feast long ago, whichever king and queen it had been. The Sulcliffe painted shield dominated the wall above the hearth. Its spears cradled a dogwood blossom and sea waves, the symbolism pure Coslett: land and sea, the sacred elements.

For many minutes now she had seen no one. It was as though the castle had long been inhabited by a chosen few, and as they grew old and died, it left fewer and fewer until none would remain.

Up the stairs to the third tower. Powell's.

31

1:35 PM. Martin had gone back for a second helping of beans in the food tent and was standing in line when the fat man caught his eye. This was the bloke who'd talked to him in the village, and who was on the same bus to the castle.

Martin nodded at the fellow. When he reached the front of the line for the beans, he took his plate outside and sat on a rock across the grounds. A bunch of regular-looking stones were set in a circle, with a mound of built-up dirt in the middle. Spooning the beans in as fast as he could, he watched the grounds for Miss Kim. When the old woman had come a while before, he thought Kim might be with her, but there was such a crowd, he couldn't see if she was. He couldn't even see the baroness properly, except that she was as old as the librarian in Coomsby, maybe older.

He watched for the fat man, too. He didn't want to explain to him why he wasn't with his parents, like he said he would be, joining up with them at the fair where he'd claimed they'd gone

ahead. At the time the fellow looked like he didn't believe it.
And worse, now he was seeing how Martin wasn't with anyone
after all.

Where was Miss Kim? He had thought it would be easy to
find her, but now he might not have much more time, if the fat
man grabbed him by the collar.

He watched the camp, considering whether it was better to
stay where he was or try to get into the castle.

The fat man was still watching him from the opening of the
big tent. Martin left his plate lying in the grass and strolled
away. Once behind one of the bigger tents, he used it for cover to
dash into the trees.

PENGEYLAN

1:40 PM. Alice had long ago learned that cemeteries were full
of memory. She stood on the far edge of the churchyard, by the
vicarage, with a clear view of the entire grounds. In the churchyard, people stood by headstones, sometimes with heads bowed,
sometimes chatting with friends, in the way of holidayers.

But for many, memories came, tender, bitter or brutal. The
latter were the sort that would descend on Alice. It had happened
often enough in the cemetery at Uxley, when the churchyard
had visitors. Today she was in danger of seeing events that
would block out the memories of her target. Perhaps when
Idelle came into the churchyard, she could get close enough to
the old woman to forestall interference from others.

Idelle would likely require a cue from Alice to turn her
thoughts to Flory Soames. And having heard the cue, Idelle
might put two and two together and think she was under

scrutiny and run off or alert someone. If old Awbrey had driven her, he would be no match for Alice, though. She thought she could outrun a seventy-five-year-old man, even if he was in the peak of health.

A swift reconnoiter of the gravestones had not yielded Bowen Coslett's, but much of the statuary was thickly matted with moss. There were several grave monuments to keep watch on: a soldier in bronze, a commanding Gaelic-looking stone crucifix, a sleeping angel carved from granite.

Across the churchyard, a car, sleekly black and decades old, pulled up to the pavement in front of the church. A man stepped out from the driver's side. From the several pictures in the dossier Alice had studied, it was Powell Coslett. He opened the door for a diminutive woman of advanced aged. *Right-o*, Alice thought with a yank of excitement. *Idelle*. Lady Ellesmere's sister-in-law.

They shared a few words before Powell Coslett got back in the car and drove away. For a moment Alice had been prepared to shift her focus to Lord Ellesmere, to find a way to establish a conversation with him at graveside. But now he had driven off.

Instead of entering the cemetery, the old woman came up the footpath to the church and entered. Alice followed, entering the cool shadows of the nave and finding Idelle seated in the front row gazing at the altar. It was impossible to exploit the moment, for conversation would be out of the question. Slipping back out, Alice waited until Idelle emerged from the church and crossed the graveyard toward the monument with the reclining angel. It flitted through Alice's mind that one did not often see angels asleep on the job.

Idelle stood before the grave. As Alice made her way closer, she saw that the angel was not depicted as sleeping, but rather prostrate over a headstone pediment, as though collapsed in sorrow. One arm of the stricken angel was thrown forward of her head, in abandonment to grief. The wings draped protectively alongside her and the pediment beneath.

Alice pretended to pay respects at a nearby grave, rehearsing in her mind her approach to Idelle. She must choose her moment with care.

1:45 PM. Lloyd Nichols nursed a pint in the corner of the White Bell next to the Penrhyn Inn. He'd been lucky to get a table, with the weekend crowd packed in. The bar man squeezed around the smoke-filled pub, handing out plates of sausages and chopped turnips, and keeping the regulars well oiled.

A man came in, obviously the minted sort, wearing a good jacket and his chin in the air. It must be the baron. Lloyd hailed him with a wave, wishing he'd waited to order his beer so the toff could pay for it.

"You're Lloyd Nichols?" Coslett took a seat, putting his hat on his knee, not wantin' to soil it on the table.

"That's right. Come from London, and at my own expense. I figured you'd want to know about the Tavistock woman. Happy to set the record straight."

The baron looked around him. "Keep your voice down, man."

"Right." Lloyd leaned into the table, to be heard above the din. "So, like I said when I rung you up, that Tavistock woman that wrote your spiritualist piece, she's got a sideline, she does." He took a long pull at his glass.

"Sideline?" As the bar man approached, the baron waved him off.

"You might stand for my drink. I come a long way to save you a particular aggravation."

A coin appeared, snapped down on the table, and Lloyd nodded. He'd better pay for his train ticket, too.

"So, like I said, a sideline. Turns out Tavistock is workin' for an unnamed government office, and this unnamed government office relates to certain *clandestine* jobs for Whitehall."

"That's absurd," the baron said, but without conviction. "The article came out a week and a half ago. If you're wasting my time, I assure you I shall have a word with the *Register*."

"Don't mind if you do. Me and my editor—a total arse—parted ways, we did. Had a blazing row over her takin' my story." Lloyd got the barman's attention for another pint. "But I did a little investigatin' and found that Maxwell Slater—my waster of a boss—is an acquaintance of Richard Galbraith, and this same Richard Galbraith is well known to my sources in Scotland Yard as bein' right up there in the Foreign Office. In fact"—he leaned in further—"quite possibly in the intelligence line."

"Intelligence? Do you mean to say spying?"

"Too bloody right." By the look on the baron's face, gone stiff and pasty, he had him now. There was nothin' the gentry hated quite so much as bein' taken for fools. "What utter nonsense!" Coslett said. But he wasn't convincing.

"Maybe so, maybe not. But seems my former boss got a call some weeks ago from a highly placed official—the selfsame Richard Galbraith—and after this conversation, Slater takes me off the story and puts her on. And before you know it, she's got an appointment with you, like I had. So, the *Register* runs the story, all regular-like, because Tavistock *is* a reporter, though bear in mind, one that's been *sacked* from certain establishments. But now, what with her sideline, she's investigatin' you, or Ancient Light, and nosin' around for a cockup or whatever it is you're tryin' to hide."

The baron didn't care for the allegation, because he sat

back, narrowing his eyes. "You'd be well advised not to say these things in public. It won't go well for you." Coslett looked out the window, as though the Tavistock woman might be lurking around the pub.

"I haven't said anything. Just to you. I took offense at her making a balls-up of a noble profession, and I thought you might want to know."

A fresh pint appeared before him, and the baron brought out a new coin, which disappeared into the barman's apron pocket.

Coslett's mouth curved into a sneer. "No doubt you expect me to pay you for this information."

"I don't want your money. I just want to set the record straight. And you can do with it what you will."

The baron stood up. "I have nothing to hide. But if what you say is true, it was good of you to let me know." He paused. "Please allow me to cover the expense of your trip." He reached into his jacket.

"I didn't come for your money."

"But you'll take it?"

He set down ten quid on the table. Then he turned and practically fled through the crowd to the door.

2:10 PM. At last, just as Idelle turned away from the grave, Alice approached.

"I couldn't help but notice the lovely statue. Exquisite. I hope you don't mind my saying so." Idelle would not speak, so she must act as though she didn't notice this.

"How tenderly the sculptor caught the emotions of loss. I'm sure it's a consolation to many who come to St. Albans." Alice nodded to the grave where she had been lurking. "I've lost a dear friend. It's very difficult to bear."

Idelle looked at her with what might be a flicker of compassion.

"Her name was Flory. That's not a name you hear every day, is it?"

Alice hoped Idelle would not check out the name on the grave, but she needn't have worried, because Idelle had gone so still she looked like statuary.

"I hope I didn't upset you," Alice continued. "You don't know a *Flory*, do you?"

The old woman's eyes widened, shining hard and dark. As the two of them locked gazes, Idelle's face trembled, as though she were trying to hold something inside her, the memory that she could not release, could never tell.

Idelle backed up, shaking her head, as though to say, *No, no, I mustn't say.*

But she had already said all that was needed. Because she was leaving something behind: a full-color, exquisitely detailed *trauma view*.

Alice saw: *A young girl, perhaps eleven or twelve years old, standing in a cavernous hall built of stone. Beside her, an enormous darkened fireplace, and above, a coat of arms in yellow and green. From an upper gallery, some thirty feet away, someone was watching. The girl had said her name was Flory Soames, run away from the orphanage, and they had taken her in for the night, half-starving and covered in filth and brambles.*

Bending over the girl was a solidly built woman dressed in widow's black. She had pinned the girl onto the floor with her knee. In her hand was a broad knife. Panicking, the observer—Idelle Coslett—ran down the corridor, and then down the stone stairs. She rushed into the hall, colliding with the woman in black, who still held the knife, now bloody. "Dorothea, no!" The shout filled the great hall, but it was too late. The girl lay dead. Idelle pulled the great hunting knife from the girl's breast.

Idelle knelt beside the child, rocking on the bloodied floor, saying "No, no, no . . ."

Dorothea Coslett watched as the blood pooled. Then she retrieved a wheelbarrow from the recesses of the hall. Together, they lifted the body and placed it inside.

Out of the great hall they went, Dorothea pushing the wheelbarrow, and Idelle opening the oak doors, her thoughts slamming into each other. The girl dead, the knife in her chest, the blood . . . They maneuvered the wheelbarrow down the stairs, almost dumping the body when they lost control for a moment. Once in the yard, the barrow's wheel lost traction in the mud, and they both had to push. After an eternity, they rolled it to the edge of the cliff. It was very dark, but Idelle heard the body slide out of the pan. The girl fell like a stone angel. Down, down, into the pounding sea.

Dorothea turned to her and said, as calm as could be: "You can never tell. You understand that, don't you?"

Idelle looked into the hated face, but she didn't answer. She would never speak again.

As someone approached, Alice shook off her vision. A man walked toward them from the footpath beside the church. Powell Coslett. Entranced by the *trauma view*, Alice hadn't noticed the car pull up and park on the street.

Idelle saw and went to join him.

Alice drifted to the headstone she had pretended belonged to someone named Flory. She hadn't known that Flory Soames was dead. She had just used the grave as a pretext to bring up the name. But now she knew: Flory Soames was indeed dead. Slain without mercy by Dorothea Coslett.

From a few feet away, Powell Coslett regarded Alice for a

few seconds, then took Idelle by the elbow and led her to the car. He seemed in a great hurry as he handed the old woman into the car and sped away.

But Alice was already rushing back to her lodging to make a telephone call to Owen. Kim must be put on alert. The old woman had killed a girl; it made her a stronger suspect than ever, of course. And Kim must be warned to stay on her guard.

The lady of the castle was truly the bloody red baroness.

32

2:20 PM. Kim slipped the key into the door of Powell's room, and the tumblers gave way. With a stitch in her chest, she knew that this was the room that Idelle meant for her to be in. She entered.

The bow of the turret commanded the far side of the room. Tall windows framed views of the sea, blue and silky and stretching forever. A cushioned window seat nestled into the curved wall.

On the oversized bed lay a coverlet embroidered with the family emblem. Two button leather arm chairs, a writing table, the massive wardrobe, a faded Turkish rug. In a quick glance she took it all in, remembering her training. The surface things first, the secrets hiding in plain sight.

If Idelle was acting rationally—and of course she might not be—there was something in the room that she meant Kim to see. She wished that Idelle had given her more information, even if it was in writing, but perhaps the arcane clues were an expression of ambivalence. Perhaps she feared what it would mean for her. Or for Powell, whom she genuinely appeared to love.

Kim quickly took stock of what lay in the open: a discarded tweed jacket, books cast aside here and there, and on a crowded desk, letters and sheets of writing paper. The topmost letter was to a solicitor regarding bills. Another was to an acquaintance or member of Ancient Light thanking him for hospitality. In cubbyholes of the desk, she flipped through envelopes of correspondence. It was odd to think of Powell having this many friends to write to, but glancing at the contents, Kim realized they were letters from Ancient Light admirers. They might be evidence of *attraction*, in Powell's mind.

Turning to the chests of drawers, she pulled drawers open, some on old and uneven tracks. She probed through stacks of sweaters, socks, vests.

At the armoire, the doors squeaked dreadfully and would not remain open. Shouldering one of them aside, she pawed through jackets, suits, formal wear, and starched shirts, patting the pockets and releasing a faint whiff of Powell's cologne.

What could she expect to find? Suspicious train ticket stubs, perhaps: Portsmouth, Stourbridge, Avebury. Or notes from Talon: *Meet me in Cambridgeshire. . . .* She closed the armoire. Pulling out the bottom drawer, she found a woman's shawl and a small box containing a set of pearl earrings. A photograph of a young woman standing on the terrace with a twenty-five-year-old Powell. So, this was Margret. Where was she now? Scared off by Dorothea before Powell could bestow these gifts. She scraped the doors back into place, wincing at the sound.

In growing frustration, she stood in the center of the room. *Idelle. Just tell me. Just tell me.*

A bookcase in the corner. Dozens of books; she could not riffle through them all. Two shelves were given over to Powell's own creation, *Earth Powers*.

How long had she been here? It was 2:34. Fourteen minutes. It felt like an hour.

The window seat drew her attention. On closer inspection, the facing, trimmed out as five separate panels, appeared to be freshly painted compared to the yellowed walls. Kneeling down, Kim ran her hand along the edges of the trim, tugging. The middle one sprang open on hidden hinges.

Pulling it fully open, she found a compartment. Inside was a metal box some fifteen inches high and ten wide. On its front panel were dials, a toggle switch, and meters. Ventilation louvers pierced the sides.

She sat back on her heels, heart racing. A wireless transmitter. Powell wasn't a ham radio operator, or he wouldn't have hidden it.

He was communicating with his handlers.

He had means to signal—likely Germany—and was keen to hide it. Although she had expected to find something, the discovery of the transmitter galvanized her. She reached into the recess but found nothing more, nor could she open the other panels. She closed the compartment door and stood up.

The room was very still, the only sound the thud of waves pounding on the headland, perhaps enough to muffle the sound of a scrape on the stairs if someone was coming.

To stay too long risked losing everything, and she now knew about the transmitter. Very damning. Still, she wasn't satisfied.

Her gaze swept over the bed with its coverlet bearing the Coslett sigil. They were proud of the symbol, though it was no true coat of arms. The dogwood blossom, the curl of symbolic

waves. The three swords jutted from the stylized castle, pointing outward.

What was it that Dorothea had said? *People are besotted with
stones and barrows. But they're all connected by the sacred ground.*

Connected. Something flickered half-seen in Kim's mind. She
mentally reached out toward it. *Connected by sacred ground.* All
connected. So, it wasn't only hills and henges and barrows that
were important but what lay between them. The lines between.

Well, what of it? The murders were all over the countryside. What kinds of lines could be drawn? In her imagination,
she concentrated on the map of England, but it truly did not
seem . . .

She looked at the bedspread again. Staring at the Coslett
emblem, her view softened, and the design lost its simple, even
crude layout. It became a mute message, trying to speak.

The dogwood. That was for earth. The waves. For the sea.
Sitting between, the castle. Human habitation. The center of
spiritual life. And from that powerful node, the swords piercing.
But they had a direction, pointing away. Where did they lead?

She was out the door and heading down the spiral staircase
before she had quite decided to move. Reaching the landing, she
pushed into her room, shutting the door behind her, locking it.

Leaning against the door, she closed her eyes, her mind
snatching at insights before they evaporated. She knew what she
needed, though. A map. She was in most acute need of a map
of England. What were the chances there would be one in the
room? Surely, a book with a handy representation of England?
But there was no bookcase, nor were there books lying about.
No handy basket full of tourist information.

Except. By God, there *was* a map. It was in her LNER timetable with its helpful map of the railway lines of Britain.

She snatched the timetable from the nightstand and turned to the page with the map of the British Isles. Holding the booklet open by placing the bedside lamp on the spine, she made a dark dot with her pen on the location of Sulcliffe Castle. Then central London. The approximate spot along the River Ouse in Cambridgeshire where murder number two occurred. Stourbridge, number five. Avebury, number three. Portsmouth, number one.

She had packed her copy of Powell's *Earth Powers*. It would do for a straightedge. Laying the book edge next to her dot indicating Sulcliffe Castle in north Wales, she drew a line from there to the murder site in Cambridgeshire near the town of Ely.

That done, she was rather crestfallen. It was a line with two points. It meant nothing. You could connect any two points in the world by a line. But she had four more sites to go.

Keeping the book edge fixed on the location of Sulcliffe Castle, she pivoted the edge until it connected to London.

A frisson of amazement passed through her. The line to London intersected Stourbridge. She knew, then, what the third line would show.

Again, she kept the straightedge at Sulcliffe and found Avebury. She drew a line connecting the two points and extended it to the south of England. Straight into Portsmouth.

She had three lines spreading out from Wales, pointing directly at the sites of the five attacks.

Turning the map so that Sulcliffe was at the top, and the lines she had drawn pointed down, it matched the trajectories of the swords on the Coslett emblem.

For several minutes, she sat on the edge of the bed staring at the map. One reason no one had seen this before was that one was accustomed to seeing England with Scotland at the top and the English Channel at the bottom. Once you turned the map, the lines from Sulcliffe were obviously the same as on the family shield.

Someone was killing young people along lines that, beginning at Sulcliffe, connected places of imagined power. It was no proof, but in her mind everything was falling into place. Was Powell the killer and working with a second man, an accomplice? Were ritual killings how an earth worshipper might hope to receive the power to lead?

She lay the timetable down on the nightstand, closing it. The castle emblem. It had been in front of her everywhere: reproduced on the flatware, monogrammed on pockets, hanging over the fire pit in the great hall that was never used. Her heart thumped loudly in her chest. She had to tell someone about this in case something happened to her, but the phone was dead, and she was without a car. To spend another night here was out of the question, unless she could tell someone—Alice, Owen, *someone*—what she had learned.

The conspiracy would surely all come unraveled now. The Cosletts would be questioned, and the truth at last could be tracked down.

She had taken Idelle's key from her pocket and was gripping it rather hard. When she opened her hand, an imprint of the key remained in her palm. Idelle's key had unlocked more than just the room. She must have known that Powell communicated using a wireless. Idelle slipped around the castle, silently, often dismissed as incompetent, but sometimes keenly aware of what went on.

A click in the lock of her bedroom door.

Kim dropped Idelle's key on the carpet and kicked it under the bed.

Turning, she saw Lady Ellesmere standing on the threshold. Behind her stood Donald and Royce, red-haired Donald looking cross indeed, and Royce as though he were terribly disappointed in her.

Her shoulder bag with her gun lay on the table across the room.

She stood up, marshalling her lies, her witless innocence, her cunning.

"Lady Ellesmere," she said.

PART IV

BURNING BRIGHT

33

3:15 PM. "We can get you out. If I signal them now, they can have a boat here tonight."

Dries had heard Coslett's report with growing alarm, but Coslett himself was subdued for a man who had murdered and now was attracting the attention of the police or the security service.

"But how much do they know?" Dries asked. He did not like retreating in the face of an English advance. He would rather continue to outwit them.

"They know enough to investigate us! They are gathering evidence, they've planted an informer, a spy in our midst! They'll find out everything. I want you out of here."

"Baron, you must calm yourself." The police *would* find out everything if Coslett fell apart. "They have not found me. If they had anything, they would storm the castle!"

Coslett stared at him as though seeing him in a new way. A most unfavorable one. "It was never true, was it? My gift. It isn't coming, is it?"

Why not abandon pretense? Coslett had lost the will to continue and would be a liability in his present state. "Alas. I do not see evidence. There were times I thought that I did. But no, you are right."

Coslett closed his eyes for a moment, absorbing this confirmation of what must be his worst fear. How much did he blame Dries for their needless enterprise? Of course, it was needless only to Coslett. To Dries, it had been of the essence.

The baron steadied himself with a hand on the back of the overstuffed chair, shaking his head, to and fro, to and fro. "I knew you were a monster, I knew," came his hoarse voice.

"*Ach*, more than you, sir?"

The distraught fellow turned on him, staggering forward a few steps. "Yes, more than me! You lied to us. We never would have done this if it hadn't been for the 'flickers of light' you saw around me, my powers waiting to flood in! Lies, oh lies . . ." He looked bleakly at Dries, perhaps hoping, even now, that they were not lies.

Dries could not afford to alienate the man. "You must remember that Hitler believes you have done the Third Reich a great service: the damage done to British morale, the fear instilled in people to register as Talents. If war comes, it will have been a critical operation." A small lie. Himmler would have preferred adult targets here.

But it was though the baron had not even listened. "We are finished here," he said. His words were dispassionate, as though the man were speaking of other people's lives and not his own, disfigured fate. "You must leave tonight."

Dries was being sent away. Well. He could not work here without the Cosletts' support. And it had been grand while it had lasted. To his surprise he felt a smattering of regret that he had used Coslett so. "Perhaps, Powell, you should get out, too."

"No. Never mind about me." It did not seem to have sunk in that if he feared the authorities would uncover it all, then he was in danger of hanging. Coslett looked around the room as though trying and failing to find something to hold on to. He sank into the overstuffed chair. "She lied to me."

Ach. So that was it. The girl. He had—how did they say?—*fallen for her.*

"*Godverdomme,* man. She has been trying to put your neck in a noose!"

Ignoring this, Coslett said, "I haven't told Mother that you'll leave. She's in high temper right now."

"*Will* you tell her?"

Coslett stared at the floor. "I wish we had never done these things."

"If it is over, then it is over. One must be philosophical." Coslett had been the perfect dupe for the intelligence service, or the Security Service or whoever the woman worked for. "You are heartbroken, of course. The future wife, your chance for happiness."

"She was never that. She was . . ." Coslett's words ran out.

"A spy, alas."

"There was something about her. . . ." He shook his head. "When the fellow from the newspaper called this morning, wanting to meet me, saying it was about Kim, I had a bad feeling. I disabled the phone. A bad feeling about her."

"It is an old trick, Baron, using a woman to lower the defense. Did she offer to come to your bed?"

"No." A frown of disgust.

That he could find it within his murderous heart to be offended by a salacious remark was so *British*.

"Well, then. You must make the call for the ship. Perhaps we should lose no time."

Coslett rose from the chair, squaring his shoulders. "They'll wait for you in deep water. A small boat will approach but stay out beyond the surf. You will have to swim. That was the plan." He looked at his watch. "Once I signal them, they will need at least six hours to move into position. Hide in the cove if you think the cabin is too exposed."

Dries sighed. The operation was over, then, truly. "So. What will you do with her?"

"Do?"

"With your reporter."

"When I get back, Mother and I will decide." His haunted look belied his upper-crust composure.

As Coslett moved to the door, Dries said, "You should come with me. Our German friends would welcome you."

He did not answer, slipping out of the cabin.

Dries had a long wait ahead of him. He began collecting his things, slipping them into a rucksack. Calmer now, he admitted to himself he had grown disenchanted with the British killings. It had been different when Himmler had asked him to undertake the mission. But his conversation with the old woman yesterday had soured him on the enterprise. He did not like, did not at all like, for her to prescribe his methods: no churches, no stone circles. It exposed his essential dilemma: how could one take revenge on the British *for* the British?

† † †

SULCLIFFE CASTLE

3:20 PM. As Kim stood up to face her, Lady Ellesmere closed the door.

"I thought you would be down at the fair," the dowager said. "How odd that you have spent so much time at the castle, when the activities are all on the field."

A surge of anxiety yanked at her chest. "Oh, I was just leaving to join the festivities."

"Were you? We did wonder where you had gotten off to. I gave a little speech at the stone ring. I'm afraid you missed it." She came farther into the room and sat on the edge of the bed. This brought her rather too near the LNER timetable. Kim sank into a chair, bracing for the worst.

"What is it, exactly," Lady Ellesmere said with elaborate politeness, "that you are looking for here?"

"I don't know what you mean."

"Is the name Lloyd Nichols familiar to you?"

Her mind racing, Kim tried to think how the reporter from the *Register* could be a problem. "He's a former reporter for the *London Register*."

"So I gather. Unfortunately for you, he has been investigating your involvement with the Earth Mysteries assignment."

"Has he? In what way?"

"Mr. Nichols tells us that you are working for the authorities. In fact, that you are acting at the behest of the intelligence service."

Kim struggled to look perplexed instead of chagrined. "He's trying to make trouble for me, then. I got the assignment he wanted, you know."

"Oh, he has definitely made trouble for you. He has brought facts to our attention, quite convincing facts."

"Facts? What facts? Lloyd Nichols is a drunk and has threatened me. Surely you're not going to listen to someone like that!" What, she wondered, could Nichols possibly know?

"Young lady. I do not wish to discuss your loathsome little charade any further. We believe him. That is all you need to know. My instinct told me that you were hiding something. I should have listened to it."

She was exposed at some level, but perhaps not in conjunction with Crossbow. Coslett might be thrown off the scent if Kim claimed she was investigating something else. Because if the woman thought it was the youth murders, she might not let her leave.

"All right," Kim said. "I have come on false pretenses." The baroness drew herself up, eyes hateful. "You are being investigated for banking and tax fraud with Ancient Light revenues. We have already assembled a mountain of evidence, so sending me away won't be the end of it."

The dowager regarded Kim with lofty disdain. "It is an outrage that you have been sent here under a false flag. My solicitor shall be apprised of your tactics, and there will be swift consequences." She heaved herself to her feet. "You will pack your things immediately. I will have the car brought around when Awbrey comes back from his supply errand in the village. Until then, I must ask you to stay in your room." She made her way slowly to the door, the shaking of her hand on the cane the only disturbance to her bearing.

At the door, she turned. "I *told* Powell that you were not our sort. Breeding always rings true."

As Lady Ellesmere left the room, Kim saw that Donald was standing guard outside.

Her mouth had gone dry. She was being kicked out, and all

because of Lloyd Nichols. Somehow the man had penetrated the operation at least to the extent of divining a connection between the *Register* and . . . what? How could he know there was a connection to the *authorities*, much less the intelligence service? She didn't think they would hurt her. If they thought she was with the police or the intelligence service, they would not dare.

At least, she acutely hoped so. She pulled in a few steadying breaths. Coslett had said she would be sent away. It would be all right. At the bedside, she reached underneath, finding Idelle's key. Opening the window a crack, she let it fall.

That done, she replayed in her mind the uncomfortable scene with Lady Ellesmere. The old woman had given a splendid performance in self-righteousness and wounded faith.

But if Kim's part of the operation must end early, at least it had happened after her visit to Powell's room. The lines of the swords in the castle emblem: not proof, by a long measure. But the Sulcliffe Castle symbol was used in orchestrating the murders. Someone with the Coslett family or Ancient Light wanted the murders to reinforce those sword lines. And though it was a breakthrough, she wanted so much more.

But she knew the old woman could hardly wait to see her gone.

THE SULCLIFFE ESTATE

3:25 PM. Dries had been stalking the boy for several minutes. He had gone to the cliffs to look at the beach in the clarity of daylight and had noted the steep descent that he would have to make in the dark. It was a question of whether he should go to the beach now when he could see his path more clearly, or wait.

Then, leaning against a stunted tree that afforded some camouflage from observation, he noted that on the cliffs some half-mile away, someone was standing. It looked like a young man.

And he shone.

For a few moments Dries stood in the shelter of the tree and stared. It was a beautiful thing, this dance of light that sprang forth even in the bright sunlight. A thing he loved to see. *Ach.* He had known this for a truth throughout the long years. One could not keep one's eyes from the halo of power.

And *this* halo. It was the strongest he had seen since arriving in England.

Dries slowly made his way back the way he had come. He must return to the cabin to collect his things. What he had in mind was daring, perhaps foolish, but he knew he would do it.

Once inside the hut, he uncapped the jar of chloroform and soaked a cloth with it, jamming it into the right-hand pocket of the jacket Coslett had brought him. The plan had come to him in a moment, fully formed. First, overpower the boy. He was skinny and would be no trouble. Then, after dark, and one last time in Britain, he would perform the act of revenge. To do so here at Sulcliffe, Dorothea's complicity would be strongly suggested, even proven. It would give this last slaying a particular sweetness.

It would have to be timed exactly. The body left in a location on the estate where it would be sure to be discovered: the stone circle in the field. He would need cover of darkness. And also, it must not be too early, lest the police come and, searching, find him. Nor could it be so late that afterward he had not enough time to rendezvous with the ship.

Dangerous, yes. But with any luck, by the time they found the boy, he would be at sea, on his way to Germany.

Of course, he would have to ask for Himmler's forgiveness for betraying the baroness. One did not go against such a master, but they needed him in France and Poland, did they not? Himmler's displeasure would be the worst of it. It gave him pause. Then he chuckled. The old serpent deserved this; it would be the perfect farewell.

Back in the woods, he made his way down a slope to a gully between the jutting rocks, then up the other side to the outcropping where he had seen the boy.

No one stood on the bald cliffs. Dotting the headland here and there were crooked firs, some lying almost horizontal from coastal storms. These gave way to long grasses bending in the wind, and then, in a glen below, a stand of trees.

Between the black trunks, light moved. Dries skidded down the embankment, following.

He was still a hundred yards away when the boy turned around. Dries waved, and with this friendly gesture, he was able to approach. It was remarkable: the face and hands sheathed in a muted, pulsing light. Underneath the light, the dark hair, the thin face on a neck with a prominent Adam's apple.

"Are you from the fair?" Dries asked. "I imagine you are. I, too."

"I was just looking around," the boy said, in the manner of someone who'd been caught at trespassing. He squinted as the sun shone into his eyes through a gap in the trees.

"A fine day for a walk. My name is Dries. And you?"

He hesitated. "Martin."

"Where are your parents, Martin?"

"I'm old enough to be here by myself. I'm eighteen."

He was much younger than that. But how excellent if he did not have parents who would search for him.

"I will walk back with you, then," Dries said. He stepped a

few paces closer. A mistake. The boy looked into his face and instantly knew his peril.

The youngster made a savage turn to flee, but even as he did so, Dries whipped the reeking cloth out of his pocket. He wrapped his free arm around the boy's chest, imprisoning one of his arms. With the free arm flailing, the boy struggled, trying to thrust up a knee. After a few moments of struggle, he weakened, allowing Dries to aim the rag squarely over his nostrils. He sank against Dries, still managing a muffled scream.

Dries laid him out on the ground and knelt for a few minutes, catching his breath. His wounded shoulder ached terribly from where the boy had hit him in the struggle. Looking up the hillock toward the cabin, Dries steeled himself for the labor of carrying his prize.

He not only had to make it to the cabin but then, under cover of darkness, to get to the stone circle. He should be able to enter it without anyone noticing; from his observations of the fair, people did not usually enter the circle except for ritual events. It was also very close to the line of trees at the edge of the field.

He heaved the boy onto his good shoulder and with a mighty effort stood up and lurched away through the woods.

34

3:30 PM. Gustaw Bajek's first experience of London was only three hours old, but so far it had been exemplary. The British intelligence service had thoughtfully directed him to the Lamb and Flag pub, where he was now enjoying a pint of ale and the excellent Stilton pork pie.

He had not eaten since setting sail from Calais and was just tucking into his meal when a man entered the pub, wearing a bowler hat and with a book under his arm. At the bar, nursing a pint, he glanced from time to time at a good-looking woman at a table under the window. When he left, Gustaw followed him.

Within a few blocks the man in the bowler hat entered a fruit and vegetable market. Here on this minor street, dodging horse droppings from farmers' cart horses, Gustaw caught up to his contact as the man examined a cantaloupe for ripeness.

Without looking at him, the agent said, "We'll take the

underground, old boy. Stick close, we'll make a dash for it."
With that, they crossed through the market stalls and passed
under a round sign outlined in red. They descended into a
noisy rail station. Letting the first train pass, the man stood
well back. When the second train pulled in, he waited until all
the passengers had boarded. At the last moment, he slipped on,
Gustaw right behind him. Within two stops they alighted and
took a train in the opposite direction. Once at street level his
man hailed a taxicab. Gustaw thought it all rather elaborate for
an SIS meeting with a low-ranking Polish intelligence officer.

The cab swung through a warren of streets, the driver
expertly navigating a steady onslaught of cars, double-decker
buses and hairpin turns. Within a few miles they were headed
through the tree-lined North London suburbs, where eventually
the taxi deposited them in front of a white-painted home. The
paint had chipped, revealing the brick underneath.

"One of our best," the agent said, noting his passenger's gaze.

"I am honored," Gustaw dutifully responded.

The agent ushered him inside the house, redolent of good
pipe tobacco. The entry hall led to an empty dining room, and
then the parlor. Gustaw entered this room, where he found someone waiting for him.

Julian Tavistock sat smoking a pipe and reading the *Times*.
He stood up, nodding to dismiss the agent. "Monsieur Bajek,
good to see you again."

"Gustaw, I insist. And you, Julian, you are better dressed than
I remember."

Julian smiled. "Not my finest hour."

"It was a bad day for all of us."

A bottle of whisky on a sideboard. Julian brought three
glasses, Gustaw noted.

They chatted for a few minutes as they waited for the third glass.

Gustaw wondered if the room was wired to record. There was nothing he could do if it were except to leave, and he had already decided he would not do that. And, besides, if he asked if it was wired, Julian would be forced to lie about it, and he would rather it didn't come to that. A little trust was needed, now that they finally were on the right trail.

"You've come a long way," Julian said. "You said that you have news, important news for us."

"I do. Once I received your letter about the murders here, I knew I had to come. To tell you about a man called Dries Verhoeven." Nodding at the glasses, he said, "I will tell you when your company arrives."

Julian poured Gustaw a drink, and one for himself. Then he knocked the ashes out from his pipe and tucked it into his breast pocket. Whoever was coming did not like pipe smoke.

Swirling the fragrant liquid, Gustaw said, "I am sorry that *Nachteule* has come to England."

Julian flashed him a startled look. "Has it?"

"I believe your murders and mine are committed by the same man."

"By Christ. What makes you think so?"

They were interrupted by voices in the back hall. An aristocratic-looking man entered the parlor. Older than Julian, he was impeccably dressed, with a trim mustache and a long, patrician face. He cut a decidedly military figure, Gustaw thought.

"This is my associate, Richard Galbraith," Julian said. "Richard, Gustaw Bajek."

Gustaw rose and shook hands. This certainly was Julian's superior. He took the best chair, which Gustaw had left empty when he had first entered and noticed that Julian had not taken it.

Julian began, turning to Gustaw. "Your news is related to a possible common assassin for both sets of murders. . . ."

Richard Galbraith narrowed his eyes. Yes, they were most anxious to know. Julian went on. "Let me just say first that we now know that Dorothea Coslett personally murdered a child, although it was not one of the recent killings. I said in my letter that we have an asset in place at her residence in Wales."

Accepting a whisky from Julian, Galbraith said, "I understand we have you to thank for putting us on to Dorothea Coslett."

Gustaw nodded. It would have been helpful if they had returned the intelligence favor sooner, but why quibble? Here they all were.

"Up in Pengeylan," Julian went on, "a few miles from the Coslett estate, we've just managed to engage a member of the Coslett family for a *trauma view*. It was a stunner. The view disclosed that Dorothea Coslett murdered a youngster some years ago. Flory Soames. The memory was from her sister-in-law, who helped cover up the murder."

"By God," Galbraith said. "Our mystery girl was killed by the dowager baroness."

"Yes. She used a knife, rather brutally. Our *trauma view* asset thinks the dowager must have been some twenty years younger at the time. This intelligence came in about an hour ago."

"So, the old woman has committed at least one murder of a child." Galbraith shook his head. "Still . . ."

Julian looked at Gustaw. "Now, if you would tell us your side of things, Gustaw. We'd love to have a decent lead."

Gustaw took a sip of the very fine whisky, savoring it. "I believe what I have to say gives you at least partial answers. It began with you, Julian. The uncle of Tilda Mazur told you that a man had followed his niece, a man with a Dutch accent. And he knew about old dolls." Gustaw sighed. "We had talked to this same uncle, but he did not trust our intelligence service. Instead, he trusted *yours.*"

Galbraith shifted in his chair, uncomfortable. Of course, sending agents undercover against one's allies and getting caught was always awkward.

"I followed this small lead," Gustaw continued, "to Belgium. There are many repairers and makers of dolls, but one in particular stood out. His name is Dries Verhoeven. He was on holiday when I tracked him to Beselare. He was not at home, but a villager who knows him well told me a clarifying story. Dries Verhoeven is an individual with a special Talent, one we have never seen before. He perceives those with Talents."

Silence, as the two men looked at him in some skepticism.

"I am saying that he can see them, you understand. They are as clear to him as a lamp that has been turned on."

"By Christ," Galbraith murmured.

"How do you know?" Julian said. "People claim things."

"Yes, but it is common knowledge in his village. As a youth he got in trouble over it. The villager, an old woman, told me they call it *aura sight.* In fact, she said, his eyes themselves are odd, even deformed. A crooked light." He shrugged. "So it is said.

"During the war there was a great crime in this village. The British shelled a school, deliberately, having had word that the school was a front to hide military ordnance. It was no front, only a school. Many children died. Verhoeven and his mother, a teacher there, almost escaped, but when she threatened to expose their bombing of the school, British soldiers killed her in front of her son." He saw that he had their rapt attention. "So, you see, Verhoeven is not just following German orders, he has a personal stake here in England: revenge."

He ended by telling them that there had been no new deaths of military Talents since the middle of July. "The youth murders began shortly after?"

"They did," Julian said. He glanced at Galbraith. "We have the man's identity, then. Dries Verhoeven. And we know at last how he identified Talents here." He shook his head wonderingly. "He can *see* them."

Galbraith nodded. Gustaw could almost see the man's mind trying to work it all through. It was a break, but they might still be a long way from capture.

Julian said, "If the killer is the same for both sets of murders, then the English deaths are, what, a sideline to the German *Nachteule* plot?"

"This is my belief," Gustaw said. "Perhaps Monsieur Verhoeven says to his Nazi handlers that he will continue working for them, but he would like to include the English in the list of targets, and young people, in order to avenge the young who died at Beselare." He shrugged. "Perhaps he soon comes back to Poland and carries on the true Nazi purpose."

"Or, it might not have come from Verhoeven," Julian said, "though he was happy to participate. Suppose that Dorothea Coslett, knowing highly placed Nazi officials and having some particulars of the *Nachteule* operation and its prized assassin, begs to have Verhoeven for a couple of months. For her own purposes. The Germans, in no hurry, indulge her."

That surprised Gustaw. "What purposes could the woman have?"

"Power," Julian responded. "And a demented belief that killing innocents at key places will accrue power to the slayer." He must have noted Gustaw's incredulous look, because he went on. "Dorothea Coslett is deeply involved in a spiritualism cult. It has taken a turn down a very dark path. Her son, Powell Coslett, is a man looking for his Talent—which Ancient Light believes is a gift of the earth itself. In some kind of mystical sense."

Gustaw shook his head. The world was going mad again. Sacrificing youngsters. It was not only the Nazis whose theories were unhinged.

Julian looked at Galbraith. "We go into Sulcliffe for an open investigation?"

His boss shook his head. "The circumstantial evidence is compelling. But we have nothing hard. Your theory of key places tying the murders together . . . You have no telling pattern in the geography. That aspect remains for now sheer conjecture, Julian. But we do have two things to help us make a case: Verhoeven's motive: the murder of his mother and the schoolchildren. As well that the baroness was funding murders in Poland and France and committed one herself, though some time ago."

Gustaw was astonished at this temerity. "The facts so far are surely strong enough to question Dorothea Coslett."

Galbraith shook his head. "Unfortunately, *trauma view* would not be admissible in court."

"It would not?" Gustaw asked.

"The British justice system has not quite accepted visions."

"For now, I want to put Sparrow on alert," Julian told his superior. "This is not just a fishing expedition anymore. She could well be in a nest of vipers."

Galbraith said, "Perhaps pull her out."

"At this point we need her on-site more than ever. They aren't likely to harm a reporter on assignment. But she should

be put on her guard that there is at least some chance that the
assassin is hiding at Sulcliffe."

Gustaw interjected, "He is?"

"More conjecture," Julian's boss said.

"Perhaps," Julian said. "But what better place to recuperate
from his wounds?"

"He is wounded?" Gustaw was trying very hard to keep up.

"Yes. The latest victim survived and his father got off a
lucky shot." Julian glanced at Galbraith. "We've not had a call-in
from Sparrow today. Telephone service is out at the castle, but
not elsewhere in the vicinity. They might have severed outside
communication."

"All right," Galbraith said. "Take a team with you and put
Sparrow in the picture. If all is well, we leave her in place.
Meanwhile, I'll bring what we have to the Secretary"—he glanced
at Gustaw—"of the Foreign Office. He'll be gone by the time I get
back, but first thing in the morning."

He stood. "I warn you, what we have so far is highly suspicious but may not be convincing up the line. Let's hope that the
threat of another adolescent murder will be enough to let us
investigate the Cosletts."

Julian rose as well. "My people can be on the train within
the hour."

His boss paused to consider. "Your cover, Julian. A bit of a
problem there."

"I can stay out of sight. I'll think of something."

Gustaw was losing the thread, but it was their show.

Galbraith gave the slightest of resigned shrugs. He and
Julian seemed to have a shorthand way of communicating. Well.
The ranks of British intelligence were famous for their tight-
knit, essential English character, all belonging to the same clubs,

attending the same colleges, and drinking at the same bars. These two had been members of the intelligence clique for a good number of years, he guessed.

As they prepared to leave, Gustaw interjected, "If I may, I would like to come along. In case of trouble, another person to back you up." Julian's superior gave an almost-imperceptible shake of the head. "We are allies," Gustaw said. They could bend the rules.

"If it were up to me," Julian said.

Gustaw was genuinely disappointed. He thought the English were on the verge of finding the assassin, and if so, he longed to be there.

"Bring Verhoeven to justice, Julian," he said. And even though he knew the English had their own wounds, he added, "For Tilda Mazur."

Julian gave a solemn nod. "She is not forgotten."

35

4:00 PM. Powell returned the wireless to its cubbyhole. It had taken his German handlers a half hour to find a ship within reach of the north coast of Wales, but he had his answer. A boat would approach the cove at 9:10 that night.

He closed and locked his door. Then he made his way down the winding staircase, his mind reeling.

Thank God at least Verhoeven would be gone soon. The Verhoeven nightmare. The one that Powell himself had helped create. Oh God, he couldn't bear to think of it.

But he did think of it; it was all he could think of. The boy by the river; the youngster in Portsmouth. And the girls, the young girls, the horror of their corpses . . . Had it not been for Verhoeven! The man had not killed for Hitler; it had been a pleasure to him, Powell was convinced of it. To put out the lights. He should have known, should have known. . . .

At the bottom of the turret stairs he hesitated. He could go to Kim's room now, to confront her, to get it over with. But he couldn't bear to. Even though it had never been mutual with Kim, not as it had been with Margret, still, he shrank from seeing her, seeing the true Kim, the one who had fooled him.

He found himself standing at the entrance to the chapel. The gouged walls, the ruin of the decorative pilasters. It was a fitting emblem of what his life had become. He was a defaced soul, a man whose conscience had slowly leached away, year by year, entrapped by the desire, the need, to be worthy. And at the end? A man whom every person would despise.

He went in. Going to the remains of the altar, he knelt. Did he even know how to pray? Closing his eyes, he found within himself a silent, quiet place, not quite a place where God might visit, but it was all he had. Gone was his chance to carry on Ancient Light. Gone forever, his peace. It had all been for nothing, the blood, the ghastly expressions of the dying, the sickening danger of discovery. All for nothing, nothing. He covered his face with his hands, trying to keep the chattering, harpy thoughts from continuing their assault.

Time passed. The cold of the stony room seeped into him, a welcome lethargy descending. He looked up at the scored and chiseled walls. Though he was now without hope, he had found a silent, internal place that exerted a strong pull on him. How strange for emptiness to provide such comfort.

And now, there were things he still had to do.

When he stood, he found that his mother was standing in the chapel doorway. She seemed fully in command, as always. Just as she had been when he had told her about the newspaperman's revelations.

"I have never found that God answers prayers," she said.

Standing in the doorway of the chapel, she looked like a

stone effigy. He could discern no humanity in her. "Sometimes you ask anyway."

"Have you said your goodbyes to her?"

"Not yet."

"It may be a mistake to let her go. Who knows what she's learned with all her snooping here? We could wait for dark, then a slip on the cliff edge. Easily explained."

Even with all he had seen of death, the idea horrified him. "No, no. I forbid it."

"*You* forbid?"

"Yes! Yes, I do. I would report you myself."

Indignant, she drew herself up. "Ridiculous. Listen to yourself!"

Had he only listened to himself, and not her. "She will leave this afternoon. But first, I have something I must do." He fixed her with a stare. "I do want to say goodbye to her. You won't begrudge me that."

She shook her head. "When will you get over being so dependent on these women?"

These women? There had only been a few. But his mother's reality and his own had always been far different.

She came closer. "What is it that you think you have to do?"

"Arrange for the next phase."

"Phase?"

"A German U-boat will pick up Verhoeven in five hours."

Her startled reaction gave way to incredulity. "Pick him up? But why?" She shook her head. "You radioed them. By God, you did. But why, why on earth, Powell? We have more we must do. We're not done!" She came forward to rest a hand on his arm.

He stepped back, avoiding her touch. "But we are done." Getting Verhoeven away had assumed an urgency in his mind. When he was gone, it would truly be over.

He thought of telling her that he had no gift, had never even been close, but the shame of it kept him silent. "I'm calling an end to it." He walked past her, throwing off her outstretched hand.

She followed him, hobbling, the cane surely ready to break beneath her weight. "Powell, what are you thinking? You mustn't give up!"

He turned, wearily. There was no way to avoid all the things that were coming. "What am I thinking? I'm thinking that I have wasted my life. I'm thinking that I should have married Margret and left you to your besotted followers. I could be living with her now in a cozy little cottage. Sussex, perhaps. As far from you as I could get." Watching her incredulous expression, he thought how affronted she must be to hear him renounce her. That she could be outraged, pretend to be injured, left him shaking. "It's a rather large thought, so I decided to pray about it."

She looked at him in consternation, as though she could not take his utterances seriously. She landed on one more familiar: "That dreadful woman married someone else."

"Yes. Well. There is that." He turned and strode away.

"You're not my son!" she shouted after him, her words echoing down the passageway. "You are not worthy!"

Well, he thought, *that was settled long ago.*

A CABIN, THE SULCLIFFE ESTATE

4:36 PM. Dries had not wanted Coslett to see the boy. He had opened the door just a little to hear his departure time. Tonight. 9:10.

But then the boy had thumped his feet against the floor, and Coslett had heard it.

"My God, man, what have you done?" Coslett said when he saw the boy.

Looking at the young man, bound, gagged and lying on the slatted wood floor, Dries thought it was rather obvious what he had done. "This one, he shines very brightly. If only you could see how they look! After a while, when you have been killing them, you are fascinated by how the light seeps away at the end."

"You can't do this! It needs to be over!"

Oh yes, Powell was upset. And how much more upset he would be if he knew Dries's plan to slash the youngster's throat in the midst of the Ancient Light camp. On Dorothea's property, so untidy for her ladyship, who wished to come away from all this with clean hands.

"You can't kill another one," Powell moaned.

"But I can. I have plenty of time before the 9:10 boat."

"I told you we were done!"

"*Ach.* So you did, so you did." He turned his gaze back to the boy cringing and lighting up his corner of the cabin. "But then I met Martin. And I could not resist."

The baron looked at him in new alarm. "Martin? Good Christ!" He rushed to the boy and began tugging at his ropes. Dries charged at him, yanking him away. A surge of strength seemed to come over Coslett, and in a mighty heave he flung Dries back, sending him sprawling into the table.

"*Fok!*" Dries cried. He grabbed the scalpel from the table and rushed back at Coslett, smashing his foot into the man's side. Coslett toppled. When he looked up, Dries was standing over him with the knife.

"Don't be foolish," Dries said. He gestured Coslett to move away.

Slowly, he complied. The boy was watching all this, fully alert, eyes huge.

Dries said, "What difference does one more make?"

The baron spat out, "Because now it is for no *purpose*."

"You mean no purpose for you, now that your gift will not arrive. That is true. Your game is over. But mine, you see, is not." He looked back at the boy. "Mine is never over."

Coslett whispered in a harsh, ragged voice, "What is it you want?"

"I wish my enemies to know what it is to suffer."

"Is this boy's family your enemy?"

"Yes. They are British."

"*I* am British," Coslett threw at him. "Will you kill *me*?"

Dries threw the scalpel onto the table. "*Ga nau!*" Come on! "Of course not you. But get out before I change my mind." They stared at each other for a moment, the baron's face pale as milk, glistening in sweat. "Don't try to bring anyone to rescue him; it will be too late. The game is in motion now. We must play it to the end."

Coslett's anguished face gave Dries pause. He needed some hope that life was not over. "You could flee tonight, with me. The boat, Powell. Germany would welcome you." The man didn't seem to be listening. "Think about it. A new future, in a nation that would admire you."

Looking at the boy in the corner one last time, Coslett swung away and stalked through the door.

THE TRAIN TO PENGEYLAN, WALES

4:40 PM. "Eddie," Julian said, stopping by the table where Fin and Elsa sat. The train swayed and clacked as it sped through the countryside, the late-afternoon light knifing through the windows.

"And Violet," Julian went on. "You and your son off on holiday?" Yes, indeed. A good weekend, a bit of a late start, and would he join them at table, they pleaded. He did. If anyone Julian knew saw them, they were retainers of an old friend at a country estate in Hendon. While they were in the second-class dining car, it was only decent to sit with them for a meal, given their long acquaintance.

It was a lengthy slog to Wales. Three and a half hours. It might have been faster by car, especially if Elsa drove, but it would be less reliable. Punctures. Breakdowns. No, it had to be by train.

Julian had been wrong when he'd told E that the team could assemble in an hour. It had taken an hour and fifteen minutes. With the extra time, Elsa Rampling, alias Egret, had managed to acquire a tent. Fin Hewett, alias Dancer, had met them at Euston station with no luggage but having purchased the tickets, including a private compartment, first class, for Julian.

They didn't know the plan, for there wasn't one, but they knew where they were going: Sulcliffe Castle.

"Lovely necklace," Julian observed to Elsa. It was not only exceedingly ugly but large as well.

She fluttered with delight. "Oh, I like it ever so much. My Dorset great-aunt's." The rest of her costume was a long, flowered skirt and shapeless tunic. She would fit right in at the gathering of mystics.

Fin, wearing a V-neck sweater and flannel trousers, lit a new cigarette from the stub of the old one. "So then, do you fancy the rarebit, sir? Or there's the sole. Might have a go at that one myself."

As they sped on through Northamptonshire and dinner was served, the clack and rattle of the train covered their conversation. Conversing at table would have to do, since it might attract attention were they to assemble in Julian's compartment.

"Violet," Julian said as he picked at the roast turnips, "you're staking out the fair."

"Fit right in, you will," Fin said happily.

"We'll arrange a car hire in Pengeylan," Julian said to Elsa, "so by the time we arrive at the station, you'll have the route down cold. No time to lose haring across the Welsh countryside, looking for a turn-off."

"Right," she said. "The fair. The road to the castle."

"If you find Sparrow, get her report and update her on Talon and Flory Soames. She's to stick to our targets, hoping for a breakthrough."

Julian turned to Fin. "You'll be the one to ask for her at the castle. She may recognize you from your stint at Summerhill, but she'll know something's up, and you'll confirm that as soon as you've got her alone. At the door we'll need a reason to have a conversation with her. Perhaps a family matter, and with the phone out . . ."

Fin blew a stream of smoke. "Family matter such as?"

Elsa brightened. "The dog died. What's his name—Shadow. She loves dogs."

"It's not as though she'll miss the bloody *funeral*," Fin said. "No, that's bollocks. How about beloved housekeeper Mrs. Babbage went down with a heart seizure."

Elsa deadpanned, "Servants die."

"True," Fin acknowledged.

"We'll think of something," Julian said.

Elsa looked at him. "And you'll be where?"

"Fin will drop me off out of sight. I'll make my way on foot, close enough that I'm there in case something's happened. If all's well, after contacting Sparrow, we have a look around the environs for Talon, and nobody the wiser."

The reconnoiter wasn't authorized by E, but not forbidden, either, Julian reasoned. If they found nothing, they'd wait in Pengeylan for E's go-ahead to question the Cosletts. That was the ideal, which, as soon as the plan was set in motion, could unravel like a bad sweater.

The pudding was served, and they still had not broached the main subject of how to proceed if they discovered Dries Verhoeven on-site. People filed into the dining car now, the practical souls who decided to take an early meal.

Julian paid the bill. The train was slowing for a station. Where the hell were they? It was only Birmingham. Christ. They should have driven.

Fin lit up another after-dinner cigarette, asking the question that was on all their minds. "So, if we see a thirty-five-year-old man with heavy glasses and an accent, do we take him?"

Elsa watched Julian with hungry interest. "We might only have one chance before he does a fade."

"If you see him, take him," Julian said.

36

6:15 PM. The packing had taken five minutes, but now that she had shut her suitcase and was ready to go, she found red-haired Donald barring her way on the landing.

"She told you to wait," he muttered, acting the part of the castle guard, though wearing a silly puffed-sleeve shirt and leather jerkin.

Back inside her room she sat at the table, her handbag close to her feet. If they had searched her things, they would have found the gun, not that it would have surprised them at this point. But if they had found the marked-up map in the LNER booklet, that would have given them pause. They wouldn't do her harm, she kept telling herself. But images of the dowager throwing Christian effigies off the battlements came to mind.

By her wristwatch it was 6:16. The last train left Pengeylan at 8:35. She had plenty of time to catch it, but still, why were they keeping her? Even if they knew she'd been in Powell's room, they could not reasonably know she had seen the wireless. She listened at the door. Opened it. Donald was still there. She stepped out.

"Really, Donald, I think it's time for someone to drive me to the station. My whole family will be quite upset if they think you detained me a moment longer than I wished to be." As a matter of fact, she had been a prisoner in her room for two and a half hours.

He looked taken aback by this forthright speech. "His lordship wants to speak with you. He'll be here."

She tried to act imperious. "Very well. But . . ."

The sound of footsteps on the stairs. Powell appeared.

"She just came out to complain of her treatment, Your Lordship," Donald said.

Powell glanced at her without expression, then turned to Donald. "Bring the car around. I'll run her down to the station." A moment passed where the men locked gazes. Then Donald ducked a bow and left.

Powell looked sallow and hunched, his eyes wild. It could not just be that Nichols had exposed her as an undercover officer. What had been happening while she had been confined to her room?

He gestured her inside. When he had closed the door behind him, he whispered, "Is it true?" He gazed at her as though trying to recognize her, to reconcile who he'd thought she was with this new image of spy and rotten friend. "Is it?"

She kept it simple. "Yes." He closed his eyes for a moment, and she went on: "Ancient Light's finances are under investigation. Some of this money has been transferred to Germany, and the circumstances may be more troubling than the Crown had first thought. My job is to discover how deep your Nazi ties are."

He was shaking his head, trying to sort it out.

"I'm sorry, Powell. I never meant to hurt you. Sometimes I don't like what my job is."

"Your job. What *is* your job?"

"I'm with the police." By his expression, it wounded him, even though he had already been told something of the sort. She watched him carefully. Was he capable of killing her? She had rejected him romantically, perhaps an additional incentive. Picking up her handbag with the Colt, she placed it on the table to be within reach.

"I knew there was something wrong when Mother told me you had a gift. All our conversations, and you never told me that. What is it?" He looked at her with something between longing and desperation. "Charisma?"

"Yes." How could Dorothea have known that she had a Talent?

Powell took a step toward her. "There's something you should know. It's about Martin." The room grew coldly quiet. "There is a person here. At the cabin."

What a strange beginning to something that had to do with Martin!

He looked in what might be the direction of this cabin. "If you follow the line of the cliffs, you'll come to the knoll where the highest cliff juts out. It's the headland surrounding the beach I took you to."

She listened, perplexed and growing increasingly anxious. How could this be about Martin?

"In a cabin nearby the cliff is a man, the one who has killed all the youngsters. He has a boy named Martin."

Her intake of breath was like a fist jammed down her throat. Impossible, it was impossible. "Martin is here? Martin Lister?" And with the killer?

"Dark hair, a lanky, thin frame." He said, without expression, "He is going to die."

How could Martin . . . it was the Dutchman . . . but Martin . . .
had run away. Her thoughts swarmed like wasps. "Stop him,"
Kim said. "Stop him."

Regarding her, Powell looked dazed, aggrieved, as though
she owed him something more than he got.

"Get to the phone, Powell, and call the police."

"I'm not going to do that." His words, flat and exhausted.
"There is Mother to consider. Police crawling over the castle. A
desecration."

"Powell. Another youngster is going to *die*." How could
he think of the dowager's feelings at a time like this? But how
twisted it all was for Powell, and always had been.

"And I have things to take care of here. Rather important
things."

Martin was in terrible danger, and she was the only one who
could help him. She had a gun. She knew the location. Martin
was there. "Then let me go."

He nodded. "I'll give you a lift down to the village. On the
way, I'll just let you out of the car. You can make your way
through the woods. Stay clear of the field. Don't let anyone see
you." He reached behind into his waistband and drew a gun.

Kim started in alarm.

"You'll need a gun. I presume at your *job*, they taught you
how to shoot." He offered her the pistol, a .38. "It's loaded."

"I have a gun." She picked up her handbag and camera case.
He returned his gun to its place in his belt but made no move to
leave. "We have to hurry, Powell."

His gaze had drifted to the view out the windows. He seemed
like a ghost of himself, a man who, even in this crisis, couldn't
pay attention.

"Powell. We have to hurry," she repeated.

He turned back to her. "His name is Dries Verhoeven. He can see Talents. Like lights, he says."

Lights . . . Oh, God. It was all as she had surmised. But it wasn't Powell who could see Talents; it was the man at the cabin.

"The killing," Powell said, barely audible. "I helped him. You may have figured out."

The confession. Whether a *spill* or a man's unburdening when he had given up pretending, here it was at last.

"It never did any good."

"What good did you think it would do?"

"To bring me my gift. So she said."

"Your mother?"

"Yes. She was wrong. I was never going to have it. And Verhoeven lied, saying he could see the lights coming into me, getting stronger with each death. He bolstered Mother's belief that we could feed the ley lines with the blood of innocents."

"Ley lines?"

He waved his hand. "Never mind. I just want to tell you that the fellowship of Ancient Light—they didn't set great store by the lines, not like Mother did. They were all about the usual places of earth power. They knew nothing of the killings. It was never Ancient Light." He barked a laugh. "Just Mother and me."

The dowager and the baron. Of course it was both. One the deluded mastermind, one the gullible executioner.

She had to get him moving. Walking over to where he stood, she handed him her valise. "Let's go."

If he were man enough, he would take her to this cabin. But Powell Coslett was a stew of emotions, and whether he even knew his own mind, she could not be sure. She was on her own.

Taking her valise, Powell stopped for a moment, as though

he wanted to say something. But there was nothing to say. He was the accomplice, the man who had helped to kill four young people and tried to kill a fifth. Perhaps he repented now. But no one would forgive him, least of all her. Still, she pitied him. "I'm glad you told me, Powell. It was the right thing to do."

He closed his eyes for a moment, as though trying to sort through whether he could accept thanks. Whether redemption was even possible.

"You know if you go up to the cabin, he will see you coming."

"Yes. Like a light." There was no help for it. In the dark, she would be an easy target.

He nodded, then he opened the door. Standing on the landing was Idelle.

"Aunt . . ." he said. They stared at each other a long moment.

Looking at her nephew, Idelle's lined and narrow face was softened by a profound tenderness.

How long had she been outside the door? If she had heard Powell's confession, she did not seem horrified or even surprised. Perhaps she had always known.

Then she looked at Kim, and shook her head in a way that looked like despair.

Kim and Powell descended the stairs to the gallery hall.

Powell was temporarily lending her a hand. But he was also an accomplice to murder. Outwardly, he was a pleasant-faced aristocrat with at least a modicum of charm who bought his clothes in Savile Row and pursued an eccentric interest in mysticism. But she had learned how little one knew of others' inner lives when she had fallen under the spell of the disturbing and elegant Erich von Ritter. How little she knew of people, despite the *spill*, that great magnifying glass turned to secret things.

Lady Ellesmere waited for them in the hall. Beside her were

Donald and Royce. Old Awbrey too, looking at Kim as though she were a vile abuser of hospitality and, worse, an American.

The dowager took one look at her son, and was taken aback. "Heavens, Powell." She came up to him. "Get ahold of yourself!"

After a pause, he said, "I'll give her a lift into town."

"Donald will take care of that."

"I would rather do it myself."

"Perhaps you would. But Donald has his orders. He is to wait at the station until she has boarded the train and is gone for good." She nodded to Donald, who strode forward and took the suitcase from Powell.

Kim's nerves were stretched so tight, she thought she might scream. It was not supposed to be Donald; it was supposed to be Powell.

Incredibly, Powell met her frantic gaze and shrugged.

She was in the most dreadful hurry. The awful plan came into her mind of killing Donald at a bend in the road. Or wounding. Yes, wounding.

"I'm ready, and would like to leave immediately."

"I imagine you would," Lady Ellesmere said, ice in her voice. She lifted a hand to signal Donald to escort her away.

She followed him out to the terrace, and then down the stairs to the driveway. *Martin*, she kept thinking. *Martin*. Then, forcing herself to be deliberate: they would drive a mile or two, and then she would place the gun against her escort's neck. *Let me out of the car.* They would pull over. She would tie him up. A lot was wrong with that.

Meanwhile, Donald was putting her suitcase in the boot. They drove off.

Out of the jaws of the castle. The world opened up, with sky and fresh air, all overlain with the most urgent panic. As they made their way down the approach road, they were heading in the wrong direction—away from the cabin.

As they drove, Kim saw that getting back unseen across a plateau with only grasses for cover would be nearly impossible. The view from the castle commanded the road for several miles. Furthermore, she would have to pass the castle, or go through the field of the gathering, unless she made an elaborate detour into the adjoining valley.

But there was one way to take a direct route: let an hour pass for the cover of darkness. If Dries Verhoeven would wait to kill.

And would he?

The sun had dropped behind the headland. The last light spilled across the water, out of sight, but still surging brightly in the great mirror of the sea. She pulled back her sleeve to check her watch. 6:34.

They approached a small stand of trees. She reached into her purse and pulled out the Colt revolver.

"Donald. Pull over the car. I have a gun, and I will use it."

He jerked his head around and flinched at what he saw.

"Just pull over. Do it *now*."

The car jostled into a small ditch at the side of the road and the motor died.

"What . . . what . . ." he stammered.

"Throw the keys onto the road. Carefully. I want them in the middle of the road."

He rolled down the window and tossed the keys onto the dirt road.

Kim let herself out of the car, leaving her door open in case he tried to lock himself in. "Get out."

She was shaking. *Damn, damn.* It didn't help her plan of scaring him into compliance. *Steady, now.*

"Open the boot."

He looked at it in panic.

"If you try to run, I will shoot you. At this distance I can hardly miss, I assure you." He went to the boot and opened it.

She gestured the gun at it. "Take the valise out and get in."

He shook his head.

"If you cooperate, I'll be back in one hour to free you."

He was breathing hard, his eyes darting, looking for rescue. There might indeed be one, if anyone came along the road. The road was well traveled this weekend. She had to hurry.

"If you don't get in, I'll shoot you. Starting with your legs." She cocked the gun.

At last he moved to comply, removing her suitcase and stepping into the boot. Once he was curled up inside, she slammed it shut. She had lied to him. It would not be one hour. She would have to wait an hour for sunset.

And that was just the beginning.

37

A ROAD NEAR SULCLIFFE
CASTLE, WALES

7:35 PM. Dusk had many shades, Kim learned. The difference between soft and deep evening, or a heavy, blanketing dusk was excruciating. Each moment of waiting could put Martin in mortal danger.

She had driven the car off the road, as far into the heavy shrubbery as possible, but the vehicle still looked conspicuous. Nightfall would camouflage it entirely, if it would only come.

At seven forty-five, heavy, nearly impenetrable dusk blanketed the plain. She left the road and began to cross the flats leading to the castle, a clear landmark in the gloaming shadows. She knew her way to the headland from the castle, having gone that way with Powell during her first visit.

Beyond the walls of Sulcliffe lay the steep cliffs and treacherous hillsides. She told herself that on the headland, she would have the last of the light from the setting sun, but she had waited for dark, and now it was exactly that. How could she find her way in such terrain and through the woods to a cabin she had never visited? It was obvious now that that her decision was unforgivably incompetent. She should have rung up the police from the village. Or she should have doubled back to the castle when she had put Donald in the boot. With luck, at least at that time of day, no one would have been looking out from the terrace or a castle window.

At last the north curtain wall of Sulcliffe loomed up before her. In the shadow of the castle face, all light had drained away. She could creep by the entrance unseen—no one would look straight down from the terrace to see her. She moved around to the eastern wall. Along the foot of the castle, a slope of loose rock made for hard going. She had one advantage: she still wore her walking shoes that she had chosen for tramping around the fair that afternoon.

Oh, Martin. Why did you come here? How was it possible that he had done the very worst thing he could do? It had come full circle: his parents rejecting his abilities, his lying about them, reading Robert's journal to fake his visions. And now, paying the dreadful price for having a light after all. The light of his Talent. Why had he lied in the first place? How sad if he thought that telling her about her brother would make him more valued, would have secured his place at Wrenfell. They would have loved him without such things. Would have loved him for himself.

The minutes sped by as she moved along the castle wall. Why would Talon—Dries Verhoeven—wait to kill Martin? Surely, there would be no reason to delay. Perhaps she was already too late. But she crept forward, anger alternating with panic. Martin had been under her care. Her care. And by God, he still was.

A flash of light ahead. Kim flattened against the wall. Who

was outside? Had Dorothea Coslett put Royce or Awbrey on watch out here?

The light came closer. Someone carrying a flashlight. By its wobbling light, she saw a person picking their way along the foot of the castle wall. She backed up. No matter what, she was not going back to her turret room. Reaching into her handbag, she removed the gun.

The person stopped a stone's throw away. Whoever it was, they had seen her. The beam of the flashlight flashed upward to the face.

Kim lowered the gun. "Idelle," she whispered.

The old woman came closer, sending rocks skittering down the slope. When she stood before Kim she said, her voice a strangled rasp, "I . . . know . . ."

They stared at each other. "What do you know?" Kim whispered.

"The way."

By God, the way to the cabin. But they dared not speak. "Turn off the flashlight." When Idelle did so: "Which direction?"

Idelle pointed along the line of the castle wall.

In the heavy dark, they crept forward, Kim steadying the old woman on the uneven ground. They crossed the road, picking their way in the dark, until they came to a dip in the hillside, where Kim thought they could not be seen from a castle window.

"The light, Idelle."

She turned it on. Kim saw that the woman was dressed in workmanlike trousers and a cable knit sweater. So, she was not quite the Victorian woman Kim had imagined.

"At the cabin there's a killer," Kim said. "He holds a young man. You know?"

Idelle nodded.

"Is the boy alive?"

A worried look and a shrug.

How involved was Idelle in all this? But now that the fear of discovery had subsided, Kim knew. "You were listening at the door. When Powell told me about Martin and the cabin, you were listening. Is that right?"

A nod.

Idelle was the guardian angel of her mission. The key. Meeting her out here. Even with her fading grasp on everyday things, she might well have known how her nephew had been driven to terrible crimes and his anguish about it.

"His name is Martin Lister. And we have to hurry if we are to save him. Are you ready?"

Idelle nodded and led the way. They were in a narrow ravine, with steep shoulders on either side. Kim took Idelle's arm, but she shook it off. The old woman was more sure-footed than Kim would have thought. The beam of the flashlight flashed over their path, showing them their next steps. A rivulet of water slid down from a ridge. Idelle pointed the way, and they began ascending the hill, following the trickling cascade of water.

At the top, Idelle was out of breath. They sat on a rock, not yet in view of the sea.

"How far now? Is it close?"

Idelle nodded.

"What is this cabin? Does anyone live there?"

"My brother," Idelle whispered. "It was . . . his. His place. Peaceful."

This remarkable speech gave Kim hope that she would say more. "Do you know if the man in the cabin is armed?" She had forgotten to ask Powell that.

"I . . . don't know." Idelle rose, and they continued. They faced a black ravine and descended into it. At the bottom, they were in a thick stand of trees. Here, the dark was absolute, their beam of light a golden tunnel that showed only a square foot of their path. They picked their way through the trees, Idelle stumbling on the more uneven ground, at last leaning heavily on Kim's arm.

At length, Idelle snapped off the flashlight and pointed. Ahead was a crack of light from an imperfectly covered window. Idelle sank to the ground, propping herself against a sapling. It had taken all her strength to come so far.

Kim could make out the cabin's outline, even obscured as it was by darkness and trees growing beside it. The door, however, was not visible.

"I'm going in," Kim whispered. "Stay here." She took Idelle's hand in hers. It was damp and trembling. "You've been very brave. Thank you."

She circled around the cabin, staying under cover of the trees, looking for a window that might allow her a glimpse inside. She cocked the gun and moved forward.

Nearing a window, she stopped, listening intently. The utter silence seemed unnatural. The day's wind had vanished. No crickets sang.

A chink in the window coverings beckoned her. She looked in, her heart pounding against her ribs.

In the corner, a rumpled bed. Beside the window, a large table scattered with books and papers. An upholstered chair. There was no one in her line of sight, but she couldn't see the whole room. She would have to go in.

Crossing around to the only door of the cabin, she put her hand on the latch.

There was nothing to do but charge in. She pushed through the door, sweeping the gun from side to side to find her target.

No one was there. Except: Martin lay on the floor to her left. Gagged and tied up.

He moved. He was alive.

She crept over to him, pulling him to a seated position. As she removed his gag, she put a finger to her lips. To untie him, she would have to put the gun down. She placed it at her side. Why had she left the door open? A mistake.

The rope binding his wrists was strongly knotted. Pulling at it, she found it loosening and yanked the knot free.

He looked unhurt but wild-eyed with fear. Nevertheless, he had to help her. She placed the gun in his hand. Whispering, she said, "If he comes in, shoot him. Just aim and pull the trigger. You understand?"

He nodded.

As he pointed the gun at the door, she worked the rope on his ankles. "Is he armed?"

His voice cracked as he whispered, "A knife. He has a knife. He killed Jane Babington. I saw it in London at that church, because I *do* get views of things. And the man in the picture helped him."

"In the picture?" At last, the ropes fell free. She took the gun back from him.

His words came out in a rush. "The one that's a baron. You have to believe me, it's him."

"I believe you. I'm here to stop him." He stared at her. "I'm working with the police. Do everything I tell you, do you understand, Martin?"

He nodded, looking at her in some astonishment. He had almost died, and the fact that she was working with the police had the power to dumbfound him.

"Can you walk?"

He could. Taking him by the arm, she helped him to his feet.

"We're going through that door and then we'll make a dash to the right. Stay close to me. If shooting starts, run to the trees and keep going."

She pulled him into the doorway. In the next moment they rushed outside, Kim holding Martin's elbow. She ran with him toward the line of trees. A flash of light. Idelle must be signaling. With a fierce grip on Martin, she crashed with him into the stand of trees. Idelle was still sitting on the ground.

Crouching, Kim darted looks into the dark. Where was Verhoeven? Moonlight laced through the trees, but still, the woods could hide a gang, or an army. Verhoeven could be nearby, hiding in the shadows.

And they, of course, were shedding a most terrible light.

"Who is she?" Martin asked when he saw they were not alone.

"Her name is Idelle Coslett. She is the baron's aunt, but she has helped to save your life."

"You're a police officer?" Martin whispered at her.

"Never mind about that now. We have to get you out of here."

"Because the murderer is going to escape. I heard the baron say there'd be a boat to pick him up."

A boat? The Germans were getting their man out. "What do you know? Tell me quickly."

"The man said it was coming at nine ten tonight. And the baron didn't want him to kill me, but the man with the knife said it was too late, and he was going to anyway."

Kim put a hand on his arm and turned to Idelle, taking the flashlight from her. She shone it briefly on her watch. It was 7:56.

Dries had seen them approach. The dark one, the light one. Two women at the tree line, watching the cabin. *Godverdomme.* They had taken his boy.

He had been waiting for hours outside the cabin, waiting to see if Powell would return to try and stop the last kill. He had been about to go back in the cabin and load up the cloth when the women got there.

The reporter. It was she, he knew it, for he never forgot a light.

She had a gun. He would have cornered her in the cabin, if only she had not been armed. And now she had the boy. Alas, for his plans, his elegant last gesture to England!

The three of them lingered on the edge of the woods. Anger built in him with tiny licks of flame. If he trod carefully, he might get within striking distance of them. But the moon was rising over the tops of the trees, shedding enough pallid light to form shadows. *Godverdomme*, he was done, then. He would not have to face a displeased Heinrich Himmler. Perhaps best. But how sweet it would have been to do two of them at once.

Dries slowly began threading his way through the woods toward the beach. He wondered how the woman had known he would be here. It must have been Powell, his erstwhile patrician helper who had so badly fallen apart, lost his nerve.

One way or the other, the man was intent upon driving him from England.

Such was gratitude.

SULCLIFFE CASTLE

7:56 PM. "Powell, open the door." Her voice had grown hoarse from pleading. Her feeble raps on the door had continued for a long while.

Go away, he thought. *Leave me in peace.*

"I beg you. Call off the ship."

That was the one thing he had done right. To get rid of the monster.

She twisted the doorknob, but he had bolted the door. "The woman has nothing! No proof. Please, Powell. We can go on."

Through the windows, the sky had fallen into a purple dusk. He saw himself reflected there, a strange being, one living in glass. Perhaps this was the man his mother had wanted him to be. She had believed so strongly in him. This was a different Powell, the one in the glass. It was the son she should have had.

You are welcome to him, Mother. But it's not me.

Kim would alert the police and they would come. He didn't hate her as she thought. In fact, it even felt right that she was the one to bring it all to an end.

Mother jiggled the door, shaking it on its hinges. "Powell."

There would be no peace with her out there. He opened the door.

She stood before him, a disheveled woman, strands of hair fallen in her face, her eyes rheumy with tears. "Why are you so cruel?" she whispered.

"I was never kind." He turned from her and descended the stairs. He could hear her following, the *click click* of the cane, her feet shuffling.

"Call your contacts back. Tell them not to come. Verhoeven doesn't need to leave, don't you see, Powell? You aren't ready yet. Call them."

He stopped at the bottom of the stairs. "I don't want the job, Mother. Leading Ancient Light. Give it to Helena or another of your happy followers." He headed for the terrace, to watch the police arrive. Just to see them coming, to know it was over, as it had been over for him the moment Verhoeven had told him the lie. His gift beginning to blossom. The nightmare of the murders. All for nothing.

She followed him down the gallery hall like a Greek harpy. "But it must be you, Powell, you were destined to lead."

"Actually, that was a lie. Verhoeven lied about it."

"He didn't!"

Rian was just coming out of the sitting room with a feather duster. Seeing the two of them arguing, she hurried down the hallway and disappeared.

His mother lunged forward, grabbing his arms to force him to look at her. "I don't believe you!"

She would not stop talking. She had been talking to him for thirty years and had never listened to him. Yanking away, he rushed down the hallway, covering his ears as she pounded after him, calling his name.

Awbrey came around from the dining hall and stopped at the sight of their argument. Powell turned away from him, rushing up the stairs of the turret. The door to his mother's suite was open, and he plunged in. If they would all just leave him alone! He threw himself into the chair by the fireplace. Peace and quiet was all he wanted.

But here she was at the door. She trembled from the exertion of having walked so far and up the stairs. She crossed to him, leaning heavily on a wingback chair to catch her breath.

"Donald hasn't returned," she said. "He should be back by now. Something has happened."

He looked up at her. "The police are coming."

She lowered herself into the chair, closing her eyes for a moment. When she opened them, all that was left was resignation. "You told Kim. Didn't you."

"She's bringing the police."

Her face sagged into perspiration-slicked exhaustion. She whispered, "Then go, Powell. Save yourself. Get on the boat. I beg you."

"I can't."

She looked at him in dismay.

"The boat can't come in to shore. It means a swim to get out beyond the surf."

Her forehead fell into very deep creases, as she put it together. "You . . . can't . . . swim."

"You remember how you never wanted me to go to the beach? You were always afraid of me drowning." He shrugged. "I never learned to swim."

As this sank in, she stared at her knuckles where she gripped her cane. At last she looked at him with the most unreserved contempt. "My God, you can't do *anything*, can you?"

"There's one thing I can do." He stood up and strode to the French doors of the balcony, bursting them open.

8:14 PM. Fin pulled the car to a stop in front of the main castle entrance. Julian and Fin had dropped Elsa off a quarter mile back, where a few stragglers were heading down a path toward the encampment.

On the train ride, somewhere between London and Pengeylan, Julian decided to change the game plan. Kim would receive her briefing from him. For three and a half hours he had mulled over the circumstances tying the dowager to the murders, and found himself increasingly convinced of the woman's complicity. The ley lines, as E said, just conjecture, but spiritual power derived from such sites—which might not be known Neolithic sites, which might be assigned import by deluded cultists—could not be dismissed. All his instincts told him that Kim was in the most immediate danger. And if she was, they might only have a few minutes alone to assess what they must do. The lead on this had to be his, not Fin's.

He knew what that meant, his cover with her blown. E wouldn't like it. He'd deal with that in due course.

He and Fin got out. A feeble electric light glowed over the iron-clad door. Fin disappeared into the darkness to keep watch. Julian looked up the great wall of the castle. He could see no windows, but one story up was the crenellated edge of a battlement.

It was the worst situation for them to be in, not knowing what they would face inside. The out-of-order phone line suggested trouble. And Kim might or might not be inside. She might have been exposed and detained, or she might still be keeping her cover. Nor could they know whether Verhoeven was inside.

He knocked on the door.

What would Kim think when she saw him? And when, in private, he revealed his true role? It was a moment he had thought about many times since his daughter had come back to England.

For three years he had looked at his reflection in Kim's eyes and seen a weak, gullible patrician, leaning to fascist philosophy and keeping his own counsel. Oh, very much keeping his own counsel. This was the web of lies that he had learned to consider normal. Normal procedure, comes with the territory. These were the clichés of the service that had made him not just one who appeared to be empty, but who was empty indeed.

He banged on the door again.

At last it opened. Standing before him was a very old man.

"I'm Julian Tavistock. I've come for my daughter, Kim."

The old man looked at him suspiciously. "For who?"

"Kim Tavistock. She's staying here for the weekend, but there is a family emergency." He was prepared to say it was her uncle Owen. A farm accident. By this she would know that he knew her connection to Owen Cherwell. She would know he had always known.

"Well, Miss Tavistock, she left. She's not here."

"Left? When did—"

A scream came from upstairs, distant and muffled.

Julian pushed past the old man and raced up the stairs. He was on a broad veranda with battlements. Stabs of light fell on the flagstones from a row of narrow gothic windows. An ornate double door led inside. He threw it open, and entered a long hallway.

Another scream. It was a woman's.

He ran toward the sound, down a corridor, past darkened rooms. A staircase led up, winding in circular fashion. He took them two at a time, arriving at a landing. A door lay open. Moving through, he found a lavish room with four-poster bed, a portrait of Hitler, and windows thrown open to a balcony.

An old woman knelt on the floor, facing the French doors. She barely registered his presence, seemingly unaware that he was holding a gun. Surely this was Dorothea Coslett.

"Where is Kim Tavistock?" he demanded.

"Gone," the old woman said. She looked at the balcony. "Gone."

His chest constricted in a sudden vise. He went out onto the deck. He looked over the side. There was nothing but the thudding of the heavy sea on the stone or rock below.

Slowly, each step painful, he walked back inside. Standing before Lady Ellesmere, he managed to say, "Who is gone?"

"My son." Then again, "Gone."

38

8:25 PM. Kim had fallen twice, once so hard her handbag had come loose from her shoulder and slid down an embankment. She found it again, but the gun could have fallen out and been lost. She lodged it in the belt of her trousers.

Moving more carefully, she continued in the direction of the cliffs. Each time she got to the crest of a hill, she thought she would be in view of the sea. But every hill was followed by a ravine, and so down again, and then up. The jagged landscape had grown more barren, with tufts of grass in protected pockets. The surf came to her ears in soft, rhythmic crashes.

She hoped that Idelle and Martin had made it back to the fairgrounds. He would support the old woman and she would know the way. Unfortunately, Idelle was also the one who could have led her to the cove.

Kim had visited one of the coves along this headland. She remembered the one that Powell had taken her to, accessed by a narrow path nicked into the cliffside. Would the cove have a beach tonight?

She knew that rock outcroppings split up the beaches in this area. Would she find the right one? Her hope was that from the edge of the final cliff she could see the running lights of the ship waiting for Verhoeven. In the moonlight it might be possible to see the rescue ship. She thought they would have to use a rowboat to come to shore.

She came to a ledge and crouched for a moment. A light up ahead. A man stood on a nearby cliff, holding a lantern.

He walked slowly along the line of the cliff. Verhoeven, she guessed. She skidded down an incline until she was out of the man's preternatural sight, but kept him in view. The light went out. Perhaps there was a trail to the beach, and he had gone down it. Scrambling across the last of the shelf, she lay on her stomach overlooking the sea. Moonlight did not touch the water, black and crashing.

As she peered down the cliffside, she saw a light, the lantern, slowly descending a path.

Out to sea, nothing. No sign of a ship. But that didn't mean it wasn't there. Sweat slicked her hands as she peered down the cliff face. Was there a beach?

If Verhoeven escaped, he would continue his slaughter of Talents. That must not happen. What a great pity it was that no one else more competent was here to stop him. She would do it then, she would. It was such an easy thing to say. The wind off the sea cooled her face and hands and her heart.

Before paralysis overtook her, she stood up and walked along the cliff edge.

In the thin moonlight, she searched for the start of the trail. If only she had the flashlight, but Idelle and Martin had needed it more. And it would only have made her more obvious to Verhoeven. She found the start of the path, barely visible. The moon gained strength as it rose, but the night was still lavishly black. Looking down, she saw the lantern preceding her, throwing a sickly light on Verhoeven's face and raised hand.

A beach, below, a wide one. The sound of the waves was close, but the cove was much bigger than she had remembered it. She waited for her moment to descend. He would be watching out to sea, but he couldn't fail to see her coming down the cliff. Nor was she a good enough shot to take him out at a distance, and at night.

She let him finish his descent. Facing the sea, he held up his lantern and waved it to and fro.

SULCLIFFE CASTLE

8:31 PM. Julian stood in the hall with its windows overlooking the terrace.

The caretaker, Awbrey, had said that Kim had left Sulcliffe to catch the train two hours before. A man named Donald had given her a lift to the village, and though he should have returned by now, he had not. Julian could believe it or not believe it, but he didn't have the manpower to search the castle.

Standing before him, Awbrey asked in a quaking voice, "Is it true? Lord Ellesmere is dead?"

"Lady Ellesmere has said so. I'm sorry." Awbrey looked entirely lost. All the staff were frightened and bewildered by what had apparently been a terrible argument between mother and son—and now shock. Julian went on. "Someone has disabled the telephone, Awbrey. You must fix it if you can, and call the police."

Awbrey ducked a bow and left to accomplish his task. Within

a few steps, he turned around. "Miss Coslett, she's not to be found anywhere."

"Idelle Coslett?" Julian asked. Awbrey nodded. Powell Coslett's aunt. "Thank you, Awbrey." The man nodded miserably and hobbled off. The staff had taken Julian at his word that he was with the authorities, and were eager to follow directions.

Meanwhile, Julian was left with the apparent suicide of Powell Coslett, and a hysterical Lady Ellesmere, who had collapsed in her room. Julian thought that Lady Ellesmere might be at risk of suicide. He put Fin in charge of her and someone whom Fin had encountered outside the castle walls. A man named Royce had come out rather on the worse end of an altercation that had left Fin with a dislocated shoulder. Still, Fin would be able to keep the dowager and her thug under guard.

He did not trust that Kim had gotten to the train station. Was the lift to the village a ruse, and she had been silenced in the woods along the road? The critical pieces of this long day eluded him. Idelle Coslett was elderly. That she was missing was surely part of the story here. He went out to the terrace to see if, in the moonlight, he could discern the Ancient Light gathering or any sign of Elsa.

A gibbous moon had risen over the distant trees, showering a fey light over the plain. He could just make out the road crossing the flats, but nothing moved upon it.

Something had happened here tonight to cause Powell Coslett to kill himself and Kim to go missing. If Awbrey could not fix the telephone, Fin would have to take the car into Pengeylan and call the police, but that would take an hour. Verhoeven was likely here. Kim was missing. And Lady Ellesmere might be the only one who knew what was going on, but she had received a sedative from her nurse and was useless for questioning.

In the distance, a light from a flashlight. It bounced along, approaching the castle.

He went down the stairs to the main door and opened it. There, standing in the car park, was Elsa. A very thin old woman stood by her side.

And Martin.

THE SULCLIFFE ESTATE

9:03 PM. Distant flashes of light confirmed that the ship lay offshore. His rescuers.

Dries put the lantern on a rock so that the crew of the boat would have a beacon. The shoulders of the cove on either side reared up, jagged and black, cradling the shore. In this embrace, the beach sloped down toward the crash of the surf, visible in the distance as a white lather folding onto the sand.

And there, very far out, a small light bobbing on the sea. The dinghy.

The water would be very cold, yes, but he would be exerting himself, and it would just be a few minutes. He removed his boots, stockings, and jacket.

The tide was coming in. They had timed this very well, his German friends. Another half hour and there would be no beach.

As the boat drew closer, its crew waved a flashlight. It was time.

He took off his glasses—now he would not be able to see much of anything—tucking them deep into his shirt, and buttoning the top buttons. He began walking toward the sound of the waves. It took all his courage to wade into the vast sea, an inky, lurking presence, invisible to him.

The cold water shocked his calves, his thighs. *Verdomme*,

verdomme, that it had come to this graceless departure, swimming out to a miserable rowboat. He hoped the boat would be able to see him once he swam closer.

Hip-deep in water, he turned to take one last look at England. It was a profound blur.

Except—was it real?—a pale glow on the side of the cliff. It had the look of a Talent shining. Very feeble, without his glasses. But still.

He knew who this was. The girl, the reporter, the informer. Incredibly, she had followed him, not just content with driving him away. Now she wished to end the thing.

Strange. That was the very thing he wished, as well. To end the thing with a decisive act. It had galled him more than he had wanted to admit that she had taken the boy from him. But this woman, this dogged, relentless creature who had brought it all down, she would serve even better.

She was half American, he had been told. That gave him pause. Of course, she was half English, as well.

He turned back to the beach, fumbling at his shirt for his glasses. She wished to find him, and find him she would. There was the gun, yes. But he would claim to surrender to her. She would not kill him, how did they say, *in cold blood*. The blur of light had made it to the sand. It moved to the south end of the cove, away from him. She could not see him yet.

He cut back at a diagonal in her direction. As he left the water, the icy air bit at him. The beach sucked at his feet, a soup of sand and water that made for slow going.

A few jagged rocks that he hadn't noticed before lay in his path. He detoured around them. The girl, the light, had stopped moving and turned toward him. He raised his hands in a gesture of surrender.

As he took his next step, his foot sank very deeply into the sand. Yanking it out, he plodded on. The girl must have seen him. She raised her gun.

"Don't shoot!" he started to say, but his next step went very deep into a muddy, wallowing depression.

When he tried to lift his foot, the other went in deeper. Panic struck. He flailed his body forward, only to sink deeper, up to his knees. It could not be, but it was. The beach was not firm. It was pulling him down.

Kim heard the man cry out. Somewhere down the slope of the beach he shouted to her. She followed the direction of the voice.

There were dark, looming shapes before her. The sea henge. Exposed. Those rocks with their tooth-like shapes, and there, not far from them, her target on his knees in the sand.

"Help me!" he cried.

She held her gun at the ready and approached. The moon had come over the cliffs revealing the sloping beach, the rocks of the henge, and Verhoeven, kneeling. As she came closer, she saw that he was not kneeling but rather up to his knees in sand.

"I am sinking!" he cried. "Help me!"

He twisted back and forth, but it did no good. "Throw me something," he shouted. "I cannot move!"

It was a sinkhole of some kind, a place only loosely filled with sand, and deep enough to hold him captive. Shoving her gun into the front of her trouser waistband, she yanked off her jacket and edged closer to him. He was afraid, she saw that at once. But if she saved him, in the scramble of getting him out of the sand, he would surely turn on her.

"Hurry!" he grunted.

He appeared to harbor no doubts that she would do the noble thing, but she hesitated.

"You can't leave me like this!" He turned his shoulders to look behind him. "The tide!"

In the moonlight, the crashing surf approached across the gray sand.

But if she pulled him onto his hands and knees clear of the sinkhole, she would be at risk. She must have her gun drawn before he could attack. With no more plan than this, she switched the gun into the back of her waistband.

How close could she get to him without entering the sinkhole? With a tentative step forward, she gradually placed her full weight on the foot. The ground held.

She looked at Dries Verhoeven, trapped in the sand, a man who deserved to die, who *would* die at the hands of a British court. The tide was coming in, and fast. To die was to die. Did it matter how?

"You killed them," she said. "The children."

Silence from Verhoeven.

"You killed four young people. Say it."

His eyes wild, he looked at the jacket that she held in her hand. "I did. I killed them. But where is British justice? To die like a dog!"

Already the sand had come partway up his thighs. She nodded. It was important that he say it. She lay down on the sand and threw one end of her jacket toward him. He snatched at it.

Too far away. The tide approached.

Stretching out the full length of her body, she felt the sand giving way beneath her elbows. She could go no farther. Holding onto the sleeve, she threw it again, straighter this time.

He grasped it with clawed hands.

Then began a dreadful pulling. It was no good to lie on her stomach. It gave no leverage to her arms. She sat up, leaning forward to pull.

"Harder!" he barked. But he had sunk to his waist, terrible to see. Turning around, he shouted in the direction of the sea, the direction of the boat: "Help me! Help! I am drowning! Come in to shore!"

Kim looked up in alarm. She could not see the boat.

"Lean toward me," she said. "Lean hard!" As he did so, she jammed her feet into the sand to anchor herself and pulled with all her strength. He came forward a few inches, but she could not keep tension on the jacket, and it slipped from her grasp. He fell back, up to his chest.

This was how he would die. The tide was close now, coming in along one side of the cove more than on this side. He looked at it in terror.

Out in the surf, no boat appeared. They would not risk coming to shore.

Time slowed, counted off by the waves collapsing and retreating on the beach. She was covered with wet sand and shivering hard.

There was nothing she could do. She looked to the top of the cliffs, where help should come. But who would come? There was only her and Verhoeven, and out in the bay, the German boat crew who could do nothing.

When she looked back, his arms had disappeared into the sand.

"Kill me," he said. "You have the gun. You must do it!"

She stared at him in horror.

"Quickly! To have it over. Quickly!" He swiveled his head to see the tide slicking forward.

She heard her voice, strangled deep in her throat. "No . . ."

"But yes!" he cried. "Do not let me die like this. The water. I hear it behind me. Do it!"

The rocks of the sea henge reared up, darker shadows against the black. They stood like silent watchers. *Leave him. Leave him to us and the sea.*

And why shouldn't she?

"God in heaven," he pleaded. "You must do it."

Though he was a slayer, monster, sadist, she could not kill him. She could not.

"Make it quick! It is justice, you see?"

Make it quick. Justice was to drown slowly. That was justice for all he had done. Except.

He was sinking in mud. He would die in a way that had kept her awake nights without counting. So many nights lying awake thinking about Robert's last moments. The horse thrashing, the heavy mud like iron manacles around its legs, and then around Robert's, anchoring him as the sides of the crater gave way. The mud moving toward him . . .

She drew out the gun from its nesting place in her trouser waistband.

He had closed his eyes. His lips formed the word *please.* . . .

He did not deserve this mercy. A finger of tide reached his neck.

Please, his lips formed.

She aimed the Colt.

9:23 PM. Julian and Elsa were just topping the ridge when they heard the sound of a gunshot.

They searched for the cliffside path, as Idelle had described it. Now that they had seen a lantern burning on the beach, they knew where Verhoeven was making his escape, but where was the trail?

Then he saw it. Julian shouted, "Elsa, here!" He plunged down the narrow trail, faintly outlined in moonlight.

Down, down, he went, hugging the side of the cliff, his gun drawn. As he descended, rocks fell away from his feet, skittering over the side in a cascade as he stumbled and slid down the path. He came to a place where the trail disappeared. Stepping over the gap, he found where the cut resumed.

He jumped the last distance, hitting the hard-packed sand.

A lantern rested on a rock. And from the edge of the water, a figure walked toward him. It was Kim. A gun was in her hand, her arm hanging down, pointing the weapon at the sand.

She noted him and stopped. Her face in the lantern's soft light was washed of all expression. In a hoarse voice, she asked, "Who are you?"

"Kim. It's me, your father."

Instead of answering, she turned back to the sea. In the near distance, jagged rocks thrust up from the surf as it rolled in.

He came to stand next to her at the tide line.

"There's a German boat out there," she said, her voice flat. "I don't think they'll come to shore."

He squinted into the blackness, watching. "Is that who you shot at? The boat?"

She looked at him, as though noticing him for the first time. "What are you doing here?"

"I came for you."

"Why?"

"I thought you were in trouble."

"I was." She gazed at him a long few seconds. "How did you know? How could you possibly know?"

"Because I've been keeping rather close tabs on you."

She frowned, seeming dazed. "You shouldn't be."

"Yes, I should. We are working for the same people."

"Who do you think I'm working for?"

"The Office, Kim."

"You . . ." She shook her head.

"I'm with the Office. Owen works for me."

A very long pause. For a moment he thought she hadn't heard him, but at last she responded with a soft, even voice. "That's . . . good. I worried."

"I know you did."

She kept watch on the jagged rocks, where the whitecaps broke upon them. Her reaction to what he had just told her gave the impression that it hadn't penetrated. "This beach is going away in a few minutes," she said. "The tide is coming in."

"Was the murderer here?" he asked.

She looked up as she noted Elsa on the beach. "Verhoeven. His name was Dries Verhoeven, who killed the young people."

Julian ventured: "He got away, then."

"No. He fell. In a mudhole."

"Here, in the cove?"

She didn't answer.

"Then he drowned?"

She looked at the gun in her hand, the Colt revolver she had been issued. Julian supplied: "He fell in a sinkhole and drowned when the tide came in?"

"He didn't drown."

Good Christ, she had shot him. While Verhoeven was trapped on the beach, she had shot him.

"He asked me to kill him. And I did."

"Oh, Kim." He had begged for death, and she had given it to him.

"I killed him." As the tide streamed onto their shoes, she

handed Julian her gun. "I suppose it was wrong. But I'm not sorry."

He wanted to say that he understood, but he didn't think she was looking for his approval. She was staking out her place in events, and in her own heart, her concept of herself. She'd killed him. In some twisted way, she'd had to.

With Elsa in the lead with the lantern, the three of them climbed up the side of the cliff.

39

10:30 PM. By the time they had made their way back to the castle, the local police had arrived.

The sorting-out of authority, Julian knew, would not be simple. It was both a police matter and a national security one. Julian would have to take control, but the Wales police must be handled with tact. One thing was certain: he would not allow Kim to be interviewed tonight. They needed a few hours to plan the story they would tell.

Kim had the presence of mind to tell the police there was a chauffeur in the boot of a car down the road, and the man was soon retrieved. She had needed to immobilize him in order to make her way secretly back onto the property to save Martin Lister. Martin had told the police about the kidnapping and the threat to kill him.

Julian arranged for the police to transport Kim to a suitable hotel in Pengeylan, accompanied by Elsa. She was under no circumstances to discuss what had happened with the officer in charge, Chief Constable Stanley Voyle of the North Wales Police.

Voyle was not much impressed by Julian's connections to Scotland Yard and the Secret Intelligence Service. SIS had carelessly inserted itself into a murder investigation, possibly contaminating evidence, tipping off a fugitive, and even driving Lord Ellesmere to suicide by pushing their way into the castle in the dead of night. But as long as Kim was not leaving the area, Voyle would wait to question her. She was the only one who seemed likely to have the full picture.

Julian had only a few pieces of the puzzle, but he had not yet revealed to Voyle what Kim had told him on the way back from the beach: that Powell Coslett had been a murderer. When he did, it would not be in front of the other police officers.

Near midnight, Julian drove with Fin and Martin into the village. Finding Fin a doctor at last, Julian secured two rooms in the same hotel as Kim and Elsa. Then he made a telephone call in the hotel lobby.

The special exchange put him through to E's residence in London. The telephone, as he knew, was by E's bed.

"Chief. Dries Verhoeven was hiding in a remote cabin on the Sulcliffe estate. He's dead."

"Ah." A long pause. "Kim?"

"We've got her. Powell Coslett killed himself. He was the second murderer. And the dowager helped to plan it."

"By God," E murmured. "How do you know?"

"Powell confessed everything to Kim."

"I see."

"The Welsh police are on the scene."

A long silence. "Julian, you know how this must be handled. If we have no proof, the Crown may not be willing to prosecute

Lady Ellesmere. Do what you must to settle the local police, but this will not be public."

It would be the devil to keep it quiet. "The baron's suicide..."

"That can be released," E said. "The murderer captured and killed, the murder spree over."

"We can say he was a foreign national, we're looking into it further."

"Yes, along those lines. You must do your best to assure that no one talks about the details until we determine how to manage it."

"I'm afraid I have to bring the Chief Constable here into it."

"Impress on him how it will be handled."

"Right, then," Julian said.

"How did the bastard die?"

"It's complicated. I'd like to give you the report in person. But shot on the beach while attempting to escape." That was the short version.

"Well done, Julian. I'd promote you, but I'm afraid the next step is a desk job."

Julian hoped E would be in as good a mood when he heard *how* Verhoeven had been shot. Not quite the heroic apprehension of a criminal that would burnish the service's reputation. Tonight he'd have to come up with a better version.

It was very late. Tomorrow, the Chief Constable would be brought in on the facts—most of them—and promptly told to forget them. Julian could imagine how that would go over.

He turned to find that Alice was waiting for him in the lobby. He had summoned her from her hotel; no point in trying to separate her from the group, preserve his cover, when he'd need to debrief her. Keeping his cover with Alice was the least of his concerns right now.

When he explained why he was here, he was taken aback when she seized his hands with unfettered joy. "You aren't one of them, then!" she blurted.

Not a fascist, Hitler-loving apologist, quite right.

Good God, how people must view him.

PENGEYLAN

Despite the lateness of the hour, Julian knocked on Martin's door.

Martin answered promptly, looking askance at the constable sitting in a chair in the hall. "Am I under arrest?"

"For your protection." Julian gestured for them to go into the room. The police officer was treating Martin as a runaway, and was under orders to make sure he didn't leave his room.

Martin was disheveled, the circles under his eyes giving him a sunken look. Julian wished they were home, where Mrs. Babbage could work some of her magic with a Yorkshire pudding or bangers, and Martin could be in familiar surroundings. But that would have to wait.

Julian broke the silence. "We have some things to talk about, Martin."

"I'm sorry I ran away."

"Yes, well. That is a problem. But before I mention that, I need to say that you have done a tremendous service to a police investigation—"

Martin interrupted, "I have?"

Julian went on. "—despite not knowing how to do it quite properly." He gestured for Martin to sit on the bed, while he took the only chair. "From what you told the police, you had a remarkable *site view* at St. Mary-le-Bow."

"I really saw it. I wasn't lying."

"I believe you. It's why you came to the castle. To warn Kim. As it happens, Martin, that was a very foolish thing to have done."

"I know."

"But Kim learned you were here, and because of that, she was able to prevent the killer from escaping. But it could have ended differently."

Martin nodded. He, more than anyone, knew how close he had come to being another victim of Dries Verhoeven.

"For tonight, let's leave it at this: your parents will be very upset with you, and with us for not supervising you properly. You will have to go home and face the music."

"But they—"

"None of that, now, Martin." From what Alice had told him, he had a clear understanding of one of the reasons Martin didn't want to go home: the boy's father had struck him, and likely more than once. But they would have to work with the family he'd been given.

"The way this is going to work is that you will tell your parents exactly what you did, and that when you ran to London, you thought you might be able to see details of Jane Babington's death. However, I would like you to refrain from saying that you saw anyone specific in your vision."

"But I did!"

"We will talk more about this tomorrow. But for now, all you need to know is that *site view* is not admissible in court. Any unproven allegations against a peer of the realm would not be well received, Martin. I would also like you to apologize to your parents for how you behaved."

Martin by now was looking very glum.

"If you do that to your parents' satisfaction, I will arrange for the police to pay a visit and say that you were a substantial help in catching the youth killer. Which—in a way that will remain unspecified—could not have happened except by knowledge you gained with your Talent."

"Which they think is a lie."

"They do think so. We all thought so, because of some of your own actions. However, if the police explain that your *site view* was helpful in the apprehension—it may help reconcile your parents, particularly your father, to your special ability."

"You'd do that? The police would?"

"I'm going to arrange it. But I have some conditions."

"Anything, sir."

"Well, let me make clear what the expectations are, and then you can decide. First, you're going to have to work at earning back your reputation. And I think you can do it, as long as you step up to whatever penalties your father imposes. You did run off from Wrenfell, where your parents trusted you would be under supervision. Secondly, I am going to ask the police to speak to Vicar Hathaway and apprise him of your notable Talent and the damage done when you are accused of lying about it."

"But—"

"Let me finish, Martin. The vicar does not give credence to Talents, but he may come around a bit if the authorities inform him that Talents played a role in ending the youth murder spree. Even if the vicar doesn't change his stance, you will resume your conversations with him, and on a new footing. You will undertake to become more trustworthy, giving up the Adder club until such time as the school might approve such things. I believe your parents will be reassured if you take instruction from the vicar, who is their close friend." The lad's expression became quite downcast. "We know that your father can be . . . harsh."

Martin flashed a look at him. Julian could not say how he knew.

He went on. "That is going to stop, with the vicar's help and with your new attitude. So, you will go home at the start of the school term, and the vicar will monitor how things are going."

"Will he be on my side? Because before—"

"I've known James Hathaway since he came to Uxley fifteen years ago. He has genuine care for his parishioners and for young people, and especially those in need. He has not had the full picture up to now, Martin, but he soon will if you agree."

Slowly, Martin nodded. "All right, then. Yes. If you're sure I can't stay with you?"

"We would love to have you, Martin, truly. But it's time for some family healing. And you can visit Wrenfell. As you continue to prove yourself at home, I think it would be allowed."

"Maybe the police would like my help again. You know, on other cases. I could be a big help."

That was quite possibly true. From what Julian had learned of what Martin had seen at St. Mary-le-Bow, he might be a profoundly strong *site view* Talent.

"If you ever want to work for the police, you'll have to get good marks in school and earn a solid recommendation from the headmaster. Maybe even go to university. So, if that's your goal, you'll have to start doing things differently."

The boy started to perk up.

"And if you buckle down in school this year, keep your nose clean, I'll ask your parents for permission to have you tested for Talent capacity."

That got his attention. "Would you, sir?"

"Yes. One last thing, Martin. You must never tell anyone that Kim was assisting a police investigation. She was working undercover with her reporter role. This is not something either she or I want anyone to know. Not your schoolmates, not Vicar Hathaway, no one."

"Are you with the police, too?"

"Martin. You are never to mention me in this capacity again. I do help out from time to time. But this must be our secret. Do you understand? If there is any breach of this trust on your part, even to your parents, I will take it very seriously indeed. Do I have your word?"

Martin nodded slowly. "I swear it."

Julian smiled at the youngster. "Get some sleep now."

"Yes, sir. Thank you, sir." He frowned. "Can I tell the chief inspector that you're with the police, though? They acted like they didn't understand that."

"Martin. You must never purport to know anything about my role in this, other than I came up here to look for my daughter."

"Yes, sir. Sorry, sir. I'm just tired, or I would have known that."

Julian was surprised the boy could put two words together, much less keep all of this straight. "Good night, Martin." He nodded at him, making firm eye contact. "You did well, son."

Martin did something that Julian hadn't seen before. He smiled. He looked fifteen again. Rumpled and tired, but a healthy, resilient fifteen.

When he came out into the hallway, Kim was waiting for him.

"They said you were in there."

"No secrets tonight," Julian responded, looking at her with great affection.

Elsa stood at the doorway to their room. He nodded at her, and she closed the door.

"Shall we take the air?" Julian suggested.

They walked out into the cool August night. It was almost September, and the air bore a promise of the season to come. They made their way slowly down the silent street, Kim wearing Elsa's jacket, several sizes too large. The village was lit only by streetlamps.

"Elsa hasn't told me anything," she said, "so I guess you'll have to do it."

"Well. It's the world's most secret club."

"Are we in the same one, then?"

"Yes. I knew when I came up here that there was a chance I'd blow my cover. I wanted to avoid it if possible."

"And it wasn't possible."

"Maybe it was. The fact is, it did no good for me to come looking for you. You had it all wrapped up without me." He cut a pleased look at her as they walked. "Well done."

They approached a village green encircled by cobblestoned streets and the frontages of eating and shopping establishments. They took a path into it.

"You've played your part very well," she said. "I was totally convinced."

"Yes. That hurt, rather."

She looked at him in chagrin, and he gave her a one-armed hug. "I don't mean it. What else could you do except believe what I said, that I admired them?" The Nazis.

"It had been so long since I'd seen you," Kim said. "I didn't know you anymore. And a lot of people are German sympathizers."

"That isn't me, Kim."

She stopped for a moment. "How could you let me believe you were a Nazi sympathizer?"

"It's the way of things. But it was very hard, Kim, I want you to know. Very hard."

She took a deep breath, trying to sort it.

He held her gaze. "Do I still look like a Nazi?"

"Yes." But she smiled.

"Good. The moment I don't, the service will cashier me."

She looked at him with a new sort of expression. He thought, if he wasn't mistaken, it might be admiration.

They sat on a bench. The view straight north was out to the bay, a black mass at this distance, pinched by the narrow street.

"What is your job, exactly? I presume it's all right to say now?"

"I'm a case officer. I work at SIS headquarters in London, and I run a team of agents, some of whom you've met, others whom you never will. It's been eleven years since I was brought into the Office. I frankly jumped at the chance to do something useful." In for a penny, in for a pound. "Walter Babbage is one of ours, running courier for me and odd jobs."

Her voice was incredulous. "Walter?"

"He's not a trained agent. An asset of mine, in the terms of the trade. We can rely on him."

"Does he know about me?"

"Yes."

She shook her head.

Julian didn't blame her for her reaction. Once the clandestine world started to cast off its disguises, it often left people blinking and wondering. If Kim stayed in the business, she would become familiar with the undercover world in all of its layers: The truths, half-truths, and outright deceptions. In the cracks between were things viewed aslant. To walk among the layers and keep your bearings was one of the great tests of the intelligence services.

There were others. But she seemed to be doing all right so far.

"I'm sorry that I had to deceive you," he said. "It's been hell on our view of each other. But it did help my credibility as a fascist, that you were so outraged. Unfortunately, in this line of work we take advantage of everything. It's nasty and unforgiving."

"I'm learning that."

He wondered what she had learned. Now they would be able to talk about these things. It filled him with a measure of relief that surprised him, a gauge, perhaps, of the loneliness he'd experienced.

"Powell Coslett killed himself. Is that true?"

"Yes. He jumped off an upper-story balcony. It may take days for the body to wash up, if it ever does."

She shook her head. "A bad way to die. So alone."

"He was with his mother."

"Oh, God. Even worse." She rubbed her wristwatch, the Elgin her mother had given her that he never saw her without. It was her habit when distressed.

"He said that he helped in the killings for the spiritual power. That was the last time I saw him, when he came to my room to drive me to the station. He told me that he'd been wrong about how the power would come to him. He and his mother had been wrong. So, it had all been a ghastly mistake. I don't know how he figured that out, but I think it was why he killed himself."

"Ritual murders along special paths." Julian shook his head. "Symbolized in the Coslett emblem, you said?"

She nodded, staring out into the distance. "Another part of this, maybe the thing that started it coming unraveled for them, was when Lloyd Nichols showed up."

She told him how Nichols had discovered her connection with the intelligence service and had exposed her cover to Powell Coslett, and how she believed that action had been the catalyst for Verhoeven deciding to escape.

"What will happen to Nichols?" she asked.

"We'll pay him a visit. Put the fear of God into him."

"He knows who I am."

"Not for long. He'll be made to understand that it's in his best interests never to have heard of us."

The moon had set, and the park slumped into a profound, tarry night. But Kim made no move to go back.

"I keep replaying it," she said. "The cove."

He took her hand in his.

"I never would have found him if not for the lantern. I knew he had gone to the cove, because Martin had overheard. I didn't know exactly where the cove was, but I'd been there with Powell, and thought it would make a good landing spot. I saw someone standing on the headland with a lantern. When he went down, I followed him."

She had told him this, in bits and pieces, as they'd made their way back to the castle last night, but she needed to talk about it, and he wanted to hear.

"Verhoeven waded out into the surf. But he turned around and saw me. He held up his hands to surrender. Then he got pulled down into the sand. It was in an area that Powell told me one must never go. Because it was sacred. A circle of stones only exposed at low tide. But that reputation wasn't about being sacred; it had always been about the danger, where the ground looks solid, but is just a batter of water and sand. I tried to pull him out, using my jacket as a rope."

A new detail. By God, she had tried to save him.

"Every time he tried to move, he sank deeper. He saw the tide coming in and was crazy with fear. He begged me to shoot him."

They sat in silence for several minutes. It was awful to think of, that she had been faced with this decision, she of all people.

"I raised my gun and took careful aim, afraid I would miss."

They stared into the night.

"I didn't."

Julian would have let the bastard drown. She had only had a few moments to make up her mind, but perhaps her actions were never in doubt. One thing he knew: it shouldn't have ended that way. But since it had, they must deal with it.

"This won't be our story, however," Julian said. "The German boat came in, and seeing that Verhoeven was about to be apprehended by you, they killed him to keep him from being interrogated. Then his body fell into the water. The tide was coming in fast, and you ran up the beach to escape hostile fire from the German boat. You don't know about the sand trap. That will be a surprise to you."

"I can't say that. I'm not trying to escape what I did."

The wind had come up, bringing a briny smell from the water. "I'm sure you are not. But that's how it's got to be."

She shook her head. "Your boss says so? The Prime Minister says so?"

"The PM will get a briefing on the whole Crossbow operation. And he'll hear that the Germans killed Verhoeven."

"You'll lie to the Prime Minister?"

"We'll provide him with deniability. And save the intelligence service from an embarrassing investigation. Which the Office does not want, His Majesty's Government will not want, and you and I certainly do not want. What we need is a perfect end to the murder spree, one that will satisfy everyone, not leave people thinking it should have gone otherwise." He got up. "Time to head back." She faced questioning tomorrow. She'd need some sleep, if she could.

When they got back to the hotel, she stopped at the entrance. "Julian. I don't think I can. Lie about it, I mean. I did it, and I knew what I was doing. I just want . . . to take what comes."

He paused. The next part was hard to say. "It's an order, I'm afraid."

"I see." Her gaze slid away from him.

This was the other thing she had to learn about the clandestine services. There was a chain of command. He knew she wouldn't like it. She had never been good about obedience and tended to act according to principles strictly her own. It had begun with setting the animals free from the pound when she was eleven, and she might not be over it.

"Another thing," he said. "And you're not going to like this one, either. But we don't have a strong case against Dorothea Coslett. Nor Powell Coslett, for that matter. In fact, we do not have any evidence of the sort that could hold up in court."

She made a rumpled smile. "I know we don't."

He put a hand on her shoulder. "We will, however, lay out the facts for Chief Constable Voyle. This is his jurisdiction, and he will hear what happened. With the exception of how Verhoeven died."

"And what then?"

"Then the Crown's prosecutor will be given all the facts and will make a judgment about whether a conviction of Lady Ellesmere is likely. If the case will not go to trial, then we will remain silent. All of us."

She thought she knew what the government would make of Powell's verbal confession and her theory on the alignments of the murders. She understood at one level, the logical one. "But what about justice?" she said. What had it all been *for*, then?

"Two killers suffered and are dead. An old woman has lost her son and is dying of cancer. Sometimes that's what justice looks like."

She turned away, murmuring, "How can you stand this job?"

"It's the best there is, Kim. You'll remember that after a good night's sleep."

They went in.

40

SUNDAY, AUGUST 30. The North Wales Police had taken over the dining room of the hotel for its inquiry. As Kim came down the stairs with Elsa, she saw that Martin and Awbrey were seated in the vestibule, waiting their turn. She smiled at Martin and he gave her a thumbs-up. He had nearly died but seemed remarkably cheerful about it.

Alice sat there too, prepared to tell what she saw, for whatever the police would make of it. They exchanged looks. Her friend's characteristic smirk and slow, eloquent nod were enormously heartening.

The door opened and a police officer with a notepad came out, looking flustered. He closed the door behind him and took a position next to it.

After a few minutes, Julian opened the door and motioned for Kim to come in.

Waiting inside, sitting behind a large table, was the man

from the North Wales Police, Chief Constable Stanley Voyle, a man so tall he looked folded over, sitting in his chair. His muttonchop sideburns made his long face even narrower.

In a black uniform with gold braid, Voyle looked very official and no happier than he had been the night before to find a local castle overrun with SIS agents and a peer of the realm dead. Kim nodded to Voyle. "Chief Constable."

He half-rose to greet her as Julian took the chair beside him.

Voyle invited her to sit in a straight-backed chair facing the table. "This is a preliminary inquiry, Miss Tavistock. You'll be asked to give further evidence to the National Task Force. For now, we want to sort out a few facts in the death of Lord Ellesmere and the kidnapping of Martin Lister. I believe you can help us do that."

"Yes. I expect so."

"Agent Tavistock here has filled us in on the larger issues of a series of murders on the Continent. We won't touch on that side of things."

It was so strange to see Julian there in his new role. She felt three years of doubt and hostility crumbling away, leaving her with a father she would have to get to know all over again. Thank God.

The Chief Constable sat back in his chair. "You may notice that we do not have someone here to take down the testimony in writing. If you find that unusual, rest assured that I do as well. But Mr. Tavistock"—here he looked at Julian with undisguised resentment—"has made it clear that we will proceed in secrecy."

He fixed Kim with a stare he must have perfected in long years of subduing police underlings. "That being the case, you are also sworn to secrecy; the things that you know of this case, and what is discussed here, unless to the proper authorities." He raised an eyebrow, letting her know she could speak.

"Yes sir, I know. That is, I swear I won't divulge anything."

Voyle had obviously been given to know in no uncertain terms who was in charge, and he was still sputtering over it. She could imagine that Julian had used words like "the national interest" and "the Crown's prerogative." Looking over at Julian, she found him completely relaxed, as though they were at tea.

The Chief Constable began. "I understand you were under-cover at Sulcliffe Castle, following a lead that Lady Ellesmere had transferred funds to the German Nazi Party. Funds that had found their way into an assassination conspiracy."

She only nodded, not having been asked a question that required more. Julian had warned her to be circumspect and not appear to hold opinions. The local police would be understandably skeptical of Coslett complicity and for a few hours more would have jurisdiction, or a semblance of it: an attempted murder and a suicide in their constabulary.

"Pick a thread and lead us into this maze, Miss Tavistock."

"Well. For starters, Lloyd Nichols."

She described how the day before, Lady Ellesmere had come to her, saying that a newspaper reporter had accused her of false pretenses in her reporting assignment, claiming that she worked for the intelligence service. Julian then joined in, relating how SIS had arranged for Kim to take Lloyd Nichols' place to write an article about Ancient Light for the *London Register*.

Voyle glanced at Julian with some satisfaction, saying, "Things not as hush-hush with your lot as you might wish, then."

Unperturbed, Julian made an almost imperceptible nod. She

was sure Nichols would receive a stiff interrogation about how he'd penetrated the operation.

Kim went on. "Lady Ellesmere acted outraged and sent me to pack. Powell came to see me in my room. He was agitated, and told me that Martin—who he knew had run away from our home in Uxley—was being held prisoner in a cabin in the woods. He said he would help me elude his mother so that if I could manage it, I could save him. I don't think he cared about consequences at that point. He seemed to have quite given up."

She glanced at Julian, to see if she had overstepped in offering an opinion about Powell's emotional state. He gave her a reassuring smile.

"I believe that Verhoeven heard about my identity and decided to escape by boat and, before that, to kill one last time. Powell—that is, Lord Ellesmere admitted to me that his mother was behind the idea of gathering spiritual strength from the . . . spilling of blood."

Voyle fixed her with a look of distaste. "The spilling of blood."

"As in blood sacrifice, I suppose you would call it."

"Let us just call it murder for now, shall we?"

"But it goes to motive." She saw Julian's gaze drop to his lap. She must be *circumspect.*

"I'm sure that you have your theories, Miss Tavistock. However, the facts will be decidedly more helpful." He did not like to think of a prominent family being involved. Still less that the details were sensational. "Why would Lord Ellesmere admit involvement to you when you hadn't confronted him with evidence?"

"Well. It's just a theory. . . ."

She got a nod from Voyle.

"I think he saw his involvement in the murders as a travesty.

Somehow, he had discovered that there had never been a possibility for him to have a Talent. Perhaps Verhoeven told him.
That would mean that everything he had done would have been
for nothing. And so his life was over from that moment."

She led them through the events of the previous evening:
Powell's warning of Verhoeven's ability to discern an aura when
looking at Talents, and therefore revealing how the slain youngsters had been singled out—as well as the danger she was in
with any attempt to hide from the man. She went on to recount
her disabling of her driver, Idelle Coslett's help in finding the
cabin, and the freeing of Martin.

Voyle let her talk now without interruption. She began to
feel that she had worn him down with her unspooling of the
facts.

When it came time to talk about the cove, she had decided
that she would obey orders. It felt wrong, even cowardly. A part
of her wished for punishment, but whether she should have to
pay for murder or mercy, she didn't know.

When she finished that piece of her tale, Julian looked satisfied but not, of course, relieved. He had a lifetime's practice
in not revealing his feelings, both as a member of his class and
also as an SIS officer. It helped immeasurably with deception,
not to feel anything. If you didn't feel it, you couldn't show it.
Unfortunately for her, she must pretend to the utmost.

The Chief Constable did become stuck on the subject of
how a German boat could come into the cove in the heavy surf.
She responded that it was very dark, and she didn't know how
close the boat had actually come. When she heard a shot fired,
she ran.

Voyle nodded as though he could well imagine her running at the sound of gunfire. "If he had been taken alive, he

could have confirmed Lord Ellesmere's involvement and that
of the dowager baroness," he said with a deep sigh. "As it is . . .
the evidence against them so far is merely your claim of a
verbal confession." Verhoeven also had admitted his crimes,
something she could not relay. But it suffered from the same
downside. In legal terms, the confessions were hearsay. Lady
Ellesmere could be tied to the murder of Flory Soames, if
Idelle agreed to testify and if the Crown would consider her a
reliable witness.

This wasn't a trial. The Wales police, at least this officer, was
being accorded the courtesy of a reasonably full discovery of the
facts. She had the satisfaction of being able to tell him. Also the
annoyance of bearing his skepticism.

But she had one more piece, and it was a doozy.

To tie it all together, the whole sordid plan, Kim needed a
map of England.

Julian had found a sizeable map somewhere. An agent of
the Office should be able to find a map of Great Britain, even
in Pengeylan, Wales, on a Sunday, and indeed he had. She asked
him to unfurl the map.

"With your indulgence, Chief Constable," Julian said. "We
have an exercise we think you should see."

Voyle waved his permission, and Julian brought forward a
tall oriental screen that had partitioned off the entrance to the
kitchen from the dining room. He hung up the map with pins.
Finishing this, he affixed white squares of paper on the five crime
sites where young people had been slain or attacked.

While he did this, Kim said, "If you don't mind, I need a
yardstick. Perhaps the proprietor or his wife may have one."

Voyle went to the door, conferring for a moment with the
constable, then returned to his seat.

Kim took Powell Coslett's book, *Earth Powers*, out of her handbag. She tore out one of the front pages, the Sulcliffe emblem.

Voyle frowned at the map of Britain with its paper squares. "We know where the crime sites are. The sites were random, and the victims selected as opportunity provided."

"Except," Kim said, "they're all connected with Sulcliffe Castle."

With barely concealed sarcasm, Voyle said, "How, if you don't mind saying?"

In answer, Kim placed the shield design, with its castle and sword points on the map in the Irish Sea. She pinned it up so that it hung askew, swords pointed from Wales to Kent.

A knock at the door, and the constable came in, bearing a cane. "They didn't have a ruler. But this is pretty straight."

Kim took the cane, a well-crafted one of polished wood with a hawk's head on the top. Julian held one end of the cane on the location of Sulcliffe Castle near Pengeylan. Kim moved the other end of the cane until its length passed through the town of Ely near the River Ouse in Cambridgeshire. Removing a pen from her pocket, she held the cane along this tangent and drew a line.

Shifting the cane south, she drew another line through the white square at Stourbridge in the West Midlands all the way to the one in London. Moving the cane so the line angled further south, she lined up Portsmouth and Avebury, drawing another line.

"They all connect in a straight line to Sulcliffe," she finished. "And they're the same angles from Sulcliffe as the lines formed by the swords in the Coslett emblem."

She looked at Voyle. While she hoped for a flicker of police interest, she steeled herself for disbelief.

"Well," Voyle said, not unkindly, "how long poring over a map did it take you to come up with this?"

"About five minutes after I found the radio receiver hidden in the window seat in Powell's room. Once I was willing to concede the high possibility of his guilt, I went with my hunch."

The awful events of the summer might well take on the name the "ley line murders." *Ley lines*, a term that she learned from Julian, that was coined over a decade before when someone thought, probably mistakenly, that such track lines were used by Neolithic peoples as routes to important centers. But by whatever name, the lines held import to Dorothea Coslett, and she had persuaded her son that they would be his salvation. They must have known that if they spilled blood at the places like ancient cairns, standing stones, and barrows, it would have made groups involved with earth mysteries more suspect. But as lines connected with Sulcliffe, lines that they kept secret, they could exploit ancient power without drawing attention to themselves.

Voyle rose to inspect the map more closely. He turned a questioning look at Julian.

Julian gestured to the map as though to say, *It's all there, take a good look.* After a time Voyle straightened and looked at Kim with a mixture of perplexity and revelation. "By God," he muttered. Then: "Unfortunately, it will never hold up in court." He went on. "From your acquaintance with Lady Ellesmere, what would you say the chances are that, confronted with this, she might confess?"

"She would never confess. In her view, police investigators would not have spiritual authority or understanding. Especially commoners."

A knock at the door. The constable came in. "Scotland Yard

special unit just arrived, sir." Receiving a nod from his superior, he left, closing the door behind him.

Voyle glanced out the parlor window where several cars had pulled up. "I'm afraid we'll have to go through it all one more time, Miss Tavistock."

Julian stood. "I have to demur, Chief Constable. We will not bring anyone else into the picture until the Foreign Office approves. That briefing comes next, in London."

"What do you expect me to tell the task force? It's their bailiwick."

"Actually, it's ours." He fixed Voyle with an expression devoid of ambiguity. "What you have heard this morning, you did not hear. If word of some aspects of the Coslett involvement comes up— aside from the assassin's taking up a hiding place on the estate, which could well have happened without Coslett knowledge— you will deny it."

The front door of the lobby slammed. Voices outside the door.

"Please refer their questions to me," Julian said. "Chief Constable, it has been a pleasure to meet you." He extended his hand, and despite his misgivings, Voyle shook it.

Constable Voyle turned to Kim. His stern face softened with a small smile. "If you get sick of the intelligence service, Miss Tavistock, and want honest work, give me a call."

As Kim and Voyle shook hands, the door opened. Three men and a woman entered, a few carrying briefcases. A man in a good suit with a poppy in his buttonhole looked at Voyle.

"Well," he said. "Let's get to the bottom of this."

Voyle turned to Julian. "May I present Julian Tavistock, with His Majesty's Government."

† † †

Kim and Alice huddled over their tea on the hotel's screened-in porch. It had taken a full pot of Darjeeling, but Alice had finally accepted that Kim could not say what precisely she had learned during her stay at the castle. Reading between the lines, she concluded that the Cosletts would "go free," as she put it, though one of them had already paid with his life.

"What happens to the dowager," Kim said, "is a decision London will make."

Nor was the discussion of the Dutchman's end more satisfying. Kim relayed her pursuit of Verhoeven down to the beach and how the Germans had shot him when they realized he could not be extracted. It was the story she'd been ordered to tell and, truthfully, she didn't want to talk about what really happened.

"Fancy your father being one of us!" Alice was saying. "I'm so happy for you, Kim. Now when you talk politics at table, you can just *pretend* to argue." She shook her head. "He was very good indeed at playing the role, wasn't he."

"Yes." Completely convincing, she thought with some irritation. "So, how will we ever keep all the secrets straight?"

Alice leaned over the table. "We shall. And it will be jolly fun, too." She sat back. "I imagine you're gaining quite a reputation for being the golden girl. Apprehending the bad guys in two big operations in under six months."

"You helped. Seeing the murder of Flory Soames."

"Well, a magistrate will never hear *that* piece of evidence."

There was so much the courts might never hear. "It brought an SIS team to my rescue, though."

"Kim." Alice fixed her with look. "You caught Verhoeven without any help from them at all."

"But I might have needed them. And your view of the

baroness killing the girl—that *trauma view* will be known to the Crown. Some people will at least understand that she murdered a child."

Alice stared at the dregs of her tea, turning serious. "Wish I could read tea leaves. Now, *that's* a Talent I'd like to have."

In the ensuing quiet, Kim murmured, "You spoke to James."

"Indeed I did." More silence.

"It didn't go well, then."

Alice met her gaze. "Right-o. It did not. He tried to convince me I was mistaken. When that failed, he drew on shame and scripture."

"Oh, no—"

"And then apologized, actually. Hearing that helped, but it's hard to forget what he did say. I mean, when you bring *God* in on it . . ." She shook her head. "James has a lot to think about, and I left him to it."

"Alice, I'm sorry. I thought that maybe . . ." She trailed off, wondering if she *had* been confident in James, sure that he would finally accept the reality of Talents. That he would accept Alice in a more profound way than either of them had previously allowed.

"Well. It's a relief to have told him. The subject had been festering like a boil, so I ought to have had it out with him long ago. Funny. When the worst happens, sometimes it's not as bad as you thought." She sighed. "Maybe he'll change his tune when he figures out I no longer care what he thinks."

"But is that true? You don't care?"

"Maybe I don't. He's not the only one who has to sort things out." She shrugged. "The world is . . ."

"Bigger now," Kim finished.

Alice nodded and looked around the scattered tables on

the veranda—mostly empty, except for a few policemen. She frowned that no servers could be found.

It was time for a wee dram, Kim thought. "Shall we retire to the pub across the street?"

"Oh God, let's."

41

TUESDAY, SEPTEMBER 15. Julian had been walking through Hyde Park for the better part of an hour when he finally decided to take the short walk to Olivia's house in Bayswater. It was late, but he thought he might risk dropping by unannounced.

He had to talk to her. Could he persuade her to stay with him? He knew what that would take. To continue openly, one of them must leave the service.

Perhaps he was going to be cashiered. At Sulcliffe he'd dropped his cover with Kim, and that might have consequences. But he couldn't hang on forever. At his age, he hadn't that long before he would be expected to retire. So, for the sake of four or five more years, for the sake of the importance of the work, he was staying on, despite the damage to his personal life. On the one hand; on the other. It was a jumble for him tonight.

He walked up Queensway, knowing he should have called.

But Olivia might have said she couldn't see him, so he would rather knock on her door and take a chance she would answer. He turned onto her tree-lined street, still not settled upon what he would say to her. *Olivia, my dear.* No, too officious. *Olivia, I know you are engaged, and I feel awkward to . . .* No, no apologies. *Olivia. Is it too late for us? If one of us must give up the service, and if you love it so much, then I will be the one to go.* And God, would he? *If you'll have me, Olivia. If you can forgive me for not knowing sooner that I love you with all my heart and am not afraid to prove it.*

A gentleman would not say this to an engaged woman. She wore Guy Ascher's ring. It was official. But, by God, they weren't married yet.

The life of the service had crept up on him over the years. At first, something to do, a nice clubby enterprise, and Richard Galbraith asking it of him as a favor. Make the rounds of the hunts, move in the right circles, see what you can turn up. From there he had been inducted officially, began to run agents, took a flat in Albemarle Street, let Wrenfell go to seed, leaving it to the Babbages for upkeep. Julian had become a Londoner. Like a fallen tree that had gradually exchanged wood for stone, he had become something other than what he had been: husband, father. His wife gone; his son. What else was he to be?

Perhaps a husband again.

He was sixty-two. It seemed likely that Olivia was his last chance at a companion in his life. Gradually, he had come to see that this mattered. He saw it now, at any rate. Damn convenient, he knew, at a time when his career might be in jeopardy.

He had stubbornly held on to the service, blind to the fact that he was too old for the game. He wasn't tough enough to let his daughter hazard herself in the same way as Julian had risked himself countless times. To be done with it, at last; how odd a thought. He felt a stranger there on this familiar street, as though he had been carrying his world with him, inside his mind, and now walked down the busy street, seeing it as it really was.

He stood across the street from her flat housed in a brick Georgian with stairs leading to the front door. The house was dark. She must have retired. It would not do to stand here and watch, as though keeping the place under surveillance.

Hadn't he had his chance, that night she had come to him, after the party in Mayfair? She had forbidden him to speak. They would be together that evening without having to define themselves. He had taken her version of it, glad to be excused from turmoil.

A cab moved down the street. Instinctively, he faded back against the wall of the building opposite. The cab stopped and Olivia got out with someone.

Julian waited for her companion to say goodbye, to get in the taxi. But Guy Ascher went up the stairs with Olivia, and the cab departed. She had her keys out and worked the lock. They went in together.

He wondered what she was doing staying out so late on a Tuesday night, but wasn't that how lovers were, needing to see each other every night? She was engaged, committed to Ascher, perhaps even in love. It was something that he hadn't wanted to believe.

But he believed it now. The impulse to bare his soul, to ask for forgiveness, died away. And all it had taken was the thought of them together tonight in her flat. So much for courage. Affairs of the heart, a beastly game, and one that he had lost. He watched the building as a light went on in one of the windows. She had chosen. And so had he.

A light rain had begun to fall. Julian pulled his collar up and turned back down the street toward Queensway.

The next morning he asked E to meet him in St. James's Park.

What he wanted to say was that things had to change.

He'd made an error in judgment about extracting Kim from Sulcliffe himself. It was possible that he had let his relationship with his daughter unduly influence his decision to go himself rather than assigning another agent to pose at the door with a summons home.

But wasn't it better that he and Kim could communicate directly?

E listened without interrupting.

Julian said that he wanted to run Kim as an agent from now on. It was no different from being an army officer and commanding one's own son in battlefield conditions.

E measured Julian with a long gaze. Perhaps he knew that there was only one way to keep two of his best people in the fold.

When they split up on Horse Guards Road, Julian had his way. It was the first time he'd bucked Richard and argued hard for something the man was solidly opposed to. He hadn't been sure he'd come out of it with his job intact, but he had known without doubt that he was going to fight for what he wanted. It was never too late to learn the wisdom of that.

Working for the Office was a life he'd loved. He still had that life. *All right, Kim,* he thought. *Let's see how this is all going to work out.*

He walked the distance back to his flat.

Within a few days the engagement announcement appeared in the *Times*.

MONKTON HALL,
NORTH YORK MOORS

WEDNESDAY, SEPTEMBER 23. Kim sat in Owen Cherwell's office, holding the *Bloom Book* in her lap.

"They're always a few steps ahead of us," she said, noting where *aura sight* would be catalogued: under Mentation, taking its place beside *hypercognition, precognition, object reading,* and *site view.*

Owen leaned against the side of his desk, trying to establish a more relaxed tone to their first discussion since she had learned that her father worked for the Office.

He glanced at the *Bloom Book.* "Yes, deucedly annoying. What I wouldn't give to have been able to hook Dries Verhoeven up to the dynograph. Shame they killed him."

"Yes, too bad." It was the only part of the story that Owen was not to know.

"*Aura sight.*" He brushed his fingers through his hair to no effect. "What exactly was the man *seeing?*"

"'Some people shine more brightly' was how Powell Coslett put it. He said that Verhoeven couldn't determine what any particular Talent was, but he had a sense of its strength."

"Intriguing. Perhaps we'll find another of those." He smiled at Kim. "English this time."

She rather hoped they wouldn't, but that was entirely selfish.

"And the man's motive," Owen said. "The awful British shelling of the school during the war." He shook his head. "Of course, that's another aspect the public will never hear about." The Foreign Office was quietly burying that piece of the story.

And the Crown, in their decision not to prosecute Dorothea Coslett, had set the stage for the whitewashing of both the

Cosletts. Nothing would be made public about a criminal involvement that would not be prosecuted. Julian had warned them it might fall out this way, and Kim had tried very hard to be reconciled to it.

She had given testimony to the prosecutor behind closed doors. Introduced as Agent A, and with several other people present who were not introduced but whom Julian had implied were "the higher-ups," Kim had told her side of it. It had taken a good part of a day. And she had revealed all, setting aside that she shot Verhoeven point-blank in the head as the tide swept in over his sandy prison.

The newspaper on Owen's desk drew her attention. DUTCH AUTHORITIES DISAVOW YOUTH KILLER. She had read the article this morning, how Verhoeven had been a troubled individual; a German sympathizer; acting alone, etc., conveniently similar to what His Majesty's Government had said or implied in its own statements.

Owen noted her gaze. "People are so easy to fool."

"There are at least five families," Kim said, "who are still asking questions." Including George Merkin's. The boy would recover, but his life might never be the same. "They want to know who the second man was. The one seen at the Merkin attack."

Owen raised a finger. "And the answer is?"

"We don't know."

"Exactly. Let them assume it was another foreign national."

"German, is what people think," Kim said. People in Uxley had been talking about little else for three weeks.

"An assumption the Foreign Office is all too happy to allow people to make, while officially saying there is no evidence of German participation."

Kim was mightily sick of hearing *no evidence.*

"If it's any consolation, Dorothea Coslett is now confined to her bed. She has taken a turn for the worse, and we hear it's ugly."

He stood up and walked to the bow window, overlooking the derelict garden. "Even if we couldn't convict the old woman, it was a stunning success for the secret service. Needed it, I think, with budget restrictions being bandied about." He turned to her. "Well done, Miss Tavistock."

Kim handed him back the *Bloom Book.* "What will happen, I wonder, to Idelle Coslett once the dowager dies?"

"I can't imagine she'll stay at the castle," Owen said. "I understand her voice has come back, though."

"Yes. Everyone assumed her silence was a vow she made after Bowen Coslett's death in the war. But I don't think it was. It was because of Flory Soames. The shock of witnessing the murder, dumping the body . . . It must have been quite traumatic."

"Perhaps that's why she helped you. She didn't want another murder on her conscience."

Kim had often thought about Idelle Coslett, and how she'd had to bear the awful knowledge, at least that last day at the castle, that her nephew had been involved in murder. It was something she must have heard at the door when he confessed, unless she'd known even before.

"The Ancient Light group has been named in the baron's will," Owen said. "They will manage the estate, with an eye to opening the castle for tours as well as allowing the public to view the standing stones on the beach . . . What did you call it?"

"A sea henge."

"Yes. I'd like to see that myself."

"It's a dangerous beach."

At Owen's raised eyebrow, she said, "And not just because

the Germans descended on it to grab their assassin. It has . . . sinkholes."

"Does it. Well, I'm sure they'll take precautions. View it from the cliff, that sort of thing."

They gazed at each other for a few moments as the subject they'd been avoiding hung in the air between them. "I couldn't tell you about Julian, you know," Owen said.

"I know." She sighed. "Next, I'm going to learn that Mrs. Babbage is with the Foreign Office."

"I can't comment on that," Owen said mischievously.

Kim smiled. But it was very difficult to get over having been so deceived. It had caused no end of discomfort, thinking her father a fascist and, at times, suspecting him of treason. They were just finding their bearings with each other again.

"No one has the full picture," Owen went on, no doubt satisfied that he knew quite a bit of the picture.

She thought of the one piece he didn't know. How it had all ended on the coast of Wales. She hoped it wouldn't haunt her, making worse the brutal knowledge of how her brother had died at Ypres. That was the strange essence of her dilemma, that she didn't regret killing Verhoeven because of taking a life, but because she had given him mercy for Robert's sake.

It was all so twisted.

A sudden longing to be home overtook her. To have a quiet supper with her father and then curl up on the sofa with the London and North Eastern Railway timetable.

She had a new copy.

POSTSCRIPT

THE BLOOM BOOK

ADDENDUM.
(GROUP 2: MENTATION)

Aura sight. *The visual perception of individuals with meta-abilities, presenting as an apparent luminosity. The ability manifests only within normal visual distances, regardless of light levels. Practitioners are not thought to be able to distinguish classes of Talents. However, a general impression of strength of the perceived Talent appears to the practitioner as greater or lesser brightness. A manifestation of the darkening Talent does not disrupt the ability. Underlying ability. Rare. No case studies; field observation reports only.*

Ref: Ley line murders. MADM 4749.55.

Historical Archives and Records Centre (HARC), Monkton Hall, September, 1936.

ACKNOWLEDGMENTS

They say that a writer's craft is a solitary one, and at some level this is true, but it would be a harsh vocation without friends and associates who care about so humble a thing as one's current novel. My profound thanks to my husband and first reader, Thomas Overcast, for his support and faith in this series and this book. I have, in addition, been fortunate to have friends and teachers who have advised, critiqued, and helped me hone my craft. My thanks to Steven Barnes, Larry Brooks, Andy Dappen, Dan Gemeinhart, Louise Marley, Theresa Monsey, Pat Rutledge, Ben Seims and Sharon Shinn. To Veronica Rood, for our enduring friendship and for help with all things Polish. My gratitude to my agent Ethan Ellenberg for believing in my story and finding the perfect home for it. Special thanks to my editor Navah Wolfe who brought this story into the light of day with exacting care and inspired insights.

This is a work of fiction, although readers will recognize some historical figures. Though some of the towns—and the castle in Wales—are of my own devising, I strove to create a realistic setting and an accurate 1930s historical context. In this I received generous advice and assistance, but in the end, any errors are entirely my own.

TURN THE PAGE FOR
A SNEAK PEEK AT
NEST OF THE MONARCH

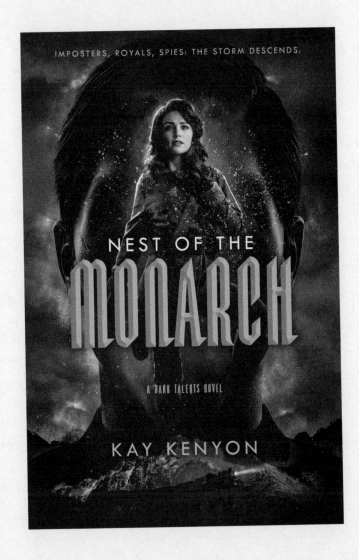

IMPOSTERS, ROYALS, SPIES: THE STORM DESCENDS.

NEST OF THE

MONARCH

A DARK TALENTS NOVEL

KAY KENYON

1

FRIDAY, APRIL 24, 1936. A silver light painted the faces in the cinema's audience. The villagers sat expectant and rapt as the MGM theme song boomed out. Watching from the back of the theater, Hannah Linz counted heads in the audience: Forty-six! And only moments before she had despaired of a decent house for the German-dubbed version of *The Great Ziegfeld*, very dear to rent in Deutschmarks and Nazi disapproval.

She wished her father were here to see the number of people daring to entertain themselves on a Saturday evening. But Mendel Linz had gone to Stuttgart after receiving a summons from the Propaganda Ministry to take delivery—at exorbitant rates—of a few *proper* German films. "Otto is here to help you," her father had told her. Otto, who ran the projection booth. "Three days. I will be back on Sunday, *mein rotes Mädchen.*" My red girl, as he called her, for her flame-red hair, like her mother's.

Just before Hannah closed the velvet drapes leading to the lobby, Frau Grober came through with her daughter Klara, Hannah's closest friend. As Hannah shone the light of her flashlight on the nearest empty seats, Klara whispered to her, "I'm sorry we are not on time!"

"No, don't worry," Hannah said. "Otto began the film late." Everyone there tonight had risked Nazi displeasure to attend a film from the West, and for that, Hannah was grateful. But wasn't it absurd to be moved by such small acts of courage?

With her father, Hannah owned and managed the Oasis, a cinema built for the Black Forest Retreat and Spa that had gone out of business during the Great War, and now, under her family's refurbishment, had ambitions to present a summer cinema festival. It would bring filmmakers, actors, tourists, and their money to Aschried.

But the cinema committee had split on the question of whether to include films showing infidelity, cripples, homosexuals, or women working—all contrary to German ideals. The *new* German ideals. At the screenings, the committee took notes of objectionable scenes. In the end, they compromised: a sprinkling of heavy, Nazi-approved films to placate the officials of the Propaganda Ministry's film division. "Give them a little, and they will be happy," Mendel Linz had said.

But they were not happy. She and her father learned this one day last month from a man with a too-long face.

When she had opened the door of her home to the knock, she had found an SS officer standing before her. He wore a black uniform with red armband, and beneath the peeked hat, a pallid face bearing a dueling scar that bisected his right cheek from eye to chin.

"Yes?"

Lieutenant Becht would speak with Herr Linz. Since she had no choice, she opened the door and led him into the parlor, feeling his eyes on the back of her neck, as though she had left the door open and a bear had padded in.

Her father, who had been reading the newspaper, stood at the library door holding that day's edition of the *Aufbau*. Removing his spectacles, he took in the unlikely view of an SS officer in their sitting room.

Lieutenant Becht sat on the divan, her father in the best armchair. A silence fell upon them. The curtains were closed against the bright afternoon, leaving the parlor in murk.

Hannah faced them, standing behind a chair, gripping the carved back. "Tea, Papa?"

Becht flicked a hand to dismiss the offer, as though it were his house. The parlor, overwarm, imposed an odd, forbidding drowsiness. As Hannah looked at their visitor, she tried to grasp what sort of man this was. The black uniform and red armband proclaimed his SS status, but this officer had a strange appearance: his pale skin and the pronounced scar, a prominent chin, long and rounded, as well as a very high forehead, revealed when he took off his hat and placed it on the divan.

"You are a widower, Herr Linz? Your wife died during the war?"

"Influenza."

Becht nodded. "And you have lived in Aschried how long?"

"Five years." Her father lifted his gaze to Hannah, then pulled back, as though hoping Becht would not notice her.

"Previously you were employed at a university, were you not?" The officer crossed his legs, getting comfortable.

"Cologne. But I am retired from the position now."

"I think retirement was not your choice, however. It was a profession not suitable for a Jew."

"Some deemed that so."

"A disappointment for you, naturally."

"I do not complain, Lieutenant."

"No? But perhaps you thought that, so far from Cologne, you could protest with impunity. Using the cinema."

"The Oasis, you mean?"

"Certainly. It is the only movie house in town. Therefore it has a certain cultural significance, you see. We have become aware of matters regarding it."

Hannah was preoccupied with the crocheted antimacassar draped along the back of the divan. She must try to pay attention. What had the SS officer said? Something about the cinema. A lethargy had fallen upon her, a feeling that she at first mistook for sleepiness. But how could she feel drowsy with an officer of the SS sitting in their living room?

Her father seemed to be receding into his chair. He was not a large man, and he now became smaller, quieter. Hannah felt a great need to throw open the drapes, open a window.

Becht went on. "Matters such as the showing of degenerate films, decadent movies from the West. Inappropriate for German citizens who should be viewing our own films, celebrating patriotism and the fatherland." He paused, inviting comment, but one could not disagree with the SS, nor really could they bring themselves to agree.

"And then we have the name, the Oasis. And the mural in the foyer, where you have palm trees and pyramids. These are not German scenes." He shook his head. "Camels."

This was too much for her father, who had grown unnaturally still but now seemed to jerk awake. "What would you have us do? The Oasis has been here for thirty years."

Becht drew out a paper from his pocket and unfolded it. "Here is a list of approved films. You will want to conform to higher cultural standards."

Her father sank back into his chair to read the document. At last he looked up. "I do not know these filmmakers. Who are they?"

Becht leaned forward. "You mistake me, Herr Linz. Your approval is not required. Your ownership of the theater is not recognized."

"Not recognized?" He frowned, and in the long pause that followed he seemed to have forgotten what he was saying. "I have papers," he finally whispered.

"I will take those papers. For review, in Stuttgart." Becht made a sweeping motion with his hand. "Get them now. I will wait."

It took some time for her father to absorb this order. At last he stood, looking stooped and far older than his fifty-five years. He shuffled from the room.

Becht stood, turning to Hannah. He was quite thin, his tailored uniform emphasizing a narrow waist. He regarded her with an expressionless stare. *What did he see?* she wondered. Not a person, not even an enemy, but someone utterly dispensable.

"Living with your father, Fräulein Linz, you have no need of a job, is that not correct?"

She struggled to pay attention. He had asked her a question—what was it?—about employment. It was imperative to remain alert, but the whole atmosphere of the room felt heavy with confusion. She struggled to gather her wits. "He . . . he lost his pension," she managed to say. "My father could not take his pension. Under your rules."

He smiled, causing the long scar on his cheek to bend. "You are bitter. Your father will conform, but you—"

"I manage a cinema . . . I do not go to university. I do not live near my friends in Cologne. I have no prospects." Her hands, slick with sweat, curled around the chair's wooden scrollwork. On his collar the curious insignia of a bird with a long, curved neck, and wings swept back like a cloak. It was a vulture.

"So many curtailments," he said. "But even here"—Becht gestured to embrace the house, the village—"even here, we take notice how things are done. Even in the Black Forest! You see, there is no place where you can poison us, where we will not . . . *notice*."

She shrank back from this attack, a wave of heat rolling over her skin. Time slowed, the room thickened. What should she say?

Her father returned with the bill of sale. They learned that he was to consider himself a temporary manager, not owner.

Did Herr Linz understand? Lieutenant Becht watched her father, a pleasant expression on his face, a demeanor that could quickly change, Hannah knew. Her father nodded, mumbling his understanding, his agreement.

To Hannah's relief, Becht seemed content and gave her a small, flat smile as she accompanied him to the door. The smile was mocking, and she did not return it.

Waiting by the Mercedes, the lieutenant's driver opened the door for him, and he departed, the tires spitting gravel as the car sped off.

In the cool night air, Hannah's lethargy evaporated. Closing the door, she turned to her father. "Papa! We own the cinema. Why did you give him the papers?"

"He asked for them." The words soft, self-explanatory: *Because he asked for them.* He ran his hand through his hair, sighing as if waking from a nap. "I could say nothing."

"But to give them away!"

Looking at the door where Lieutenant Becht had been standing, her father said, "He has the Talent. *Mesmerizing.*"

Ah, now she put it together: how when Becht entered, a fog of unreality had descended on them.

Her father went on. "It was the strongest demonstration I have ever witnessed." Yes, he would know, Talent research having been his specialty at Cologne.

"But why does he waste this Talent on the likes of us?" Hannah asked. "He could have taken the papers in any case."

"Because," her father said, "he wanted to enjoy our fear."

Perhaps it was enough for Becht and his superiors in Stuttgart that he had taken the cinema. They would still have a small stipend to live on. Aschried was very far to come just to terrorize two Jews.

That had been a month ago. The disturbing memory lingered, casting its shadow over the happiness of a good reception for *The Great Ziegfeld.* The film was not on the list. They had ordered two propaganda films to satisfy the ministry, but *Ziegfeld* had already been rented.

In the projection booth, Otto made a seamless transition to the second reel. Hannah watched in the back of the house near the drapes screening off the lobby. The whirring of the projector, a faint susurration from the booth. On the screen, William Powell was charming Myrna Loy into joining him, promising her the publicity she had always dreamed of. So handsome, William Powell, the ill-fated promoter, young and self-assured—

The film snapped. A groan went up from the audience. Fortunately Otto was a master at splicing celluloid and would soon have it up and running.

Someone came through the drapes. It was Frau Sievers, who

tried to give Hannah her ticket money. Hannah waved it away, since she had missed much of the film, but Frau Sievers insisted on paying. Finally Hannah accepted a few Deutschmarks and helped her to find a seat in the crowded middle, where Frau Sievers preferred to sit.

A loud thud came from the booth, then a crash. Something had fallen. Hannah slipped from the auditorium. If Otto had dropped the second canister, it would mean a tangle of film and an awkward delay. As she pushed through the drapes into the lobby, she noted a man just leaving through the main door. A black leather coat. A bloodless, long face.

He didn't see her as he strode away. But she recognized him. Becht.

She rushed up the stairs. The projection booth door lay ajar as it should not be during the program. She could hear the film up and running again and whirring on the reel.

Entering the booth, she found Otto on his hands and knees struggling to get up.

Screams erupted from the audience. Leaving Otto sitting upright, she rushed to the aperture to look into the house.

There, on the screen, a scene that was not from the programmed film. A birch woods, with fog drifting, snow remaining in patches on the ground like scabs. And there, some fifteen meters away, a man—what was this?—a man tied against a tree. The movie camera zoomed in closer.

Hannah gasped. It was her father who was bound against the trunk, ropes around his chest and legs. No, no . . . it could not be. But yes, he was roped to a tree, his shirt stripped from him. And oh, the blood gushing from his torn neck . . . It could not be, it could not. "Papa!" came her strangled cry.

A close-up of the knife as a figure walked into the frame. The knife stained red. Held in the hand of the man with the too-long face, the man who had just left the cinema.

Was it her own screams or was it the people in the theater? She could not tell. People jumped from their seats to flee, while others sat rooted in place. She forced herself to watch the screen, willing it to be gone, to be a dream, a nightmare, but no. There was the birch woods, the tree, her father. So much blood, still pumping, the life leaving him. Still the film ran, the camera coming ever closer to his stricken face, until his head dropped down to his chest.

The film flickered off, the end of the spool slapping against the reel again and again.

She staggered from the booth into the corridor outside, her mind black, her breaths harsh and loud. Down the darkened stairway to the foyer. The crowd pushed past, slamming against her in their rush to the exits. She fell to her knees. A moment of stunned immobility overtook her as she stared at the carpet, sandy brown, studded with palm trees and popcorn.

Klara rushed up to her, kneeling at her side. Men were leading Otto down the stairs. He staggered over to Hannah and she held him as he wept. "What is happening," he cried. "What is happening!"

But she knew what was happening. The National Socialists had taken notice of Aschried and its cinema.

She held Otto, comforting him. Thank God she could think of someone else at this moment, because if she thought of her father . . .

He had left for Stuttgart, but it was unlikely that he had been called by the Ministry. She felt certain that he had been lured away and stopped along the road. Her thoughts became stone, as though the world had solidified, never to change after this moment.

Klara helped her outside, away from the theater lights, into the darkness. People were shouting, some clumped into groups, consoling each other. In the cold April night, Hannah's tears turned icy on her face. Then Hannah and Klara were walking along the pavement toward home. Her friend would stay with her. She must have tea, Klara said.

But when they got to her house, she saw the windows shattered, and inside, the furniture upended and ripped.

Klara was aghast, but Hannah looked on the chaos without reacting. How could she care about upholstery and china when her father had died, died alone in the deep woods, tied to a tree?

The SS had come for Hannah and her father and life could never be the same. She must leave here. Tonight. Glass crunched under her feet as she climbed the stairs to her room.

Packing a small suitcase, she dressed in trousers and a sweater and her father's leather jacket with ivory buttons. He had been a small man, and the jacket fit her.

An hour later she left Aschried. Some people had not been afraid to help her. She drove Klara's father's truck, to be picked up tomorrow at the railhead. Driving to the station, she held to one thought: that she would not be solicitous, passive, or silent again. Klara had given her the names of friends in Leipzig. At the station window she bought her ticket, but it was not for Leipzig. That city was not the source of this horror.

It was Berlin. Where they would *notice* Hannah Linz.

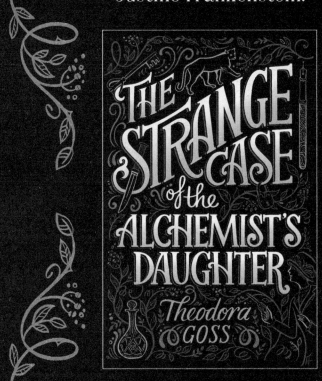

WHAT IF THE UNITED STATES DEVELOPED
THE ATOMIC BOMB A YEAR EARLIER, IN 1944?

TUESDAY, JUNE 6, 1944

AMERICAN ATOM BOMB
ANNIHILATES NAZIS

THE
BERLIN
PROJECT

A NOVEL

GREGORY
BENFORD

Unprecedented Weapon Unleashed on German Capital | AMERICAN SCIENCE
Allied Bombers Deliver Pillar of Fire and Smoke; Tens of Thousands Perish in Seconds; | CHANGES THE COURSE
German High Command in Ruins; No Sign of Adolf Hitler | OF THE ENTIRE WAR

STUNNED DISBELIEF | Roosevelt Says that
AT THE SUDDEN TURN | Victory is Near; Berlin

PRINT AND EBOOK EDITIONS AVAILABLE
SAGAPRESS.COM

A
CRIMINAL
MAGIC

A NOVEL

LEE
KELLY

"A smart, absorbing read, with a deft take on Prohibition,
engaging characters, and an utterly believable and fantastic
version of magic that is as splendid as it is dangerous."

—KATE ELLIOT, Nebula Award-winning author of the Spiritwalker trilogy

SAGAPRESS.COM